ROSIE MEDDON

A Wartime Welcome

CANELO

First published in the United Kingdom in 2023 by

Canelo
Unit 9, 5th Floor
Cargo Works, 1–2 Hatfields
London SE1 9PG
United Kingdom

A CIP catalogue record for this book is available from the British Library.

Print ISBN 978 1 80032 657 6
Ebook ISBN 978 1 80032 656 9

Cover design by Debbie Clement

Cover images © Arcangel, Shutterstock

Look for more great books at www.canelo.co

Printed and bound in Great Britain by Clays Ltd, Elcograf S.p.A.

I

Exeter, England

May 1942

I. Loss

Chapter 1

'Huh. So much for coming back to save our belongings. Look at it all. There's nothing left. Those Jerry bastards have destroyed the lot.'

Clemmie Warren stared in disbelief. Pearl was right. There was nothing left of Albert Terrace except a mound of charred timbers and smashed masonry, here and there among the smoke and the debris the sorry remains of people's possessions: an iron bedstead; someone's tin bath; the mangled frame of a lady's bicycle. That last item she recognised as the old boneshaker Mrs Dawes rode home on from her job at the public baths every evening and then left propped overnight against the front wall. As a little girl, she'd warned the old dear that one day someone would steal it and she'd have to go to work on foot. Granny Dawes had laughed. *Folk on Chandlery Street might not have much to their names*, she'd said as she'd bent low to pinch her cheeks, *but they respect one another's property*. It was more than could be said of Jerry.

Her eyes continuing to scan the devastation, Clemmie gave in to a despairing sigh. After two and a half years of war, and more false alarms than anyone could reckon, the drone of bombers last night had come as a shock, it taking her a while to recognise the low and oscillating hum for what it was. Even when the first incendiaries had come whistling out of the night sky, their elder sister May had

5

tried to play down the danger. The Luftwaffe, she assured them, were only interested in places like the quayside and the railway yard; being some way up the hill meant Albert Terrace was unlikely to suffer anything worse than the odd shattered windowpane and a few dislodged roof tiles. Having seen pictures in the newspapers from the time Plymouth was bombed, she claimed this as fact.

Clemmie had wanted to believe her. But when the incendiaries had stopped and, in the eerie silence that followed, the *crrrrrump* of the first HE to explode nearby had made her ribs rumble, she'd sensed it was going to be worse than May was letting on. And now, in the smoke-filled light of day, it was plain her doubts had been well-founded: Jerry hadn't given a damn where the bombs fell, much less for the families whose homes and livelihoods they obliterated.

Her head pounding from lack of sleep, the back of her throat dry from the dust, she heaved another despair-laden sigh. Four hours they'd cowered in that dank little public shelter on the corner of Friar Street, forced to listen, helplessly, to the destruction raging overhead: to the boom of explosions; the crashing of glass; the rush of masonry collapsing into the streets. Four hours she'd clung to her sisters, praying with each ragged breath that it wouldn't be her last; that, against all the odds, they would live to see another day. But standing there this morning, she had to wonder what it was they'd been spared *for*. With neither home nor belongings, what were they to do? Where would they even go?

As the reality of their plight sank in, she started to cry. How could this be fair? What had the three of *them* ever done to the Germans? If a single stray bomb had flattened just Albert Terrace, then the three of them might have found refuge with neighbours. But even with a veil of brick dust hanging in the air like a November smog, Clemmie could see that the rest of Chandlery Street was gone too; even Mundy's the bakers, where she'd worked six mornings a week selling bread. To make matters worse, all she could make out of the Sovereign Hotel, where May had been employed as a cleaner, was a blackened outline of the facade. Pound to a penny the Plaza had been destroyed too, leaving Pearl without her job as an usherette. If none of them had work, how would they buy food? Essentials of any sort? They had nothing but the clothes they stood up in.

Catching May looking across at her, Clemmie reached into the pocket of her jacket, pulled out her handkerchief and blew her nose. 'What are we… going… to do? Everything's… gone. All of it. All of it…'

'Yeah.' Stabbing at the rubble with what looked to be a fire poker, Pearl agreed. 'Ain't so much as a matchstick to be saved from this lot.'

Unusually for May, her response offered little comfort. 'No.'

Dearest May. When illness had left their mother too frail to continue to care for them, without questioning the fairness or otherwise May had quietly assumed responsibility for everything, from paying the rent to looking after their ration books, from putting meals on the table to ensuring they had clean clothes. For all her pragmatism and determination, though, Clemmie imagined even *she* was going to struggle to make things right this time. Where would she even start? Those two rooms on the ground floor of that crumbling old terrace might have been rat-infested and damp, but they'd been their home, within its walls what precious few belongings they'd so far avoided having to sell.

'You know...' At the edge of the debris, Pearl's prodding had lost some of its vigour. 'There is *one* good thing...'

Clemmie frowned. Amid all this devastation, there was a *good* thing?

Beside her, May looked equally puzzled. 'Really? Not sure how you fathom that.'

'Well, you got to think we've seen the last of Charlie.'

Dear God, yes, her stepfather, Mr Warren. When the air raid siren had started up its nerve-shattering wail, they'd crept past him slumped over the kitchen table, reeking of the Stoker's Arms and snoring like a hog. Was it wicked to pray that Pearl was right – to hope the Luftwaffe really had put an end to him? Given his habit of showing up more times than a bad penny, she doubted they could be so lucky.

Desperate for reassurance, she turned to May. 'You think he were definitely still in there, then? You don't think he could have got himself out *before* the bombs started falling? He couldn't have... he couldn't have woken up after we'd left and took himself off to shelter someplace else?'

'Think about it,' May said as she cast a glance to where Pearl – the only one of them to have Charlie Warren as her real father – was now clambering over the rubble. 'When the three of us left, he was snoring fit to wake old Mrs Tuckett on the top floor. So, no, I reckon that skinful he had yesterday was his last, and that when he came stumbling in, cursing and lashing out as usual, it was for the final ever time.'

Pearl was of the same mind. 'Yeah. There's *no way* he could have got out. He's gone. Dead and buried. And I for one shan't mourn his passing.'

To hear Pearl talk so coldly about her own flesh and blood made Clemmie wince. 'But—'

'Face it, Clem.' Continuing to poke about in the rubble, Pearl was unrepentant. 'That foul-mouthed bastard might have been my father, but he was rotten through and through. And yes, I know you're not supposed to speak ill of the dead, but you're not supposed to tell lies, either. So, let's none of us pretend we'll miss him. You might have been the one to feel the back of his hand most often but weren't none of us spared his wrath. It was me he swore at for fighting off the drunks he brought home. It was me he told not to be so prissy every time I complained about one of them putting a hand up my skirt or trying to reach inside my blouse. And if I can't forgive him that, then why would I mourn him? And you, May – don't tell me you weren't brassed off with him constantly helping himself to the coins from your purse…'

'Trust me,' May said stoutly, 'many's the time I could gladly have taken the carving knife to that man—'

'…or that you, Clemmie, weren't browned off with him sending you out with your own money to fetch his fags or his booze.'

To Clemmie, that hadn't been the worst of it. 'I daren't never disobey him.'

'See, that's what I mean. So, no, I shan't lose sleep over him being dead, and nor should either of you.'

Clemmie dabbed her eyes. While Pearl might have a point, it still didn't seem right for the man's own daughter to wish him dead.

'It's true,' May picked up again. 'He don't deserve to be neither mourned nor remembered.'

But if Clemmie was to rest easy, she needed to know, beyond all possible doubt, that Charlie Warren really had drawn his last breath. 'Even so…'

'Look,' said May. 'You've had a shock. You're tired. We all are.'

'Besides,' Pearl went on, rising to her feet and gesturing about her, 'we've more important things than the demise of Charlie Warren to worry about. I mean, what the hell do we do now? Where do we even go?'

Before their discussion had turned to the fate of her stepfather, Clemmie had been wondering the same thing.

'Well,' May replied. 'When we came up out of the shelter, that warden told us we were to go up the church and wait there. So, I suppose we go and see what the arrangements are – see if a rest centre's been set up, like that time last month when those stray bombs fell on Marsh Barton. I don't see as we have a choice. I mean, look about you. High Street's flattened. Fore Street's burned out. Even Bedford Circus is gone. There's nowhere left.'

Turning her attention back to Pearl, Clemmie watched her tug something from the rubble. As it glinted in the light, she recognised it as the sort of little mirror to hang in a birdcage. She supposed it must have belonged to Mrs Duncan upstairs, what with her keeping budgerigars.

Letting the mirror drop from her fingers, Pearl picked her way back across the rubble. 'So,' she said, brushing the dirt from her hands, 'that's what we're going to do, is it? Go up the church?'

May nodded. 'It is. We'll go and see what's what. And we'll do it now, early, before every other soul does the same and we're left to traipse here, there and everywhere in search of any old place that'll have us.'

'Which makes me proper glad then,' Pearl said, and with which Clemmie noticed her half-sister's lips curl into a grin, 'that on the way down the shelter last night, I thought to grab this.' When she held aloft her pink vanity case, the sight of her sister's most cherished possession made Clemmie start crying again. 'Because at least I shan't be without my curlers or my toothbrush. Nor lipstick and mascara.'

'Yes, because let's face it,' May said, glass crunching under her shoes as she turned away from the ruins, 'looking your best really ought to be your biggest concern when you've just lost your livelihood, your home, and everything that was in it.'

Turning to see her sisters picking their way over the firemen's hoses snaking up from the river, Clemmie risked a final glance back at the ruins. *Dare* she believe Mr Warren was dead? Had they really seen the back of him? She supposed only time would tell.

Chapter 2

She really didn't know why she was there. May would probably say that losing their home had left her needing to seek comfort, and she could well be right. All Clemmie knew for certain was that this morning, when she'd woken up in that narrow little camp bed in the rest centre, she'd felt drawn to come.

Poking a strand of hair behind her ear, she reached with her other hand to trace a forefinger over the inscription carved onto the otherwise plain headstone. The letters of her mother's name were crisper than those of her father, the latter worn shallow over the seventeen or so years he'd lain there. *In loving memory of Frederick Sidney Huxford.* More recently, the three of them had scraped together the money to have a stonemason inscribe underneath, *& Maude Annie, his wife.* When the vicar had agreed they could lay their mother to rest with their father, they'd been enormously relieved; ensuring she rested in peace seemed the last decent thing they could do for the poor woman. That Charlie Warren had deserted them more than a dozen years previously had been handy in that regard, since he hadn't been there to insist they bury her separately, nor to demand that she be immortalised as Maude Warren. It wasn't as though he would have covered the cost of doing either: whatever money that man came by was only ever spent on Woodbines, brown ale, or the bookie. And that had to be why, the moment he'd learned of Mum's passing, he'd turned up again: to see whether she'd still had anything of value he might pawn or sell. When it quickly became apparent that she hadn't, he'd moved back in anyway and taken to thieving from the three of them instead.

That he, too, was now dead she was still struggling to believe. To know they need no longer fear his wrath was more than she could have dared hope. His temper had been bad enough at the best of times; no matter how quickly she moved, it was never fast enough. But when he'd been drinking – and when hadn't he? – it was so very many times worse. *I won't tell you twice*, he would bawl, his hand raised in reinforcement of his point. May said the reason he'd picked on her most was because she was small and fair; bullies were like that, she'd said, always quick to single out the slight or the frail.

Dear May, she'd tried so hard to shield her from the man's fury, as had Pearl. But sometimes, when she'd finished work and was home on her own, he would turn up without warning. When that happened, May had said she was to grab her purse and go off up the street, or go down and wait in Mundy's. But if he started on her the second he staggered in through the door, finding the right moment to give him the slip wasn't always possible. And he didn't always pass out straight away, either. Anyway, as they'd seen nothing of him since they'd fled to the shelter on Sunday night, she could only suppose he really was dead.

She returned her eyes to the headstone and let out a sigh. 'It's all gone, Mum. Albert Terrace is just a pile of rubble, the rest of Chandlery Street the same. And I don't know what we're going to do.'

You'll be all right, love, she imagined hearing her mother reply. *You're stronger than you know.*

But *how* would they be all right? Albert Terrace might have been a rat-infested dump but, Mr Warren aside, it had been their home. Moreover, the three of them had all worked nearby, meaning they'd just about been able to scrape together the rent every Friday and have enough left over to buy food. But now, without work, they would be destitute, and she couldn't see how they were going to be all right at all. While her future might never have been exactly bright, at least she'd had one. As Miss Treadgold at school had said, *the best* you *can hope for, Clemmie Warren, is to make someone a good wife.* And although she'd known hostilities were looming, she'd been pinning her hopes on doing just that; she'd only ever assumed that, when all the young men came home from war, she would meet one of them, someone kind-hearted but ordinary, someone with whom she would make a home and start a family. And she would have been happy with that. Still would be. But who knew how many of the young men who had gone off to wage war – some of them as far back as the summer of '39 – would even come home? Would there be any sort of man left to marry, let alone a kind and gentle one? That the war continued to rumble on was bad enough. But now, with the city in ruins, who knew what was in store for them? How they were going to get back on their feet now, she had no idea. She doubted May did, either. And if there was anyone who could be relied upon to be optimistic, it was May.

The weight of her gloom sagging her shoulders, she let out a despairing sigh. One thing was certain: standing at her parents' graveside wouldn't solve her problems. No, sadly, there was nothing for it but to head back to the rest centre and see what arrangements the authorities were making for people. And by that she meant people like the three of them, who'd been left without so much as a stick to their name.

–

'This is ridiculous. We'll be stood here for ever.'

Inclined to agree with Pearl's assessment, Clemmie nodded. She, too, had been eyeing the queue snaking ahead of them through the doors into the school hall, concluding that they would be lucky to reach the front before nightfall.

The waiting around was taking its toll on May's patience, too. 'Oh, for heaven's sake, Pearl.' A glance at her expression made Clemmie glad she'd kept quiet. 'It's not as though you've anywhere else to be.'

'Happen you're wrong. Dreckly we're done here, I'm going up the Savoy to try an' persuade them to take me on.'

'Yes, well,' May grumbled, 'admirable though that is, you know as well as I do that just because the place is still standing doesn't mean they'll be able to open. Even if they can, I can't imagine their most pressing need right now will be new usherettes. Not with the city in this mess.'

'You don't *know* that. They might have lost some of their—'

'Pearl, just this once, do as I ask. We can't go on without clothes. Nor money nor ration books. And while I can't speak for the two of you, and grateful though I am for the roof over my head, I'd prefer to sleep someplace that doesn't involve being woken up by some baby grizzling, worse still by some complete stranger snoring.'

Inwardly, Clemmie had to agree; if the only course open to them was to throw themselves on the mercy of the authorities, they might as well get on with it. If it took all day for them to reach the front of the queue, so be it.

A glance at Pearl, though, suggested she wasn't persuaded.

'But the Savoy *might* be open. And they *might* need staff. For all you know—'

'They might well. But if you're not here when our turn comes, odds are you'll miss out on getting a new ration book, which will mean—'

'Can't you get one for me? You usually do. You fetch *all* our new ration books when they come in.'

'That's different. These aren't new ones, they're replacements. If you *lose* your ration book you have to sign a form to get another one.'

Listening to May explaining, Clemmie stiffened; if you lost your ration book, you also had to pay a fine.

'Do you think they'll make us pay?' she asked. It hardly seemed fair.

Beside her, Pearl scoffed. 'They'd have to give us the shilling to pay with first.'

'Can't see it would be right to fine us,' May replied. 'Anyway, when I asked that WVS woman, she said everyone has to come in person. So, Pearl, do you want a new ration book and the chance of some clean clothes or are you not bothered? Because if you're happy to keep washing out that same pair of drawers in the washbasin for ever more…'

Evidently seeing sense, Pearl huffed. 'All right, all right. Keep your hair on. I'll wait.'

Her younger sister's irritation apparently blown out, Clemmie stood in silence, the whiff of disinfectant reminding her of her schooldays, when she had existed in a state of near perpetual dread of putting a foot wrong and being given the cane. As it happened, the worst she'd ever had was a rap across the knuckles with a ruler for staring up at a butterfly trying to get out of the window, when she should have been writing out her six times table. The humiliation had stuck with her; to this day, it was rare for her attention to wander. This morning, though, concentrating on anything was almost impossible. And she guessed that the people around her felt the same, those queueing to either side of them tutting and fidgeting and shifting their weight, raising their eyebrows at one another in weary resignation.

She glanced along the row of tables where people were being helped to fill in forms. The officials and volunteers assisting them all seemed of a certain 'type': exclusively female, they were generally grey-haired and clad in the green cotton overalls of the WVS. The two younger women in ordinary skirts and blouses she supposed to be childless newly-weds, wanting to *do their bit* while their husbands were away fighting. And hovering behind the tables, watching proceedings closely and directing or intervening where necessary, were two supervisors who looked as though, between them, they could run a dozen emergency committees and still make time for more. Their uniform flannel dresses and low-heeled shoes marked them out as organised and efficient, the seriousness of their expressions suggesting to Clemmie that they were women who brooked no nonsense. Even just watching them put the fear of God into her.

When, sometime later, a distant clock chimed midday, she once again scanned the queue and, counting just three families still ahead of them, studied the appearance of the volunteer talking to the family at the front. Another capable-looking woman, her striking ash-brown hair was fashioned into a loose bun. On her nose she wore a pair of gilt-rimmed glasses; resting on her maroon WVS jumper lay a single strand of pearls. But what fascinated Clemmie most was the elegant way she held herself. Without realising it, she straightened her own spine and lowered her shoulders from where they had become hunched up around her ears. Oh, to have such polish and poise. Oh, for such confidence. Here was a woman who hadn't grown up with schoolmistresses telling her that if she didn't buck up her ideas she wouldn't even get a job as a char, and that even a housewife needed to understand arithmetic if she was to avoid being 'done' by a stallholder in the market. Still, Clemmie reflected, she'd fared all right behind the counter in Mundy's; it wasn't often she'd had to scribble down a customer's purchases to arrive at the amount to charge them.

'Now, my dears,' the woman in question addressed May when the family ahead of them in the queue was finally directed to a vacant desk, 'what do you need?' She had, Clemmie noted, very neat fingernails.

'To be honest,' May replied wearily, 'everything. Our home in Albert Terrace, and what few bits we had in it, are all gone. The whole lot of it.'

'Oh dear, I'm so sorry to hear that.' *What a lovely voice*, Clemmie noted. 'So, you truly are in need of our help.'

Together with May and Pearl, Clemmie nodded and then, feeling tears welling, held herself rigidly; weeping would only make her look childish.

'I'm afraid so,' May agreed.

'Then let's see if we can get a few of your most urgent needs taken care of. For certain we can do something

18

about food. Shortly now, our temporary kitchen will be dishing up hot meals. And clothing donations are trickling in all the time. We also have a couple of officials from the local Food Office here today, so you'll be able to apply for new ration books. And someone from the Registration Office is here to help with lost identity cards. You'll also be able to apply to go on the list for rehousing. Look, there you go,' the woman said, pointing to the far end of the row of desks, where an elderly couple were getting up to leave, 'that's our Mrs Hughes. She'll get you started.'

To Clemmie, the paperwork for even the simplest of things seemed complicated beyond belief.

'I know all these forms and questions are the last thing you want at the moment,' Mrs Hughes said after a while, her manner kindly, 'but we have to make sure those asking for help are genuinely entitled. Unfortunately, these days there are some poor sorts around, not to mention a few out-and-out rogues.'

Eventually, by the time the smell of boiling vegetables was wafting into the hall and Clemmie had begun to feel almost sick from the headache hammering away in her skull, a few of their most pressing needs had been taken care of.

'Thank goodness they were able to give us temporary ration books,' she remarked as they joined yet another queue, this time for a bowl of split-pea soup and a couple of dry crackers.

'Not that we've any place to keep food, nor to cook it, let alone the means to buy it in the first place.'

May had a point. She was also, Clemmie could tell, still hopping mad over the discovery that Pearl had lost her identity card.

'What?' Pearl asked, when she caught May glowering at her.

'Well, for goodness' sake, how many times have I reminded you about your blessed ID? Over and over, I told you that when you turned sixteen you had to apply for an adult one. Still, I suppose it's my own fault. I should have known you weren't listening. The morning of your birthday, I should have marched you up the Registration Office and *made* you do it. Worse than yours being out of date, though, is the fact that each and every time that blasted siren's gone off, I've said to both of you, *don't forget your identity card*. But the one and only time I didn't say it, what do you do? Rather than check you've got the important things, you grab your vanity case. So now, not only do you need a new identity card when you shouldn't, but, because your old one wasn't even still valid, we've got to traipse all the way up that bloomin' Registration Office to fill in a load more forms when it could have been done here, now, today.'

Their soup eaten, the three of them had gone next to apply for rehousing. Clemmie found the process both fraught and dispiriting: what few billets were available were being given first to families, then to the elderly without relatives nearby, then to childless married couples. Single women like the three of them seemed almost not to make it onto the list at all, which, since it wasn't *their* fault they had no family to take them in, she thought unduly harsh.

'I don't know what we're going to do,' she had whispered to May after a particularly depressing encounter with a woman from the city corporation. 'I don't want to be put somewhere on my own. I shouldn't like that at all.'

May's response had done little to reassure her.

'Well, hopefully it won't come to that.'

Pearl, Clemmie had noticed, was also oddly quiet, her silence leaving Clemmie to wonder what hare-brained scheme her younger sister was cooking up now.

–

In the wake of that particularly trying day, the rest of the week dragged: each subsequent dawn coming on the back of another largely sleepless night in the church hall; each new morning bringing watery porridge for breakfast – or, occasionally, a slice of toast and marge – the remainder of the day either stretching emptily ahead or else occupied with a further round of form-filling, none of which made Clemmie any more hopeful. And as the three of them sat watching another family, or another older couple, gather up their few belongings and leave the rest centre for the last time, they could do nothing but envy them their good fortune.

'That lot,' a girl Clemmie had come to know as Maggie remarked of the latest departures, 'have given up waiting and are going to stay with her sister down near Sidmouth. And the tall red-haired woman with the little boy got found a room in a house up near Exwick. And that other lot further over – you know, them in the corner with the tearaway kiddies – well, the authorities found *them* some place out on the Cowley Road. Gawd, didn't the mother moan.' Casting her eyes about the room, Maggie lowered her voice. 'You should have heard her. "What do we want with going all the way out *there*? We don't know a soul out there." Ungrateful so-and-so. I felt like saying that if *they* didn't want to go there, I'd gladly take it. Anything beats hanging around here.'

To Clemmie, the more she found out as the week went on, the less well it boded; if the corporation were having to send people several miles out of the city, then the likelihood of them being kept together felt increasingly slim. And with no job to tie her to a particular location, she could easily end up not only separated from her sisters, but somewhere she didn't know anyone else, either. Ungrateful or not, she found herself in sympathy with the woman who hadn't wanted to be sent up the Cowley Road.

The other thing making her uneasy was the fact that, these last few days, May seemed to be becoming more and more withdrawn. She'd told herself it was natural – just her sister's way of coming to terms with the shock of losing their home. A woman she'd got talking to in the rest centre had said that's what happened; you thought you were going along all right and then bang – it hit you all over again. And while all three of them were, by turns, either heartily browned off with their situation or else fretting and fearful of what lay in store, May was usually the *last* to succumb to despondency. *She* was usually the one keeping their spirits up. But there could be no denying she was quiet. Still, perhaps soon, there would be news of a place to live and then they could start to look for work and begin to get their lives back together. In truth, hoping for it was the only thing keeping her going.

'Don't you have *any* family?' the worn-out volunteer asked when, yet again, they'd traipsed along to the War Damage Information Bureau to enquire as to whether there was any word about a billet for them.

'Have you thought about joining up?' another suggested, her voice lowered to a conspiratorial whisper.

'Only, the WRNS have such a natty uniform, don't they? And one hears naval officers are terribly dashing.'

This last visit having proved fruitless, Clemmie left the emergency centre in a fog of despair. She had to do *something*; she couldn't go back to the rest centre and perch on that little camp bed, counting down the hours until it was time to eat whatever soup or stew was on offer next. She wasn't complaining. She was grateful for everything they were being given; driving her crazy was the endless sense of *nothingness*, the sense of drifting, pointlessly, from one day to the next.

'Well.' Pearl arrived to stand next to her and said, her tone as weary as Clemmie's mood, 'As usual, that was a waste of time.'

Coming to join them, May nodded in agreement. 'But no one's fault.'

'Happen not,' Pearl went on. 'But since the Savoy don't want me, I've decided to look for something else. Seems to me the only way any of us is going to get a roof over our head any time soon is to find it for ourselves, something that strikes me would be a good deal easier with a wage. So, I'll see you two back at the rest centre later.'

'Well, just have a care,' May said, her concern seeming rather less than Clemmie might have expected. 'Just be back before supper, else you'll go hungry.'

'Do you think she's right?' Clemmie asked as she watched Pearl trot down the steps and head off up the road. The idea of her younger sister getting herself fixed up with a job and a home through her own endeavours made her feel both envious and inadequate. 'Are *you* minded it's the only way we'll get back on our feet?'

With an air of resignation, May nodded. 'Beginning to seem that way. Look, I've something I need to go and do, and since there's no point you trailing around too…'

'Where are you going?'

'Nowhere important. And I shan't be long. Go on back to the rest centre and I'll see you there. All right?'

Something about May's tone made Clemmie feel like crying. Was this it? Was this the end of them always being together? Was this damnable war going to see them split up and going their separate ways? If so, which was *her* way? More than once lately, Pearl had accused her of lacking the courage to say boo to a goose. Since she wasn't wrong, how could she expect to get a job? The Mundys had only taken her on because they'd felt sorry for her mother – and because they'd only had to pay her a pittance. But if both of her sisters were going to find work and get on with their lives, where did that leave *her*?

Watching May follow Pearl's route down the steps and, without looking back, turn up the hill, Clemmie blinked away tears. No, it couldn't end like this. It wasn't fair. There had to be a way they could all stay together. Pearl finding a job and going off was one thing but May deserting her was unthinkable. Without May, how would she manage? All she'd ever done was walk the few steps to Mundy's each morning, serve customers wanting bread – for which there was no complicated system of rationing to operate – and walk home again. And yes, she *had* needed to try to stay one step ahead of Mr Warren and his drunken temper, but that hardly qualified her to live by herself, or even with someone she didn't know.

At a loss to know what else to do, and fearing she might properly cry, she ducked her head and hurried down the steps. She would do as May had said and go back to the rest centre. She certainly had nowhere else to be.

When she arrived back at the church hall, she went in through the entrance to find a woman struggling with a dilapidated cardboard box. At the top of it, she could see what appeared to be fabric.

'Oops! Watch out ahead!'

Stepping smartly out of the woman's path, Clemmie watched her squeeze sideways into a little room off the porch. 'Sorry,' she said. 'Do you need a hand?'

Setting the box down on a trestle, the woman nodded. 'Goodness, yes. If you have a moment or two to spare, that would be marvellous.'

With a rueful grin, Clemmie nodded. 'Time is something I have aplenty.'

'Excellent. Then there are more boxes outside, all of which need to be brought in for sorting. Follow me.'

Parked at the kerb was a dark-blue van, its rear door thrown wide. And when Clemmie stepped down into the road and peered inside, she saw a dozen or so boxes, their contents spilling onto the floor.

'Goodness,' she breathed, watching the woman pull the next box towards her. 'Are these all donations?'

'They are indeed. Some newly donated, some we'd previously rescued from a store we were using over at St Thomas's. When those few bombs fell over that way last month, part of the roof fell in, so we moved the contents to my friend's garden shed. But now we really do need to get them sorted and dished out to those in need. Not too heavy for you, that one?'

'Not… this short distance… no.'

'I don't suppose,' the woman said when they'd both put their boxes on the table, 'you happen to be at a loose end?'

Clemmie smiled. 'Pretty much all the time. Since we were bombed out, I've been sleeping here in the rest centre. So, unless we need to go and see some or other official, or queue for something, I've nothing to occupy me at all.'

'Have you thought about volunteering?'

Clemmie stiffened. 'Well, I—'

'Sorry. That came out rather sharply, didn't it? I rather meant that, if you're looking for something to fill the hours, you could do worse than join our number.' When Clemmie frowned, the woman went on, 'The WVS. We're the merry band of women in green who see to anything that needs doing.' With that, Clemmie recognised her as the supervisor from the aid centre. 'Our motto is "The WVS never says no". There's a team of our ladies running the kitchen through there, another that helps with evacuees, and I'm currently trying to whip up a gang to get a clothing centre up and running. We're helping to man the information bureau as well. Unfortunately, Hitler has scattered our members to the four winds and flattened a good number of the buildings we used to borrow – the one we had earmarked as our emergency cooking depot included – so it's proving tricky to say the least. But, after food and a bed, clothing is probably the single most important need.'

Clemmie nodded. 'The thing is, I'm not very useful. What I mean is—'

'My dear girl, you're a fit young woman with two hands, a brain and spare time. I can't think what better qualifications there could possibly be.'

Clemmie liked this woman. She was straightforward. And bumping into her again like this did have to make her wonder about fate. 'All right then.'

'Excellent. I'm Miss Evercott. Dorothy. And as well as being Exeter's WVS centre organiser, I'm standing in this morning as clothing officer.'

When the woman extended a hand, Clemmie shook it. 'I'm Clemmie.'

'Pleased to meet you, Clemmie. Let's get the rest of the boxes brought in and then I can show you what needs to be done.'

Goodness, Clemmie thought, as she followed Dorothy Evercott back out to the street. Whatever would May say? She'd be surprised, that was for sure. And Pearl would doubtless mock her. But what did that matter? Not only would volunteering give her something to do, but she would be helping other people, bombed-out people like themselves. And already, the prospect was lifting her spirits.

–

'Blimey, these dumplings are stodgy.'

'For goodness' sake, Pearl, keep your voice down.'

'I just meant that the ones you make are a lot— *were* a lot nicer.'

With a shake of her head, May scoffed. 'Yes, well, no doubt having to make a gross of the things in a temporary kitchen is a darn sight harder than knocking up just a handful in your own home. Besides, in our situation, it's a case of worse where there's none.'

Her head bent over her bowl, Clemmie watched through her fringe as Pearl stabbed with her spoon at one of her dumplings. To her mind, the admittedly rather grey-coloured little balls were just fine, hot food of any sort being far and away preferable to yet more paste sandwiches made with day-old bread.

27

'Any luck with your search for work?' May looked across the table at Pearl to enquire.

Clemmie smiled; changing the subject was a tactic her sister inevitably employed when she'd grown weary of one of them complaining.

Dropping her spoon into her bowl, Pearl let out a frustrated sigh. 'Do you think if I said I couldn't eat the dumplings they'd give me some more stew?'

'If you go up and tell them you don't rate their dumplings, I'd be surprised if they serve you anything ever again. Anyway, your search for work…'

'Actually, yes,' Pearl replied, her tone lifting. 'I do have something up my sleeve. But since I have to go back for a proper interview, and since I don't want to jinx it, I'm not going to talk about it until after I've been. But I'm sure I'll get it. I could just tell.'

Clemmie's smile this time was a wry one; if *she* hadn't wanted to jinx something, she would have been careful to sound neither so boastful nor so confident. But then that was the difference between her and Pearl – and why Pearl would probably get the job where she herself wouldn't.

'*I* have some news—'

When Clemmie spoke at precisely the same moment as May, they both laughed.

'You first,' May went on, scraping the last spoonful of stew from her bowl.

'I'm volunteering with the WVS.'

When May looked back up and smiled, Clemmie recognised genuine warmth.

'Well good for you. I thought you looked perkier when I came in. Was that this afternoon you joined up?'

Clemmie nodded. 'By chance, I bumped into one of the organisers and got to talking. When she asked me if I could spare some time to help out, I said I could. I mean, it feels only right. It's WVS volunteers who run this canteen and this rest centre. And she told me that since the bombings, they've also been helping out at the hospital with the casualties, and helping folk to get their belongings from their damaged homes and make them safe against thieves.'

'All well and good,' Pearl remarked. 'But not much use if they don't pay you.'

'I don't intend on doing it for ever.' Clemmie rounded on her younger sister. 'Just while I wait for a proper job to come along.'

'Take no notice,' May said. Reaching across the table, she patted Clemmie's hand. 'It's very kind-hearted of you. No doubt they need all the help they can get. And I'm sure they'll be as grateful for your time as we are for theirs. Besides, who knows what meeting new people might lead to – who you might meet that knows of someone with a vacancy?'

'Exactly.' In truth, it was a possibility Clemmie hadn't considered; but now May had pointed it out, she felt even better about her decision to get involved. 'So, what's *your* news, then?' Her question posed, she braced for her sister's reply. If May had got herself a job, she very much doubted it was locally; she couldn't think of a single undamaged hotel anywhere even close – certainly not one that would need staff, what with so many cleaners and maids having lost their jobs at other hotels.

'Well, I too have a job.' From her pocket, May with-drew an envelope and put it on the table. 'The letter offering it to me came this morning.'

Under the table, Clemmie curled her fingers tightly: so much for having crossed them in hope. Not that May's news was a surprise; she'd guessed there was a reason for her sister being withdrawn these last few days. She'd known *something* was going on.

'I see you're calling yourself Huxford,' she said, nodding towards the envelope.

'I'm not *calling* myself anything,' May replied. 'I'm simply using my own name – the name our father gave to our mother.'

Clemmie frowned. 'But our names were changed to Warren.'

'Not properly, they weren't. Mr Warren just insisted we use his. Reckon he didn't want Mum reminded of Dad. I've been meaning for years to change it back. And now I have.'

'But—'

'You're welcome to stay as Warren if you want.'

Stay as Warren? Not bloomin' likely. No, if May said it was all right for them to use the name they'd had when they were born, then she would change hers back, too. From now on, she would tell everyone she was Clemmie Huxford. She would think of everywhere that had her down as Warren and tell them to change it, starting right here, in the rest centre. She would have nothing more to do with that odious man.

'This new job in Exeter?' Pearl asked. 'Only, I can't think there can be many hotels left here taking guests.'

'Actually,' May said carefully. Clemmie studied her sister's expression. 'It's not in a hotel, and it's not in Exeter. I'm going to be housekeeper to a farmer and so it will mean moving away.'

Listening as May went on to explain that this new employer was expecting her on Monday, Clemmie ducked her head and blinked back tears. *Monday*. Her sister was going as soon as that. Then this was it: at just eighteen years of age – in the eyes of the law still some way from being considered an adult – she'd lost her father, her mother, her home, and now she was losing May, too. And no doubt, before much longer Pearl as well. With a dismayed shake of her head, she sniffed. Ironic really, that in the space of a single night Hitler had achieved what a lifetime of hardship had so far failed to: he had split up what remained of their little family.

Feeling the cold hand of fear clutching at her insides, she wrapped her arms across her waist. From now on, then, she would be on her own in the world. And golly, how the prospect terrified her.

Chapter 3

It was no good. She could hold herself as stiffly as she liked but the sight of May's bus pulling away was too much for Clemmie to bear; nothing she could do was going to prevent tears. Her sister was going to start a new life without her. And the pain in her heart hurt more than she would have thought possible.

By contrast, beside her Pearl was dry-eyed. 'Hey, c'mon. Don't get upset. She'll be back. Mark my words.'

With a sniff, Clemmie met her half-sister's look. 'I'm not so sure 'bout that. You know what a stickler she is for keeping her word. If she's told this farmer she can do the job, she'll make good an' sure to do it.'

Pearl raised an eyebrow. 'Always assuming the place turns out to be what she was expecting. For all she knows, this feller could be tuppence short of a shilling. Or a German spy... or an axe murderer.'

'Stop it. Don't say that.'

'Well you've got to admit it's peculiar. I mean, who offers a woman a job in their home without even meeting her? Anyway, look,' Pearl went on, her tone softer this time, 'I have to go and see about this job again. They said if I called in today, they'd tell me if I've got it. But since I don't know how long I'll be, why don't you go on back to the rest centre and I'll see you there later on?'

Clemmie replied with a disconsolate nod. 'All right. But just be careful. Don't do anything rash.' She could do without both sisters going off on a whim.

'You be careful too.'

Watching Pearl walk away, Clemmie sighed. She wished she believed May would be back. While she didn't want her sister to have a nasty surprise when she got there, nor for her to hate every minute of her new employment, she wouldn't mind in the least if, come the end of the week, she decided it wasn't for her and came home. *Home.* Huh. How was it possible, two weeks on from losing everything, that she was still thinking in terms of 'home'? They had no home. Nor, with the way things were going, could she see how they ever would again – certainly not the three of them together. That said, if Pearl's news turned out to be good, she must try to be pleased for her. Turning in the direction of the rest centre, she gave herself a talking-to. *Stop rueing your plight and buck up. Try an' be a bit more like May and Pearl and show some spine.*

As it happened, one of the WVS volunteers, a rather gossipy woman called Beryl Trobridge, had said that today some bundles of household items were coming down on the train from the WVS central store in London, and had gone on to ask her whether, since they would need sorting out, she could lend a hand. With nothing better to do, she had agreed that she could. So, to take her mind from her despair, she would look forward to being of use with that.

'Oh, there you are, love,' Beryl Trobridge said when Clemmie went into the little side room off the hall and was standing unbuttoning her jacket. 'I hoped you hadn't forgotten.'

Clemmie shook her head. 'No. I just had… private business.'

'Private business. Ooh. Everything all right, is it?'

If Mrs Trobridge thought she was going to share family secrets, she was sorely mistaken. 'Fine, thank you.'

'Then let's get going, shall we?'

'All right.'

By listening to Beryl explaining, Clemmie gleaned that there were householders on the outskirts of the city willing to offer rooms to homeless families but who lacked sufficient supplies of the staples such as towels, pillows and blankets. This, Beryl was hoping, was what had arrived for Clemmie to divvy up.

'So, you understand what you've got to do? Work down the list for each billet and put together what they need.'

Clemmie nodded. 'Yes.'

About to leave her to it, Beryl turned back. 'Remember, stick to the list. Every item is precious.'

Inwardly, Clemmie sighed. Did she look incapable of following instructions? Did she really look like the sort to give out things willy-nilly?

'Of course.'

'And if there's not enough here to go round, then give every billet one less than they've asked for. Better to have more needs *nearly* met than some not at all. While it's good of these people to offer to take in strangers, there *is* a war on. If they're short, they'll have to get by as best they can.'

Really? There was a war on? 'Yes.'

'We've all got to manage with what we've got. And I've no time for scroungers.'

'Me neither.'

When Beryl left her to it, Clemmie wasn't sorry she'd gone; the little bit of power had clearly gone to the woman's head. Struck by a thought, she giggled: what was the betting that, behind her back, Mrs Trobridge was referred to as Bossy Beryl?

Having studied the sheet of paper containing the names and addresses of the householders and a list of each of their needs, Clemmie glanced about the room. The best thing would probably be to push together the three trestles and make a separate stack of goods for each household. If she kept to the order they were written down in, then in the absence of anything to label them with, she would know which was which.

The tables dragged into position, she turned to the first bale of goods. The string securing it was knotted so tightly that it took her several minutes to undo. Among the items that had arrived were plenty of blankets, which, although she could see they were made from salvaged wool, appeared otherwise unused. There were also items that had clearly been donated: a couple of eider-downs; several bedspreads; an assortment of pillowcases, largely thin and well-worn but perfectly serviceable in the circumstances. Towels were significantly fewer in number but, before long, she was standing looking at almost two dozen stacks that reasonably closely matched what the recipients had requested.

'Goodness. Well done.' Realising the voice wasn't Beryl's, Clemmie spun about to see Dorothy Evercott in the doorway. 'Are these for the new billets?'

Clemmie nodded. 'Not quite enough for everyone to have everything they've asked for but not far off.'

'Better than nothing.'

'For certain.'

'Well, if you need anything,' Miss Evercott said, gesturing to the main hall.

'Well, actually…' She might as well ask; no sense doing half a job. 'I think each bundle should be tied up so as not to get all muddled. But I'm going to need more string. I doubt what I've salvaged here will be enough.'

'String. Yes. Good idea.'

'And some paper and a pen to mark each parcel with a name.'

Dorothy Evercott grinned. 'You've done this before, haven't you?'

Feeling her cheeks colour, Clemmie shook her head. 'Never.'

'In that case, all the more well done. I'll go and see what I can find. Then if tomorrow morning I can commandeer a van to deliver some of it, we'll be able to get a few more families into their billets.'

Moments after she'd left, Dorothy was back with a ball of string, a pair of scissors, a pen and some cardboard labels. And when she looked in again sometime later, Clemmie was just tying up the last bundle.

'My word, you've done well. Time for you to get off home.'

Clearly, Miss Evercott had forgotten. 'Actually, I'm still sleeping here, in the rest centre. So I suppose you could say I'm already home. My sister, Pearl – well, more properly my half-sister – should be back soon. She went to see about a job.'

Miss Evercott didn't immediately respond, leaving Clemmie to wish that she hadn't prattled on. After a moment's thought, though, Miss Evercott said, 'I imagine you're hoping to be found somewhere together.'

'I should like to have been billeted with my older sister. But this morning she went off to take up a job as a housekeeper on a farm somewhere. And I'm minded

Pearl will find her feet all right without me. So, to be honest, I've reached the stage now where I'll be grateful for a bed wherever one can be found for me.'

Miss Evercott continued to look thoughtful. 'I see. Well, if you feel inclined to lend a hand again tomorrow, we'd be glad of your help. But now, if you're all done, I need to go and fetch the key to lock this door against pilfering.'

'People steal from donations?'

Miss Evercott nodded. 'Some from genuine desperation, others simply from greed.'

While she knew the war had brought about a lot of shady goings-on, to steal from people trying to help those with nothing struck Clemmie as appalling. 'That's awful.'

'It is. Anyway, thank you for your time. I hope we see you again tomorrow.'

Clemmie smiled. 'I'm sure you will.'

Following Miss Evercott from the room, Clemmie decided to see whether Pearl had returned. But as she pushed open the door to the main hall, she recoiled in distaste; with so many people packed into a space with so little fresh air, the odour of clothes in need of laundering and bodies in need of a wash grew more pungent every day. Doing her best to ignore it, she looked around. Pearl was indeed back.

Threading her way towards her, mindful of the families clustered in a bored fashion about their few belongings, her contentment from an unexpectedly meaningful morning began to give way to trepidation; she was about to learn whether Pearl had got the job she'd been after and whether, as a result, she would be left to languish here alone. Taking in the way Pearl was so casually reclined on her camp bed, she practised sounding pleased. *You got it? Oh, Pearl, well done.*

At that moment, Pearl looked up. 'Oh, there you are.'

Perching beside her, Clemmie felt a lump in her throat; while she might have steeled herself for Pearl's news, the sight of the adjacent camp bed stripped of its blankets served as a stark reminder that May had already gone.

'How... did your interview go?'

Casting aside the dog-eared copy of *Woman's Own* she'd been leafing through, Pearl grinned. 'I got the job. But then I told you I would.'

Clemmie's heart sank. So much for preparedness. 'Another cinema, is it?'

Still grinning, Pearl shook her head. 'Nope. Something *much* better than being an usherette. For a start, I shall be earning a good deal more money *and* rarely need to work a late night. On Monday, I start ten days of training—'

'Ten days?' What on earth sort of job had Pearl talked her way into? Not shop work, that was for sure. Nor cleaning.

'It's a highly responsible position requiring proper and thorough training.'

Proper and thorough training? Now she was plain baffled. 'So, what is it you'll be doing then?'

'Well, since I'm on a month's trial – during which I have to pass an assessment and then do two weeks without a hitch – I still don't want to jinx it by telling anyone.'

Clemmie stiffened. 'What, not even me?'

'Sorry. Not even you. But as soon as the job's properly mine, you'll be the first to know.'

Golly, Pearl could be infuriating. 'Will you even tell me where it is? I mean, what about somewhere to live?'

'It's here, in town.'

'And do they know you're homeless? Did you tell them?' It would be just like Pearl to have played fast and loose with the truth.

''Course I told them. I had to fill in three pages of application forms. They're very thorough.'

'And they don't mind – that you're homeless, I mean?'

'As it happens, they were most understanding. They even said that if I take to the position well enough, they'll help me find lodgings. I'm going to need to live close by.'

Weighed by a mixture of despair and dismay, Clemmie shook her head. *Need to live close by?* 'Please, Pearl, won't you tell me what it is? I don't like being kept in the dark. If nothing else, I could do with knowing what I should do about taking up an offer of somewhere to live, should I get one. I mean, what do we do if they offer us a billet but it's not in the city? If you turn it down, should I turn it down too?'

Pearl shrugged. 'I suppose we have to wait and see what they come up with. But I can tell you that if they announce we're to go out to Exwick or Alphington or Matford, like we saw happen to some of the families here at the beginning, then I'd have to say I can't go that far for reasons of my employment.'

For reasons of my employment? What on earth had happened to suddenly make Pearl so grown up? 'I see…'

'Look, all I can say is this. If you get offered somewhere to stay, you should probably take it – not worry about me and then risk losing out. One way or another, I shall be out of here before long anyway.'

Seemingly, then, this was it. Without so much as a backward glance, both of her sisters were moving on without her; thanks to Hitler and his ruddy Luftwaffe, not only had she lost her home and her work, but she'd lost the little bit of family she'd had left, too. And she didn't know which felt worse – the ache in her heart from being so easily abandoned, or the cold clutch of fear she felt when she tried to picture what might happen to her next.

Chapter 4

'Right, then, love. All this lot's salvage. But what not everyone realises is that there's a difference between salvage and salvage*able*.'

The following morning, listening to Beryl Trobridge explaining what she wanted her to do, Clemmie swallowed her indignation; the difference between salvage and salvageable was one she understood perfectly – probably far better than Mrs Beryl Trobridge, truth be told. Mum had been forever drilling into the three of them that nothing was ever to be thrown away until it was completely and utterly beyond all conceivable use. Growing up, the only clothes Clemmie had ever known had been hand-me-downs from May, which, even when May had been put in them, were unlikely to have been new and which, as often as not, went on to be worn by Pearl. Pillow slips were darned and redarned and then cut into squares and hemmed into handkerchiefs. Towels were used until they were threadbare and then still cut down to serve as either wash flannels or cleaning cloths. Outgrown jumpers and cardigans, or those worn to holes, were painstakingly unpicked and reknitted into something else. And her mother's dresses, having been taken in, let out, or darned as far as was respectable, were eventually fashioned into pinafores or skirts for whichever daughter was in greatest need. Yes, in their household, the mantra *waste not, want not* had been with them since long before the war. *It's perfectly serviceable for a while yet*, her mother would routinely observe of the result − whether it was darned socks or teacups with chips glued back on.

'Yes, I know the difference,' she nevertheless said to acknowledge Beryl's remark.

But as she had come to discover was the woman's way, Beryl wasn't listening; she was far too fond of her own voice for that.

'A sheet that's worn thin can be cut down the centre, turned edges-to-middle, and joined with a seam—'

Unable to resist, Clemmie interrupted. 'Yes, my mother did that all the time. You end up with a sheet that's smaller but does just fine.'

'Yes. Well. Then you shouldn't have a problem sorting this lot. Dorothy wants three piles − one for things that are perfectly fine as they are, one for articles that would be serviceable with a little attention from our Make-Do-and-Mend group, and one for items truly beyond repair. Think you can manage that?'

Despite the instructions striking Clemmie as something a seven-year-old could grasp, she nodded demurely. 'I'll do my best.'

'Then I'll leave you to get on with it.'

But Clemmie hadn't been at it long when Miss Evercott herself poked her head round the door.

'Thought I'd find you here. I trust our salvage officer, Mrs Trobridge, has explained what's needed.'

Clemmie smiled. 'Most thoroughly.'

'I know it might seem a tedious task, but, if we're to continue to endure the shortages, good housekeeping of limited resources is ever more vital.'

'My mother brought us up to be thrifty.'

'Women like your mother, leading by example, are something else that's vital.'

'Yes.' Noticing how Miss Evercott then appeared to hesitate, Clemmie waited.

'You're Clemmie Huxford, aren't you?'

With a sudden hope that she wasn't in trouble, Clemmie nodded. 'I am, yes.'

'Since the list revealed only one Clemmie, it seemed safe to assume it was you.'

Clemmie frowned. 'The list?'

'Oh, yes, forgive me – so many thoughts in my head all at once these days. The list for rehousing. When I was talking to our billeting officer yesterday, I took a peek to see whether you are close to being found somewhere.' Gripped by a mixture of surprise and anticipation, Clemmie held her breath. 'Alas, while I wish I could tell you otherwise, you're right at the bottom.'

Although she had hoped for better news, it was really no more than she'd been expecting. 'So… there are still a number of people above us.'

Dorothy Evercott nodded. 'A good many, I'm afraid. Although, obviously, since we're moving people into places all the time, and the loudspeakers are driving around the outlying areas asking for households to volunteer billets, there are slightly fewer above you than a week ago. Anyway, my reason for raising the matter is that I have a spare room. And before you get too excited, I should point out that it's terribly small. I always think that whoever built the house must have had in mind a nursery. But it does have a bed, and I might just be able to squeeze in a modest chest of drawers.'

Was she really being offered a billet? 'So…'

'If you like, you can have it. It's a crime to let it stand empty with so many young girls in need.'

How was it possible to feel both relieved and disappointed? 'The thing is,' she said, immediately spotting a snag, 'I don't have a job. So I can't see how I would pay the rent.'

'Oh, goodness, I'm not asking rent. It's far too small a room for that. No, I just thought that rather than languish here, you might prefer a little comfort. And privacy. And use of a proper bathroom. As for food, well, in the short term we'll get by.'

Unable to believe what was happening, Clemmie found herself struggling to reply. A room in this nice lady's house? With no rent to pay? It seemed too good to be true. 'Well…'

'And in case you're wondering – because, in your shoes, I know *I* would be – the house in question is mine and mine alone. I'm unmarried, childless, naturally, and have one other lodger. She's a young lady called Gwen, a little older than you, but who was in similar straits. She's been with a me a week or so now and, entirely through her own endeavours, has just found herself a new job.'

'Yes,' Clemmie said, fearing that if she thought about it for too long she'd come up with any number of reasons to decline. 'Yes, please. I'd like that very much.'

'Excellent. Do you know Topsham Road?' When Clemmie nodded, Dorothy went on, 'My house is in Buckingham Crescent, some way along on the left. Number twelve. It's a little under half an hour's walk from the city centre and on the route of several buses, when they're running.'

'Thank you,' Clemmie said. 'It sounds—'

'Look, this afternoon, I have to attend a meeting of the relief committee at the corporation. And these things do tend to drag on. So, why don't you have a hot meal here and as soon as I'm done, I'll come and find you? That way, we can walk back together, and you needn't fear getting lost. Would that seem sensible?'

'That would be very kind of you.'

'Right. Then I'll leave you to your sorting and I'll see you later.'

'Later. Yes. Thank you.'

When Miss Evercott left, Clemmie reached to the trestle and tried to calm her excitement. Had that really just happened? Had she really been offered somewhere to live? True, she felt mean accepting when Pearl didn't have anywhere yet – she was already in a fret about having to break the news to her later. But Pearl was full of talk about this job she'd just got, and how it would require her to live close by. She'd also said that if she, Clemmie, was offered somewhere to lodge, she should take it. So, while none of that did a scrap to ease her conscience, she would grasp the opportunity being so kindly offered and hope, as she usually did with Pearl, that the girl knew what she was doing.

–

'So, Miss Evercott says you was bombed out.'

Adopting what she hoped was a friendly smile, Clemmie nodded. 'That's right.'

From where she was leaning in the doorway to the tiny bedroom, Gwen Brewer gave a dismayed shake of her head. 'Me too. Ruddy Jerries. If I could get my 'ands on even just one of them… well, let's just say they'd pretty quickly wish it had been *them* on the receiving end of their HE.'

Pulling open the top drawer of the small chest at the foot of the bed to look inside, Clemmie gave another nod. 'I feel the same. Hitler took everything we had. And it wasn't much to start with.'

'Same here. Where did you live?'

Her few underthings placed in the drawer, Clemmie persuaded it closed. 'Chandlery Street.'

Gwen thought for a moment. 'Oh, yeah. I know it. Just up from the quay.'

'That's right. Where were you?'

'Bedford Circus.' Unwittingly, Clemmie raised an eyebrow. Gwen Brewer neither looked nor spoke as though her family had owned – nor even rented – a home in the city's smartest crescent. 'Me mum kept house for a gentleman.'

That explained it. 'I see.'

'Her job needed her to live in and so we had a couple of rooms in the basement. When the siren went off that night, we stayed put. Had a Morrison shelter, see. And being in the basement we thought we was as safe there as anywhere. And Mr Lloyd-Digby, being the night owl he was, couldn't never be bothered to stop what he was doing for an air raid anyway. Had it in his head the Luftwaffe wouldn't be interested in Bedford Circus – that they would go after the railways and the factories and the gasworks. Anyway, when them first bombs started falling, Mum said she didn't like the idea of him sat all the way up there. He had his bedroom and his study on the third floor 'cause he liked to be up above the noise of the street and whatnot. Anyway, she went up to try and persuade him to come down the basement with us. In the moments she was gone, we were hit. The bomb landed two houses along, but the blast and the debris took both her and Mr Lloyd-Digby instant. The warden what eventually found her said she would have been gone straight off. And yet me, I was helped out of the rubble with no more than a few grazes on my arm and a cut on my leg.'

Feeling tears welling, Clemmie looked down hastily. 'I'm so sorry. That's awful.'

'What about you?' Gwen enquired. 'You lose anyone close?'

Knowing that the only person they'd lost wasn't in the least close made her flush with guilt. 'No,' she whispered, determining not to mention Mr Warren. 'Me an' my sisters were in the public shelter on the corner of Friar Street. Somehow, despite just about every building around us being flattened or burnt down, we made it out.'

'You got a job?' Gwen went on to ask. Reaching to the bedstead, she fingered the sleeve of Clemmie's jacket. 'This is nice.'

Clemmie shook her head. 'Not any more. I used to work in the bakery at the bottom of Chandlery Street. But an HE that fell nearby demolished the front of it. Somehow the yard out the back, where the ovens were, stayed standing. Next day, the Mundys were back baking again – until the corporation stopped them on account of the building next door being unsafe.'

'I was in Woolworths.'

Clemmie's eyes widened. 'I always fancied being a Woolworths girl. I even went in once to enquire about vacancies, but they said they didn't need anyone and already had a long waiting list.'

'Yeah. It were popular. I made a lot of friends there. The manager was real strict but it were fun.'

'Where do you work now? Miss Evercott said you've found something new.'

Gwen pulled a face. 'Parachute factory. Fulling's Road. God-awful place. For a start, it's bloomin' draughty. And the supervisor on our section is a proper witch. Still, as war work goes, it could be worse. I could have been sent up the Midlands to an armaments place. By all accounts, they're the pits. We think the witch is strict, but the stories coming out of some of them places make me count my lucky stars. It's the reason I got myself up there pretty quick – you know, to get in before everyone else from Woollies did.'

'Good idea.'

'So, are you registered?'

Clemmie shook her head. 'Not yet. I'm only eighteen. My older sister, May, she had to register. Although as it happens, the other day, she went to a job keeping house for a farmer, some place up near Crediton. She said she'd write once she got settled but I haven't heard yet, so I've no idea how she's getting on. My younger sister, that's Pearl, she's still in the rest centre. Although, according to her, she's about to get a new job too. She lost her old one at the Plaza. It was burned out by a fireball.'

'Must be tough, being split up.'

'It is.'

'My sister's married with two kids. And my brother used to be down the gasworks, which put him in a reserved occupation. But he hated it there so much that last year he went in the merchant navy as a stoker. Mum's beside herself – *was* beside herself – you know, with all that keeps happening to our ships. Anyway, so far as I know, he's all right. The authorities are trying to get word to him about Mum. They said next time he's in port he might be able to apply for a couple of days compassionate. But to be honest, it don't seem worth it. I mean, she's buried now.'

Before the war, Clemmie would have been horrified to hear someone talking so matter-of-factly about losing a member of their family; it just went to show the effect that almost three years of terrible events was having on everyone.

'So,' Clemmie said. While talking to Gwen, she had found homes for all her belongings apart from her toothbrush and face flannel, both of them given to her at the rest centre. Glancing beyond Gwen along the landing, she lowered her voice and went on, 'What's Miss Evercott like? She seems nice.'

Gwen smiled. 'She is. But real particular. Likes everything in apple-pie order. If you were to ask me what she can't abide most, I'd say slovenliness. Can't bear it. Nor untidiness. And she's terrible quick-witted. As clever as any man, more so than many. And kind. I don't know what you'd call it but when you talk to her, she listens proper, and you can see she's thinking about what you've got to say. She don't dismiss you, neither, nor pooh-pooh your fears… or whatever. And so far, she hasn't taken a penny from me for food or rent. She said once I've worked my week in hand, and I see what's in my pay packet, we can agree on *a suitable contribution*. Kind, see. Some folk would want everything you earned and still not be happy.'

Clemmie knew the feeling. 'Seems more than fair.'

'All you got to do is leave things as you find them and make a proper go of looking for work. Oh, and show an interest in the war. She can't abide folk who bury their head in the sand. Says it's up to us to keep abreast of what's going on… to be *informed*, as she puts it, and to have an opinion on it one way or another.'

This last discovery put Clemmie on less certain ground. As far as possible, she avoided anything to do with the war, or what the government were doing about it, so much of it being either beyond her to understand or simply too frightening to contemplate. But Dorothy Evercott was right; if families were giving up their menfolk to it, it did rather behove those left behind to understand where they had gone, and why.

The following morning, though, it was with some trepidation that Clemmie went down to the kitchen. Although it was still early, already there, with the back door thrown wide, was Dorothy.

'Good morning, dear,' she said as Clemmie hovered in the hallway. 'Come on in. How did you sleep? I should imagine you found it all quite strange.'

'Actually,' Clemmie said, starting to relax a little, 'I had my best night's sleep in ages.'

'No doubt catching up after so long in No. 1 rest centre.'

'Yes.'

'Now, if you're all right with toast,' Dorothy went on as she popped two slices of bread under the grill, 'we can manage for breakfast today. But perhaps this morning, you could take your ration book along to the shops. I've written out for you where Gwen and I are already registered, so just get them to add you to my account. Simpler that way. The list's there, look, on the side. The shops in question are all on the main road. As for a meal at lunchtime, if I give you a shilling, how do you feel about going along to the British restaurant and having a hot one there? When we're all back here tonight, we can have a chat about routines and so on. While she's still training, Miss Brewer is assigned to the early shift, which starts at six each morning and finishes at three, so she's usually home sometime after that. As for my own hours, well, they rather vary. But in the morning I like to be well under way by eight, and home by six.'

Clemmie nodded. Miss Evercott was certainly organised. 'I understand.'

'Have you had any thoughts about a job?'

'Well…'

'Don't worry, I'm not expecting you to find something today. From a purely selfish viewpoint, you are a tremendous asset to our WVS team, and I shouldn't want to lose you. But we must all earn a crust, mustn't we?'

Clemmie smiled. 'I'm hoping to find shop work again, but it's going to be hard.'

Dorothy sighed. 'With so much of the High Street destroyed, you'll certainly face plenty of competition. On the other hand, as more and more young women are called up, smaller shops are being left in the lurch. You're presentable and you've a tongue in your head, so you could do worse than ask everywhere you go.'

'Oh, yes,' Clemmie said. 'I shall.' Her eyes flicking to the grill, she quickly pulled out the tray.

'Well done. You narrowly averted having charcoal for breakfast. And while bread might not be rationed, I do hate to see it go to waste.'

'Me too.'

'Well, then. I must leave you to it. I need an extra-early start this morning. If there's anything you need, just have a good hunt about and I'm sure you'll find it.'

'Thank you.' As expressions of gratitude went, Clemmie knew hers was woefully inadequate. 'I can't believe how kind you're being.'

'Everyone deserves a helping hand. Besides, I minded that you're the sort of young lady who will more than repay the favour.'

'I'll certainly do my best.'

'Then I shall see you this evening.'

When Clemmie heard the front door close moments later, she let out a lengthy sigh. Against all expectations, she'd been plucked from the grim atmosphere of the rest centre and brought to this lovely home, where she had the luxury of a bedroom all to herself. Miss Evercott, a kindly stranger whom she had met quite by chance, had given her the opportunity to get back on her feet. So, with May having already found her way into a job and a home, and with Pearl making it plain she wouldn't be far behind her, the three of them seemed slowly but surely to be getting themselves sorted out.

So why, then, she wondered, with life for each of them beginning to look up, did she have tears running down her cheeks and a dull ache in her chest? Why, if their lives were all taking a turn for the better, did everything this morning feel so unbearably sad and so horribly, horribly wrong?

Chapter 5

Having never before seen taps that could be polished to a shine, Clemmie let out a little sigh of contentment. In a home as nice as this one, doing the cleaning was almost a pleasure; a smart semi-detached dwelling with semi-circular bay windows and a front door recessed behind a brick arch, she guessed it couldn't be any more than ten years old. With all its mod cons, it was certainly a far cry from Albert Terrace.

It was now the start of Clemmie's second week lodging with Dorothy and Gwen in Buckingham Crescent but, despite having asked in almost every shop she passed, she had yet to find one in need of staff, let alone be interviewed for a position. And while it was true that she'd crossed her fingers beforehand and prayed to be turned away, she'd even enquired in the little laundry she'd seen near the barracks; slaving away in there all day would surely have tested both her stamina and her resolve.

Sometimes, in her quieter moments, she felt a creeping desperation; while more than happy to do the housework, she would prefer to earn a wage and start properly paying her way. *I will not accept charity*, her mother had always vowed. Given how badly they were usually struggling, Clemmie had found her mother's pride plain daft. But since being bombed out, she had come to appreciate how accepting charity left you feeling helpless, worthless. Not to mention beholden.

Hanging her apron on the back of the door, she glanced about the kitchen: all clean and tidy. So far this morning, she had washed up and dried the breakfast things, dusted everywhere except Dorothy's bedroom, wiped down the bathroom – such a luxury after the indignities of the kitchen sink and a shared outdoor lav at Albert Terrace. She had run the Bex Bissell over the carpet in the front room and the runner in the hallway and had polished the ornamental panes of glass to either side of the front door. And now, since it was approaching ten o'clock and to leave it any later was to invite disappointment, she would walk round to the grocer's and see which of the items on Dorothy's list were to be had.

'Pilchards?' she asked, more from hope than experience, when it was her turn to be served.

'Sorry, love. Plenty of snoek, though. Cheap, too.'

Without needing to look, Clemmie knew that Miss Evercott's list said _No snoek_. 'Thank you, no. I'll do without. Is there any sugar?'

'Supplier still hasn't got any,' the weary assistant replied. 'Try again next week.'

'Right.' _Try again next week_ – along with every other housewife who'd run out. 'Disinfectant?' A modest-sized bottle landed on the counter in front of her. 'Spam?'

'You're in luck. Came in yesterday.'

'Two please. Vinegar?'

'Not seen any of that in weeks.'

'Oh dear. Suet, then.'

'Big or small?'

She glanced to the list. 'Large. And toilet soap. Imperial Leather if you have it. If not, then Cussons.'

'This lot for Miss Evercott?' When Clemmie nodded, the woman bobbed down out of sight, and from under the counter came the sound of her scrabbling about. Reappearing with something in a brown paper bag that she placed alongside Clemmie's other goods, she winked. 'Sorry, love, no, only Cussons again.'

'All right. Thank you. That's it then. On Miss Evercott's account, please.'

It was only when Clemmie got home and was unpacking her paltry haul that she realised how, despite the assistant's assertion that there was none to be had, the bar of soap was indeed Imperial Leather. Putting it aside to take up to Dorothy's room later, she smiled.

'You'll find,' Dorothy had remarked of the grocer's the other day, 'that if they receive a stock of my favourite items, they generally put one by for me. Nothing black-market I hasten to add – and nothing for which I'm not registered with them, nor for which I don't have sufficient coupons. It's just what they do for those customers who, shall we say, not only spend well but do so without fuss – and settle their accounts without having to be reminded.'

To Clemmie, it didn't seem an unreasonable way of carrying on; shops had always taken care of their 'best' customers.

Her little bit of shopping put away, Clemmie glanced to the clock: ten minutes to twelve. She didn't really like an early lunch but the queue for the British restaurant when it opened at midday was a good deal shorter then than at half past. And with Gwen able to take her lunch at the factory canteen, and Dorothy usually eating at one of the British restaurants closer to her work, it made sense for her to eat at one too. As Dorothy had pointed out, it might seem an expense and a privilege, but it left them with more rations for their meals at the weekend. And, although the choice of hot dish – if on any given day there *was* a choice – could be somewhat repetitive, the food was always freshly cooked and of passable quality.

When she arrived at the drill hall, the menu chalked on the blackboard outside read *Sausage, Mashed Potato, Peas & Gravy, 8d*. Feeling her stomach rumbling, she joined the dozen or so others already queueing to get in and, when her turn came, handed over a thruppenny bit and five pennies, for which she received a ticket. With only one main course on offer, the queue moved smartly along, and she was soon seated at the end of an oilcloth-covered trestle. At home, sausages had always been something of a treat; if, come Friday morning, there had been not only sufficient money to pay the rent collector, but a few extra coins left over, then when she finished her cleaning shift at the Sovereign, May would pick up a link of them for their tea. Unfortunately, of late sausages seemed to contain more cereal than pork and had become something of a let-down. It was rumoured they were going on the ration soon anyway; before long, there wouldn't be any foods that weren't.

Her meal eaten and her plate returned to the trolley, Clemmie retraced her steps to Buckingham Crescent. Dorothy had suggested she treat herself to a pudding after her main course: *It's only another thruppence*. But she didn't want to appear to be taking advantage. This way, by going three days without, she could tell Dorothy she had enough left to pay for another day's main course. It was a small gesture, but one that made her feel less awkward about being fed by someone she barely knew.

Arriving back at number twelve, she let herself in, and only narrowly avoided stepping on two letters from second post. When she bent to pick them up, the first turned out to be a stiff ivory-coloured envelope for Miss Evercott. The sight of the handwriting on the second made her gasp: May had written.

Having propped up Miss Evercott's envelope on the hall table, Clemmie kicked off her shoes and padded through to the kitchen, where she pulled out a chair from beneath the table and sat down. In keeping with the 'Please Forward' instruction May had written at the top, someone had crossed through the address of No. 1 rest centre and written *12, Buckingham Crescent*.

Pulling out the sheet of notepaper, she began to read.

> *Dearest Clemmie,*
>   *I hope you are well.*

Two lines down and already she was blinking back tears. How stupid to cry over a letter from her sister!

> *I have now been here just over a week and I suppose you could say I am as settled as can be expected. After the ruins of Exeter, this place do truly feel like another world. Not long after I got here, the apple trees all burst into blossom at once. It is quite the sight. And there is so much space and so much quiet that my first few days I felt a proper fish out of water. But already I am grown used to it.*

What a relief to read that May was all right. It would have been truly terrible if she'd got there and found the place to be a dump of the worst order.

She read on.

So far away from everything, there are very few signs of the war. Other than grumble about rationing, folk seem to carry on much as they always have done. We have rabbit and pigeon to eat, and I'm told sometimes lamb from the farm next door, though I have not had the fortune to have any of that yet. There is also plenty of cheese from there, too, if you don't mind it being made from ewe's milk.

From what I can gather, there have been no air raids here, though apparently, when we had those first ones in Exeter back in April, a single bomb fell near the cattle market and around that same time, a Jerry plane came down in a farmer's field.

On the farm are land girls called Bonnie and Nessa. Two more different souls you would struggle to find. The farmer, who is called Mr Beer, is the most private and secretive man I ever met. He has no time at all for the land girls. But I think that is because they are here to grow vegetables and he has no interest in doing that. Seems to me, his apple trees are his whole world. He's a funny feller all right. Anyway, now that I have the place a bit more up together, the work is not too bad and leaves me some time to myself.

When a tear dropped onto the middle of the page, Clemmie fumbled about in her pocket for her handkerchief, mopped at her eyes and blew her nose. While it was a relief to know that May was all right, having to accept that her sister was settling down without her seemed only to deepen the chasm between them.

Trying to ignore the ache pulling in her chest, she read the final few lines.

Well, I hope this letter reaches you without too much delay and I am sorry I did not get around to writing until now. I did sorely mean to, but you will know how it is. Are you still ~~volent~~ volunteering with the WVS? Do you see much of Pearl? Please let me know soonest where you are staying and how you are going along.

  With warmest love,
  Your sister May

Clemmie's immediate thought was that she must write back. However, unless she wanted May to think her morose and lost, it might be best to wait until she didn't feel quite so tearful. Besides, this afternoon she had vowed to visit the shops on the other side of the main road. After all, if she didn't keep looking she would never find work. And then, in the morning, she was going to help at the rest centre. If she timed it right, she might even see Pearl there; the day she'd moved out to take up Miss Evercott's offer of lodgings, she'd scribbled the address on a scrap of paper and asked someone to hand it to the red-haired girl called Pearl Warren. She'd also made sure one of the volunteers had recorded the address alongside her name in the register of displaced people. That way, if Pearl lost the note she would still be able to find her. She'd had no word, though, and on each of the occasions she'd been back there, Pearl had been out. But now she wanted to let her know that May was all right.

Well, one thing at a time. Since she was the last of the three of them to find a job, she'd better get off her behind and have another go. After all, sooner or later her luck had to change, didn't it…?

Chapter 6

'Now, you're clear about what it is you've got to do?'

Clemmie met her supervisor's look. 'Yes, Mrs Trobridge. You explained it real thorough. I'm to write in this register the details from these evacuee forms.'

'Except they're not evacuees, they're—'

'Bombed-out families who've been found billets. Yes. You said.'

'These were the only forms we could think to use to record who's gone where.'

'Yes.'

'Poor souls.'

It was the morning after yet another afternoon's fruitless search for work and, having already suffered Mrs Trobridge explaining this latest task at least three times, Clemmie checked her impatience. 'Poor indeed. No doubt in a minute I shall find my own name on the list.'

Beryl Trobridge's expression didn't change; clearly, the woman wasn't even listening.

'Because it's important the register is both up to date and accurate. You can't imagine the number of telegrams still coming in to the police, the ARP, the town clerk, all of them from folk desperate to know what's become of their relatives.'

Itching to be left to get on with it, Clemmie sighed. 'Yes.'

'Write neatly and be sure not to spell any of the names wrong.'

'I will.'

'And have a care not to miss anyone off.'

'I shall take every care.'

'Well, yes,' Beryl Trobridge blustered. 'Then I'll leave you to it.'

When Mrs Trobridge finally left her alone, Clemmie looked about the room and, spotting a folding chair, carried it to the trestle and sat down. Then she opened the register, the smell wafting from its pages suggesting it was kept somewhere damp. When she then glanced at the forms, completed in various hands and with varying degrees of legibility, she had an idea: she would sort them into alphabetical order by surname; that way, anyone looking for a particular family ought surely to find them more quickly.

That done, she removed the lid from the bottle of ink, unscrewed the fountain pen Mrs Trobridge had given her, dipped the nib into the ink and squeezed the bladder to fill it up. At school she had always enjoyed cursive writing lessons but, these days, she found herself with scant reason to write a thing. Today was a chance to practise.

Once she'd set to, the morning flew, such that when she went through to the main hall to peer at the clock she was shocked to see it was almost midday.

Spotting Clemmie arrive, Mrs Trobridge bustled across, a clipboard tucked under her arm. Clemmie suspected she carried it to look important, and tried not to giggle.

'Have you finished?'

'I have. I've written up all the names and checked the forms to make certain I haven't missed anyone.'

'No doubt you're off home now then.'

Noticing the edge to Beryl's tone, Clemmie hesitated. 'Well…'

'No, it's all right. You go on. It's just that when Miss Evercott returned from checking on No. 2 rest centre up at Sidwell, she brought a whole sheaf of forms from there to be done as well. But if you have somewhere important to be I'll keep them for you to do tomorrow.'

Golly, Beryl Trobridge had a sharp side to her tongue; perhaps she'd once been a schoolmistress.

'Then I'll be here first thing.'

–

The following morning, waking at five thirty to the click of Gwen closing the front door as she left for work, Clemmie forced herself straight out of bed to wash and dress. Then she padded downstairs, put on her apron and slipped silently out of the back door. She might have promised Mrs Trobridge she'd make an early start, but not before she'd got on top of the housework.

For the first time since the bombings, the dawn air had an unexpected clarity to it and, as she stood drawing deep breaths, she realised how in Albert Terrace it had been rare for anything to ever feel clean and fresh. As often as not, laundry that had hung on the line all day came in covered in coal smuts; the air had a perpetual odour – the gasworks and the sewage farm chief among causes; windowpanes were continually obscured with grime. And yet here in Buckingham Crescent, which, as the crow flew, had to be barely more than a mile distant, she'd noticed how each morning brought a welcome newness. As for the way the dew sparkled on the tips of the blades of grass, well, she'd never witnessed such a thing; until now, the only grass she'd seen was on Cathedral Green, and at this time of the morning she would have been heading in the opposite direction, down the hill to Mundy's.

Experiencing a wave of something she couldn't put her finger on, she sighed. There were aspects to living in Albert Terrace she genuinely missed: the sisterly companionship of May and Pearl; the cosiness of the bakery on a cold morning, Mrs Mundy handing her a chunk of crust, fresh out of the oven and dabbed with dripping; the sense of family – not just her and her sisters pulling together to scrape by, but the spirit of her mother, even a sense of her father, whom she was too young to remember. She also missed having some money in her purse. Come Fridays, she might only have had the odd copper left – and only then if she'd been able to keep it hidden from Mr Warren – but she'd rarely been completely penniless, nor had she been beholden. Miss Evercott was lovely, kindness itself, but being dependent upon her didn't sit easily. This afternoon, she must redouble her efforts to find a job. Surely someone, somewhere, wanted a shopgirl?

Not helping in her search for work was the low-key manner in which she was having to go about it. Just recently, the government had introduced yet another new rule, the upshot being that those aged eighteen and nineteen were now no longer supposed to change jobs without first going to the Labour Exchange. May said it was so the authorities could put pressure on even younger girls to go into factories, a fate she herself was desperate to avoid.

Back indoors, she rinsed and hung out the tea towels she'd left soaking overnight in soda, cleaned the ground-floor windows inside and out, and swept the front path. Just as she was finishing, Dorothy came downstairs.

'My word. *You* made an early start.'

Untying her apron and hanging it up, Clemmie returned her smile. 'Mrs Trobridge said there's a sheaf of forms from No. 2 rest centre needing to be entered in the register. She seemed put out I wasn't staying on yesterday afternoon to see to it.'

A flicker of recognition crossed Dorothy's face. 'So that was *your* handwriting. I couldn't think whose it was.'

Clemmie blushed. 'Sorry. Was it untidy? Only if it was, then this morning I'll try harder—'

'Untidy? Goodness, no. It was neatness itself. But tell me, was it your idea to list the surnames alphabetically?'

Oh dear. Why had she meddled? 'I was minded it would make life easier for anyone wanting to find a particular person.'

'And it will. Infinitely. I just wish someone had thought to do so earlier. You know, carry on like this, Miss Huxford, and I might have to conscript you into the office – steal you away from the clutches of Mrs Trobridge and her little coven!'

Escape Beryl Trobridge? If only. 'Mm.'

'The WVS was set up to be an organisation of equals, with very little by way of hierarchy. But, while there will always be natural leaders, there are also those driven to grasp power. I suppose what I'm saying,' Dorothy went on, 'is that you mustn't let Mrs Trobridge browbeat you. She does tend towards officious. But she's also unstinting with her efforts and we'd be lost without her.'

Despite knowing she would never be able to stand up to a woman like Beryl Trobridge, Clemmie nodded. 'All right.' At least she hadn't upset the way the records were kept.

'And while we're on the subject of effort, much as I'm impressed by your diligence this morning, please don't wear yourself out with housework on my account. Clean and tidy, yes. Collapsing from exhaustion to keep the window glass sparkling, no. Even before Gwen came, the house ran well enough without me here all day to see to it. If this war has demonstrated anything, it's that women have been unpaid drudges far too long.'

Clemmie didn't disagree, but she also knew that few women had the luxury of choice. For most who'd grown up as poorly educated as she had, becoming an 'unpaid drudge', as Miss Evercott put it, was inevitable, went hand in hand with being wife to a working man and mother to his children. But she wasn't sure how her landlady would react to having that pointed out. Instead, she settled for murmuring her agreement. 'Mm.'

'Men being shipped off to war shows just how valuable women can be when they're allowed to venture outside of the home. And so please don't become a slave to the cleaning cloth.'

'I just didn't want you to think I put volunteering before my effort to repay your kindness,' Clemmie said. 'Because I don't.'

'You needn't fear that. Quite the contrary. Now, how about some tea and toast?'

Realising she'd been stood idling, Clemmie spun about. 'Yes. Sorry. I'll fill the kettle—'

'No, *I'll* fill the kettle. You sit down for a moment.'

'Well…'

'And since you've got everything here tidied, how about, this morning, we walk into town together? That way, when we get there, I can give you what Mrs Trobridge referred to as the *sheaf of forms*. Imagine the look on her face when she arrives to find you already hard at work.'

Get one step ahead of Mrs Trobridge? 'Yes please,' she said. 'I'd like that very much.'

–

Striding along the main road with Miss Evercott, Clemmie realised there had been more behind her land-lady's suggestion they walk in together than getting a head start on some forms; it was plain now that she'd also wanted a chance for them to get to know one another.

'Forgive my prying,' Dorothy said to that end as they skirted bricks from a bomb-damaged garden wall that still lay strewn across the pavement. 'But were you baptised as Clemmie, or are you more properly Clementine?'

'My birth certificate says Clementine Alice, though I've never known anyone call me anything but Clemmie. Or Clem, if you're my sister Pearl.'

A few paces further on, makeshift barricades around a bomb crater forced them to cross the road. 'And do you have a boyfriend?' Dorothy asked as they reached the other side.

Clemmie felt her face redden. 'Heavens, no. I'm too young for that sort of thing.' But the enquiry triggered a question of her own, and she asked, 'What about you, Miss Evercott? Do you have a young man?'

A glance at Dorothy's face told Clemmie she was strug-gling not to laugh.

'I have neither a young one nor an old one. And to spare you the torment, I shall tell you the two reasons why not. Firstly, so many of the men of my generation were lost in the last war that not only were the odds of meeting anyone severely reduced, but so were the usual avenues for doing so. Families who might once have hosted house parties or tennis weekends to get young people together no longer felt it appropriate while they were in mourning for a son, or a brother or nephew. Often, more than one. Dinner parties became few and far between. When they did take place, a single male would attract the attention of four, five, six young ladies. Even if he was nothing special, he really did have his pick.'

With the way this current war kept dragging on, Clemmie could see herself ending up in the same situation – just without Miss Evercott's start in life.

'My father was a soldier in the last war,' she said, preferring not to dwell upon circumstances she could do nothing to change. 'Many years after he died, my mother became ill and my sister, May, said Mum confessed that though she had loved Dad very much, when he came back from the fighting he seemed little more than a husk, and she didn't know how to go on with him.'

'I'm so sorry to hear that. Sadly, her circumstances were not unusual. War doesn't just affect those who serve, it does wretched things to their loved ones as well.'

There was no need, Clemmie decided, to mention how, left a widow, Mum had made the mistake of going on to marry Mr Warren; she'd vowed never to speak that man's name again. Instead, flattered that a woman of Miss Evercott's standing should consider her worthy of being spoken to so openly, she asked, 'What was the second reason?' When Dorothy frowned, Clemmie went on, 'You said there two reasons why you never married.'

'Oh, yes. Well, the second rather came from the first. The longer I remained single, the more I grew to fear that marriage would cost me my independence.'

While Miss Evercott's response raised more questions than it answered, if she was to enjoy her company in the future Clemmie knew she mustn't pry. Her landlady was intelligent and shrewd; someone from whom she could learn a great deal.

Discreetly, she studied Dorothy's outfit: a no-nonsense navy-blue skirt with a hemline that fell just below the knee; a timeless blouse that looked as though it might be silk; a navy and cream checked blazer; a businesslike handbag and matching court shoes. Elegant. Stylish.

When they arrived at the rest centre, Clemmie went ahead of Dorothy up the steps. But as she reached for the door, it flew open, and she had to sidestep someone bowling smartly through from the other side.

'Whoops. Sorry!'

'*Pearl?*' She might not recognise the outfit, but the red hair was unmistakeable.

Already halfway down the steps, Pearl cast a look over her shoulder. 'Oh, hi, Clem. Didn't see you there.'

'Where are you—'

'Can't stop. Mustn't be late for work.'

Left to stand and frown, Clemmie watched Pearl dash away up the hill. 'My sister...' she said to Miss Evercott, and reached again for the door.

Passing through ahead of her, Dorothy smiled. 'Thank you. I must say, I wouldn't have known.'

'No,' Clemmie mumbled as she followed her in. 'Everyone says that. We're not much alike.'

Once seated with the register open before her, Clemmie was annoyed to find herself struggling to concentrate, her mind repeatedly wandering back to Pearl. Her sister's outfit – dark grey trousers and a tailored jacket – had to be that of a clippie. Was she to believe

Pearl had gone on the buses? Was *that* what her interviews had been in aid of? If so, she didn't know what to feel most – shock or admiration. One thing for certain, Mum would have been speechless. To be fair to Pearl, though, even in the relatively short time since Mum had died, war had made all manner of things that might once have been unpalatable now seem quite acceptable – indeed, to be encouraged, women taking on men's jobs a case in point.

Forcing her attention back to the register, she let out a sigh. Well, good for Pearl. Having to toe the line in a responsible job might be the making of her; might instil some much-needed discipline and curb her tendency to flightiness.

–

Back in Buckingham Crescent later that afternoon, though, her mind *still* kept going back to Pearl and her new job. Why had her sister chosen to be so secretive about it? It was hardly because she feared courting her disapproval; Pearl knew she wasn't the judgemental type. Well, next time she saw her, she would make a point of asking how she was getting on. With her bright and cheery manner, she'd probably be a very good clippie. Of the three of them, Pearl always was the one people took to first.

Staring out through the kitchen window, she exhaled heavily. May and Pearl getting jobs only drew attention to her own lack of direction. While her sisters were getting on with their lives, what was *she* doing? Granted, she had somewhere to live – somewhere that was both comfortable and welcoming. She was also enjoying volunteering. But when it came to employment, there hadn't been a single sniff. And if she continued to stand there all afternoon, there never would be. No. So, she would tidy herself up and endeavour to put that right. She would reply to her letter from May, walk round to the post office for a stamp, and check in the window for any new cards advertising vacancies. If she was to avoid taking her chances at the Labour Exchange, the time had come to find something double quick.

Her reply to May eventually written, she skimmed the contents.

> *My dearest sister May,*
>
> *Thank you for your letter. I am pleased to know you are settling in all right. Sometimes I try to picture what you are doing there but not knowing anything about farms, all I see is cows and mud. Since you didn't say nothing about cows, maybe you don't have any.*

As she read on towards the part where she described what she'd been doing for the WVS, she wondered whether to mention Pearl. In truth, her sister's news wasn't hers to tell but, since she doubted Pearl would think to write and reassure May herself – she certainly hadn't asked for her address – she added a postscript:

> *P.S. Pearl is well. She has a job but I will give her your address so she can write and tell you about it for herself.*

Having walked to the post office and bought her stamp, she dropped the letter into the postbox and turned to browse the postcards in the window. Unsurprisingly, none of them were advertising anything suitable: written in a shaky hand was a request for a window cleaner; the one below it wanted a gardener; one was advertising for homes for tabby kittens; another was selling a piano *Buyer to Collect*. Not one wanted even a char.

In despair, she turned away. But, as she crossed the road to head home, movement in the window of the shop opposite caught her eye: a hand was sticking something to the inside of the glass. She darted across to see what it said.

Wanted
Girl to work mornings
Apply within

She glanced up. The sign above the window said *Cedric Narramore, Grocer & Tobacconist*. Unable to believe her luck, she reread the card. Then, glancing over her shoulder as though fearing someone might beat her to it, she pushed open the door and stepped inside.

The owner of the hand, now back behind the counter, was a man in his fifties with thinning hair. Over a greying white shirt, the sleeves of which were rolled up above his elbows, he wore a woollen waistcoat, its buttons straining to stay done up.

'Yes, love?' he said, his eyes appearing to make a quick assessment of her form. 'What can I do for you?'

She swallowed. It was vital she made a good impression. 'Good afternoon. I've just seen the card in your window advertising for a girl.'

'Six mornings a week, seven till one.'

His accent didn't strike her as local.

'I should like to apply.'

'Yeah? How old are you?'

Clemmie tensed; she hated lying – hadn't stepped through the door intending to – but admit to being eighteen and he might wonder why she wasn't registered at the Labour Exchange. 'Seventeen.' Now she just had to hope he wouldn't want to check. Thankfully, he looked like a man who viewed officialdom as something to be skirted at every opportunity.

'And how come you wants a job?'

'I was employed on the counter at Mundy's, the bakers on Chandlery Street. But it was bombed out. Our home, too.'

'What brings you all the way over here then?'

'Someone who lives in Buckingham Crescent took me in.'

At the mention of Buckingham Crescent, he raised an eyebrow. 'You married?'

Married? Her? At seventeen? With a shake of her head, she offered up her ringless fingers. 'No.'

'And you can reckon up in your head.'

'I can.'

'Worked in a bakers, you say?'

'Started at six every morning and was never late once.' There was no need to tell him she'd lived less than fifty yards up the hill, making it almost impossible to be anything *but* on time.

'I was really hoping for someone who knew how to do the ration forms for the Food Office.'

Desperate not to lose out simply because she'd only sold bread, which wasn't rationed and didn't involve paperwork, she adopted a smile and racked her brain for a response. 'I understand that. But I'm a quick learner. Show me a thing once and I'll remember it. While I've been looking for work, I've been volunteering mornings at No. 1 rest centre with the WVS. I've been keeping their registers, and the supervisor there said they've never been so orderly. She also said—'

'All right. Week's trial. You get paid on Fridays, week in hand. Bring your own apron. If you're still here come Saturday, I'll get you a shop one. My wife takes over the job at one o'clock. Doesn't mind doing a few hours in the afternoon but won't do mornings – too busy. You don't leave till she comes down – late or not.'

'I understand.'

'Start Monday morning.' Moving to turn away, he added, 'To be honest, I was hoping for someone a bit more… womanly, if you know what I mean. So, for Gawd's sake, put on a bit of lipstick. A bit of sass brings in the gents for their ciggies. And with them being in such short supply, well, let's just say they're one of the few things that still make me any money.'

If jobs for girls like her weren't scarcer than hens' teeth, she'd tell him where to poke his vacancy. And his lipstick. Instead, with this being the only job she'd found, she forced a bright smile. 'I'll see you Monday morning.'

Besides, she told herself as she made her way back to Buckingham Crescent weighed by a sense of unease, *don't be a prude. There's a war on. It's either this or take your chances at the Labour Exchange.*

What's more, she thought as she paused at the kerb and then crossed the road, it might not hurt to take a leaf out of Pearl's book anyway; the odd bit of simpering always seemed to open doors for her.

So, yes. She would look upon this as giving her the best of both worlds: a wage for her labours in the morning, and time in the afternoons to volunteer. The job might not be quite what she'd been hoping for but, since beggars couldn't be choosers, she would thank her lucky stars.

II. Opportunity

Chapter 7

'Right then, love. Rationing.'

In an attempt to hide her nerves on this, her first morning behind the counter at Cedric Narramore, Grocer & Tobacconist, Clemmie smiled. 'Rationing, yes.'

'Now, you don't need me to tell you that to get goods needing coupons, you got to be registered with the shop where you want to buy them.'

So far, so good. 'No.'

'At present, I've got thirty-eight families registered.'

'Right.' To Clemmie's mind, thirty-eight didn't sound too bad.

'But they come and go.'

'Yes.' She supposed they would. Having only recently moved there herself, she was proof of that.

'Where it gets tricky is that not all families register to get all their goods solely from me.'

'Right.'

'And not even all the members of one family register for the same things.'

Clemmie frowned. 'Golly. That must take some keeping on top of.'

'You're not wrong. You got to keep your wits about you. I've had customers try to pull a fast one, an' then I got others just too plain daft to remember which of the family gets what from where.'

'I see.'

'Take butter and cheese. You'd think, wouldn't you, that if you got the one here, you'd get the other, too? But no, we've got sixty-eight counterfoils for butter but only sixty-four for cheese.'

Maybe, Clemmie thought, not everyone who bought butter liked cheese, but she couldn't see how it would help to point that out. Instead, she said simply, 'Right.'

'Now, as you know, since the Ministry keeps changing the allowances, your ration book don't state the amounts you're entitled to. So, you got to keep *them* in your head.' In support of his point, Cedric tapped a finger on his temple. 'And when a housewife wants the rations for, let's say, five family members all in one amount, you got to be able to tot that up.'

Clemmie nodded. 'I can do that.'

'You'd better be able to, because for every restricted good I sell, I only get a permit based on totalling up how many folk I've got registered to buy it each month – along with a fraction over on some goods for what they call cutting up.' When Cedric looked directly at her, Clemmie nodded her understanding. 'Cutting cheese off the block, for instance, means you lose some in crumbs. And if they didn't make an allowance for that, I wouldn't have enough to go round. But you still got to be careful. Cutting exactly two ounces off a block the required number of times takes some doing.'

Already, Clemmie's head felt full. Perhaps she should have thought to write some of this down – although that might have given Mr Narramore reason to doubt her ability, when what she desperately needed was to make a good impression.

Trying to commit to memory the last thing he'd just said, she once again nodded. 'I understand.'

'Now, on the matter of ration books, you look to me like the sort of girl who always writes the shop's name on her counterfoils—'

'Oh, I do. Always.'

'But a good number of folk don't. Some forget. Some can't be bothered. You'll quickly get to work out who's who. Ignoring that you're not supposed to do it for them anyway, you can imagine the tutting and grumbling from folk in the queue if you stop serving to do it for someone who can't be bothered, 'specially when we're busy. So, take a firm line. Point them to the pen I've tied to the counter there and serve someone else. The only exceptions are old Miss Short – blind as a bat – and Widow Hodge. Dear old biddy's lost most of her marbles and hasn't a soul in the world to help her.'

'Miss Short and Widow Hodge. Right.' How she'd know them from Adam she had no idea. She supposed she'd spot them from the names on their ration books.

'Needless to say, keep firm hold of the counterfoils. Once a month, my wife has to get them all together, check they're all proper completed, and sort them for the Food Office. If that ruddy lot of pen-pushers finds they're wrong, we'll be called in front of them for a knuckle-rapping and made to explain the difference. And trust me, that's trouble I *don't* need.'

Clemmie could quite see why. 'Of course not.'

'Right then. Next, we've got goods on points.' But as Mr Narramore was about to launch into an explanation, the bell on the door announced the arrival of a women in a headscarf and flowery housecoat. 'Mornin', Mrs Parker,' Cedric greeted her. 'What can I do for you?'

'Got any sardines?'

Without needing to even glance along the shelf, Cedric shook his head. 'Sorry, love. Wholesaler didn't have any.'

Mrs Parker tutted. 'Still?'

'Still.'

'As I was saying just last night to my Dulcie, where's the use in giving us points if there's nothing to be had with them?'

'Can't tempt you with a nice tin of salmon instead?'

'Salmon? Pah. That's all well and good for a Sunday treat for me an' Ron, but a waste of points giving it to the boys – pair of gannets.' Just as Clemmie thought Mrs Parker was done moaning, she heard her start up again. 'You know what gets my goat?'

Flashing Clemmie a quick grin, Cedric shook his head. 'No, love. What's that, then?'

'All these women writing in the newspapers about how to eke out meat rations with everything from breadcrumbs to them bloomin' split peas. Honestly, did you ever read such claptrap? Messing about with perfectly good food, that's what Ron calls it.'

'And there's many as would agree with him.'

'So, when *will* you have sardines, then?'

Cedric shrugged. 'If I knew that, Mrs Parker, I'd be laughing.'

'Utter shambles if you ask me. Bloomin' Food Ministry – wants a woman in charge, that's what it wants. Things would jolly soon be sorted out then, I can tell you.'

'I dare say you're right, Mrs Parker.'

'Well, just me tin of Carnation and some matches, then. Oh, and while I'm here I'll take me sweet biscuits.'

Watching Cedric deal with Mrs Parker, Clemmie wondered how, having come into the shop for sardines,

Mrs Parker proposed to make do instead with Carnation and sweet biscuits. She could only suppose she didn't.

After that, the morning provided Clemmie with a steady flow of customers who came in through the door, eyed her with a mixture of curiosity and suspicion, and then proceeded to buy what struck Clemmie as 'dribs and drabs', pointing her to where on the shelves she might find the things they wanted.

'No, not that big one, for heaven's sake. I'm not made of money,' one woman chided her.

'Haven't you got any Hudson's?' another asked when Clemmie presented her with the only type of household soap on the shelf.

'How many points is it for All Bran?' a particularly exasperated old dear shuffled in to enquire.

'Three,' Clemmie replied, having peered at the hand-written ticket stuck to the shelf.

'Does it do any good?'

'I'm sorry. Any good for...?'

'Lord, it's all right for you youngsters.' Leaning across the counter, the woman hissed, 'For constipation.'

Trying to hide that she was blushing, Clemmie ducked her head. 'I'm sorry, I couldn't say.'

'How much is it?'

'Sevenpence ha'penny.'

'Don't you have a smaller packet?'

Clemmie gave the woman a sympathetic smile. 'Sorry, no. I suppose you could try the chemist for something else—'

'Walk all the way down there? No, I'll stick with this ruddy rabbit food.'

As the morning continued in a similar vein, Clemmie reflected on the differences between the customers here and those she had served in Mundy's. No matter the early hour, the women who popped in for their loaves had been bright and chirpy. By contrast, here, although none of the customers she'd served had been rude or short with her, neither had they been overly friendly – despite her permanently fixed smile. In fact, they mostly seemed grumpy and exhausted. It just went to show what a neighbourly little place Albert Terrace had been. Still, who knew what troubles these people had at home? And anyway, it didn't do any harm to treat them with courtesy. In truth, she had no choice but to: she was only on a week's trial and Cedric was watching her every move.

Thankfully, although business turned out to be steady, Clemmie found herself with time between customers to look along the shelves and familiarise herself with the jars and bottles, packets and tins – and, just as helpfully, with those items of stock for which there were just gaps. From listening to Cedric, she learned that Monday was the quietest day, custom gradually gathering pace through the week until Friday – the day the old-age pension was paid, and things got really busy. She also discovered it was pensioners who griped the most when something wasn't available. Since they were the generation who had lived through the hardship of the last war, she found this odd, particularly their unwillingness to grasp the fact that having sufficient coupons or points, or indeed an entitlement of any other sort, didn't guarantee you the goods; just because the Ministry of Food said you could have it didn't mean there *was* any.

'No, I'm very sorry,' she said for the umpteenth time that morning, 'we don't have any eggs and aren't sure when we will.' To the same grumbling from each of the customers, she would go on to reply, 'Yes, I can assure you Mr Narramore harangues them continually about it. And no, he doesn't put them by for special customers. Nor does he keep them all for himself.'

On the fourth or fifth such occasion, Cedric came through from the back.

'Mrs Widger, trust me, I complain every time I go up there. I'm as desperate for my allowance of the bloomin' things as you are. Have you used up your ration of dried?'

Mrs Widger huffed. 'Dried? No ruddy use buying that stuff. Mr Widger wants proper eggs.'

'As do we all.'

'You know, one of these days, I shall march up that Food Office and treat them to a piece of my mind.'

'Mrs Widger,' Cedric replied wearily, 'please do.'

'I bet their sort gets eggs. Them with their polished shoes and their fancy blouses and their rubber stamps. Pound to a penny *they* don't go without. Needs someone to write them a raging letter, that's what it needs.'

When, still mumbling, Mrs Widger eventually left, Clemmie sighed. Was this it? Was serving behind a counter in a scruffy corner shop to be her lot until, well, until what? Until fate decided otherwise?

'Cheer up, love,' Cedric said, and jostled her arm on his way past. 'Come one o'clock, *you* get to go home. *I* have to put up with their moaning morning, noon and night.'

She supposed there was that. In a couple of hours, she could turn her thoughts to the WVS. Besides, of her two occupations, this was the one that actually paid. And it had to be better than nine or ten long hours, six days a week in the parachute factory… didn't it?

'Survived your first week at Narramore's, then.'

From where she was sitting on Gwen's bed, watching her get ready to go out, Clemmie nodded. Only moments earlier, she had been reflecting on the same thing, coming to conclude that, as settling into a new job went, it could have been worse.

'It would seem so.'

Having licked the tip of her forefinger, Gwen traced it in turn over each of her eyebrows. And then, shifting her focus in the mirror to look directly at Clemmie, asked, 'Think you'll stick at it?'

'Unless something changes, I don't have a choice. I was lucky to find it.'

'Yeah. And it can't be worse than where I am. Wages might be decent, but they certainly want their pound of flesh. If anyone dares grumble, even in the canteen, some or other supervisor will pop up and point out, "there's a war on", and that anyone not keen to pull their weight should "take a long hard look at themselves in the mirror and remember the brave pilots who have given their lives so we might all be safe from evil".'

'I suppose they have a point,' Clemmie said, watching as Gwen smoothed her skirt down over her hips. Her legs, she noticed, had been treated to a stain of something brown. 'You going on a date again?'

'I'm seeing Ken.'

'The one you met last week?'

Gwen nodded. 'We're going to a dance with one of his pals and another girl. Some little place that's just opened up over Heavitree after being bombed out from down near Deller's.'

'What's Ken like?'

Reaching for her handbag, Gwen shrugged. 'Bit quiet for my taste if I'm honest. That said, least he's not constantly trying to put his hands where he shouldn't. I suppose you takes your choice.'

'Mm.'

'Seems it's the one or the other.'

'Well, anyway,' Clemmie said as she got up from Gwen's bed, 'you look nice.' With her height and her striking dark hair, though, Clemmie imagined Gwen turned heads even without the need to paint her nails and daub her lips with Victory Red.

'Thanks. But really,' Gwen replied, turning to leave, 'I could have done with washing my hair. Still, if the place we're going is as dark as most of them are, no one will notice.'

'I daresay not,' Clemmie replied as she watched Gwen pad away along the landing and start down the stairs. 'Well, have a good time.'

Already in the hallway, Gwen called back over her shoulder. 'You should come with us one night. I'll ask Ken if he's got any unattached pals.'

'Um…' But before Clemmie could summon a reply that didn't sound curmudgeonly, Gwen had already let herself out through the front door and was trotting up the path to the gate. Perhaps, while she was on her own, she should put on her thinking cap; better to be ready with a reason to decline such an invitation than to be caught on the back foot and end up going along with Gwen's idea purely for want of knowing how to get out of it.

Heaving a resigned sigh, and not really sure what to do with herself now that Gwen had gone, Clemmie went downstairs and, finding no sign of Dorothy in either the living room or the kitchen, went out through the back door and into the garden – a generous strip of land that faced almost due south and had a cinder path running down the right-hand side to a gate into an alley. A portion of ground at the far end had been turned over to growing vegetables, the section nearest the house remaining as an area of lawn, which Dorothy herself kept neatly cut with a little hand mower.

'I aspire to stripes,' Dorothy had remarked of the grass when she'd first shown Clemmie around the house. 'But for that it needs a mower with a heavy roller. And I fear I should quickly tire of using something so cumbersome.'

Where the two areas of garden met stood a lattice screen, home to a profusion of rambling roses that, if she remembered correctly, Dorothy had said were a relatively new variety called 'Albertine'. In the warm evening light they looked stunning, the salmon-red buds having given way to clusters of copper-pink blooms.

'They smell so lovely,' she remarked, approaching where Dorothy was currently deadheading with a pair of secateurs.

Without looking up, Dorothy nodded. 'Don't they? Their fragrance is incredibly rich, almost fruity. I make a point of saving some of the petals to put in a little bowl on my dressing table. Their scent fills the whole room, especially on a warm evening. Help yourself to some if you like.'

'Thank you.' Bending to pick a single petal from Miss Evercott's little wooden trug, Clemmie rubbed it lightly between her fingers and held it to her nose. The fragrance was heady to the point of overpowering.

'Come September, this whole trellis will be covered in dark-red hips. The blackbirds and thrushes can't get enough of them.'

'Goodness.'

'So, how are you?' Dorothy changed the subject to enquire.

Still fingering the rose petal, Clemmie smiled. 'Fine, thank you.'

'You've settled in with Mr Narramore?'

'In so far as I ever will, I suppose. Turns out there's a good deal more to groceries than bread – on account of the rationing, I mean. Some households are registered for all of their groceries, some for just one or two goods like tea and sugar – and they're the women who keep you on your toes because, if the shop they're registered with for other things – say, jam – hasn't had any in a while, Mr Narramore says they come and try their luck with him and hope he doesn't notice they're not registered for it. He says I have to be on the lookout for all their tricks. But it strikes me some of them genuinely forget where they've registered for what. And with the points system now as well, it *is* confusing. Least, it is to me.'

'You know, I find that in general people are creatures of habit, especially when it comes to their basic needs. Give it another week and you'll know all the customers' little foibles – not to mention the price of everything in the shop.'

Clemmie smiled. 'I hope so.'

'Do you find the work tiring?'

Thinking Dorothy's question an odd one, Clemmie paused for a moment. 'Not through being on my feet all morning. I'm used to that from Mundy's. But at times it does give me a headache.'

'But you think you have it in you to keep volunteering in the afternoons?'

Was Miss Evercott asking for any reason in particular? Clemmie wondered. 'I don't see why not. I enjoy it – far more than working for Mr Narramore.'

Secateurs poised to snip off the next fading bloom, Dorothy looked thoughtful. 'I ask because in the WVS, women who just get on with a job as quietly as you do are a rare find. It won't have escaped your notice that we have plenty of would-be chiefs, but rather fewer Indians.'

Miss Evercott wasn't wrong. 'Yes.'

'And would-be chiefs are given to spats over territory. Or over how a thing should be gone about. Silly, really. However, in my role as the WVS centre organiser for Exeter, I've been approached by the city corporation about a new committee that's being set up. I don't think I'm telling you anything I shouldn't – although perhaps keep this to yourself for a while – but the south-west of England is to become home to various units of American servicemen. And it's likely the first of these will be US Army Air Force chaps joining the operation at RAF Exeter.' Evidently reading Clemmie's frown, Dorothy went on, 'You know – out at the airport.'

Although she didn't know, Clemmie nevertheless nodded. 'I see.'

'Apparently, there might eventually be as many as several thousand personnel.'

Several thousand? From what she knew of the airport, it was little more than fields. 'Golly.'

'Precisely. And it doesn't need me to point out that such an influx, while undoubtedly bringing benefits to the local villages, will also create headaches. For a start, I'm given to understand that American servicemen are rather better paid than our own chaps, and that, when they're a long way from their homes and their loved ones, they are wont to spend their leisure in pursuit of a good time. Wine, women and song, if you will.'

Clemmie felt herself blush. 'I see.' She still had no idea why Miss Evercott was telling her any of this.

'Hence the idea to form a committee – a small group of people to represent various local interests, who can work together not only to plan how to cope with the sheer number of personnel and spot potential areas of… well, shall we say, *difficulty*, but also how to make these chaps feel welcome. As it stands, the proposal is to draw committee members from the city corporation, from the police, the Chamber of Commerce – already rushed off their feet after the bombings – to have someone represent the mayor, someone from the RAF, and so on.' Looking directly at Clemmie, Dorothy continued, 'And since, when it comes to welfare and upheaval – both civilian and military – the WVS has considerable experience, they've asked us to take part.'

'I see.' But if only she did.

'The proposal is to hold a meeting one evening next week and, obviously, I have been invited. But I should like you to come with me.'

In her surprise, Clemmie took a step backwards. '*Me?*'

'No need to look so terrified. This first meeting will just be to introduce everyone involved and learn what's proposed – hopefully understand a little more about the numbers of men, the possible dates for their arrival, the sorts of issues their presence might spark. After that, it would be usual for a second meeting to be held for everyone to share their concerns and to pool ideas. From thereon, the more detailed arrangements are usually assigned to smaller groups to work out. And when I thought about who might take on that task for us, you were the person who came to mind.'

'But…' She genuinely didn't know what to say. Be on a committee? Come up with ideas? Her? Was Miss Evercott mad?

'Miss Huxford, you are bright and personable. You have an eye for detail. You're thorough.'

'Yes but—'

'What's more, you're not tainted by long-standing grudges or rivalries. And of course, I am on hand to assist you – every day of the week if needs be.'

'Well, yes…'

'Look, I shan't just throw you in at the deep end and walk away. We can introduce you as my assistant. I doubt any of the officials who attend the first meeting will go on to do much of the work themselves, anyway. There will be subcommittees. Or working parties to which they will second or assign juniors from within their offices. Indeed, should no one suggest that as a way forward, I shall. It's my experience that more gets done that way.'

Clemmie continued to hold herself rigidly. Golly, how hot she suddenly felt. If she thought Miss Evercott would take 'no' for an answer, she would decline this very minute. What on earth qualified her, little Clemmie Huxford, to talk to anyone about anything – let alone something to do with the war? She'd left school at four-teen. She was a shopgirl – a nobody. Could Miss Evercott not see that to put her in charge of anything more than a grocery list was a recipe for disaster?

Trying to work out what to do for the best, she gave in to a despairing sigh. 'But I wouldn't know what to do, where to even start with such a thing.'

'My dear girl, that makes two of us. My expertise is with evacuees and the displaced. As far as I know, I have never met an American. I shouldn't imagine any of the other invited parties have either. This will be new for all of us. That said, there's unlikely to be a person among us who hasn't at some time found themselves in unfamiliar territory, separated from family, or in a situation where they feared putting a foot wrong' – That, Clemmie thought, described pretty much her entire existence just lately – 'and were grateful for a friendly face to help steer them right.'

She would concede to the truth of that. Since the night of the air raids, a sense of being lost and uncertain was something she and her sisters had come to know all too well. But take charge of something? Her? Alongside strangers? *Grown-up, professional strangers?* Dear God, it made her feel faint even just thinking about it.

'The thing is—'

'You're bound to have concerns. And no doubt rather a lot of questions, too.'

'So many I don't know where to start.'

'But the best way to allay your fears and get some answers is to come with me to this first meeting. When we know a little more about what's proposed, you and I can decide how we think the WVS might help, if at all, and whether we might rustle up the necessary resources to do so. Once matters are a little clearer, we can see how you feel about continuing to be involved.'

Since she couldn't see how Miss Evercott might otherwise be deflected, Clemmie gave a reluctant nod. 'All right. I'll come with you to see what's what.'

'Good girl. Now, since it's far too lovely an evening to be cooped up indoors, how about, while I go and pop these prunings onto the compost heap, you go in and pour us each a little sherry? We can sit on the steamer chairs and watch for bats. And yes, I know the sun's about to sink down behind the house and it will start to grow chilly but, if you bring a couple of rugs, we can be toasty warm and enjoy the dusk, hm?'

Clemmie smiled. 'All right.' At least if they were seated out here, then, once she'd taken a polite sip or two of the sherry, she could discreetly empty the rest onto the grass.

To her surprise, though, once reclined against a cushion, her legs cocooned in a rug, Clemmie found her terror from earlier turning to pride: Miss Evercott thought her capable of something purposeful and worthwhile; as she'd heard people say of others, she *saw something in her.* And no one had ever done that before. Despite considering her landlady's faith in her completely misplaced, she nevertheless felt a warm glow. And no, she didn't think that was down to the sherry. Although, she would admit to enjoying *that* rather more than she'd been expecting, too. And if she was getting a taste for something she'd always assumed she wouldn't like, then who was to say there weren't other things in life she might also take to, given the chance...?

Chapter 8

'Well, that was interesting, don't you think?'

Walking beside Dorothy as they made their way back to Buckingham Crescent after the meeting to discuss the arrival of the American airmen, Clemmie was surprised to find that she agreed. Once she'd got past the notion that she had no right to be among such important people, she'd found the discussions fascinating.

'It was,' she said. 'I knew America joined the war on our side, but I never gave a thought to their men coming here to Britain. It seems such a long way.'

'I don't suppose many of us had reason to even consider the possibility. I, for one, hadn't realised that some of their number have been here since January.'

Matching Miss Evercott's pace as they continued along Topsham Road, Clemmie nodded. 'But if their ways are different to ours, then it's good that we should all know how to treat them. In fact, if there's to be so many of them, I'm surprised the government hasn't seen fit to tell us exactly how to go about it. They've issued a pamphlet for just about everything else.'

Dorothy laughed. 'How to grow a carrot...'

'How to keep pigs.'

'How to darn socks and reinforce the elbows of cardigans.'

'Yes! As if such a necessity wasn't already known to women the world over.'

'But when it comes to how to welcome our foreign allies, they have nothing to say on the matter. They leave us to bumble along as we see fit.'

'I suppose,' Clemmie said, noticing they were about to turn the corner into Buckingham Crescent, 'if they sent out instructions, we'd all simply moan and accuse them of interfering where there was no need.'

'Very possibly. For once, I think the corporation's idea is a good one. Bring together all the organisations who might help. It's just a shame the war has done nothing to change Austin Young.' When Clemmie frowned, Dorothy went on, 'The chap from the corporation who's setting this thing up. Our paths have crossed many times over the years, and on every single one of them he's come across as a pompous windbag.'

Clemmie pictured the man in question: thin; balding; his complexion a match for the colour of his grey flannel suit. 'He was quick to warm to your idea of working parties.'

'As I recall, he's quick to embrace anything that lightens his own load. By contrast, I thought Roger Marshall seemed very willing. Made a lot of sense, too.'

Already struggling to remember which name went with which face, Clemmie continued to frown. 'The man from the Chamber of Commerce?'

'That's him. He said to me afterwards that they're currently stretched rather thinly. Hardly surprising, given the state of the High Street, and how many factories and businesses have been lost. But I think he'll have some good ideas. He'll certainly be useful when it comes to finding out who to call upon for anything we might need – or any*one*.'

'I thought he had a nice manner. But I don't mind admitting that police inspector terrified me.' Of all the people to whom Clemmie had been introduced, it had been Inspector Lethbridge who had made her feel a fraud – hopelessly out of her depth and as though she had no place being there.

Dorothy regarded her sideways. 'Henry?' When Clemmie nodded, she went on, 'Oh, he's all right. The first time I met him was back in '38, when it was first mooted the WVS assume responsibility for preparing women for civil defence work. He's a good deal more reasonable than his uniform makes him look.'

Clemmie smiled. 'I suppose it wouldn't do if policemen looked too friendly.'

'I suppose not. It's a shame no one was there from the RAF. Of everyone, they're probably best placed to give us an idea about what to expect. I mean, I know we have Polish pilots stationed out at the airport, but for the most part they keep themselves to themselves. From what I'm led to believe, we'll find the Americans altogether more gregarious.'

Left to guess at the meaning of 'gregarious', Clemmie nevertheless nodded. 'Mm.'

'Still, Mr Young said there will be someone from the RAF present next time – a former pilot, I believe. Apparently, the chap in question underwent part of his training in America. Before the war, that is.'

'Goodness. Then he should be real helpful.'

'We can only hope. Anyway, how about, once we get indoors, we have a little sherry and then put our heads together to think of ways the WVS might help this *influx of Americans*, as Austin Young kept calling it? It would be good to go back next week with some ideas we've thought through in advance.'

'Yes,' Clemmie replied, latching the garden gate behind her and following Miss Evercott up the path to the front door. 'That's a good idea.' To her surprise, the prospect of going to another meeting didn't terrify her nearly as much as she would have thought. But then neither, to her relief, did the prospect of joining her landlady for *a little sherry*. In fact, she realised, when matters were out of your hands, it was surprising just how quickly you could become accustomed to new ways of carrying on.

–

'So, tell me again about this thing Miss Evercott's dragging you to?'

This evening, Clemmie was going to attend the second meeting of the committee on what, between them, she and Dorothy Evercott had come to refer to as *The American Situation*. And now that she had seen how professional the other members were, she wanted to look her best; make an effort, and people were more likely to take her seriously. It was just a shame that the better of her two skirts didn't look right with her only jacket.

Heaving a vexed sigh, she glanced to where Gwen had come flouncing in and thrown herself onto the bed. 'Not seeing Ken tonight?'

Gwen grimaced. 'I dumped him.'

'Oh.' It wasn't the answer she'd been expecting. 'What did he do to upset you?'

'More a case of what he *didn't* do.' From the dismissive way Gwen shook her head, Clemmie detected irritation and displeasure. 'Do you have any idea how tiring it is having to lead a man every step of the way?'

Angling the little mirror on top of the chest of drawers, Clemmie tried to get a better look at her outfit. 'But I thought you were glad he didn't keep trying to put his hands all over you. If I remember rightly, you said something about it making a refreshing change.'

Gwen scoffed. 'Turns out I was wrong. Turns out, having so narrowly escaped the Luftwaffe's attempts to blow me to smithereens, what I want when I go out at night is a bit of fun.'

To Clemmie's mind, surviving an air raid didn't constitute reason to throw caution to the wind. That said, she had no wish to come across as prudish. 'Hm. So, what did he say when you dumped him?'

'Only had the nerve to tell me he'd already been thinking I wasn't right for him. Well, you can imagine, can't you?' Despite not being able to imagine anything of the sort, Clemmie nodded sagely. 'That did it. I told him we were finished.'

'Goodness.'

'I'm not bothered.' With a sudden liveliness, Gwen swung her legs over the edge of the bed and sat up. 'Got my eye on someone else. His name's Jimmy Woodley and he works up the railway sheds. Reserved occupation. He's tall and dark-haired. Real good looking. And the other day he smiled at me.'

Clemmie tried not to laugh. 'Did he indeed?'

'Been going out with this girl from the factory, he has, but I happen to know he's looking for a change.'

As satisfied as she could be with her appearance, Clemmie returned the mirror to its former angle. 'You happen to know this.'

'I'm friends with a friend of his sister. And she told me. Although, when you meet these American pilots you and Miss Evercott are always going on about,' Gwen went on, getting to her feet and smoothing a hand over her hair, 'feel free to put in a good word for me. Don't mind doing my bit to make some Yank feel welcome.'

'I hate to disappoint you, but I can't imagine *me* getting to meet *any* of them,' Clemmie replied as she watched Gwen open the door and saunter away along the landing. In fact, if they were as boisterous as everyone seemed to think, she *might* have to go out of her way to ensure precisely the opposite...

–

What on earth would May and Pearl make of *her*, at a meeting where one of the other attendees was the mayor? Seated alongside Dorothy in the little room behind the church hall, she could scarcely believe it herself.

This evening Austin Young, from the city corporation, had brought his secretary to minute what was discussed and agreed – which just made Clemmie think her own presence there all the more incredible; anything she dared to contribute tonight would be noted for all to see. Not that she was likely to breathe a word – she simply didn't have that sort of courage. Pearl, yes. Her and May, never.

'With certain caveats,' she became aware of Miss Evercott remarking, 'I believe the WVS could assist in that regard, yes.'

Alarmed to find she had allowed her attention to drift from the matter under discussion, Clemmie forced herself to concentrate.

'Thank you, Miss Evercott,' Austin Young responded. 'WVS to the rescue.'

'Hardly unusual,' the mayor added warmly. 'Although, I do feel moved to go on the record as saying that while it is our collective wish to make these fellows feel welcome, and to aid mutual understanding, we must guard against getting carried away, against being too ambitious in our aims. With hundreds of the city's traders having gone out of business, and with so many families still lacking proper accommodation, we cannot be seen to be spending money on pomp and ceremony, nor on lavish spreads.'

Dorothy was nodding with some vigour. 'I agree, Mr Mayor. But fear not, the WVS is well used to fashioning something out of nothing.'

'I think you'll find that the US Army Air Force are not short of either money or resources.' The voice joining the exchange was new and came from the far end of the table. Craning to see its owner, Clemmie realised it was the man she'd seen earlier being helped out of a motorcar and into a wheelchair. In his smart navy blazer, he looked intelligent and businesslike, his voice deep and commanding but warm. Given the distance between them, it was hard to decide how old he was but, if pressed, she would guess at about thirty. 'Naturally, as their hosts, we feel obliged to provide. And that's understandable. But, if it's social functions you envisage holding, then I think you'll find the Americans more than willing to chip in, be that with refreshments, facilities… ensuring their chaps behave themselves.'

'Do you have a contact among them?' Austin Young enquired. 'Someone whose brains we might pick, so to speak?'

'I do. I've been given the name of…' Glancing at a sheet of paper in front of him, the newcomer replied, 'Major James D. Hogue of the USAAF. I'm given to understand he's coming over with the ground echelon but isn't expected to arrive for another week or so.'

'And can you tell us anything about the sort of set-up they're going to be establishing here?' Roger Marshall from the Chamber of Commerce asked. 'Any idea of numbers and so on?'

'At this stage, none. The only thing I know so far is that the unit will comprise a fighter group of P-38 Lightning aircraft.'

'Is it true it could mean several thousands of men descending upon us?'

To Roger Marshall's subsequent question, the young man looked thoughtful. 'Not being privy to operational details, I couldn't say. It's possible. But I think it safe to assume they won't all arrive at once.'

'I do hope not,' Dorothy whispered as an aside.

Clemmie hoped not, too. 'No.'

'So, Squadron Leader, it will be through you that we deal with them?'

Listening to Austin Young enquiring, Clemmie wondered about the title 'squadron leader'. It sounded important.

'In the early days, certainly. And in case you're all wondering why it has fallen to me, I should perhaps explain that although I am recently retired from the air force, before the war I spent a while training in Texas alongside what was then called the US Army Air Corps. I can only imagine that led somebody somewhere to believe the experience affords me an insight into the American character.'

'And does it?' Roger Marshall asked.

'To a degree, I suppose. One thing I can state without reservation is that, in their military capacity, they are as disciplined and as efficient a fighting unit as any of our own. I can also say that, as individuals, you will find them unreservedly warm and friendly.' Looking around the table as though to reassure them further, the squadron leader went on, 'I suspect it is they who will be bamboozled by *our* inherent reserve far more than *their* open and easy-going manner will flummox us.'

'Useful to know,' Dorothy observed. 'Something we will try to bear in mind.'

But as Clemmie sat nodding in agreement, the thought going through her own mind was how Gwen would react to learning that Americans were warm and friendly. Perhaps, she concluded, it was a fact best withheld for the moment. In any event, Gwen supposedly had her eye on some fellow called Jimmy. And it might not be a bad idea to conceal the news of *warm and friendly Americans* from Pearl, too.

–

'Terribly good of you to come, Squadron Leader.'

'Miss Evercott. Miss Huxford. Good afternoon. Not at all. It was good of you to suggest we meet here – gives me a chance to see the formidable ladies of the WVS in action.'

'Well, just be on your guard,' Dorothy said, a hint of mischief in her tone. 'Sit still too long and you'll find a ball of wool and pair of knitting needles thrust into your hands.'

When Squadron Leader Dunning laughed Clemmie noticed how, in an instant, his demeanour went from serious to boyish. Such a terrible shame he was in a wheelchair; since no one had mentioned it, she could only suppose he'd had an accident of some sort.

'You're not the first person to warn me of the danger of being press-ganged. I'm given to understand the WVS is a force to be reckoned with.'

'Second only to the RAF, Squadron Leader.'

'Miss Evercott, I think you're being modest.'

It was a couple of days later that same week, and, at Dorothy's suggestion, Squadron Leader Dunning had arrived at the WVS centre to discuss ideas for welcoming the American servicemen. And with the three of them now settled around a table in the dusty little room that more often served as a store, a tray of tea things in front of them, Dorothy went on, 'I was most interested to hear you have personal experience of life across the Atlantic.'

Squadron Leader Dunning nodded. 'I do. A year or so prior to the outbreak of war, I was sent to America for a spell of training on a new aircraft they'd been developing.'

'Is it true what you said about them being friendly?' While Clemmie knew she risked sounding forward, if she was going to be of any use in this endeavour she might as well know what she was up against and start speaking to some of the people involved. So far, she'd been too afraid of making a fool of herself to even open her mouth. At least this particular man didn't seem too frightening.

'Absolutely. Those I had the pleasure to meet were warm-hearted, open and generous to a fault.'

Then she could relax: having to deal with strangers was terrifying enough; knowing they were unlikely to be cold and stand-offish could only help.

'The impression I'm getting,' Dorothy said, 'is that they're rather less formal than we are. Rather less... how shall I put this? Wooden?'

'When they're removed from the business of war, I'd say that's true, yes.'

'Which leads me to thinking,' Dorothy picked up again, 'that perhaps, rather than arrange the traditional welcome – with speeches and the attendant ceremony – we should go for something a little less, well, stiff and starchy.'

Evidently considering Dorothy's point, Squadron Leader Dunning angled his head. 'Perhaps there's room for a mixture of the two.'

'Do go on.'

'Something I learned early on about Americans is that one of the things they find fascinating about us – as a nation, I mean – is our pageantry and rich history. For their own part, they have nothing quite like it.'

'So, a speech by the mayor in all his regalia…'

'Precisely. A short speech, a presentation of some sort, an exchange of pennants or badges or similar, and then quickly into a band and some dancing.'

'An event along those lines would be well received?'

'I believe it would be just the thing.'

'Hm.' Now it was Dorothy's turn to pause and think. 'Tell me, would you restrict invitations solely to officers or include some of their men as well?'

'All I can say, Miss Evercott, is that were *we* to be guests of the Americans, they would invite everyone, regardless of rank.'

'Maybe we could hold it somewhere very old.' When her companions turned to regard her, Clemmie reminded herself not to get flustered. 'You said they like our history – the Americans, I mean. So, while I know everywhere has been badly bombed, there must be an old building somewhere we could use, even just this once.'

'Oh, good idea,' Dorothy replied. 'Yes. How about, Clemmie, you ask the mayor to suggest somewhere? Were it not for the state of the High Street, the guildhall would have been terrific... but behind all those sandbags, I'm not sure it's still open. Yes, explain to him we're after a location that will provide our guests with a taste of our place in history.'

'Coming into the heart of our city would also give them the chance to see some of the devastation,' Squadron Leader Dunning added. 'Would help them understand what we've been through – what we're still going through.'

'Show them why they're here,' Clemmie remarked as the thought struck her.

'Show them why we're relieved to see them,' Dorothy agreed. 'Even if the general feeling is that they did rather take their time.'

'Hm.'

'Once we have a venue,' Dorothy went on, adopting what Clemmie had come to recognise as her purposeful tone, 'we can determine the number of guests it will comfortably accommodate, and help us to decide on the key people from each side. We don't want anyone's nose put out of joint.'

'And when we have a better idea of that,' Squadron Leader Dunning chipped in, 'I'll try and contact this Major Hogue fellow – get his thoughts on the matter.'

Dorothy smiled. 'Excellent. Well, I think we now know where to start. Clemmie, why don't you go straight along to the mayor, get him to put his thinking cap on and let us have his ideas in the next day or two? It would be nice to be able to report back to the next meeting that we have the beginnings of a plan. That way, if everyone agrees on it as the way forward, we can get cracking.'

Go and see the mayor? Her? The prospect alone was enough to make her tremble. But, if she was going to be a part of this thing, she supposed she had to start somewhere. Besides, with a bit of luck the mayor would be out, and she could get away with leaving a message with his secretary.

Or, she thought, as she realised that Dorothy was getting to her feet, signifying that the meeting was at an end, she could try to be a bit more like Pearl – show some backbone and simply get on with it.

—

'Got any razor blades?'

'No, Mrs Wright. I'm afraid not.'

The following morning, back at work in the shop, Clemmie wished heartily she wasn't. So far today, most of the women who'd come through the door were after something of which there was no stock, Mrs Wright being a case in point.

'So, what's Bert supposed to do for a shave?'

Struggling to appear sympathetic, Clemmie shrugged. 'I really don't know. There's a shortage everywhere. The rep told Mr Narramore he has no idea when the next delivery will arrive. It's down to the government commandeering all the steel for more important things.'

'More important things. What – making sure Churchill and all his cronies get to shave every day, you mean?'

'I think perhaps they mean for ships and… things.'

'Huh. Then please God, tell me you've got Bert's cigs in. If there's none of those either, I might as well not bother going home. Never hear the end of it.'

'Player's Navy Cut, isn't it?' Clemmie lowered her voice to ask. Shooting a glance towards the door, she flipped back the lid of a wooden box beneath the till, pulled out a packet of twelve and slid them across the counter. 'For goodness' sake, don't tell anyone. Mr Narramore put them there just for you.'

'Tell him I said ta,' Mrs Wright whispered back, in one move sweeping the packet off the counter and into the pocket on the front of her apron. 'And tell him I'll settle up Friday.'

'Very well.' While Clemmie was still making a note of Mrs Wright's purchase in Cedric's account book, the bell tinkled again, and through the door this time came Mrs Barrett.

'How much do 'e want for them caulis outside?'

Despite having now been working there for several weeks, Clemmie still found that very few customers directly acknowledged her presence, 'Mr Narramore got any…' or 'Did Cedric put by any of those…' being their usual manner of addressing her.

'Thruppence,' Clemmie replied. 'Has the sign blown down again?'

'Thruppence? For thruppence I'd want summat bigger than they tiddlers.'

Clemmie shrugged. 'Sorry. They're small because it's early in the year. Did you see there's spring greens out there? For the same price, they'll stretch further.'

'I'd rather not,' Mrs Barrett replied, her tone tetchy. 'They take so much getting clean. Devil only knows how they manage to get so much grit in them.'

Clemmie smiled. 'They do take a deal of washing. But they're very good for you. The Ministry of Food leaflet says they're rich in iron.'

'Happen they are. No, love, give me one of them big tins of peas. I'll use me points.'

Next to come through the door was a woman Clemmie had come to know by sight without ever learning her name.

'That came for Cedric,' the woman said, holding out a brown envelope. Seemingly in her forties, she sometimes came in with a boy of about eight.

With a puzzled frown, Clemmie accepted the envelope, the typewritten address reading *Mr C. A. Narramore, 47, Worcester Terrace, Exeter.* 'Um…'

Noticing Clemmie's bafflement, the woman explained, 'I'm Mrs Bodley – Jean – from next door. Number forty-seven.' And when Clemmie continued to frown, the woman added, 'Heavens, dearie, Cedric's my landlord. I live in the rooms downstairs with my boy, Malcolm. Old Mr Reeves is up atop.'

Clemmie gave an apologetic smile. 'Sorry,' she said. 'I didn't know. Thank you for bringing it round. I'll make sure he gets it.'

'Ta, love.'

On her way through to Mr Narramore's little room out the back, Clemmie pondered the discovery that he owned not only a corner shop and the flat above, but the whole of the house next door as well. Clearly, he was doing all right for himself.

The trail of morning customers having subsided, she took to dusting along the shelves, her mind wandering to Squadron Leader Dunning. Presumably whatever accident had befallen him must have occurred a while ago, otherwise he wouldn't be out and about again. He certainly didn't bear any signs of injury in the shape of cuts or bruises. And he seemed proficient at manoeuvring his wheelchair, too. For all he must have endured, his spirits seemed remarkably good, certainly more cheerful than those with little to bemoan above the shortage of their favourite cigarettes or the nastiness of the National Loaf. He was nicely mannered, smart too. She supposed he had his wife to thank for his clean cuffs and neat shirt collars. Him being in a wheelchair, she couldn't imagine him pressing them himself.

'Holding it near the shelf don't get the dust off, you know.'

Swivelling so quickly she almost toppled off the little step she'd been using to reach the highest shelf, Clemmie shot out a hand to steady herself.

'Mrs Narramore. Sorry. I was miles away.'

Audrey Narramore dismissed her apology with a wave. 'It's all right, love. I know you're not a slacker. Anyway, just this once, since I'm here, why don't you get off early? It's only ten minutes. I can tot up the counterfoils for the register and still keep an ear out for the bell.'

'Well, if you're sure, then yes, thank you. It'll give me time to have a bite of lunch before I have to go up the WVS. We're so busy up there.'

'You go on, then,' Mrs Narramore said before turning to go through to the back. 'And we'll see you bright and early tomorrow.'

At the sound of Cedric Narramore's heavy tread on the stairs, Clemmie nodded. 'Yes,' she said, untying her apron before Mrs Narramore could change her mind. 'Thank you. I'll see you in the morning.'

About to step out onto the pavement, though, she realised she didn't have her handbag. Honestly, she'd forget her head if it wasn't screwed on. But, as she retraced her steps across the shop and back behind the counter, she heard Audrey Narramore speaking to someone – presumably Mr Narramore – and noticed the snippiness of her tone.

'All right, all right, keep your hair on. I'm not going through your ruddy papers. I'm just after the ledger. Besides, if they're so private, happen you shouldn't leave them lying around.'

With no wish to let either of them know she was there, Clemmie reached around the doorframe to the shelf, swiped up her bag and tiptoed back across the shop, where, with the door still standing partly open, she slipped out onto the pavement. Peculiar couple, those two; Audrey with her adopted airs and graces, Cedric with his slightly shifty manner. Well, thankfully she was done for the morning; a quick sandwich for lunch and then she was free to spend her afternoon helping out at the WVS.

In fact, she thought as she turned the corner into the far end of Buckingham Crescent, it was shame she had to work for the Narramores at all; how much nicer her days would be if she could just go with Miss Evercott to the WVS each morning. Alas, there was the small matter of needing money; the wage Cedric Narramore paid her might be a pittance but, without it, she would be penniless. So, she would keep her head down, get through the mornings with a smile, and then enjoy her afternoons as a volunteer. Oh, and try not to panic too much about her part in this new welcome committee, and everything it seemed *that* was going to entail...

Chapter 9

'Well, he confirmed he'd be here. So I can only suppose something has happened to detain him.'

'That or he's got lost,' Clemmie replied to Squadron Leader Dunning's observation. 'After all, the city has barely a landmark left to go by, let alone a street sign, which must make it awful difficult for someone who doesn't know the place to find his way around.'

'Tricky, certainly.'

It was late one afternoon, ten days or so after the second committee meeting, and, having ascertained that Major James D. Hogue of the USAAF had arrived in Exeter, Squadron Leader Dunning had arranged for them to meet at the guildhall. Despite being heavily sandbagged and closed to the general public, it was still, the mayor had told Clemmie, the most suitable venue for their welcome event. Miss Evercott agreed, going on to claim that, as a building, it told the city's story like no other. But this afternoon, with the major having not yet shown up, Clemmie was beginning to wonder whether they might have been better going to the airfield and meeting him there.

'He's probably cursing that *we* didn't go and see *him*,' she said. 'Maybe my idea to invite him here was a daft one.'

Squadron Leader Dunning shook his head. 'Nonsense. If he can't find his way into the centre of Exeter, then I fear for when his pilots must find their way to France.' Noticing that he was grinning, Clemmie smiled back. 'As you said the other day, he should see the city for himself. He should see how we've been struggling – indeed, how we still are.'

'Do you think he'll like the building?' Clemmie asked.

'Can't really fail to. Have you been in here before?'

She nodded. 'When I was at school, we came on a visit. I seem to recall we were learning about kings and queens, and the headmaster brought us. The boys liked hearing about the executions, and going downstairs to the cells—'

'All the grisly stuff.'

'Yes. But *I* liked being up there, in the gallery. I liked looking down from so high up. And being so close to such an unusual roof.'

'Best place from which to view it, I would imagine. Shame I can't make it up all those steps.'

When, with a look of frustration, the squadron leader indicated his wheelchair, Clemmie held off responding. Knowing what tragedy had befallen him might prevent her making a gaffe. But dare she ask? Would he take offence? As men in authority went, he had a surprisingly approachable manner.

Deciding there was only one way to find out, she forced a swallow. 'May I ask you what happened?' Her question posed, she braced for his reaction.

'For me to end up in this?' When he looked directly at her, she gave a barely discernible nod. 'Not through doing anything heroic, that's for sure. Look, I don't know how much you know – I can't imagine you're old enough to have been aware of it at the time – but, back in the

August of 1940, the Luftwaffe mounted bombing raids over the south-east. First it was attacks on shipping in the Channel. Then it was our ports. A few weeks later, their tails clearly up, they turned their attention to our airfields. Their tactics caught us embarrassingly underprepared and cost us dearly. It's fair to say that, for a while, they had the better of us. That was when people started talking in earnest about Hitler invading.'

'I see.' He was right; to her shame, she knew nothing of this.

'When the Luftwaffe then moved on to London, our boys in Bomber Command retaliated by launching raids on Berlin. For one of those, my squadron was detailed to provide escort duty for our Wellingtons. The mission was a success. However, as we were making our way back, from out of nowhere, firing at me for all he was worth, came a lone Messerschmitt Bf 110. I thought I was gone, was utterly convinced of it, was bracing for the ball of fire. To this day, I have no idea how he didn't bring me down.'

Clemmie found herself rapt. 'But... he didn't.'

'He didn't. I made it back. On approach to land, the undercarriage wouldn't come down. I tried repeatedly, couldn't get it to work manually either, made a circuit of the airfield to have another go. In the end, there was nothing for it. I had to make an emergency landing. And, well, let's just say that in all my time behind the controls of an aircraft it wasn't my finest hour. Suddenly she was all over the place, and instead of putting the tail down first, I hit the ground with her nose. Stopped her all right. Stopped her dead. But at the cost of my spine.'

Despite being unable to picture precisely what had happened, Clemmie winced. 'Oh.'

'Since then, I must have seen every military doctor in the land. I've been poked, prodded, injected, stretched. You name it. But the sorry truth remains that, while on some days I do have mild feeling in my legs, and with the use of sticks I can hobble around the house, on other days I have no sensation whatsoever and I'm utterly useless.'

Clemmie had no idea how to respond. Her initial thought had been to remark that he was lucky to have made it back at all. But with him left unable to walk, there was always the possibility he didn't see it that way. Who was she to presume? Having never met anyone in a wheelchair, she had no idea how it must feel to suddenly be confined to one.

'I'm so sorry to hear that,' was all she eventually managed. 'That's terrible.'

'Please don't be sorry. I knew the risks. All aircrew go up voluntarily. These things happen. I'm alive. Many aren't.'

'Yes.'

'Ah, look.' Turning to see what had caught his attention, Clemmie noticed movement at the entrance. 'Major Hogue,' the squadron leader raised his voice to call across. 'Good afternoon. Welcome to Exeter.'

The man striding through the door towards them stretched out a hand. 'Squadron Leader Dunning?'

'Correct. How do you do? This is Miss Huxford. She's a volunteer with the WVS – the Women's Voluntary Service. They play an important part in just about every aspect of the war at home.'

When Clemmie's fingers were crushed in Major Hogue's grasp, she almost yelped in pain.

'Miss Huxford. Pleasure to meet you. I read in my briefing papers about the WVS. Great work.'

'Thank you.' Although she was smiling warmly back, inside, Clemmie squirmed. What a fraud. She'd only been a member for a matter of weeks. Who was she to take credit?

'So, what is this place I've trekked all the way here to see? It sure looks old.'

'It's been here more than six hundred years,' she said, delighted by the apparent sincerity of the major's wonder.

'Is that so?'

'This is where,' Squadron Leader Dunning picked up, 'all the business of running the city was once carried out. Indeed, where much of it still is.'

'Stroke of good luck it survived the Luftwaffe.'

'Indeed.'

'Did the whole city look like this once?' With an expansive wave of his arm, Major Hogue gestured to the wider building. 'Was it all so ancient?'

The squadron leader nodded. 'A good deal of it. Many of the streets in the city centre are medieval. *Were* medieval.'

'Heck, what a loss. And these raids were recent.'

'A few weeks back,' Squadron Leader Dunning confirmed.

As he continued to answer the major's questions about the air raids, Clemmie took in the new arrival's appearance. Tall and stocky, and standing as he was with his stiff-looking service cap tucked under his arm, he seemed like a wall of brass-studded khaki. He certainly looked as though he meant business. He also looked healthy, as though used to decent amounts of both food and sunshine. By contrast, Squadron Leader Dunning appeared fragile and grey.

Apprised of the air raids, the major took to answering questions about his own operation.

'And how many men will that entail initially?'

'Two squadrons plus support crews, all from the 14th Fighter Group.'

From where she was listening, Clemmie relaxed a little; while she had no idea of the size of a squadron, she guessed it was nowhere near the thousands of servicemen they had been warned to expect.

'Two squadrons.'

'Six squadrons are coming over, two of them to be based here. Since Pearl Harbor, they've been flying patrols down the west coast.'

'Right.'

'The ground echelon is expected here next month.'

Even better, Clemmie thought; they had a while longer to prepare, news that was bound to please Miss Evercott.

'And the air echelon?'

'With decent conditions, shortly after. Right about now, they're testing new drop tanks. If they work as well as we anticipate, they'll add close to a thousand miles to the aircrafts' range.'

'Any idea of the route they'll take?'

'Right now, we envisage Labrador, Greenland, Iceland, Scotland. irst time we will have flown single-seat fighters across the Atlantic.'

'Quite an achievement.'

'Sure is.'

'So, initially, the number of personnel will be quite small.'

The major shrugged. 'To start. But who can say? Things change.'

'They do indeed.'

'Look,' Major Hogue said, pushing back the cuff of his jacket and glancing at a solid-looking wristwatch, 'it's been great to meet you both. And this is one swell place. I appreciate you inviting me. I'll have to come back some time and take a proper look around. But how about next time, you come over to us? See how we're getting set up. By then, I might be able to say more, might be able to talk about dates for this social.'

'Sounds good, Major,' Squadron Leader Dunning agreed.

'Well, pleasure to meet you, miss.'

This time, Clemmie was prepared for the strength of the major's handshake. 'It was a pleasure to meet you, too, Major Hogue.'

'Six hundred years, huh? Wait till I tell them *that* back home.'

When the major had left, Clemmie and the squadron leader exchanged glances.

'I think the polite description for a chap like him is larger than life.'

Clemmie grinned. 'I'm not sure my hand will ever recover. Are all Americans like that?'

'By *like that*, I take it you mean large and loud?'

Clemmie blushed.

'Not all of them, no. But by necessity, their officers usually are.'

'He seemed friendly.'

Beside her, Squadron Leader Dunning turned his wheelchair towards the door. 'He did. I think we'll be all right with him.'

'Yes.'

'So, I'll see you at the committee meeting Thursday evening. Are you all right to report back on what we've learned?'

Despite the jolt of terror triggered by the prospect, Clemmie nodded. 'Yes. Yes, of course. In the meantime, I'll tell Miss Evercott.'

'Right, then. I'll see you there.'

'Yes. See you there.'

Moments later, turning left from the High Street onto South Street to make her way home, Clemmie allowed herself a smile and reflected on what she had gleaned. Much as she'd supposed, Squadron Leader Dunning had been injured in the line of duty. And while he was free to say all he wanted about not being heroic, she couldn't agree. To fly an aeroplane in the first place had surely to require inordinate courage; to fly one over Germany, with the attendant risk of being shot at, was fearlessness beyond comprehension. If she'd understood correctly, despite thinking he was about to drop from the sky, the squadron leader had kept flying. And then, having made it all the way home, his mettle already thoroughly tested, he'd had to land his aircraft without the use of any wheels. If that didn't constitute bravery, then she didn't know what did. But for his landing going awry, which she found hard to believe was down to an error on his part, he would have made it unscathed. But now, by being unable to do things other people took for granted – like climbing a flight of stairs – he missed out on so much. And he probably wasn't much more than thirty yet, either. How unfair was that? It certainly put into perspective her own fear of having to address the committee.

Crossing onto Topsham Road, she sighed. Well, since he had spoken to her in such a nice manner, she would give real thought to what to tell the committee members, and work hard to make sure their joint part in this business was a success. A brave man like him deserved no less.

'Here, love, you've given me sixpence too much change.'

Staring at the coins on Mrs Day's open palm, Clemmie flushed. Thank goodness Mrs Day was honest; most customers would have kept quiet. Make that sort of mistake too often and she'd lose her job.

'Thanks ever so for telling me,' she said, accepting the coin Mrs Day handed back to her.

'My reward will come in heaven, love,' Mrs Day replied before turning for the door. 'Least, that's what I keep telling myself. See you later.'

'Yes,' Clemmie said as she dropped the coin back into the cash drawer. 'See you later.'

She knew, of course, the reason for her distraction; this afternoon was the meeting of the American Welcome Committee, where she would be expected to relay to the other members what had transpired with Major Hogue. The prospect had been playing on her mind since first light, making her feel more and more edgy as the morning had worn on. But if she didn't soon find a way to stop feeling so jittery and start concentrating, her mistake with the amount of Mrs Day's change wouldn't be her last.

'Morning, love.' Mid-thought, Clemmie looked up to see Mrs Parker. 'Got any liver salts?'

Reaching to the shelf, Clemmie selected the last green and white tin of Andrews. 'You're in luck.'

'Mum's got tummy troubles again.'

'Oh dear, I'm sorry to hear that.'

'This usually does the trick, though.'

'On your account?'

'Please, love. I'll be in to settle up Friday, once Vic's been paid.'

Hot on the heels of Mrs Parker came Mrs Nosworthy. Since she was one of the customers renowned for constantly challenging – largely through forgetfulness – how many of her week's rations she'd already taken, Clemmie drew a breath and fixed a smile.

'You live round here, love?' Mrs Nosworthy asked as Clemmie was carefully weighing out eight ounces of sugar.

Having learned to her cost that saying she lived in Buckingham Crescent made her appear a bit *la-di-da*, as the locals would say, Clemmie kept her answer deliberately vague. 'In lodgings off Topsham Road.'

'Yeah? All right, are they?'

'Very convenient. Couple of minutes' walk.'

'Nice to only work mornings, I should think.'

Twisting closed the top of the paper bag, Clemmie added the cost of the sugar to Mrs Nosworthy's account. 'When I finish here, I volunteer afternoons with the WVS.'

'Yeah? What d'you get up to there, then? Don't suppose there's any eggs?'

'Sorry, no.'

'Chopped ham?'

'There is some but—'

'Couple of ounces, then, dear.'

'But it's three points per ounce, and so won't it leave you short for the rest of the four weeks?' Why, Clemmie wondered, couldn't points be allocated monthly? Twenty-four points per person per month made sense; everyone could understand that. Twenty-four points every four weeks was a nightmare, both for Cedric and his customers alike. 'But of course, it's up to you.'

'No, two ounces. I shall be all right.'

'Very well.'

'So,' Mrs Nosworthy went on as she leaned across and squinted at the scales to ensure she wasn't being diddled. 'What do you do up the WVS? Knitting, is it?'

'No, there's more to the WVS than just knitting and salvage,' Clemmie replied as she folded the square of paper over the ham. 'I started out helping the centre organiser with writing up records and ledgers and the like. But now I'm on a committee to arrange—'

'Ooh, *on a committee*.' Mrs Nosworthy winked. 'Hark at you, love, all important.'

With a good-natured smile, Clemmie picked up again. 'There's some American servicemen coming, and the committee has been set up to work out how best to—'

'American servicemen? Morning, Mrs N.'

Alarmed to hear Cedric behind her, Clemmie spun about. How long, she wondered, had he been standing there? While she might not have anything to hide, she didn't like to think of him eavesdropping on her conversations with the customers.

'Morning, Mr Narramore. You heard the latest? Your girl here was just telling me we got Americans coming.'

Cedric's attention switched to Clemmie. 'So I hear. When's that, then?'

Carefully entering the total of Mrs Nosworthy's shopping into Cedric's accounts book, Clemmie shrugged. 'We don't know yet. We think in a couple of weeks.'

When Mrs Nosworthy left, Cedric turned to regard Clemmie more closely, his expression earnest. 'Serious, love. When you find out, I shouldn't mind knowing.'

Unsure why Mr Narramore should be interested in the arrival of a couple of squadrons of American airmen, Clemmie frowned. 'All right…'

'See, I hear from those places what's already got them how your friendly Yank ain't exactly short of goodies. And not short of ways to get more, if you catch my drift. So, if you can see your way to tipping me the wink when they get here, then if anything comes of it, I'll see you don't lose out, make it worth your while.'

In a bid to cover her alarm, Clemmie treated him to a smile. Surely he had to be joking.

'Oh, I see.'

But Cedric Narramore wasn't finished. 'No need for you to get your hands dirty. I'll keep you out of it. You just put me in touch with someone, and I'll take it from there.'

With no idea what to say, Clemmie settled for nodding. Regrettably, her employer wasn't someone with whom she could afford to fall out. On the other hand, dabbling in the black market was both illegal and highly dangerous, bringing the risk not only of incurring a heavy fine but also of being sent to prison. Everyone knew that.

'All right,' she replied nonetheless. 'I'll bear that in mind.'

On his way past, Cedric squeezed her shoulder. 'Good girl. Like I said, I won't overlook it.'

The moment Clemmie was sure he'd reached the storeroom and wasn't lurking just beyond the door, she exhaled heavily. Now what should she do? She supposed that, for a couple of weeks, there was nothing she *could* do; even Major Hogue didn't know for certain when his men were going to arrive. Given the nature of this war, there was always the possibility that they never would. Real-istically, though, they were likely to be here quite soon, Major Hogue having given the impression that everything was set.

In the hope that it was almost time to go home, she glanced at the clock: not long now. Although after this she still had the committee meeting to get through.

On the matter of Mr Narramore, though, she supposed her safest bet was to string him along with a story of delays and setbacks, and then hope he forgot all about it. Yes. And if he didn't, then her only other choice was to confide in Miss Evercott and ask her advice on how to handle such a tricky situation.

–

'Good afternoon, Miss Huxford.'

Looking up to see Squadron Leader Dunning wheeling himself through the door into the little room behind the church hall, Clemmie smiled.

'Good afternoon to you.'

'I trust you are well?'

'I am, thank you. Miss Evercott has just nabbed Mr Young,' she said as though to explain why she was standing there on her own. 'Something about a family still on the housing list.'

'Ah. And what about you? Ready to impart our news?'

Her response sounded less than convincing, even to herself. 'I suppose.'

'There's really no need to be nervous. And yes, I do realise how that very statement usually only serves to make matters worse. But it's true.'

Clemmie sighed. 'Easy for you to say. But where everyone else has a proper and important job, I'm just a shopgirl.'

'First of all, Miss Huxford, you are not *just* a shop-girl. Without shops we would none of us have food, or indeed any of life's other essentials. Moreover, dealing with customers is an art form in itself. But you know that from doing it every day.'

'But serving customers is hardly going to help me here.'

'I disagree. I cannot think of a single job where an ability to successfully deal with all sorts of people isn't of the utmost importance.' Having paused for a moment, he grinned before going on to add, 'Well, apart, possibly, from being a lumberjack charged with chopping down trees in the depths of a forest. But presumably even he would have a boss he would need to get along with.'

Reflecting on his point about being able to deal with people, she realised she had never looked at it like that. 'I suppose.'

'On top of that, none of us with these *proper and important jobs*, as you call them, came to them fully competent. We all had to start at the bottom and learn. Take it from me, Miss Huxford, as you get older you will almost certainly find that life is a business for which few of us are ever fully prepared or even remotely skilled, but that much is to be learned from doing – from starting somewhere and having a go. And, of course, from making the odd mistake.'

While she didn't doubt he was right, she wasn't sure how knowing any of that helped with her present panic. 'Hm.'

'I can see I'm not convincing you. So, if you hear only one thing I say, let it be this. You have as much right to be here as the rest of us. Every individual here today accepted a task that will enable us, as one body, to achieve a common goal. Each of us went away to obtain information our fellow committee members need to know if they are to fulfil their own roles. All you have to do is tell everyone, clearly and simply, what we learned from Major Hogue. They will listen to you because they need to know what you have found out.'

'But what if—'

'If they have questions?'

'Well, yes.'

'If you can answer factually, do so. Resist the urge to embellish – not that you would. On the other hand, if you don't know the answer, say so. Don't be tempted to guess or to suppose.'

'Don't guess. Right.' It seemed sensible advice.

'But, and here's the important part…'

Clemmie regarded him expectantly. 'Yes?'

'Try to avoid simply saying *I don't know*. Instead, follow quickly with something along the lines of "Does anyone else know the answer to that?" Or, since in this instance I'll be here with you, and we were both at the meeting with Major Hogue, you can look to me and say, "Do *you* remember anything about that?"'

Clemmie rehearsed his suggestion. 'I don't know. Do *you* remember anything about that?'

'Perfect. Do you see how that's better?'

Surprised to find that she did, she replied with a vigorous nod. 'Yes. It doesn't make me sound so hopeless.'

'It also presents a chance for others to contribute. Occasionally, someone will have a pithy insight they might not otherwise wish to interrupt you to divulge, or a new piece of information they might otherwise have forgotten.'

'Yes,' she said again. 'I see that. Thank you, that's real helpful.'

'Oh, and don't forget to breathe. And in your case, smile. If *I* were to smile I would simply come across as odd. But you have a lovely smile and really shouldn't shy away from using it.'

Now she was just blushing madly. 'Breathe and smile,' she said to distract from the fact.

'Right, then, are we all here?' Turning in the direction of the voice calling them to order, Clemmie saw Mr Young from the city corporation standing at the head of the table. 'Since it would seem that we are, might I suggest we make a start?'

As luck would have it, Mr Young called upon her first. And although she was trembling so badly she thought everyone must be able to see, she conveyed her information as calmly as she could before turning aside to ask, 'Is there anything I've left out, Squadron Leader Dunning?'

When he appeared to suppress a smile, she feared she had overstepped. What if she had now come across as impertinent? Oh, dear God, why had she gone and spoiled it? Up until then, it had been going so well.

'I don't believe you have left out a thing.'

'A very thorough briefing,' Mr Young agreed. 'Thank you, Miss Huxford. We look forward to you keeping us up to date with progress. Next, then...'

After that, discussions around the table went largely over Clemmie's head. Nevertheless, when proceedings drew to a close she felt both relieved and exhilarated. She had spoken in public. She had given people important information about no less a subject than the arrival of American servicemen in Exeter. Her headmaster would be astonished; her mother, too. And Pearl would be gawping in disbelief. Little Clemmie Huxford had stood up and addressed a group of people she didn't know. She wasn't even sure she could believe it herself.

'Well done,' Squadron Leader Dunning whispered as he wheeled his way past her on his way out. 'I'll see you soon.'

'You acquitted yourself very well,' Dorothy announced when, a while later, the two of them were walking back to Buckingham Crescent. 'I said you'd be good at this, didn't I?'

Feeling her cheeks colouring, Clemmie lowered her head. 'I wouldn't have been, had it not been for Squadron Leader Dunning giving me some advice.'

'And do you know the most important part of being given advice?'

Clemmie shook her head. 'No?'

'It's only of any use if you heed it. So, well done for clearly doing just that. Keep going like this and you'll be quite the force.'

Despite considering that highly unlikely, Clemmie smiled. 'Thank you. I'll do my best.'

'No doubt you'll disagree but, when it comes to spotting young women with promise, I'm rarely wrong.'

'If you say so.'

'Now, how about, when we get home, we toast your success with—'

'A little sherry?' Unable to help it, Clemmie laughed. 'Just the thing.'

Speak at a committee meeting and then take sherry with someone as refined and composed as Miss Evercott? Go back a couple of weeks and no one would have believed her capable of either. But then, until this afternoon she would have struggled to believe it, too.

Yes, all in all, it had been a day of revelations, those giving her most pause for thought coming from Squadron Leader Dunning – a man overcoming adversity on a scale she found almost impossible to comprehend, and yet who had taken a moment of his time to help her. If nothing else, the challenges he had to face every day brought into perspective her own rather juvenile fear of talking to people she didn't know.

When she looked up and saw they were turning into Buckingham Crescent, she made a vow: from now on, she would try to learn from his example. When she felt unqualified to do something, she would push herself to try; when she feared making a mistake, she would remind herself that nothing she got wrong could possibly compare to the consequences of trying to land an aeroplane without wheels. But above all, she would aim to conduct herself with grace and compassion for others. Oh, and with humour wherever possible too, because if Squadron Leader Dunning could do it with the trials he surely faced, then what – other than a simple lack of confidence – was there to stand in her way?

Chapter 10

How strange, the business of time. When she was at the WVS in the afternoons, or talking to Miss Evercott in the evenings, it simply flew. But when she was at Narramore's, the hours did nothing but drag. Was it, Clemmie wondered, because when she was in the shop she spent all her time wishing she was doing something for the American Welcome Committee instead? Was it because, in contrast to working behind the counter, volunteering meant never knowing what she might be asked to do from one minute to the next? Or was it meeting so many different women? Exercising a good number of them at the WVS at the moment was talk of the Americans; the various working groups were humming with anticipation of their arrival.

'Apparently,' Dorothy told her one evening when they were sitting in deckchairs, watching the swallows swooping low over the garden, 'the younger housewives of the Make Do and Mend party talk of nothing else. One can only suppose they've heard the tales.'

In the soft dusk, Clemmie frowned. 'The tales?'

'There's a certain grouchy element among our population,' Dorothy replied, and then glanced about before lowering her voice to continue, 'among men especially, who not only consider America rather late to this war, but who delight in being dismissive of her servicemen.

Overpaid, oversexed and over here, seems to be the general gripe, which leads me to suspect there are those among their wives hoping to find out it's all true.'

Although Clemmie gave a little laugh, this discovery rather took the shine off her excitement. She'd imagined the Americans to be knights-in-shining-armour types, galloping to their rescue. *It'll be all right now the Americans have joined in*, people had reassured one another last year. Now she had to wonder whether that was still the case, or whether their arrival might not upset the apple cart, especially with women everywhere being so heartily fed up with feeling dowdy and drained, and longing desperately for something – anything – to bring relief to the never-ending greyness of their days. If it wasn't for her own delight at lodging with Miss Evercott, and the joy she derived from belonging to the WVS, Clemmie supposed she might feel the same way. She could certainly sympathise with the plight of some of the women who came into the shop; in a bid to be seen as supportive, she often did.

'We're hoping this week brings more news from Major Hogue,' she said to Dorothy, the arrival of the American airmen now on her mind.

'That would be good.'

'My mistake, I suppose, but to hear him talk that first time I thought they'd be here by now.'

'One imagines the plan for bringing them over must be mired in difficulty, there being all manner of obstacles to cause delays, not least the sheer practicalities of crossing the Atlantic. If what we're told by the Home Service is true, our soldiers continue to make good progress against Rommel's forces at Alamein, and both the RAF and the navy have been seeing some success out there, too. But what we don't seem to hear much about lately is the situation in the Atlantic. There might have been a bit of a lull, but I doubt Germany has removed her fleet of U-boats elsewhere.'

Whenever Miss Evercott spoke of the developments in the war, Clemmie wished she understood. The only thing she knew about Alamein was that it was in Egypt, a fact she'd gleaned from a news broadcast on the wireless. As to why the war seemed to have gone there at all, she was in the dark. And she didn't like to ask for fear of seeming stupid. She'd even tried reading about it. Spotting Miss Evercott's *Daily Telegraph* left open one morning at a page showing arrows marked on a map of North Africa, she'd tried to make sense of the situation. She'd failed, of course, it being entirely beyond her to comprehend.

Staring up into the darkening sky, she sighed. She supposed she might ask Squadron Leader Dunning; in common with Miss Evercott, he made it his business to keep up to date. But even supposing she spotted a suitable moment, how would she go about it? *I was wondering, Squadron Leader Dunning, whether you might explain to me about the war?* One poorly asked question could ruin his impression of her. Mind you, that was on the cards sooner or later anyway, since she was nowhere near the capable individual he thought her. Nor did she possess the promise he seemed to suppose; she really *was* just a shopgirl. And sows' ears were not renowned for making silk purses.

Thankfully, none of that prevented her from looking forward to the committee meetings. That she and the squadron leader had no news with which to update the other members was disappointing but couldn't be helped. Perhaps someone else would have something to tell them.

As it turned out, at the meeting the following day someone did.

'Although we are yet to learn when our American visitors will be joining us,' Austin Young from the city corporation began by saying, 'we have been asked by the War Office to establish the number and location of billets available for American officers. Clearly unfamiliar with the… well, shall we say *rural* nature of the county of Devon and, indeed, the raids that have lately come to befall our city, our colleagues on the other side of the Atlantic have expressed a preference for hotels or guest houses, but go on to state that, in the absence of such accommodation, rooms in private homes will be acceptable. To that end, our billeting officer, Mr Evans, will be visiting the villages around the airport to establish what might be made available.'

The expression on the face of Roger Marshall from the Chamber of Commerce brightened. 'Any idea how much they pay?'

Austin Young scanned the memorandum on the table in front of him. 'Officially, I don't appear to have that information. However, word *unofficially* is that they pay 10d per night.'

'Ten pence a night?'

'So I've heard tell.'

'Stone me. That's fourpence a night more than a householder would get for billeting one of our own chaps.'

'It is indeed,' Austin Young agreed. 'And so I doubt we shall be short of offers.'

'What about the men?' Squadron Leader Dunning asked. 'Where will they be accommodated?'

'In the first instance, I believe they are to live on the airfield, in something called Quonset huts. Apparently, they are more properly designed for use as warehouses and workshops but in the short term can be used as dormitories.'

To Clemmie's mind, the arrangement sounded mean.

'I should imagine any number of families would happily take in an ordinary serviceman,' Dorothy remarked. 'But I suppose it would be futile to suggest such a thing to the powers-that-be.'

'I think we should first ensure we are able to meet their requirements for officers,' Austin Young replied. 'But I shall pass on your thoughts, Miss Evercott. Unfortunately, Inspector Lethbridge couldn't attend this afternoon, but responsibility for the billeting of service personnel rests jointly with him.'

In the absence of significant further business, shortly after that the meeting broke up. Squadron Leader Dunning attracted Clemmie's attention as she headed with Miss Evercott towards the door.

Seeing him signalling to her, she willed herself not to blush. It didn't work.

'Miss Huxford, I was rather hoping we would have heard from Major Hogue by now.'

'Yes.' How ridiculous to have come over so hot. 'I just said the same to Miss Evercott.'

'But since we are no doubt a long way down his list of priorities, all we can do is wait.'

'Yes. I supposed the same.'

'Rest assured, the moment he telephones me I shall let you know.'

Clemmie smiled. 'Thank you.'

'Otherwise, I shall see you here next week.'

'Yes. You will.'

Walking home afterwards, Clemmie felt frustrated to the point of being cross. She'd had high hopes of the welcome committee; her duties in that regard were the most enjoyable part of her week. But having got excited about it, she now felt rather let down; of late, it was providing her with next to nothing to do and, thus, no reason to see Squadron Leader Dunning, in whose company she was slowly becoming more at ease.

Turning the corner into Buckingham Crescent, she inadvertently let out a sigh.

'Everything all right?'

Noting Dorothy's inquisitive expression, she smiled. 'Yes, of course.'

'Only, you seem somewhat distracted.'

'Sorry. I think I'm just a bit tired today.'

'Early night?'

'I think so.'

On the point of heaving yet another sigh, Clemmie instead raised a smile. She supposed the situation with the welcome committee would change soon enough. No doubt shortly, rather than pining for something to do she would find herself wishing she had altogether less on her plate. It was the way of the world – especially, it seemed, for women. Until then, she had no choice but to soldier on at Narramore's and content herself with whatever Miss Evercott entrusted her with at the WVS.

Of course, she reminded herself, another way to feel less frustrated was simply to stop counting down the days until her next meeting with Squadron Leader Dunning...

–

Finally, a moment of peace. Finally, there was no one to tut while they waited to be served, and Clemmie could note in Cedric's ledger the two shillings Mrs Parker had paid off her account. If his book had been under the counter as it usually was, she would have done so at the time. However, this morning it wasn't there. She could only suppose he had taken it out the back to see which of his customers were behind with their payments. There were certainly plenty of them. For a man who made so free with his opinions and was so blunt with his manner of speaking, he took a surprisingly lenient view of overdue accounts.

With a glance to check that no one was about to come in from the street, she darted through the small stockroom behind the counter to the even smaller space beyond. In his wit, Cedric referred to this tiny room as 'the office'. Barely larger than a cupboard, it was home to a hefty mahogany desk with a green leather top – not that the surface was ever visible, submerged as it usually was beneath a chaotic assortment of regulations from the Food Office and invoices from wholesalers, a good many of them stamped in red with the words *PAYMENT OVERDUE*. Even pushed hard up against the wall, the desk took up more than half the floor space; on the wall above it was a shelf upon which sat a row of box files labelled with the names of suppliers. All in all, the room was a mess. And she suspected Cedric recognised the fact because, every now and again, he would have what he rather unfortunately chose to term 'a blitz', after which, for as much as a week, the green leather desktop would glimpse the light of day. This morning, a blitz was long overdue.

Cocking an ear towards the shop and discerning only silence, she cast her eyes over the mass of documents spread across the desk. Unable to spot what she was looking for, she lifted aside a sheaf of papers; from somewhere among them, a document slid to the floor. Replacing the sheaf on the desk, she stooped to pick up what turned out to be a flimsy but official-looking booklet. Turning it the right way up and replacing it on the desk, she scanned the heavily printed title: *War Damage Commission*. Smaller typeface beneath instructed that its use was confined to 'notifying damage to land, buildings and certain fixed plant and machinery'. Puzzled, and unaware that the shop had suffered in the air raids, she glanced about. As far as she could tell, the entire street had escaped harm. In fact, a few weeks back Dorothy had remarked how incredibly fortunate it was that this part of the city was intact.

Intrigued, she flicked open the booklet's cover. Answers to the questions inside had been completed in what she recognised from the shop's ledgers to be Cedric's hand. She skimmed the details: in the section headed 'Name and Address of Claimant', and against a line marked 'Surname and Title', he'd written 'Mr Narramore', on the line beneath, 'Cedric Arthur'. Further down the page, where the question required 'Full Postal Address of Damaged Property', he had written '3, Hastings Terrace, Magdalen Street, Exeter'. Having recently become aware that Cedric owned the house next door to the shop, she could only suppose he must have others as well; Magdalen Street wasn't far from here. And she knew from having been along there that every building on it – certainly as far along as the almshouses – lay flattened. She'd also heard how a shelter behind one of the terraces had taken a direct hit and all eighteen occupants had been killed. The awfulness of it had made her realise just how lucky she and her sisters had been in that shelter on Friar

Street; she still found it hard to believe they had escaped without so much as a scratch.

With a sigh, she looked back at the form. On the right-hand page was a question requiring the claimant to state 'Interest in Damaged Property'. Against it, Cedric had written the word 'Owner'. It seemed, then, that her earlier supposition was correct; Cedric owned another house, making three in total. While she couldn't imagine how a man of such apparently meagre means could have achieved such a feat, she nevertheless had to admire that he had.

Realising with a start that she had allowed herself to become distracted, she straightened the sheaf of papers, replaced the form on the desk, and scanned afresh the disarray. Where was this blooming ledger? Ah, there it was – on the shelf. Daft place to put the accounts book but never mind, at least now she could enter Mrs Parker's two shillings and get back to the shop.

As the morning wore on, though, Clemmie found herself mulling over the discovery that Cedric owned more than just the two houses she'd already known about. He didn't seem a wealthy man, even though his wife did wear the odd piece of expensive-looking jewellery and her nails always looked newly manicured. Indeed, from the state of the shop it would be easy to think he didn't have two ha'pennies to rub together. But she supposed owning houses must be something of a burden; if it wasn't, everyone would buy them. Terrible shame he'd lost one of them in the Blitz. Still, by the look of it, the government would compensate him for his loss. Who knew, perhaps he would spend some of the money for which he was in line on the shop. Maybe he would even settle some of his overdue accounts with their suppliers.

Back behind the counter the following morning, though, the idea that Cedric had managed to purchase several dwellings when most people didn't even own one continued to puzzle her; he just didn't seem that sort of man. For a start, his appearance verged on shabby, the seat of his trousers showing the sort of shine associated with a lot of wear – and yes, she did know there was a war on, and that clothing was hard to come by. Then there was the fact that the inside of the shop was plain tatty; a couple of the shelves were dangerously rickety, and the rubber floor mat on the customer's side of the counter was a veritable death-trap. Moreover, only last week the telephone line had been cut off for several days because, according to the post office, Mr Narramore had repeatedly failed to pay his bill. Hardly the financial circumstances of someone in receipt of rents from several houses. If he did have that sort of money coming in each week, where was it going? He certainly wasn't spending any of it on himself, nor on his premises. Nor did he appear to have a soft spot for the horses. Unusually for a working man, he didn't even smoke. And he and Mrs Narramore didn't have children to cost them money, either.

Aligning a packet of gravy browning with the front edge of the shelf, Clemmie sighed. Perhaps she had it wrong. Perhaps she had misunderstood the document she had found. Either way, it was really none of her business. Although… since customers this morning were few and far between, she might just go and take another look – see what else she could find.

With a glance towards the door, she lowered the flap between the counter and the shop and crept through the store to the office. Since yesterday, someone appeared to have been ferreting about because the papers seemed in even greater disarray than previously.

Acutely aware of the sound of her own breathing, she worked her way across the desk, lifting each sheet of paper in turn to peer beneath it. War Damage Commission. Here, this was it. But when she opened the cover, she stared in surprise: this wasn't the same application form. Inside this one Cedric had given the address of the damaged property as 2, Hastings Terrace – she was sure the one she'd seen yesterday was for number three. Was she misremembering? Or did he own more than one property in the same terrace? And on a separate note, why, this morning, did the name Hastings Terrace ring a bell?

Scrutinising this new form, she saw that in the space provided for 'Postal address to which you wish communications to be sent', Cedric had written '47, Worcester Terrace' – the house next door to the shop, and the one occupied by Mrs Bodley and Mr Reeves. Why hadn't he put the address of the shop itself – Rochester Street – especially since that was where he resided?

Taking a silent step backwards, she held her breath and listened. No, she was all right; there was no one about.

Returning her attention to the desk, she searched through the papers for the original form, what she went on to find only adding to her puzzlement; in total, Cedric had completed six application forms, covering what appeared to be a row of adjacent houses. And on each of the documents, his statements were identical: he was the owner; the damage had been incurred in the early hours of the fourth of May this year, on the night of what was now being referred to as Exeter's Blitz; the damage had been caused by *Incendiary and/or direct hit from high explosives*. Towards the bottom of the documents, where he was required to describe the extent of the damage suffered, on every one of them he had written *dwelling destroyed*.

Her latest find trembling in her hand, she hastily returned it to the others on the desk. Then, as much from guilt as from fear of being caught, she pushed the whole lot under the nearest stack of papers, the topmost of which she noticed absently was the latest Schedule of Prices from the Food Office. Hurrying back through to the shop, she regretted having gone to look; giving in to curiosity was as wicked as deliberately spying. Mr Narramore was her employer, and without this work she would be lost. The job might be dull and wearying but her wage covered the amount she gave to Miss Evercott for her keep, with a modest amount left over for her other needs. If Mr Narramore sacked her, then by law she was now required to register at the Labour Exchange. And since she wasn't *so* far off nineteen, she would almost certainly be despatched to war work in a factory somewhere. If that came about, then continuing to help Dorothy at the WVS would become impossible – she'd be as worn out and grouchy as Gwen always seemed to be.

Startled by the tinkling of the bell, she looked sharply up to see Mrs Nosworthy coming through the door.

'Morning, love. Got any condensed milk?' Clemmie cast her eye along the shelf. 'I've run out of sugar and Mr Nosworthy won't so much as look at a cup of tea without it. Claims it don't even smell proper. "You'll have to have condensed, then," I says to him. So, you'd better have some or he'll have my guts for garters.'

'We do have small tins, yes,' Clemmie replied, wishing as she reached for one of the remaining two that her face wasn't burning with guilt. 'Do you have enough points?'

While much of the time she knew Mrs Nosworthy's confusion was genuine – arising from her habit of popping in for a single item every time the need arose, rather than shopping from a list two or three times a week as she would have done before the war – she also suspected the woman wasn't above using her 'me and my muddled head' excuse to try to obtain more than her entitlement. It was, Cedric claimed, *the oldest trick in the book*.

'Only the small ones?'

'Only the small ones. And there's only two.'

'Suppose you better give me both of them, then – seeing as I shan't have no more sugar ration for a while.'

Detaching Mrs Nosworthy's coupons from her book, Clemmie rather needlessly asked, 'On your account?'

Snatching up the tins, Mrs Nosworthy nodded. 'You've saved me bacon, love. Ta-ta.'

A dozen or so customers later, Mrs Narramore came down the stairs to take over behind the counter for the afternoon, and the matter of the bombed houses on Magdalen Street drew Clemmie to study her appearance. As usual, her dark hair was tidy, her lips painted bright red. But while her clothing was smart – navy slacks worn with a pale-blue sweater – they didn't look any more expensive than something that, before the war, might have been bought from any store on the High Street. If the Narramores had money, it wasn't apparent from their attire. Besides, if they did have wealth, why did Mrs Narramore work afternoons in the shop? It certainly wasn't for the conversation. The Narramores were a real puzzle.

'Anyone give you any trouble?'

Clemmie shook her head. 'No. it's been the usual sort of a morning.'

'All right, then, love. Off you go. See you tomorrow.'

'Yes. Thank you. See you tomorrow.'

When Clemmie had removed her apron and hung it in the storeroom, she stepped outside to find that a dull morning had turned into a bright and blowy afternoon. And as she crossed Rochester Street to head home, she glanced back to Worcester Terrace, her eyes coming to settle on the last house in the row – number forty-seven. Flat-fronted and with plain brick, it looked identical to every other dwelling in the street, its ordinariness giving no pause for second thought. So why, she wondered as she continued on her way, was she doing precisely that? What business was it of hers how many houses her employer owned? None. But wasn't it odd that— no! Peculiar and unlikely though it seemed, it really was none of her concern.

By the time she arrived back at Buckingham Crescent, though, she was more convinced than ever that all was not what it seemed. If Mr Narramore owned houses that had been destroyed in the air raids, he should of course get restitution. But why did the name Hastings Terrace mean something to her?

As she paused to unlatch the garden gate, and then closed it behind her and walked up the path to the front door, into her mind came a picture of a girl who had been in her class at school: Sheila Waycott. When Sheila's dad had gone in the navy, and her mum had been worn out after having another baby, Sheila had gone to live with her gran… in Hastings Terrace. Yes! She *knew* the name rang a bell the moment she'd read it on the form. A nice enough girl – if not a little slow on the uptake – Sheila had sometimes attached herself to Clemmie's little group of friends. She could see her now: pale, thin, drawn. She'd also bumped into her more recently, in Woolworths, she seemed to recall. Yes, that was right, because Sheila had bemoaned the fact that on account of her dad having been lost when his ship was torpedoed in the Atlantic, and her mum having a new man friend, she was *still* having to live at her gran's.

Suddenly, details of the encounter were coming back to her.

'I don't like it there one bit,' Sheila had confided. 'There's this man in the house at the end of our row. He's got next to no teeth and I don't mind saying he gives me the creeps. He sort of lurks about, watching. When I first went there, Gran told me I was to stay away from him and said that if he tried to talk to me, I was to go straight indoors. She said something about him being gassed in the last war and not being right in the head. But see, when you go out, you've got to walk right past his parlour window to get to the street, and every time I go by he stares at me. Worse than that, sometimes he comes in the house and there's nothing we can do about it because he owns the place. He's Gran's landlord. But I'm telling you…'

About to put her key in the door lock, Clemmie paused, hand outstretched. That was it: the peculiar man who lived at the other end of Hastings Terrace from Sheila and her gran was not only the landlord *but the owner as well*, which had to mean that, unless she was missing something, Mr Narramore couldn't be. So, what the devil was going on? Why was he claiming that he was? She supposed it was always possible Cedric Narramore and Sheila's landlord were related, or otherwise had some business venture together. What other explanation could there be?

Turning her key in the lock, she exhaled in frustration. Perhaps, if a suitable chance arose, she might make discreet enquiries of Miss Evercott and find out just how this business of compensation from the government worked – purely, of course, in the name of satisfying herself that nothing about what Mr Narramore appeared to be doing really was, well, *untoward*.

–

'May I ask you something? Something about the war?'

Seated in a deckchair alongside Clemmie's in the back garden of number twelve, Dorothy nodded. 'Of course. What's troubling you?'

'Well…' Unfortunately, Clemmie thought, this was going to call for a degree of stealth. But thankfully only a little. 'I was wondering what happens when someone loses their home in an air raid. You know, when it's destroyed by a bomb.'

With a thoughtful look, Dorothy set her empty sherry glass down on the grass beside her chair. 'Happens in what respect?'

'Well, how does the owner go about getting a new one, when everything he had is gone? How do they afford it?'

'Ah. I see. How does he recover its value? Is that what you mean?'

While she would never have thought of it in those terms, Clemmie supposed that was indeed what she was asking. 'Yes.'

'Depending upon the precise circumstances,' Dorothy began, 'they can apply to the War Damage Commission for compensation. After what happened to London in the Blitz, and the damage being suffered from the war more generally, the government passed the War Damage Act setting out what people can expect.'

'So, someone whose home has been completely flattened—'

'Can apply to be compensated for its value – its value before the start of the war, that is.'

'I see.' To Clemmie's mind, that seemed fair. After all, it was the government who'd taken the country to war.

'On the other hand, if the damage to the property is not so extensive as to put it beyond economic repair, the owner can apply for the cost to have it put right, say, to repair the roof, replace the window glass, that sort of thing.'

'Right.'

'I make it sound simple, but it can be terribly complicated. If the owner was the only interested party, he alone would be entitled to compensation of the full value. However, if there was a tenant in the house – a lessee – then that person is entitled to a share of that payment as well. As you might imagine, that's a bone of contention, for, while the tenant might feel entitled to compensation for the loss of his home, the owner is the one facing the bill to rebuild it.'

'And he might not have enough money to do that if some of it must go to the tenant.'

'That's right. There are other anomalies, too. If the owner has died – be that a result of the same bombing or through unrelated causes – then the amount in compensation will be paid to his estate, and be subject to the levying of death duties, meaning there is even less money to rebuild.'

'*That* doesn't seem fair.'

'It's not,' Dorothy agreed. 'Nor is the length of time it will take for people to receive these payments.'

'Hm.'

'Might I enquire why you ask?'

In the name of appearing casual, Clemmie shrugged. 'No real reason. I was just thinking about what happened to the place where I lived in Chandlery Street.' It wasn't, Clemmie reflected, entirely untrue; the papers on Mr Narramore's desk had genuinely brought back memories of what happened to Albert Terrace. 'I suppose I was wondering whether it would ever be rebuilt. Or what would happen there if not.'

'It's a good question. One thing for certain is that once this war is finally over, the demand for builders will be considerable.'

'I suppose it will take years for everything to get back to normal.'

'Many, many years. And the character of whole towns will be changed beyond all recognition.'

Thinking about the ancient and narrow little streets that had once made up the centre of Exeter, Clemmie nodded. 'I suppose so.'

'By the way,' Dorothy unexpectedly changed her tone to say, 'it almost slipped my mind. Just as I was leaving the office, Squadron Leader Dunning telephoned. Major Hogue has news of the airmen and has invited the two of you to go out to the airfield to see the set-up there. The squadron leader said he hopes you can make it and that he'll pick you up from the centre tomorrow at two forty-five.'

Her insides doing a somersault, Clemmie fought to hold her lips in a straight line. 'Quarter to three. Right.'

'So, finally,' Dorothy went on, 'it would seem we are to have some news.'

'Yes,' Clemmie murmured in reply.

Good heavens. She was going to the American airfield with Squadron Leader Dunning. And while part of her was thrilled, another part of her felt wholly unprepared for such an event. In fact, the prospect filled her with nothing short of complete and utter dread.

III. Taking Flight

Chapter 11

'So, whaddya think?'

When Major Hogue turned towards them, Clemmie realised it was in the expectation that they would be impressed. The trouble was, while she wasn't sure what she'd been hoping to see, it was certainly more than an expanse of Devon pasture marked out with rows of little wooden pegs, and a couple of odd-looking huts.

Fortunately, Squadron Leader Dunning was ready with a response. 'I think, Major, that if you're to be ready by the end of the month, you have a great deal of work ahead of you.'

'Well, sure we do. But these new huts are made to be put up double quick. Once a crew's done their first one, the rest are plain sailing.'

'They're impressive structures,' Squadron Leader Dunning remarked of the pair of shiny steel tunnels. 'An improvement on our Nissen type, I should think. But then our design *is* almost thirty years old now.'

'Yeah. Without the internal struts, ours require less material – a real boon when it comes to shipping them all over the world.'

'Indeed. So, on the matter of the welcome reception, I take it you don't see a problem with our proposal to hold it at the start of August – specifically, on the third, which is our bank holiday. Nor with the idea that you and your men come to the guildhall, where we met last time.'

'Sounds grand,' Major Hogue agreed. 'And once we find our feet, we'll reciprocate with a shindig here.'

Listening to the discussion, Clemmie tensed; a couple of hours on familiar territory was one thing, but an event hosted here, by the Americans? How on earth would she conquer her nerves for something like that?

'That's most generous of you.'

Despite her reservations, Clemmie agreed. 'Most generous.'

'So, Miss Huxford,' Squadron Leader Dunning remarked over his shoulder when, a short while later, they were heading away from the airfield in his Wolseley. 'It would seem we're all set.'

From her seat in the back, Clemmie nodded. 'Yes.' Today was only the second time she'd ridden in a motorcar. With its fetching blue and black trim, four large doors and astonishingly comfortable seat, it was an experience she knew she would remember for a long time to come.

'Now we just have to organise the thing.'

'Yes.'

'Major Hogue's rather a character, isn't he?'

'He is.' To her dismay, being in the confined space of his motor seemed to have put her senses on full alert, the presence of his driver only adding to her fear of putting a foot wrong or coming across as graceless. In fact, she felt so far out of her depth that the opportunities for slipping up appeared endless.

'A real live wire, as they say. Look,' Squadron Leader Dunning turned back to her to ask, 'how about we stop for a cup of tea? I don't believe it would be improper, would it? There's a little place just up here on the left. I've been there before. It's highly respectable.'

His expression in that moment was so earnest she couldn't find it in her heart to decline, which was presumably why, before she could stop herself, her traitorous voice was already answering. 'Thank you. That would be nice.'

Oh, dear Lord, *now* what had she done? Going into a tearoom with a very correct RAF officer? What *was* she thinking? She doubted it would be like any tearoom *she'd* ever been in. She had once been to Deller's Café, albeit the smaller one on the High Street; May had taken them there the day she turned twenty-one. It must have taken her weeks to save up for such a treat. But going into a tearoom with this man was so mired in opportunities for making at least one gaffe that the prospect was already bringing her out in a cold sweat.

'Right, then, Pearce. We'll stop at the Copper Kettle, just before the turn to Sowton.'

'Very well, sir.'

And that was another thing: how was she supposed to act towards the squadron leader's 'man' Pearce? 'Miss Huxford, this is my man, Pearce. Pearce, this is Miss Huxford from the WVS.' As introductions went, it had told her nothing; what, exactly, Pearce did, she had no idea. Clearly, he drove the squadron leader where he wished to go, but as to whether he also filled a wider nursing type of role she was in the dark. His erect stance and greying moustache made her suspect he had at one point been in the military himself. More than that, she hadn't a clue.

When Pearce steered the car onto the forecourt of a low thatched building with a bow window, Clemmie withheld a gasp at the prettiness of it; at intervals along the timbered facade hung baskets planted with trailing flowers of pink and white.

'I'll go and check they can accommodate you, sir.'

'Thank you, Pearce. Please do.'

Largely to break the silence that fell once Pearce had left, Clemmie carefully cleared her throat and said, 'It's very quaint.'

'It is. And very old. Once upon a time, it was a forge.'

'Ah.' Yes, giving it a second look, she could see that from its appearance. 'Prettier than the one at the bottom of Chandlery Street.' Dear God, why on earth was she talking about the forge on the quayside – horrible dirty place that it was? It could only be down to nerves. If she was to avoid a disaster, she'd have to learn to keep them in better check.

Thankfully, Pearce was returning.

'They have plenty of room, sir.'

Squadron Leader Dunning rubbed his hands together. 'Jolly good. Let's hope they also have scones.'

When Pearce then came round to open her door for her, she thanked him and went to stand a short distance away, her attention ostensibly given over to admiring the tearoom rather than watching as he assisted the squadron leader from passenger seat to wheelchair. She'd noticed on a previous occasion the chair's ingenious design, how the canvas seat enabled the steel frame to scissor flat for stowing in the Wolseley's boot.

'It's a pity they didn't have the scones you were hoping for,' she said once they were seated at a table in the window, the choice between eggless chocolate cake and eggless carrot cake leading both to opt for the latter.

'But hardly surprising. Pearce tells me wholemeal flour is hopeless for baking anything that doesn't have its own distinct flavour.'

Was she to deduce, then, that Pearce cooked the squadron leader's meals?

'It is,' she said, watching as he cut a corner from his slice of cake and popped it into his mouth. 'Ask most people and they'd say it's not even fit for making bread.'

'The dear old National Loaf is a trifle heavy, isn't it?'

'Yes. And even worse when spread with National Margarine.' There, she thought, this wasn't *so* bad; conversing while eating cake and sipping tea wasn't completely terrifying. She'd even managed to 'be mother' without spilling any, despite the unreliable dribble from the teapot's little spout.

Having finished chewing his mouthful, the squadron leader looked up. 'Forgive me if I'm mistaken in my observation, but I can't help sensing you found the airfield disappointing.'

Finishing her own mouthful gave Clemmie time to consider her reply. 'I suppose I was expecting there to be more of it.'

'An operation in full swing?'

To his response, she nodded. 'I imagined more... bustle.'

Squadron Leader Dunning smiled. 'Once the squadrons arrive, it will be very different – a proper hive of activity. You never know, perhaps once it's up and running we might be invited back. I shouldn't mind seeing the modifications they've made to the P-38s. Those are the aircraft they're going to operate from here.'

'Do you miss it – flying an aeroplane, I mean?'

Something about the way he set his knife down on his plate made her wish she hadn't asked. She *must* remember to think before speaking. With someone like this, she couldn't just blurt things out like she always had with May or Pearl or the Mundys.

'Immensely. To be able to fly was a privilege I never took for granted. I can honestly say that I miss everything about it – the purpose, the challenge, the thrill. I doubt I'll ever find anything to compare.'

'Miss Evercott mentioned that you are a tutor now.' There, that was better.

'I am. Mainly in mathematics. Before I was discharged – somewhat unceremoniously, I might add – I had hoped to be kept on to train new pilots. Ground instruction covers subjects such as mathematics, navigation, and the principles of flying. Even when pilots reach advanced level, there are still classroom lessons to be taken, and I genuinely believed I could have qualified as a ground instructor – and have become a good one, too. Sadly, when it came down to it, there were just too many mundane obstacles rendering it impractical. The Medical Board categorised my fitness to serve as *ApBp*, which is effectively the death knell because it signals one is permanently unfit for duties, both in the air and on the ground. In other words, useless to them. And so, here I am, pensioned off. By the way, this cake's not too bad, is it?'

Struck by the way he so lightly changed the subject – perhaps because there were facts upon which he preferred not to dwell – she smiled. 'I think the cake is very good.'

'So, what about you?' he went on to ask. 'I know you volunteer at the WVS but what else do you do?'

While Clemmie pondered how much about her mundane little existence to disclose, her eyes came to rest on Pearce; seated at a table in the corner, he was stubbing out a cigarette in an ashtray, in front of him a cup and saucer and a pot of tea. If only she could ask the squadron leader about him – learn more about who he was and what he did. It wasn't just a sense of nosiness that made her wonder; she had a genuine desire to understand. If nothing else, comprehending the extent of his duties ought to reduce her chances of putting her foot in it. She supposed she could always ask Dorothy. She might know.

Directing her thoughts back to the squadron leader's question – and rueing that she couldn't make the way she earned her living sound any less dull – she kept her answer simple. She was pretty certain she had already mentioned being a shopgirl anyway. But why would he remember that? 'I work mornings in a corner shop.'

Although she was watching for his expression to change, she didn't even see him blink.

Instead, he was characteristically gallant. 'Ah. Yes. I remember now. Important work helping to keep the nation fed.'

'Yes. And it's not as easy as it sounds. Just because a thing's not on the ration don't mean there's any of it to be had. But there's many as can't understand that – or don't want to. You'd think that after two years of shortages, folk would be more accepting by now.'

'We never realise how much we value a thing until we can't have it.'

She smiled. 'No.'

'What else do you get time for?'

Without meaning to, Clemmie frowned. 'Not much. I start work at seven. I go home at one o'clock for a bite to eat or, when I can be bothered to walk there, for a hot meal at the British restaurant. After that, I do a bit of housework for my landlady. Then most afternoons I go along the WVS centre. After we're done there, all I usually want to do is put my feet up.'

'I'm not surprised. That's a long day.'

'Mm.' It was also, Clemmie realised as she reflected on her account, excruciatingly humdrum. In fact, if it wasn't for the WVS her existence would be very dull and shallow indeed. But then, as everyone was forever reminding everyone else, what could you expect when there was a war on?

'No doubt you save your energies for the weekend – for dancing or the pictures.'

Was he trying to find out whether she had a young man? Mortified to even wonder such a thing, she felt her cheeks start to burn. Of course that wasn't why he'd asked. Foolish girl – he was just trying to make conversation.

'Before we were bombed out of our home in Albert Terrace, me an' my sisters did go to the pictures now and again. But then Pearl, my younger sister, she got a job as an usherette and saw all the films for free, and so we just sort of stopped going. And now we don't live together no more, anyway. Miss Evercott's other lodger, though – that's Gwen – she works earlies at the parachute factory and is forever trying to get me to go out with her. But her and her friends are a bit older than me. And she's got a boyfriend. So I decline.'

'Ah.'

'Yes.' Golly, she felt hot. Perhaps it was the tea.

'So, tomorrow evening,' he picked up. 'We have the committee meeting.'

Relieved to be back on safer territory, she nodded. 'And at last we have something to tell everyone.'

'Two weeks, and Exeter will have its first Americans.'

'Yes. Although, when Major Hogue told us how few it's going to be, I'll admit to being a mite disappointed.'

'I know what you mean.'

'We were told to expect hundreds, if not thousands. But now it seems it will be barely two dozen.'

'To start with, yes. But I still think it worth extending a welcome.'

'Oh, yes. Definitely.' While it might be a selfish way to think, without a function to arrange the committee would fold, and she wouldn't get to do things like this. She still couldn't believe she'd accompanied a squadron leader to visit an American air force base and then had tea with him. As afternoons went, it was one she was unlikely to forget.

'Although, of course, we didn't do anything similar for the Poles.' Seeing her frown, he went on, 'Perhaps you don't know – well, why would you? – that Exeter airfield is also home to the 307 City of Lwów Night Fighter Squadron, whose Polish pilots fly Bristol Beaufighters. There are several Polish squadrons in the RAF but the only night fighter one is the 307.'

'Actually,' she said, the facts sounding familiar, 'I think Miss Evercott mentioned something about them.'

'Very few people know of their presence here and yet, back in May, they managed to get four aircraft into the air and hold off at least part of the Luftwaffe attack, thus sparing the city even worse damage.'

'They did all that and yet no one even knows they're here?'

'Hardly a soul. However, in this instance they are not our concern.'

'No.'

'We have a welcome function in the guildhall to plan.'

'Yes.'

'And we also have to get you back to the WVS centre before Miss Evercott starts to wonder what I've done with you.' Turning towards the woman standing behind the little counter, he signalled to her for their bill. 'And so I suppose I had better settle up and get you back to her.'

When the waitress brought a saucer bearing a slip of paper, Squadron Leader Dunning picked it up, glanced at the total, and then placed it back down with an assortment of coins.

At the same time, across the room, Pearce rose to his feet and went to wait for them at the door.

'Where to now, sir?' he enquired when they were back in the Wolseley.

'Where to, Miss Huxford?' the squadron leader turned to her to ask. 'Back to the WVS centre? Or is there somewhere else we can take you?'

'The WVS centre, please.' Somehow, asking him to take her to Buckingham Crescent felt like taking advantage of his generosity, even though he had been the one to offer. It also felt too familiar.

For the same reason, she was grateful to be sitting behind him, where the need for either of them to try to keep up a conversation seemed less pressing, too.

As they drove back towards the city centre, though, she found herself studying how the back of his hair sat in a straight line above his collar, which led her to consider his appearance more generally. While perhaps not handsome in the film star sense, he was nice looking: his face was square; his brows flat; his neat moustache identical in colour to his chestnut hair. Moreover, in contrast to his air of purposefulness, every now and again his brown eyes sparkled as though with mischief, something that led her to imagine that, prior to his accident, he would have been lively and daring and someone with whom she would have been utterly besotted but completely unable to converse. She could be wrong of course, he might only ever have been a gentle, home-loving soul; what did she know of men? To be honest, nothing. She had no brothers and wasn't even old enough to remember her father. And Charlie Warren she preferred to forget.

'Here we are then, Miss Huxford.'

Brought back from her reverie, Clemmie glanced out of the window to see that they had drawn to a halt alongside the WVS centre, and that Pearce was getting out to open her door.

'Thank you for inviting me along. And thank you very much for the tea and cake.'

Turning towards her as she got out, Squadron Leader Dunning sent her a warm smile. 'My pleasure. I'll see you tomorrow evening.'

'Yes. Goodbye.'

Why, Clemmie wondered as she crossed the pavement towards the entrance, did she feel like skipping? Why, in her chest, was there a warm fuzziness combined with a dull ache? Whatever its reason for being there, she hoped it would go away, and soon, too, because while in some respects it was quite nice, in others it was deeply unnerving, and *not* something she would want anyone else to find out about.

–

Her feet had barely touched the ground all day, but then Thursday mornings in the shop always were busy. And now she was at the committee meeting where, finally, with only nine days to go, attention was being given to the finer details of the welcome function.

Austin Young from the city corporation looked across at Squadron Leader Dunning. 'How many guests on the American side?'

'Miss Huxford has the number.'

Finding herself the focus of all eyes, Clemmie addressed her reply to Mr Young. 'No more than fifty altogether.'

'Although, should circumstances conspire to prevent the release of all personnel,' Squadron Leader Dunning added, 'the major said he would do his best to ensure a minimum of thirty.'

From where she was seated alongside Clemmie, Dorothy shared an observation. 'Then we must have a care not to outnumber them.'

'While still making a decent turnout,' Roger Marshall from the Chambers of Commerce agreed.

From there, the discussion turned to the matter of refreshments.

'Since the number of attendees would appear to be fewer than we might originally have envisaged,' Austin Young observed, 'the corporation should be able to make a reasonable contribution. That said, if any of your members, Roger, can donate refreshments in exchange for an invitation, that would be of tremendous help.'

Roger Marshall looked thoughtful. 'Couple of chaps do come to mind. Sociable sorts who would probably think it a worthwhile investment – you know, given the possibility of supplying the camp with this and that.'

'Then I'll leave it with you.'

'Perhaps, though,' Squadron Leader Dunning remarked, 'they could be requested to be discreet. This will be our visitors' first impression of we British, and I think we should avoid making it look as though we're simply after their money.'

Roger Marshall nodded. 'Of course, of course. I'll make that plain.'

When the committee's attention moved on to the need for volunteers to serve the refreshments, Dorothy assured them she would be able to raise willing hands from among the ladies of the WVS. Inspector Lethbridge confirmed that he could draft a couple of constables to man the door and prevent 'any old Tom, Dick or Harry' from wandering in. Roger Marshall said he knew of a band who, if there was a sniff of further functions, might be persuaded to perform for a couple of hours, free of charge.

'They play all types of music,' he said, 'and I can suggest they take their lead from their audience – you know, young or old.'

It was then that Clemmie spotted a problem and, turning to Squadron Leader Dunning, whispered, 'If all the Americans are airmen, who will they dance with?'

The squadron leader grinned. 'Mr Chairman, Miss Huxford has just spotted a snag.'

Oh, *why* had he done that? Couldn't he have just relayed what she'd said? Aware that everyone was regarding her, she forced a swallow.

'Miss Huxford?'

'I was just wondering,' she said, trying to ignore that she was blushing hotly, 'how the airmen will dance without any ladies present? Those who *are* there will be tied up with serving refreshments and so on.'

When her observation met with silence, she began to wish she'd kept quiet.

'Crikey,' Roger Marshall eventually remarked. 'A gaffe like that would make us look right fools.'

Austin Young glanced around the table. 'Anyone have any ideas?'

To Clemmie's mind, he looked uneasy.

'Whatever we decide,' Inspector Lethbridge remarked, 'we'll have to be careful. Pick the wrong sort of girl and not only will it give the wrong impression of *us*, but I suspect the Americans' commanding officers will be less than impressed, too.'

'So, no one off a street corner, is that what you're saying?' Roger Marshall asked, and then sent Clemmie a wink.

'Nor, for safety's sake, anyone from the girls' high school,' Austin Young chimed in.

'By that same token,' Dorothy contributed, 'we shouldn't invite married ladies, then, either.'

'Doesn't leave many possibilities, does it?' Squadron Leader whispered in Clemmie's direction.

Unable to help it, she grinned. 'Not really.'

'And we can hardly advertise.' Austin Young's observation was met with a shaking of heads.

'The parachute factory,' Clemmie whispered to Squadron Leader Dunning and watched as he raised an eyebrow.

'Miss Huxford might just have saved our bacon.'

Lord, how she wished he wouldn't do that. 'The parachute factory,' she repeated for everyone's benefit. 'Lots of girls work there and most of them live nearby.'

'Right...'

'Perhaps we could ask the manager there to put forward, well, to suggest—'

'To nominate suitable young ladies.' The squadron leader came to her aid.

'Yes,' she agreed. 'He would know which ones were married and which ones could be relied upon to, well, what I mean is, to know how to behave.'

'By Jove,' Inspector Lethbridge replied. 'I think our young Miss Huxford is on to something. Roger, you must know – what's his name at the factory, John Dickins? Perhaps you could make an approach?'

Roger Marshall angled his head. 'I could…'

'But?'

'But might it not be better if the request were to come from a young lady? Would it not seem less patronising, more tasteful, perhaps, for Miss Huxford to ask?'

'Goodness, yes.' Austin Young looked relieved. 'Would you be able to do that, Miss Huxford?'

Thrust yet again into unfamiliar territory, Clemmie glanced to Dorothy, from whom she received a nod of encouragement. 'Yes,' she said simply.

From around the table came sighs of relief.

'Excellent.'

'Well done.'

'Let's wait and see how you get on.'

'Lastly, then,' Austin Young looked up from his notepad to announce, 'is the matter of decorations.'

But while the discussion moved on to the supply of bunting, regretting what she'd been roped into doing, Clemmie stared into her lap. How on earth was she going to go to the parachute factory to see someone she didn't know, and ask him to put forward a list of girls to invite? Where did she even start? What was 'the done thing' in such circumstances? Did a 'done thing' even exist?

With that, she looked back up to see Austin Young drawing proceedings to a close and Miss Evercott sending her a smile. Perhaps Dorothy would know how to go about it; she *had* promised to be on hand to help. She supposed she *could* even ask her to go with her, two women – one of them with some seniority – surely being better than her alone.

As she got up from her seat, though, Squadron Leader Dunning held up a finger to attract her attention. 'Miss Huxford, are you all right? You look suddenly pale.'

'Just a bit tired.'

'And perhaps wishing you hadn't been press-ganged into rounding up a bevy of young ladies?'

From her lips came a lengthy sigh. How did this man, who barely knew her, read her thoughts with such uncanny accuracy? 'Somewhat.'

'Would you like me to help you prepare your approach?'

Her shoulders sank with relief. '*Would* you?'

'Of course. If you like, I could help you to telephone beforehand. To be honest, we *could* do the whole thing by telephone, but I think it would be better if they met you.'

'Met *me*?'

'Of course. You're presentable and nicely mannered. Were you to approach me, asking for the loan of some young ladies, I would be intrigued and hear you out.'

Considering the nature of the task, the squadron leader did have a point. 'I suppose.'

'How about tomorrow afternoon at the WVS centre? I could be there at, say, three o'clock? I have a student at four thirty, but this shouldn't take us long. We'll telephone this Mr Dickins and arrange to see him on Monday afternoon. If you like, I can give you a lift.'

Give her a lift? What a relief. 'Thank you, that would be such a help. But only if it's not too much trouble.'

'It will be no trouble at all. Quite the contrary.'

'Well, all right then,' she said, her exhaustion now genuine. 'Thank you. Three o'clock tomorrow. I'll tell Miss Evercott we're expecting you.'

–

'Squadron Leader Dunning. Miss Huxford. Welcome. Come in. Miss Huxford, please have a seat. Here, Squadron Leader, allow me to move this chair out of the way. May I offer you some tea?'

Realising just how badly fear had dried her throat, Clemmie nodded. 'Thank you, Mr Dickins, tea would be lovely.'

It was now Monday afternoon and, in their *quest for respectable young ladies*, as the squadron leader had taken to calling it, the two of them had just arrived at the parachute factory. And as they settled in front of his desk, John Dickins lifted the receiver of his telephone, pressed a button, waited, and then said, 'Miss Atwill, would you please bring us some tea? Thank you.' The receiver replaced, he looked across his desk and smiled. 'Now, Miss Huxford, I have to say I found your telephone call most intriguing.'

Clemmie smiled back. His response was just as Squadron Leader Dunning had forecast. *Tell them just enough to ensure they will want to find out more but not so much they decide they've no need to meet you.*

'Not many people know this yet,' she said, sticking closely to the advice he had given her, 'but RAF Exeter is about to become home to fighter squadrons from the United States Army Air Force.'

Right on cue, John Dickins raised an eyebrow. 'You're right. I was not aware.'

Clemmie continued to smile. *As long as you don't overdo it, smiling makes you look open and friendly.*

'As yet, very few people are. In fact, outside of our committee, you are one of the first we have told.'

Now it was John Dickins' turn to smile. 'I see.'

'And since we've been charged with holding a little function to make the new arrivals feel welcome, we were wondering whether we might have your help?' As Squadron Leader Dunning had explained to her, a little flattery went a long way.

'Anything within my power, Miss Huxford.'

Realising that from there on her task was relatively straightforward, Clemmie felt the stiffness leave her spine. And as she began to explain, and saw Mr Dickins nodding, she relaxed even further. When she drew to a close, she indicated with her hand the picture in the frame standing on his desk. 'Would this be your family, Mr Dickins?'

Beside her, she thought she saw Squadron Leader Dunning shift his weight. But while she might have ventured beyond what he called 'their script', it was because she'd had an idea.

'It is. My wife, Eileen, and my sons, Kenneth and Harold.'

'Then how would you and Mrs Dickins like to join us? If you were to include among your nominations the name of one of your supervisors, perhaps a more mature lady you would trust to keep an eye on your young ladies—'

'Miss Margaret Wilford. Despite not tolerating nonsense, she's well-liked by our female employees.'

'—then you and your wife might socialise without the worry.'

'How thoughtful of you, Miss Huxford. Mrs Dickins would like that. And I shouldn't mind the chance to get the American take on our present situation – what with our business fortunes being so bound up in this war.'

'Of course. So, might we leave the matter in your hands? I apologise for the short notice but, as I said to you just now, we've only just found out the date of their arrival here ourselves.'

'No matter, Miss Huxford. As I'm sure you can imagine, my team and I have become rather expert at pulling rabbits out of hats.'

'I'm sure.' Crikey. From where was she so unexpectedly finding all this front? And how could she hold on to some of it? She'd never been so bold in her life. 'Thank you for your time, Mr Dickins. If you have any questions once we're gone, please telephone me at the WVS centre.'

'Very well. And thank you for the opportunity to help you out with this.'

When she and the squadron leader were back in his motorcar, Clemmie couldn't stop grinning.

'Miss Huxford, you were magnificent. I can honestly say, hand on heart, I was jolly impressed. Truly, Pearce,' he said, shifting his attention to his driver, 'there I was, coiled ready to spring into action should she become tongue-tied, and she didn't even falter.'

Pearce flicked her a look. 'Well done, Miss Huxford.'

'She was a natural.'

'Hardly a natural,' Clemmie corrected him. 'You have no idea how badly I was trembling. When I first started to speak, I was sure you would both hear my knees knocking.'

'But you didn't show it. Truly, you looked as though you do this every day.'

Relaxing back into her seat, Clemmie felt so relieved she thought she might cry. 'Thank you for saying so. But it was all your doing. Without your help I wouldn't even have got through the door, let alone opened my mouth.'

'Nonsense. All I did was suggest an approach I thought you might find comfortable. You did the rest. And you were terrific.'

An unbelievably short amount of time later, as she stood at the kerb watching the squadron leader's Wolseley pull away, Clemmie *still* couldn't stop grinning. Who would have imagined that, by giving up the occasional afternoon to go and sort piles of clothes and linens for families bombed out of their homes, she would end up meeting a businessman and asking for his help to entertain American servicemen? Not her, that was for sure. In fact, *had* she known where all this was going to lead her, she would never have volunteered in the first place. But it was evident now that, had she declined to accompany Miss Evercott to that first meeting – or, more accurately, had she not allowed herself to be coerced into going – then she would never have met so many nice people; people like the squadron leader, who didn't see her as just an eighteen-year-old shopgirl with no earthly right to be in the same room as him. And while in no way would she ever be his equal – or even close to it – perhaps, when this little committee had done its job, she might speak to Miss Evercott about the possibility of joining another one. It couldn't hurt. It might even do her good, especially if it meant that, once this war was over, she ended up with the confidence to apply for work that didn't involve standing behind the counter of a grubby little corner shop all morning. After all, as Pearl was always so quick to say in defence of her own aspirations, *where was the harm in having a dream?*

Chapter 12

'What do you think? Is the refreshment table too close to where the musicians will be?'

Studying the corner Dorothy was indicating, Clemmie frowned. 'Um…'

'Mrs Trobridge thinks it's convenient there for ferrying supplies from the storeroom. But I think serving drinks so close to where people will be dancing is asking for trouble.'

Finally, it was the day of the welcome function at the guildhall, and since the moment she'd opened her eyes at five o'clock that morning Clemmie had been unable to think of anything else. How she'd got through her stint at Narramore's she had no idea. But it was after she'd left there and gone home that the unsettling mixture of nervousness and excitement had really folded her into its grip. Having been unable to face anything for lunch, rather than tell the truth and then be made to eat something, she'd let Miss Evercott think she'd had a sandwich; with the way her stomach was knotted, it wouldn't thank her for forcing something down. After such close involvement with the event's preparations, she was now terrified that something would go wrong; she was convinced she had failed to do something important, leading to the sort of disaster that would be recounted in gory detail for years to come.

Thankfully, since she'd arrived at the guildhall with Miss Evercott, she'd had little time to dwell on the chances of that coming about; earlier, the caretaker and his staff had removed the wooden benches that usually furnished the Great Hall and had set up a stage for the band. Left for the team of WVS ladies were the tasks of ferrying chairs from a storeroom, arranging trestles for the refreshments, directing the hanging of bunting, and generally making the place look welcoming. As a result, she hadn't had a moment to think.

Reflecting on Miss Evercott's question about the drinks table, and feeling slightly calmer now that preparations were in hand, Clemmie glanced about.

'I think the refreshments would be better all the way back there.'

Dorothy nodded. 'I agree. So, will you tell her, or shall I?'

Alarmed at the prospect of having to tell Beryl Trobridge anything, Clemmie responded with a vigorous shake of her head. 'Oh, no. That's a job for her superior.'

'It's all right,' Dorothy replied. 'I'm teasing you.' Scanning the hall for Beryl Trobridge, she went on, 'I'll go and tell her now, before she starts laying it out. Ah, were you expecting Squadron Leader Dunning?'

With a start, Clemmie spun about to see the squadron leader wheeling himself in through the double doors.

'Me? No.'

'Pop and see what he wants, would you, while I go and find Mrs Trobridge?'

''Course.' Crossing to where Squadron Leader Dunning was coming towards her, Clemmie smiled. 'Good evening.'

'Miss Huxford. Sorry to drag you away from the preparations.'

'Oh, it's all right. We were just debating how to tell one of the WVS ladies we don't agree with where she's put the refreshments table.'

Squinting to where she was gesturing, Squadron Leader Dunning grinned. 'Ah. Tact and diplomacy required.'

'Yes.'

'I was wondering whether you might be spared for an hour?'

In her chest, Clemmie felt a thud. 'Um…'

'I appreciate the timing isn't ideal, given the preparations you have to see to, but when I telephoned Major Hogue to confirm they were still able to make it he shared a rather perceptive observation.' Clemmie frowned. 'Which was that few of his men have ever been outside of their hometown, let alone out of the country, and that, as he's finding for himself, in Britain, there are a number of things we do rather differently – even down to the names by which we refer to certain items. So, although it's rather last minute, he was wondering whether it mightn't be wise to give the men a little talk.'

She still didn't follow; was *a little talk* the same as *a talking-to*? 'A talk?'

'To give them an idea of what to expect.'

Now she was even more confused. 'I'm sorry, I'm not sure I understand.'

'Forgive me. Clearly, I'm not explaining the situation very well. He thinks it might be wise to explain to his men a little about the different ways our two nations do things so as to avoid any gaffes.'

'Oh. Oh, yes, I see.' In truth, she still didn't entirely understand; Major Hogue was the only American she'd ever met – and then only briefly – but he'd seemed to comprehend them easily enough. 'Well, I suppose if he thinks it would be wise—'

'To cut to the chase, he's asked me if I'd pop over there and lay out a few basics. Try and give his chaps a feel for who we are and why we appear as we do, you know, give them an insight into daily life after two and a half years at war, eighteen months of rationing, that sort of thing.'

'Right.'

'And I wondered whether you might come with me. I mean, obviously...'

'Yes.'

'...you're busy.'

What was she doing? Why the eagerness to go to the airfield with him? She was needed here. 'I'll have to check with Miss Evercott.' In something of a daze, Clemmie glanced about the hall. 'When are you going?'

'I said I'd be there for five o'clock. He suggested we use the mess hut before the men take their meal.'

As the reality of what was involved hit home, Clemmie rued being so quick to agree; he hadn't invited her to accompany him on a genteel picnic – although even that in itself would be causing her no small measure of panic and regret – but to stand in front of a couple of dozen American airmen. What *was* she thinking? Well, it was too late now to back out: not only had she said she would go, but she had done so with considerable enthusiasm.

'Then I had better go and find Miss Evercott.'

Squadron Leader Dunning nodded. 'Of course. I'll wait here.'

Turning away from him, Clemmie cursed her stupidity. If she was lucky, Miss Evercott would tell her she couldn't possibly be spared – might even offer to explain as much to him on her behalf.

'Yes, of course you should go,' Dorothy said when Clemmie rather mournfully explained the squadron leader's proposal. 'Major Hogue's idea sounds eminently sensible, don't you think?'

'I do. Yes. But if it will leave you short-handed here…'

'No, we'll manage. But perhaps prevail upon Squadron Leader Dunning to drop you at home afterwards, so that you might freshen up and get changed.' Christ, yes, she'd forgotten about needing to dress up for the bloomin' thing. 'We need to be back here by seven fifteen and so I'm hoping I shall be able to leave here by six, dash indoors and hotfoot it back. If you go straight home from the airfield, we can meet there and return together.'

It seemed, then, that her fate was sealed. And in which case, let her dismay at this precise moment serve as a lesson, the adage that came to mind that well-worn favourite of her mother's: *look before you leap*.

–

'I'm so pleased you agreed to come. You'll brighten up proceedings no end.'

'Don't know about that,' Clemmie mumbled as she got out of the Wolseley and stood waiting for Pearce to help Squadron Leader Dunning into his wheelchair. She felt awkward just standing there, but she could see that between them they had the manoeuvre down to a fine art. 'I should prefer to have smartened up a bit first.'

Wheeling himself towards the first of the newly erected steel huts, the squadron leader's expression changed. 'Yes.

Sorry to whisk you away like that. I forget there's rather more to being a lady than there is to being a chap. I'm rather out of practice at considering the needs of a female.'

In his tone Clemmie thought she detected remorse, which served only to make her regret even more deeply that she'd mentioned it. 'It's all right.'

To distract from her discomfort, she looked about: with it having been an especially warm day, a shimmer of heat haze was distorting the surface of the airfield to give the impression that in the distance was a strip of silvery water, while drifting towards her on the lightest of breezes was the sweet tang of newly mown hay.

'Squadron Leader Dunning. Glad you could make it.' Bowling out through the door of the nearest structure came Major Hogue. 'Miss Huxford, nice to see you again.'

'Good afternoon, Major.'

'Are you all right over this gravel, Squadron Leader?' Major Hogue gestured along the neatly aligned row of buildings. 'We're going along to number three hut.'

'Yes, thank you, Major. I've negotiated worse than this.'

'I guess so. Well, come on in.'

Since their last visit to the airfield, the steel huts had been painted in shades of green and brown. With the grass around them parched from a lack of rain, the colour served as perfect camouflage.

Once inside 'No. 3 Hut', Clemmie looked around. Large windows ran down either side. Flung open, they lent the interior a surprisingly airy atmosphere, the shadows and reflections they cast on the arched underside of the roof creating the sense of being in a railway tunnel.

As she stood taking it all in, the smell of something savoury being cooked made her regret going without lunch. Telling herself not to think about food, she continued to look around. In the central section of the hut stood two long trestles, either side of which were positioned benches at which she could picture as many as forty men, albeit tightly packed. Closer to, a couple of square tables were each surrounded by four wooden chairs. The air given off by the set-up was one of simplicity and function, the closest thing she could liken it to being a schoolroom.

Having rolled his wheelchair up a shallow ramp to get through the door, Squadron Leader Dunning came to a halt and fastened the brake. 'I'll try to keep it brief,' he said to Major Hogue. 'Cover just a few points about the British and our character generally, and then a few specifics about why we might seem rather dowdy. And by that I mean in both appearance and mood.'

'Sounds *just the ticket*, as I've heard you Limeys say. And if you can think of a few words that cause confusion on either side, that'd be swell, too.'

'I'll do my best not to disappoint.'

'Now, if it's all right with the two of you, I need to step out for a moment. But I'll be back before the men arrive to chow.' Seeing the puzzlement on Clemmie's face, he frowned and then went on, 'I guess over here you'd say "eat".'

Now she just felt silly. 'Oh. Yes. Right.'

Once Major Hogue had left, Squadron Leader Dunning turned to Clemmie, his look oddly sheepish. 'I hope you didn't mind coming here with me. Only, I did rather ambush you.'

She tried not to show her surprise. 'Goodness, no. Not in the least.'

'You see, when Major Hogue called me, I remembered that on our last visit you were disappointed by there being so little to see. And I thought you might like the chance to come back again now that the place is about to become operational.'

How thoughtful of him to remember something of so little consequence – in fact, not only to remember it but to be willing to extend the invitation. 'Thank you,' she said, rueing that she was blushing. 'It does look more businesslike now. These huts are very clever.'

With a quick glance over his shoulder, Squadron Leader Dunning lowered his voice. 'They claim the design was their own idea, but the fact of the matter is they copied the Nissen huts we developed for the last war. Cheeky scoundrels.'

Clemmie giggled. When the squadron leader laughed – something she noticed he did surprisingly often – his eyes lit up. His merriment was infectious. 'Are you coming this evening?' she asked.

'Of course. You know, if you like, we could call to collect you. Give you and Miss Evercott a lift.'

Her instinct was to thank him and accept, but as she went to reply she stopped herself; while it would be lovely not to have to walk – to arrive in style – Miss Evercott had said they had to be there early. In addition, without knowing how soon Miss Evercott would be able to get home to change, to make a firm arrangement seemed risky; imagine if she didn't have time to get ready. In light of that, it felt safest to decline.

'That's a very kind offer,' she replied carefully. 'But I have no idea when Miss Evercott will get home, which means I wouldn't feel comfortable agreeing to a time for you to collect us.'

His smile was one of understanding. 'Then perhaps—'

'So, then, folks.' Major Hogue burst back in through the door and stood rubbing his hands. 'Where do you want to be for this, Squadron Leader? Will that do you there?'

Squadron Leader Dunning looked about. 'As good as anywhere.'

'Miss Huxford, why don't you take a seat?' From beneath one of the nearby tables, the major pulled out a chair. 'And I'll go stand at the back.'

'Thank you.'

With that, through the door at the far end of the hut came a stream of men, who made their way to stand behind the benches until, at a command from Major Hogue, they sat smartly astride them. Faced with so many inquisitive stares, Clemmie quickly lowered her head and looked intently into her lap, the result being that the words of the major as he introduced them were completely lost on her. If only she'd sat in the next chair round; that way, she wouldn't be facing the all-male audience head on.

Realising that Squadron Leader Dunning had commenced his address, she forced herself to pay attention.

'—and so, firstly, although later this evening the Mayor of Exeter will extend formal greetings to you on behalf of our city, for my own part I should just like to welcome you to our shores. Some of my countrymen will tell you that you took your time getting here' – From his audience there was a deep rumble of laughter – 'but the main thing is that you're here now and you're very welcome.'

'Thank you, Squadron Leader Dunning,' Major Hogue replied. 'Glad to be here.'

'And to satisfy your curiosity about why anyone in their right mind would send a cripple in a wheelchair to talk to a group of airmen, well, let's just say that when a Messerschmitt Bf 110 comes at you out of nowhere and shoots up your landing gear, this is what happens when you come in too steep for your emergency landing when you get back.'

'But did you get him?' a voice from the benches called out.

'I certainly had a go.'

'Good on ya.'

'Now, since only a fool would come between a man and his chow, I'll try to keep this brief.' There was a murmur of approval. 'So, perhaps one of the most helpful things you can bear in mind about Britain is that, right now, we're not at our finest. We've been subject to German attacks for not far short of three years. They've bombed our homes and our places of work. They've bombed our shops, our railways, our factories. Conscription into our armed services has left our women and children without their fathers, brothers, husbands and sons. Children have been separated from their mothers and evacuated from our cities to the safety of the countryside, where they have been taken in by complete strangers, sometimes separated from their siblings in the process. People everywhere have had to put up with shortages of daily necessities such as food, clothing, even power and coal. So, I guess what I'm saying is that you'll probably find we don't match up to what you've always heard about Great Britain. For the most part, we're tired, we're hungry, we're separated from our loved ones and we're desperate for this to be over. That said, we haven't lost sight of our innate fairness, our British sense of justice, nor our determination. You'll also find that despite all I've just said, and despite our differences, you will be warmly welcomed.'

When the squadron leader paused for breath, Clemmie realised she had forgotten his audience was there, and had been listening, spellbound. No matter who he was talking to, he had such a lovely manner; he didn't lecture or preach, he spoke to you with understanding and respect. In that regard, he was unlike anyone else she had known.

'You mention differences,' Major Hogue said. 'Can you give us some idea what you had in mind?'

Squadron Leader Dunning grinned. 'Well, although the idea of a country having a king and queen might seem peculiar to you, we hold our royal family in high esteem and have a great affection for them. Having a visitor to our country criticise or make fun of them is something we don't take to kindly. And by way of illustration of that loyalty, you might note that whenever the national anthem is played, out of respect we always stand up, including at the end of a film in a cinema – or, as you might say, at the end of a movie in a theatre – even though we might all be desperate to catch the last bus home. And contrary to what you might think, we *are* a nation of sports lovers. It's just that rather than following baseball, we play rugby and cricket. And we have own version of what you call football. Another example is when it comes to food and drink. You like your beer ice cold – and, if I might be so bold, rather weak—'

'Hey, settle down,' said the major but, to Clemmie's ears, the rumbles of dissent in response to this last comment stemmed from amusement.

'Whereas our ales are meant to be drunk at room temperature – not, as you might claim, *warm* – and they're strong. In a pub, you'll probably find the beer is brewed locally and, if you're looking for a recommendation as to what to try, you could do worse than pardon yourself to someone sitting at the bar with a pint already in front of him and ask him the differences in the various offerings. We like to be consulted for our opinion but will rarely give one without being asked. What to you might seem to be reserve to us is merely respect for someone else's privacy. Equally, while we might seem quietly spoken and endlessly polite, don't underestimate us – we're tough when we need to be.'

'Sir, how do we address your women?'

Feeling her face colouring, Clemmie glanced at the squadron leader.

But without a flicker, he replied, 'Unless you want a slap in the face, I would advise against *honey* or *doll*. A safer bet is always *miss* for a younger woman or, for someone you imagine might be married, *madam*. Which brings me to colloquialisms – and I'm afraid we have many. *Bobby* is affectionate slang for a police constable on the beat. *Swank* means bragging or showing off – something for which we have little time. A *ha'penny* is one halfpenny. We don't *stand in line*, we queue – these days, we queue for everything, we're very good at it, and woe betide anyone who breaks that rule. We don't have automobiles, we have cars, and in them, were we to have a supply of any, we would put petrol rather than gas. For cabs we say taxi – unless you happen to be in London. For trucks, we say lorries. And you don't call anyone a *bum* because here, that's your behind.'

When the laughter at this last comment died down, Squadron Leader Dunning went on, 'And just as in the United States you have many different accents, so do we here, the upshot being that it's unwise to call the way we speak *funny*. Over here, you're the ones who sound funny. But the only people likely to point that out to you will be small children. So, in summation, as someone who experienced what you're going through now when I had the good fortune to visit your own fine country, my advice to you would simply be this. Show us respect and you will be made welcome. Listen more than you speak. Keep your criticisms to yourself. And do try to get to see some of our history and our beautiful countryside while you're here. I promise you, it's worth the effort.'

'Show of appreciation for the squadron leader,' said Major Hogue.

To Clemmie, the applause that rang out sounded genuinely warm.

The major came towards the two of them. 'Thanks for shlepping all the way over here to do that,' he said. 'I can tell them this stuff until I'm blue in the face but from you it carries more weight.'

'My pleasure, Major. I could stand here for an hour and barely scratch the surface.'

'Yeah, well, if the only thing listening to you makes them do is stop and think before they open their mouths in public, we might just avert a few misunderstandings.'

'Let's hope so.'

'Major Hearst, you waiting for me?'

Turning to see to whom Major Hogue was talking, Clemmie found that standing a short distance away was an officer who looked to be around thirty years old.

'Hoping for a word or two with the squadron leader, Major.'

'Squadron Leader Dunning, meet Major Hearst, pilot of one of our P-38s and squadron commander.'

As the two men shook hands, Clemmie couldn't help noticing Major Hearst's eager expression.

'I was hoping, Squadron Leader, to ask you about your experiences flying close escort duty to your bombers, if that would be all right.'

'Happy to oblige, Major. Are you coming this evening?'

'Looking forward to it.'

'Then how about we find a moment to talk there?'

'That would be swell.'

When Major Hearst walked away, Squadron Leader Dunning turned to Major Hogue. 'We'll see you and your men later.'

'You sure will. I'm just itching to see a little more of that guildhall of yours.'

'I'll see to it that you do. But now we must return to the preparations.'

'Thank you again for coming. I'll catch you both later.'

'Well,' Squadron Leader Dunning said as they left the hut and emerged into the dazzling late-afternoon sunshine. 'How do you think that went?'

'As far as I could tell,' Clemmie said as she accompanied him to where Pearce was waiting alongside the Wolseley, 'they listened to you carefully. And for the little my opinion counts, I thought you made some very good points. You even made me stop and think about how *I* view *them*.'

'Well, thank you for that. But Miss Huxford' – His statement left hanging as Pearce assisted him into the motor, Clemmie hastened around to the other side and climbed in – 'don't ever belittle or excuse your opinion. Don't do yourself the disservice. If I ask you what you think, it is because I genuinely wish to know. Not only do I consider you to be a shrewd judge of character, but I also believe you capable of critical thought. And that is a skill you shouldn't squander.'

While she had no clue what he meant by *critical thought*, on the assumption that he was paying her a compliment she ducked her head and fiddled with the strap on her handbag so that he might not see how furiously she was blushing. Squadron Leader Dunning valued her opinion. How was that even possible when she was nothing more than a poorly schooled shopgirl?

'Where to, sir?'

'Good question, Pearce.' Craning over his shoulder to look at her, Squadron Leader Dunning went on, 'Since I am instructed to take you home, Miss Huxford, you will need to tell Pearce where that is.'

'Buckingham Crescent,' she said with a smile. 'It's along the Topsham Road.'

'And you're sure you wouldn't like us to drop by later to pick you up?'

She would like it very much. 'Thank you for the kind offer but no, we'll walk.'

'Then I look forward to seeing you later.'

'Yes.' *And I*, she thought as the Wolseley slowed at a junction and she found herself staring out at the all-too-familiar words 'Business As Usual' daubed on a boarded up shopfront, *shall look forward to seeing you there, too*.

–

'You *sure* you ain't got your eye on some chap?'

'Quite sure, thank you.'

'Only, far as I recall, you've never shown so much as a moment's interest in how you look, let alone wanted to get all dolled up.'

Back in Buckingham Crescent, wishing she had given more thought to what she might wear for the evening ahead, Clemmie had asked Gwen for her opinion on her limited choice of garments. What she quickly found herself regretting, though, was letting Gwen talk her into *doing something with her face*.

'I *don't* want to get all dolled up,' she said, genuinely terrified of what Gwen might be about to propose. 'It's only a do for the WVS. All I want is to look presentable.'

'Yeah, right.'

'Truly. If there was some chap, I hardly think I'd be going with Miss Evercott. Nor would I be meeting him at seven fifteen to help get things ready.'

'Fair point.'

'Anyway,' Clemmie said, anxious to get off the subject; were Gwen to learn that she and Miss Evercott had helped to organise a dance for a squadron of Americans but hadn't seen fit to extend her an invitation, she'd probably never speak to her again. And rightly so, too. 'How's it going with Jimmy? You seem to have been out a lot of evenings this last fortnight.'

'God, Clemmie, he's...'

As she listened to Gwen describe the considerable attributes of Jimmy Woodley – sadly, no detail considered too minute nor too delicate – Clemmie's thoughts drifted back to the evening ahead. She had always supposed that, as appeared to be the case with Gwen, liking a member of the opposite sex made you go all daft and swoony. The realisation that she herself wasn't so afflicted came as a relief; the peculiar feeling that had recently taken up residence in her chest was clearly attributable to something else. And no, she didn't know what. That it had nothing to do with Squadron Leader Dunning was reassuring, though. For a start, he was a good deal older than her. And so far above her in life that, even were he to think her pretty – which, obviously, he didn't – he would never consider her someone to ask out on a date. Besides, being without the use of his legs meant he probably didn't go on dates anyway. How could he with Pearce always in tow? He should probably find a way to, though. A lovely man like him shouldn't be on his own. Besides, if he had a wife *she* could look after him instead of Pearce. Not that there was anything wrong with Pearce, but a wife would surely be better.

Trying not to wince as the hairpin Gwen was wielding scraped her scalp, she pictured the scene: a pretty young woman in a flowery dress, her hair fresh from being set, her pearls swinging at her throat as she bent low to hear what he was saying. Their imaginary smiles when he repeated what he'd said were so warm and loving, she felt a little jab in her ribs.

'Ouch,' she breathed as another kirby grip skidded off her skull. 'Are you nearly done?'

Gwen nodded. 'Almost. So, anyway, that night, his mum was up the bingo, and so he turns to me an' says why don't we see the film another night and go back—'

See the film. She supposed that was another thing the squadron leader couldn't really do. Although, hadn't she once seen a soldier in a wheelchair right down the front of the stalls? Hardly an enjoyable experience – having to sit so close to the screen.

Realising she hadn't taken in a word Gwen was saying, but noticing that she had been to fetch her hand mirror, Clemmie sent her a grateful smile. 'Thank you for doing this.'

'Best hold off thanking me till you've seen it.'

But when Gwen held up the mirror, Clemmie thought it was perfect. 'It's lovely,' she said of her neatly pinned roll of hair. 'You do it far more tidily than I ever could.'

Gwen scoffed. 'It's always easier to do someone else's.'

'So, where are you going tonight?'

'There's a funfair up the pleasure ground, least, what passes for one these days. By all accounts it's a good deal smaller than last time. But we're going up there to see it anyway.'

'Sounds like fun.'

Thankfully then, Clemmie thought as she continued to admire her hair, Gwen wouldn't be too bothered at missing what could always be reported upon afterwards as a stuffy and tedious bit of a do, with dignitaries giving speeches and little to write home about.

'Want me to put some mascara on you?'

Handing back Gwen's mirror, Clemmie gave a vigorous shake of her head. 'I'd look silly.'

'Oh, come on, you've got to. It'll make your eyes look so much wider. I mean, I know you're blonde and so you don't really have to try...'

'What?' Now what was Gwen on about?

'Put it this way, I shan't be introducing you to Jimmy any time soon. He likes blondes. Always ogles them when they walk past.'

Gwen's chap looked at women with blonde hair even when he was out with *her*? That didn't seem very gentlemanly.

'*I* don't think blonde hair is anything special. *I* like your colour.'

'Only a blonde could say that.'

'No, truly, I think—'

'Especially one with blue eyes. You wait till you start looking for a man of your own. They'll fall over themselves to get their hands on you. In fact, you're gonna have to be careful.'

'Well, thanks for your help.' Getting up from where she'd been sitting on the bed, Clemmie glanced at her alarm clock. 'Have a good time at the fair.'

'You don't want the mascara, then?'

'Not for the WVS, no. But thanks anyway.'

Gwen, though, wasn't ready to give in. 'Then at least have a quick dab of lipstick—'

'Oh, no thanks.'

'It's all right, I won't paint you like a harlot. I've got one called "First Flush". It's a real pale pink.'

While the sensible half of Clemmie's mind told her not to be daft – to resist the draw – the other half of her had a secret desire to see how she would look. The only time she'd ever tried lipstick was when Pearl had put some on her; the result had made her look like a clown. But that was a long time ago, when Pearl had been secretly experimenting with a lipstick she'd found down the back of the seat on a bus.

'All right. But just a little.'

'Course. I know how to do *understated*, as they say in the magazines.'

The lipstick applied, Clemmie re-examined her appearance in the mirror. To her surprise, the effect managed to be both astonishing and subtle at the same time, making her look more woman than girl. And quite pretty, too.

'I like it.'

'See, told you. Here, have it.'

Eyeing the little tube that Gwen pressed into her hand, Clemmie frowned. 'Have it?'

'It never did suit me. Don't know what I was thinking. With my colouring I need harlot red.'

'*Don't* say that.'

'Seriously, Clem. My complexion ain't fair like yours. I don't suit pretty-pretty shades. Never have. I need the opposite – bold and bright.'

'Well, if you mean it.' Clemmie examined the little tube.

'Miss Huxford? Are you ready?'

'Miss Evercott,' Clemmie hissed. 'I have to go. Daren't make us late.'

Casually, Gwen sauntered away along the landing. 'See you then.'

'Yes. Have a good time with Jimmy.'

Snorting with laughter, Gwen called back, 'Believe me, I intend to.'

'Ready?' Dorothy greeted Clemmie at the bottom of the stairs.

'Yes.'

'Then let's go and make our visitors feel welcome. Demonstrate to them that we're not the reserved and rather stiff people they're expecting.'

'Get off to a good start,' Clemmie added as she followed her landlady out through the front door.

'Who knows, maybe even strike up a few long-lasting friendships.'

Or perhaps, Clemmie reflected as the stirring of excitement in her stomach took her thoughts down a different path, something even better?

Chapter 13

Clemmie sighed. As she stood watching the girls from the parachute factory file into the Great Hall, she hoped they would behave, hoped they would heed Dorothy's warning to them just now about this evening being an opportunity to extend a welcome and foster good understanding, rather than being a chance to meet a husband. In their summery pastel-coloured dresses, they certainly looked fresh and pretty, not to mention eye-catching. It made her regret that she'd had nothing nicer to wear than just the better of her two skirts – navy cotton gaberdine with piping on the pockets for embellishment – and her plain white blouse with the rounded collar. As garments, they would have been acceptable for what her mother liked to call 'Sunday Best'. And while they might be clean and smart, alongside such a profusion of colour they made her feel plain and dowdy, which, when she'd asked Gwen to pin her hair for her, hadn't been what she'd had in mind.

In truth, though, what did it matter? With time since to reflect, what she'd been hoping for from the evening now felt prickle-inducingly foolish; no amount of primping and preening was going to suddenly render Squadron Leader Dunning speechless with desire for her. He was a grown man, not an adolescent. He was worldly and intelligent, serious. He was also confined to a wheelchair. She flushed with embarrassment; what on earth had she thought was going to happen between them? He was hardly going to ask her to dance. Nor to go for a stroll with him afterwards. So why, if she knew all of that, was she unable to get him out of her head? Why, just lately, had he become the first thing she thought about each morning and the last thing each night? Moreover, why, at the prospect of seeing him at a meeting, did she come over all hot and panicky? If she wasn't secretly hoping for something to happen, what was that all about?

Hearing the entrance doors creaking open, she looked up to see a line of khaki-clad young men filing in, at their rear Major Hogue and Major Hearst. And to her astonishment, already in the far corner of the room was Squadron Leader Dunning. How had she not noticed him arrive? She must go and say hello.

'Miss Huxford. Good evening,' he greeted her warmly as she drew near.

'Good evening, Squadron Leader Dunning.'

'You look very smart.'

Smart, perhaps. But not pretty; not like the girls who had dresses from before rationing.

'Ladies and gentlemen.' The hum of conversation around them fell quiet and Clemmie turned to see Austin Young from the city corporation standing on the little stage. Proceedings were getting under way, and she suddenly felt incredibly nervous. What if the evening was a flop? She scanned the room; a couple of American officers seemed to be admiring the architecture of the hall. Their men, however, seemed rather more taken with the girls from the parachute factory. 'If I might have your attention for just one moment.'

Hoping desperately for the evening to be a success, she glanced to Squadron Leader Dunning. As he so often did, he met her look with a smile.

'Can you see from there?' she asked.

'Perfectly.'

She turned back. Austin Young had just introduced the mayor; in full regalia, he certainly drew their guests' attention.

'Ladies and gentlemen, as mayor of the city of Exeter, it gives me great pleasure to welcome you all this evening to our historic guildhall. In particular, it is my honour to extend warmest greetings to the airmen of the…'

Clemmie's attention wandered away. So far, so good. But then things hadn't got going yet.

She turned her attention back to the stage. Set up behind the mayor were the piano and drum kit belonging to the band. She did hope they were up to the mark; lively music would get people dancing and help them to mingle without having to rely on small talk.

As a round of polite applause broke out, she joined in; arriving to stand beside the mayor – indeed, towering over him – was Major Hogue.

'Ladies, gents, good evening. Mr Mayor, I'd like to thank you for that warm welcome and for inviting us here tonight to this incredible guildhall of yours. To know that parts of it have been here for over six hundred years, maybe longer, sure has a way of making a man feel small.'

In the laughter that followed the major's remark – for he was anything but small – Clemmie felt a hand on her arm. Turning sharply, she found Squadron Leader Dunning looking up at her and flushed.

'Are you all right?'

'Just a bit warm.'

As applause broke out again, she looked up and clapped. Seconds later, a man in a sharp suit walked onto the stage, sat at the piano, raised the lid, and started tinkling the keys. At the same time, someone turned off the overhead lights, leaving just the twinkling of the magnificent chandelier above the dance floor and a couple of spotlights to illuminate the stage. In this softer light, the colours in the portraits around the walls took on a rich glow. She couldn't deny it; the location they'd chosen was impressive. It was just a pity no one could see the lovely stained-glass window, boarded up as it was against damage by bombs or showing a light in the blackout.

'Ladies and gentlemen, good evening.' On the stage, the man Clemmie presumed to be the bandleader was speaking into the microphone. 'We're the Eddy Edwards Dance Band and we're here to get you on your feet. So, grab a partner and don't be shy. A one, a two, a one, two, three, four!'

The eager young men of the USAAF didn't need telling twice. The moment the first chord was struck, they descended upon the girls from the parachute factory to invite them onto the floor. For Clemmie, it seemed a good moment to find the ladies' cloakroom and splash cold water over her wrists. And then maybe get herself something to drink. Having first excused herself to Squadron Leader Dunning, she headed away.

Grateful to find the cloakroom empty, she went straight for the basin, where she turned on the tap and let the paltry trickle of water run first over one wrist and then the other. When she looked up and caught her reflection in the mirror, the sight of her lips took her by surprise. The pale-pink colour really did brighten her whole face, just as Gwen had said it would. Having seen the girls from the parachute factory, though, she wished now that she'd let her apply some mascara as well. Easy to be wise after the event, but perhaps she would wear some next time – if there *was* a next time.

Feeling marginally more composed, she straightened the collar of her blouse. Heavens, how disappointingly staid it looked. Casting about to check that she was alone, she unfastened the top two buttons. In the mirror, her cheeks flushed with embarrassment. Now she just looked as though she was angling to be lured from the straight and narrow. But *one* undone button... Refastening the lower one, she appraised the effect. Yes, that was all right. Now she looked relaxed and friendly rather than stiff and starchy. Golly, what a nightmare these social occasions were. And oh, for even just a single ounce of Pearl's confidence!

Heaving open the heavy oak door to the great hall on her way back released a wall of noise; the band were playing a tune she thought she recognised from the wireless.

Casting about, she spotted the refreshments table and went towards it. 'Do you need a hand?'

The two women behind it were at that moment arranging paper cups on a tray.

'We're all right for the moment, love,' one of them replied, raising her voice above the music.

'These American cups are bigger than ours,' the second observed. 'If we're to avoid running out of drink before the night's out, we mustn't fill them past halfway.'

It had been good of Major Hogue to offer them several boxes of what he called Dixie cups. Without them, they would have been reduced to using some from the corporation's emergency supply for air raid shelters and rest centres.

'The way they're all going at it,' the first woman remarked, nodding to the dance floor, 'we'll run out anyway.'

With a smile, Clemmie turned to study the dancers. A few feet away from her, a gangly airman was partnering a girl who appeared to be around nineteen or twenty in a particularly showy version of what she supposed was a quickstep. Beyond them, she spotted Major Hearst. Seated on a chair he'd commandeered from the side of the dance floor, he was nodding as though following a technical explanation from Squadron Leader Dunning, who sat beside him, the latter angling his hand in a gesture that she guessed had something to do with aeroplanes and flying. Tonight, the squadron leader was wearing a blue-grey RAF cap – not a stiff-looking circular one with a rigid peak, more in the style of a narrow beret. Pinned to the front left was a gilt badge of an eagle, above it a smaller gilt crown. The sight of him wearing it had given her a jolt and changed the way she thought of him; rather than seeing him as the 'normal' man she had come to know, she now felt unexpectedly aware of his past. Unlike their American guests here tonight, he had already fought in this war, and been badly injured for his trouble. Now he had to sit and watch others setting off to do what he had once done, the fate of his country out of his hands. How did that feel, she wondered? Did he fear for these American pilots with their eagerness to 'get stuck in', or did he envy them?

Watching him in animated discussion, she realised there was so much she would like to ask him – not only about his time as a pilot but also about his life now. She knew something about how an existence could be so instantly and dramatically changed; after the air raids, her own life and those of her sisters had altered beyond recognition. And she supposed her mother's must have been too, when she lost her husband. But to be so intelligent and brave, and so active?

'Say, excuse me, miss. Care to dance?'

Realising the question was aimed at her, Clemmie started. 'Um, well, actually, it's very kind of you to ask but you see, I'm one of the helpers.'

Undeterred, her khaki-clad would-be dance partner flashed her a warm smile. 'Maybe later?'

Unable to summon the courage to refuse entirely, she smiled. 'Maybe. Yes.'

When the chap walked away, Clemmie exhaled heavily. But as she turned about, bent on finding something – anything – to make her look occupied and therefore unavailable to dance, she noticed Squadron Leader Dunning watching her. And although she held his look for less than a second, she felt a bristle of disloyalty. Unable to explain it, she determined not to dwell and instead set off in search of Miss Evercott. She would see what needed doing and offer to help.

When she eventually found her, Dorothy was consoling a young lady in a burgundy-coloured dress.

'Good timing,' Dorothy hissed in Clemmie's ear before, raising her voice back to normal, she added, 'This is Miss Eileen Rugge, and she's just had an unfortunate accident with some lemonade. I wonder, could you go with her to the ladies' and see what's to be done? The light in there will be rather better than it is here. And perhaps see if there's a clean cloth to be fetched from somewhere.'

Relieved to have something to do, Clemmie put her arm across the girl's shoulder and guided her towards the door. 'Eileen, is it?' Between sobs, the girl nodded. 'Hello, Eileen. I'm Clemmie.'

The girl gestured to her skirt. 'This… dress… belongs… to me sister. And… and she don't know I've borrowed it 'cos she's away in Somerset being a land girl. Mum warned me not to wear it. But I was so thrilled to be put forward to come here tonight. And all the other girls had dresses.'

Clemmie knew the feeling. Opening the door, she guided Eileen along the corridor beyond. 'Well, I doubt it's ruined,' she said. 'Let's get you into some better light and take a look.'

As it turned out, there was just one almost perfectly circular damp patch on the girl's right hip.

'Tell me,' Clemmie said, dabbing water and hand soap on the stain, 'what do you think of the Americans?'

'Ooh, real nice.'

Her ploy to distract Eileen was evidently working. 'Nice how?'

'Well, for starters, they're real good dancers.'

'Yes?' Finally, the rather alarming amount of froth she'd inadvertently made was beginning to subside. 'That's fun then.'

'And so *shiverous*.'

'*Shiverous?*' Now to try to get the wet patch to dry.

'Ever so. A real credit.'

'Good. Well, look—'

'I'm so glad I got to come,' Eileen said. 'Even though this has happened.'

'I'm sure it will dry out just fine.'

'They say the top woman from the WVS came to the factory to ask for *respectable young ladies*, you know, to be nice to the airmen who are so far from home.'

The top woman from the WVS? She doubted she'd ever be called *that* again. 'Goodness.'

'And Mr Dickins and Miss Wilford picked me as one of them. So, I can't let them see my dress.'

'I doubt they will,' Clemmie said warmly. 'It's really quite dark out there.'

'Well, thanks ever so.' Her earlier panic apparently forgotten, Eileen turned to the tiny mirror over the washbasin to check her appearance. After wiping under each eye with the corner of her handkerchief, she flounced back to face Clemmie, her voice breathy as she announced, 'I'm going to go and see if I can find that nice one called Harvey.' Opening the door, she looked back and smiled. 'Such a dreamy name, don't you think? So much nicer than John or Alfred or…'

Clemmie returned her smile. 'So much nicer, yes.'

When Eileen went scurrying back to the hall, Clemmie let out a sigh and turned back to the mirror. *I'm going to go and see if I can find that nice one called Harvey.* She did hope this wasn't all going to end in tears. The young women might have been warned this wasn't a chance to find a husband but, where young men were involved, when did a girl ever listen to reason? *Such a dreamy name, don't you think?* Harvey. As names went, it was certainly different. Was it odd, she wondered, pursing her lips to admire their colour, that she didn't know the squadron leader's first name? She couldn't even decide what he looked like – but not a Harvey, that was for sure. He knew *her* name, of course – not that he ever used it. He always addressed her, quite properly, as Miss Huxford.

She leaned further over the basin. Perhaps she would ask Gwen which mascara to buy, assuming there was any to be had; according to Pearl, pretty much all make-up apart from lipstick had become hard to find these days.

Noticing that the music had come to an end, and hearing in its place laughter and scampering feet, she opened the door, to be met by a gaggle of young ladies coming excitedly towards her.

'He never did! He *said* that to you?'

'True as I'm standing here.'

'What ever did you say?'

'What *could* I say?'

'*I'd* have given him a slap.'

Deciding she'd prefer not to know what they were talking about – largely to avoid having to intervene and come across as a spoilsport – Clemmie flattened herself against the wall to let them pass and then continued back to the hall. Apart from a few couples standing about talking and, further over, two airmen demonstrating a series of dance steps for two girls to try to copy, the room had momentarily fallen quiet. On the stage, the musicians were downing drinks, the one on the drums mopping at his brow with a towel. In the far corner, Squadron Leader Dunning was conversing with Major Hogue; a short distance away, Miss Evercott was talking to Margaret Wilford. Clemmie went to join them.

'Disaster averted,' she said as Dorothy looked at her and smiled.

'No trouble with anyone?' Miss Wilford enquired.

Clemmie shook her head. 'Some of them do seem rather excited.'

'Yes, I think we're going to have some very tired young ladies at the benches tomorrow morning.'

'It's why we thought it should finish at ten,' Dorothy replied.

As the conversation between the two women continued, Clemmie strained to hear what Squadron Leader Dunning was saying to the major but, at that moment, the bandleader came back to the microphone to announce their next song, and the floor once again filled with couples.

'Miss Huxford,' Major Hogue acknowledged her as he turned to move away.

'Major Hogue.'

'Fine do. Great way to build understanding.'

'Miss Huxford,' Squadron Leader Dunning said when Major Hogue had left. 'How are you? I've noticed you dashing about.'

Was he just saying that to make conversation, or had he really been watching her? Her non-existent experience of men made it hard to tell.

'To be honest, I am beginning to feel a bit weary.'

'I'm not surprised. You ladies of the WVS have worked a miracle.'

Pleased that he should think so, Clemmie smiled. 'The band certainly seem to be going down well.'

He smiled back. 'They do, don't they? *You* won't be too busy for a dance, I hope.' Her puzzlement evidently showing on her face, he hurried on, 'My apologies. I've embarrassed you. Trust me, there's nothing I should like more than to ask you. But, patently, I can't. I rather meant that after all your hard work, it would be a shame if the evening ended without you having found time for at least one turn around the floor.'

'Oh. Well, I…'

'Christ. Now I've embarrassed you even more. Look, at least come and take the weight off your feet.' When he patted the seat of the chair beside him, she did as he suggested and sat down. 'You can catch your breath for just a moment, can't you?' Aware that for some inexplicable reason she was perilously close to tears, she confined herself to nodding. 'So, how do you think it's going?' he went on. 'Something of a success, wouldn't you say?'

'If the dance floor is anything to go by.'

'Music usually does make for a good icebreaker.'

'It does, yes.'

'Do you play?'

She gave a vigorous shake of her head. 'No. Do you?' It seemed only polite to ask.

'I do, yes. I play piano. I also teach it.'

In her surprise, she turned to regard him. Apart from her schoolteachers, she'd never met anyone who played a musical instrument, let alone taught one. 'It looks difficult.'

'It can be. But the basics are straightforward.'

'Oh.' She was so far out of her depth now that she'd completely lost sight of the shore. And yet, oddly, she felt surprisingly at ease.

'Look,' he said, his tone gentle. 'I meant what I said about you dancing. Just because I suggested you sit down, please don't feel obliged to stay here and keep me company. Someone like you' – *Someone like her? What did he mean by that?* – 'What I mean is – Christ, I'm making a meal of this. Look, someone as young and as pretty as you shouldn't be sitting here with a stuffy old thing like me. Any number of these dashing young airmen are probably itching to ask you but won't come across while you're sat here—'

'I like talking to you.'

'Thank you. And I like talking to you. You always manage to make me see things differently.'

She turned sharply. 'I do?'

'You do. You might not say much – but then neither do I, I accept that. But, when you do say something, you display thought and consideration. When I was in the RAF, I knew people of all ages and from all backgrounds. And I found mixing with them stimulating. But now, apart from my students – who, to a boy, are generally terrified of me—'

'I don't believe that.'

'It's quite true, I'm afraid. Anyway, apart from them, I don't know anyone young at all.' As though reading her thoughts, he went on, 'And because I know you're too polite to ask, in December I shall be thirty.'

She laughed. 'Sorry. Was it that obvious?'

He grinned. 'I'm afraid so.'

'Well, because I know *you're* too polite to ask as well, *I'm* nearly nineteen.'

'Your whole life ahead of you.' His wistfulness was hard to miss.

'Unless this war sees to it otherwise. I mean, soon, now, I shall have to register for war work.'

'Do you know what you'd like to do? Do any of the services appeal?'

Clemmie shrugged. That they didn't was probably down to her ignorance of what joining any of them would entail, rather than a genuine dislike rooted in fact. 'I don't really know what's involved.'

'I've always thought that for some young ladies, the life offered could be quite a good one.'

'I suppose. I think mostly I've always been put off by the thought of having to leave home, of being apart from my sisters.'

'Understandable.'

'But since we were bombed out, we've been split up anyway. So, I suppose I ought not to fear that so much now.'

'Fear of any change is natural. And I speak as one who knows.'

She glanced at his expression. It seemed to contain a mixture of sadness and regret.

'I suppose you must do.'

'Well, like I said, please don't let me detain you.'

As the dancers left the floor at the end of another song, Clemmie glanced about. 'I suppose I *should* go and see whether I'm needed anywhere.'

'Of course. But well done, you. Your idea proved just the ticket. Mission accomplished.'

By her 'idea', she could only suppose he meant her thought to invite the young ladies. 'Happen you shouldn't tempt fate,' she said with a grin. 'The night's not over yet.'

'Nonsense. It's been quite the triumph.'

In a bid to hide that she was beaming with pride, she turned away, skirted the throng on the dance floor, and went in search of Miss Evercott. That the squadron leader seemed suddenly subdued she could only attribute to him having to sit out the dancing. After all, there were so many pretty young ladies present. And twenty-nine was no age at all.

Spotting Miss Evercott standing by the refreshments table, she went towards her; she could only hope that whatever the committee's next task turned out to be, she got to work on it with Squadron Leader Dunning. In fact, she couldn't bear to think that she might not. Without the prospect of seeing him, she would feel quite bereft.

'Ah, Miss Huxford.'

'Miss Evercott. What can I do to help?'

'Well, you could discreetly start some clearing up – scout about for paper cups, perhaps? Out the back there's a box I've labelled cardboard salvage.'

'I'll go and find it and set to.'

On the stage, the music slowed to a ballad; on the floor, the athletic dancing from earlier slowed to a shuffle. Clemmie noticed both Miss Wilford and Mrs Dickins, evidently alerted by the change in mood, get smartly to their feet and start patrolling the perimeter, clearly on the lookout for any of the *shenanigans* Miss Wilford had earlier warned the girls against. From what she could tell, the couples looked to be behaving perfectly, although she suspected that tomorrow there would be at least a couple of broken hearts.

And then, after a perfectly observed standing to attention for the national anthem, Major Hogue mustered his men at the rear of the hall, while Miss Wilford called the girls to the entrance. 'Miss Pope, come here at once. You too, Miss Boden. Miss Rugge, hurry up, your grandfather is here.'

Eventually, after a formal exchange of thank-yous, the girls were shepherded to their various means of getting home through the blackout, and the airmen climbed aboard the trucks that had brought them. On the stage, the band had already packed up all but the drum kit. To one side of the hall, two of the WVS ladies were stacking chairs.

'Miss Huxford?' From where she had been looking to see what else needed to be done, Clemmie swivelled about; Squadron Leader Dunning had wheeled himself across to join her without her hearing. 'I've spoken to Miss Evercott and suggested that we give the two of you a lift home. I would feel far happier knowing you're not walking in the pitch black. She accepted my offer.'

For Clemmie, this news came as a relief; with Cedric having chosen not to close the shop for the bank holiday, she'd been on her feet since first light, so to be relieved of the traipse home was a real boon.

'Thank you. You're very kind.'

Eventually, with the hall cleared and tidied to Dorothy's satisfaction and the front door soundly locked, Pearce guided the Wolseley at the necessary crawl through the blackout to Buckingham Crescent.

When they drew to a halt outside number twelve, Pearce got out and opened Dorothy's door.

'Good night, Squadron Leader Dunning,' she said once she had got out. 'Thank you very much for bringing us home.'

'My pleasure, Miss Evercott. Good night.'

When Dorothy walked away, Squadron Leader Dunning turned to look over his shoulder. 'Miss Huxford, would you wait here for a moment? There is something I need to tell you.' Alerted by the formality of his tone, Clemmie stiffened. 'And it would be very much easier to say were you to come and sit beside me.'

With that, Pearce arrived and when, with a frown, she got out, he opened the driver's door and directed her into the seat.

Baffled, she got in behind the wheel. 'What is it? What's the matter? Did I do something wrong?' To her mind, it seemed the only possibility.

'No, no of course not. No, it's just that now our function has been held, I shall be withdrawing from the welcome committee.'

Withdrawing? At the back of her throat, she felt a lump form. 'But I—'

'I was only asked to take part because of my service in the RAF. It was considered I would prove useful in liaison. And I like to think that I have been—'

'Oh, you have. Very much. We couldn't none of us have done it without you.'

'That's kind of you to say. But, as things now stand, the need for liaison has gone away. Contacts have been established… friendships forged.'

'But…' Struggling to believe how he could do this, she stared out through the windscreen into the thick darkness beyond. No. She couldn't let him just give up. 'But there are bound to be other things.'

'Perhaps.'

'And it would be a terrible shame if you weren't there for them.'

'It's true that I shall miss our time together.'

Not above begging, she turned towards him. 'Then please keep going. *Please*.'

'Perhaps in different circumstances, I would. But what you don't know, because I choose to keep it private, is that just lately I find my condition, my paralysis, that is, becoming more difficult to manage. Until recently, I had days when I was able to get about without my chair. With the aid of sticks, I was able to cover short distances. The doctors have always been quick to press upon me the importance of not pinning my hopes upon a recovery. And I like to think my attitude has always been realistic – has been the appropriate balance of reality and determination. But the number of occasions when I have been able to walk with sticks has grown fewer. Don't get me wrong, I have no intention of giving up my physiotherapy exercises.' With a light scoff, he went on, 'For a start, Pearce wouldn't allow it. He oversees my daily gymnastic exercise with an enthusiasm bordering upon zeal.' If he thought he could conjure a picture to make her smile, he was wrong. 'I realise that to start with, you relied upon me for guidance. And being on hand to assist you in your endeavours has been both a privilege and an absolute delight. But now that you have built up your confidence, you have no further need of me.'

What? Why on earth would he think such a thing?

'That's not true. You're wrong. I'm so terrible unworn— unword— unworldly. Even just thinking about having to go up to a stranger and ask them to do something knots my tongue and twists my insides like the wash copper tangles bedsheets. But *you* know how to speak to people. You know how to get them to agree to do a thing. They like you.'

'They like *you*.'

'It's not the same.'

'No, to be fair, it isn't. But you underestimate your abilities. Truly, you do.'

Well, if he was adamant about withdrawing from the committee, she could see nothing for it. 'Then if *you* stop, so shall I. I shan't want to do it no more. And while I'm about it, I might as well give up the WVS as well.'

'I can't help but think that would be a terrible waste.'

The ache that had come from nowhere to settle in her midriff made her want to double over and howl in despair. Fearing she might do so, she felt blindly about for the handle, pushed open the door, and extricated herself from behind the steering wheel. 'Not… as big a waste,' she gasped between sobs, 'as *you*… stopping helping… *me*.'

Brushing past Pearce waiting on the pavement, she fumbled open the gate and hurried up the path to the front door. Finding it left ajar, she went inside, closed it behind her, swiped across the blackout curtain and kicked off her shoes. Then, bending to scoop them up, and not bothering with the light, she ran up the stairs, hurtled along the landing, and shut herself in her room. In a whirl of fury and distress, she threw herself face down onto the bedspread.

How could he do this to her? How could he stop coming to meetings? And how was she supposed to go on now? The best thing in her life had been snatched away – and for no reason that made the slightest bit of sense. So, he couldn't get about with sticks; what of it? Every time she'd seen him, he'd been in his wheelchair, and it had never been a problem. And as for saying that she no longer needed him, well, it just went to show how much he knew about that. She needed him more than she needed anyone; without his company to look forward to, her life would be hollow and empty. And utterly pointless. In fact, how she was going to get through the days without him, she had absolutely no idea at all.

IV. Turbulence

Chapter 14

'Thank you, Mrs Parker. See you tomorrow.'

'No doubt, dear. No doubt.'

'Mrs Widger, good morning. Sorry to keep you waiting. What can I do for you today?'

'No point me wasting my breath asking if you've got any eggs, I suppose.'

Clemmie sent Mrs Widger a sympathetic smile. 'None whatsoever, I'm afraid.'

'Sardines, then.'

'How many tins?'

'Just the one.'

Reaching to the shelf, Clemmie grasped the nearest tin and put it on the counter. 'Anything else today?'

'No, that'll do me for now, love. Ta-ta, then.'

When the shop door clanged shut, Clemmie glanced at the clock and let out a sigh. One more hour to go. One more hour until she could go home, and then decide whether she could be bothered going to the WVS.

It was now almost four weeks since the dance at the guildhall and, for Clemmie, life had assumed a routine of unbearable monotony. The tedium of her mornings at Narramore's she could do nothing about; that her afternoons spent at the WVS centre had become similarly dull was disappointing. She knew from Dorothy that the WVS was about to be given a rent-free lease on a shop on the main road near the Heavitree rest centre. In anticipation of getting together stock for it, great bundles of clothing and linens kept arriving, all of it requiring sorting to determine what was saleable.

She didn't mind getting stuck in; someone had to get the stuff ready. No, what got on her nerves was the other women nattering away, Beryl Trobridge foremost among them. *My Arthur this, my Arthur that.* Some days it grated so much she found herself wondering whether the parachute factory might not be so bad after all. Gwen said the girls there were fun, and if the dance was anything to go by, they did seem a lively lot. At least there she would be working with people her own age, whereas most of the volunteers at the WVS centre were old enough to be her grandmother. A while back, Dorothy had suggested that once the shop was open she might like to do some afternoons there. But knowing her luck, she'd get the shifts with Beryl Trobridge, who was already talking as though the manager's position there was hers.

Resting her elbows on the counter, she let out a sigh of despair. Did all of life's decisions boil down to choosing the least unattractive of two options? Was that the basis upon which all of adulthood was conducted? If so, she was sorry to be growing up.

When the tinkling of the bell interrupted her contemplations, she looked up to see Mr Narramore's tenant, Jean Bodley, coming in.

'Morning, love.'

'Good morning, Mrs Bodley.'

'Got any tinned peas?'

'As it happens, we have.'

'One of those then and some condensed milk. Got any prunes?'

Clemmie shook her head. 'Sorry, no.'

'Custard powder?'

Again, Clemmie shook her head. 'Haven't seen any of that for a week or two.'

'Always the same, ain't it?' Mrs Bodley remarked with a weary laugh. 'Well, this'll have to do for now then.'

'All right.'

Having started for the door, Mrs Bodley turned back. 'Saints alive, no, where's my mind this morning?' Thrusting her hand into the pocket of her housecoat, she pulled out a brown envelope. 'Almost forgot. This came for Cedric.'

When Clemmie noticed that printed in the top left-hand corner were the words *War Damage Commission*, a picture came into her mind of the forms she'd seen on Cedric's desk.

'You know, until you told me,' she said, accepting the envelope and spotting her opportunity to find out more, 'I hadn't realised Mr Narramore was a landlord. Does he own the whole of Worcester Terrace?'

'Cedric? Good lord, no, love. Just number forty-seven. An' he don't never cease moaning about all the bother that comes with that, either. See, when the last owner died, Cedric offered to buy the place. By his own telling, he did so on a bit of a whim. Well, that's men for you, ain't it, love?'

Clemmie raised a smile. 'Indeed.'

'And they call *us* contrary.'

'Mm.'

'Anyway, I've known Cedric going on— well, let's just say I know him of old. So, when I found out I was expecting Malcolm and needed somewhere less mouldy than the place I was in before, he said I could have the downstairs of number forty-seven. And here we are.'

'I see.' Feigning ignorance as much as interest, Clemmie asked, 'So… he don't own anywhere else, then?'

Mrs Bodley laughed. 'No, love. Like I said just now, he claims owning next door is headache enough.' Lowering her voice, she went on, 'Mr Reeves up atop, he's the nuisance, always complaining something needs fixing or seeing to. Drives Cedric round the bend. Many's the time he's said about selling the place. But with a war on, well, nobody's buying houses, are they? I mean, who in their right mind sinks money into something that could get bombed to rubble? No, I said to him, you got to put your fancy plans on hold now till the end of the war. There's no money in houses.'

Fancy plans? Mr Narramore? To Clemmie, he didn't seem the type to plan as far as the end of the month. 'Got big dreams, has he?' Now she was relying on the woman being in the mood for a gossip.

Jean Bodley leaned over the counter. 'Soon as he can, he's going to sell up and buy a little pub in the countryside.'

It was as much as Clemmie could do not to laugh. While she could almost picture Mrs Narramore as a land-lady, she couldn't picture her living out in the sticks. Where would she get her hair done? Or her nails? 'Really?'

Mrs Bodley glanced in anxious fashion towards the storeroom. 'Uh-huh. But *I* didn't tell you.'

'Here,' Clemmie said, and reached under the counter. 'One of these got in among today's newspapers.' In front of her, she placed a *Woman's Weekly* magazine with a crumpled cover. 'I was keeping it to read later, but why don't you take it for when you get the chance to put your feet up?'

Shooting another look towards the storeroom, Mrs Bodley swiped it off the counter. 'Ta, love.' Tapping the side of her nose, she went on, 'But remember what I said. The other thing's a secret.'

'My lips are sealed,' Clemmie replied, watching as Jean went out through the door and then turned sharply to the left.

So, unless Mrs Bodley was wrong, which, seeing as she claimed to know Mr Narramore *of old* seemed unlikely, Cedric owned just the two properties. He didn't, as the forms she'd seen suggested, own any in Magdalen Street. Until a moment ago, those War Damage Commission documents, and the question of what Mr Narramore was doing with them, had slipped her mind. But now she was curious all over again.

With the shop empty, she stared down at the envelope. What a shame it was sealed. And it would *stay* sealed, she told herself as she carried it through to the office and put it on the desk. Mr Narramore's business was none of hers; thoroughly disliking this job was one thing, losing it, a rather different matter altogether.

–

'Is it just me, or are the evenings really drawing in now?'

From where she'd been staring into her sherry glass, Clemmie raised her eyes to look out through the window. 'No,' she replied to Dorothy's question, 'it's not just you. I'll fix the blackout and put on a light.'

'Thank you, dear. I can barely see to read this. It's the latest on the political situation in Spain… and this Franco

215

business. But the way it's presented here has me baffled. Conventional wisdom holds that one should read two newspapers with opposing views, to tease from between the pair of them something approximating the truth. But who has time for that these days, hm?'

With a murmur of agreement, Clemmie pulled down the blind and checked that it was properly tucked up on the windowsill. Then she felt around on the wall for the light switch. The yellowy glow from the overhead bulb gave the room an air that was barely any less gloomy than the fading daylight had been.

'Do you think,' she said wearily, 'there will ever come a day when we don't need to go through this palaver every night?'

'The blackout? I do hope so. I've grown as tired of it as everyone else.'

'It's been such a pleasure to go through the summer evenings without needing a light, or to have to black out the windows.' Spotting the calendar on the wall, she went towards it. 'Shall I tear off the page for August or do you need to keep it?'

'No, tear it off. Might as well confront September head on.'

'I suppose.'

With Gwen having gone out again this evening – three nights in a row; she must be serious about this Jimmy chap – Clemmie was once again at a loose end. She noticed the *Radio Times* magazine on the side, but was too tired to even bother looking to see what was on and sat back down at the table.

Without looking up from her newspaper, Dorothy said, 'You can go through to the drawing room and listen to the wireless if you like.'

Having just dismissed that very idea, Clemmie smiled. 'No, it's all right.'

'In a minute, it will be that variety show, *Let's Get Acquainted* – you know, the one where that American, Jimmy Something-or-other, introduces the British to the Americans and vice versa. American music. Journalists. Politicians. Rather forward-thinking of the BBC, don't you think? They should broadcast more programmes like it. Not everyone is as fortunate as we are in getting to meet Americans in the flesh.'

'No.'

'And we are all on the same side, after all.'

'Yes.' The problem for Clemmie was that thinking about the Americans reminded her of Squadron Leader Dunning – in particular, how much she missed seeing him. His company had been of a sort she doubted she would ever have again, certainly not with a man; Miss Evercott challenged her way of thinking, and for that she was grateful. But Squadron Leader Dunning had been, well… She sighed. In truth, what did it matter? He had withdrawn from the committee. Not that the committee had met for a while now. Major Hogue had said that once operations at the airfield were up and running, they would host what he'd called a 'concert party' and invite people from the town. For a while after hearing the news, she'd got her hopes up; surely the squadron leader would be first on the list for an invitation. And surely, given how well he had got on with both Major Hogue and Major Hearst, he wouldn't decline. Since the major's announcement, though, nothing had happened – not that she'd heard, anyway. Deeply disappointing, that's what it was; she'd been banking on something like that to lift her spirits.

Of course, her gloom was being exacerbated by what she knew about Cedric Narramore. Despite having vowed to push the matter to the back of her mind, it kept popping back to the fore, demanding to be reckoned with. Alas, the more she tried to do just that the more she felt certain Cedric was up to something shady. Who was she kidding? It wasn't just shady; it was downright suspicious. And if she was right about what he was doing – falsely claiming he had owned properties destroyed in the Blitz to get compensation to which he wasn't entitled – then he had to be committing fraud. She might know nothing about the law of the land, but she knew stealing when she saw it. Charlie Warren had been involved with some dodgy schemes, but Cedric was doing more than just handling the odd box of black-market soap or tea; he was trying to get money from the government – large sums of it, at that. The trouble was, she couldn't prove it. She didn't even know for sure that he'd done anything more than fill in application forms. For all she knew, he'd had second thoughts and torn them up. Although if he had, then why had a letter come from the War Damage Commission? It couldn't be for the shop, nor for Worcester Terrace. And then there was what Mrs Bodley had said about him wanting to buy a public house. Could that be what he was intending to do with the money – run away to the countryside somewhere? She shook her head in dismay. Supposition. It was all no more than supposition. And without further evidence, that was how it would remain. But should it?

Unfurling her hands from where they had become clenched into fists, she realised that while it was one thing to understand the dangers of getting involved, unless she took it upon herself to act there was every chance his scheme would prosper. On the other hand, if she went to the authorities Cedric might go to prison, meaning he could lose his shop, and she her job. Not that she liked working there – hadn't from the outset. But jobs were hardly two a penny, and without one war work loomed. Did any of that constitute reason to keep quiet, though? Could she live with her conscience if she was the one who let him get away with it?

At the other side of the table, Dorothy gave a weary sigh. 'It's no good. It's too late to make sense of this now. I'll try again tomorrow.' Closing her newspaper and looking up, she went on, 'I'm going through to listen to the wireless. Coming?'

Swirling the dregs of her sherry in the bottom of her glass, Clemmie shook her head. 'Actually, I think I'll write to my sister.' Perhaps unburdening herself to May would help; perhaps her sister would write back and advise her on what she should do. After all, a problem shared *was* supposed to be a problem halved.

'The table's all yours.'

'Thank you. I hope you enjoy your programme.'

After half an hour spent struggling to set out what was on her mind, Clemmie eventually put down her pen. She would read what she had written and then go and ask Miss Evercott whether she might go up and have a bath. Even just five inches of water ought to help her feel less tense.

Smoothing a hand over the sheet of notepaper, she started to read.

> *Dearest May,*
>   *I hope this letter finds you well. I am mainly going along well, too.*

> *I don't know about you, but I find it hard to believe we are on the verge of autumn now and do wonder where the summer has gone.*
>
> *I am getting along so-so at the shop. I enjoy seeing so many people every day and having a chat. Some of them I have got to know quite well. The owner is an odd fellow, though, and at times makes me wonder what he is up to.*

No sense worrying her sister by disclosing too much; if May knew she was unhappy at Narramore's, she might feel bad about having moved away.

She cast her eyes back down to the page.

> *Although I miss you often, at this very moment I wish more than ever that you were close by as I am in a quandary over something. It is nothing that need alarm you for, as I say, I am quite well otherwise. But I do wish you were here to lend me your thoughts. Apart from you, there is no one else I trust to be neither so honest nor so fair. Anyway, since you are not here, I shall have to rely on my own judgement in the matter. I suppose it hasn't served me too badly thus far.*
>
> *Please take every care, dearest May,*
> *Your loving sister Clemmie*

Picturing her sister reading the letter, she realised what she was hoping for most was that May would offer to come and visit on her day off. But suggesting such a thing directly would be a cheek – even between sisters. At least this way she was leaving it open for May to suggest. And yes, it was selfish to put the onus on her sister. And yes, there *was* always Miss Evercott to confide in. But, since she'd only discovered what she had by snooping, she wasn't sure what such a revelation would do to her land-lady's opinion of her. With clear-cut evidence, it would be different.

Heaving a long sigh, she folded the letter and pushed it into an envelope. All told, she didn't think she'd written anything to cause her sister alarm, but rather to make her want to find out what was going on. And by the time that happened, with a bit of luck she, Clemmie, might have chanced upon something to confirm, one way or another, what Cedric Narramore really was up to.

Chapter 15

How on earth had she let herself get talked into this? She might have grown fed up with constantly feeling down in the dumps but, as solutions to problems went, this one reeked of desperation. Even while she had been agreeing to it, common sense had told her she was heading for disappointment. Going on a double date with Gwen and Jimmy? What was she thinking?

Turning to see Gwen coming along the landing, her perfectly pinned victory roll hairstyle making her look alarmingly sophisticated, Clemmie withheld a resigned sigh. Clearly, it was too late to back out now.

'How do I look?' she greeted Gwen.

Given the stylishness of Gwen's dark-green button-through shirt dress and black peep-toe shoes, her reply came as no surprise.

'Want the truth? Like you're off to visit your gran.'

'Haven't got a gran.'

'Fortunately for you, I'm here to remedy things.'

Clemmie tensed. *Remedy things?* 'Oh, no, I don't think I—'

'Look, Clemmie Huxford, I know you haven't started dating yet—'

'Well, that's not—'

'—and so it's understandable you don't know what men like.' Unfastening her pink flowery make-up purse and ferreting about inside, she went on, 'Luckily, you've got me to put you right.' Having found what she was apparently looking for, Gwen glanced about. 'But it's too dark in here. Come back to my room and we'll do it there.'

Recalling Gwen's observations about her appearance on the night of the welcome party and the effect of the little bit of lipstick she'd let her apply, Clemmie gave in. Who knew? Maybe in Gwen's hands, she might be made to look a bit more stylish.

'Where do you want me?' she asked, glancing about Gwen's room. By dint of having a large picture window, and facing as it did to the west, it was very much brighter. It also had a dressing table with a three-panel vanity mirror.

'Sit on the stool. But turn this way, towards me.' Clemmie sat down. 'I take it you've washed your face.'

''Course I have.'

'Right. Well, you've got a nice complexion, which is all well and good, but left bare makes you look like you're off to school.'

'Which isn't what men want.'

Gwen snorted. 'Hardly. Men want you to look glamorous—'

'*Glamorous?*' Now she really was alarmed.

'I mean, think about it. Not only do they want something nice to look at for themselves, they also want the girl on their arm to turn a few heads.' *Turn a few heads?* The only person she'd ever known do that was Pearl. And that was because she had red hair and green eyes. 'Good skin is one thing. But just wait till you see it with a bit of foundation to give you that made-up look. Now, I know this colour's a bit darker than you would buy, but that's because this is for my face and it's the only bottle I've got. So, I'll just keep the layer thin.'

Unable to nod while Gwen applied foundation – on the bottle of which Clemmie could read the words *Henry C. Miner's Liquid Make-Up* – she settled for saying, 'All right.'

'I was lucky to get this. It's new. It comes in colours for six different skin tones. This one is medium, but you'll need one of the palest. Shilling and thruppence a bottle.'

'You should be behind the beauty counter.'

'I know! Bloomin' Hitler, bombing all the best shops. Still, after the war... Now,' Gwen continued, standing back to admire her handiwork. 'I don't think you should wear eyeliner. The black will be too heavy for your eyes.' Inwardly, Clemmie heaved a sigh of relief. 'And anyway, you've got good lashes. So instead, we'll put on loads of mascara, a touch of lipstick and some rouge.'

At the mention of rouge, Clemmie stiffened. 'Oh, I don't think—'

'Trust me. I know what I'm doing. I won't make you look like a clown.'

'You hadn't better.'

'I won't. Sit still. Now raise your head and keep your eyes looking about here.' With one hand, Gwen indicated an imaginary spot a couple of inches beneath her chin. 'And try holding them wide open. That's it.'

The trouble was, every time Gwen's brush neared her eye, Clemmie blinked. 'Sorry.'

'It's normal. Doesn't happen when you do it yourself but there's an art to it. And since you haven't done it before... Tell you what, I'm going to hold your upper eyelid back. Sorry, it's the only way.' Staring at Gwen's chin, Clemmie felt her eyelid growing steadily heavier.

'Now, try not to blink too much while it dries otherwise it'll flick all over your foundation, and I'll have to touch it up.'

Holding herself unnaturally stiffly, Clemmie gave the slightest of nods. 'I'll try not to.'

'Next, for the rouge. I've got a new cream one from Coty. Matches my lipstick. It cost two shillings but it's worth every penny. It's called "Magnet" and it glows a real warm red without looking too bold. As you can't fail to have noticed, the more natural look is very fashionable again now.'

Despite not having the least idea how any form of make-up could be described as 'natural', Clemmie risked another nod. 'Uh-huh.'

'You want true red colours nowadays rather than anything purply or bright pink.'

'Right.'

'This Coty one promises a milk and roses bloom. And it smells divine.'

Milk and roses? She'd heard of peaches and cream to describe a complexion but milk and roses? Ah, well. Too late now. Besides, Gwen was right; it did have a pretty smell.

'And finally, for your lips, I'll use the matching shade.'

'But the other night you said I should wear pale pink.'

'And for the other night with the WVS, that was fine. Tonight, you're going on a date. Tonight, as I keep telling you, you don't want to look as though you're going to a meeting with a load of old fogies. So, hold still and do this.' Gwen held her mouth in a broad smile and Clemmie copied her. 'Just right.' The lipstick applied, Gwen said, 'Good. Now do this.'

Doing the same as she had last time Gwen put lipstick on her, Clemmie pressed her lips together a couple of times. 'Is that it?'

'For your face, yes. But we need to do something with that blouse.'

Clemmie frowned. 'Why? What's wrong with it?'

'Well, do you see *my* buttons done all the way up to *my* throat?'

Clemmie glanced to Gwen's dress. 'Well, no, but—'

'Who are you *not* going to visit?'

With a shake of her head, Clemmie exhaled a weary sigh. 'My gran.'

'Too right. So, top four buttons. Undo them.'

'*Four?*'

'You need to show some cleavage.'

Reluctantly, Clemmie unfastened three buttons. 'I haven't *got* any cleavage.'

'Go on. Undo another one.'

Growing hot, Clemmie undid another button. 'But it just makes me feel scruffy.'

'You don't look it,' Gwen replied with a grin. 'Now, let's give that chest a bit of help.'

'My chest?'

'Look, you've got a real slim waist but nothing much by way of hips or bust. So, if we give your top half some oomph, you'll look stunning.' Turning about, Gwen opened the top drawer of the chest and pulled out a paper bag. 'I'm going to lend you some cotton wool—'

'Cotton wool?'

'—but I'm going to need it back afterwards.'

As Gwen separated a wad from the clump, Clemmie froze. 'Oh, no, I don't think—'

'No, and *that's* your downfall. What you've got to remember is that there's thirty women to every chap these days. And if you want a bloke – especially a decent one – you've got to be crafty. Blokes like my Jimmy – fellers still home 'cos they're in reserved occupations – got the choice of pretty much any woman they want. So, you've got to show yourself to best advantage, especially if you want to hang on to him once you've got him. Trust me, it'll be worth it.'

Accepting the wad of cotton wool Gwen thrust at her, Clemmie forced a swallow. 'What do I do with it?'

'Make a mound and push it into the bottom of your bra. It'll plump you up. That's it. Now, do the same with this bit for the other one. That skirt got a belt?'

Struggling to get the mound of cotton wool to sit comfortably in her bra, Clemmie shook her head. 'No.'

'I'll lend you one of mine.'

Still fiddling with the cotton wool, Clemmie frowned. 'But my skirt fits fine.'

'No doubt. But with this…' Turning back from her wardrobe, Gwen held out a wide black belt. '…we can turn over the waistband so your skirt swishes about your legs rather than hanging all limp like it does now, and at the same time cinch you in about the waist.'

'My bra feels lumpy.'

'You'll get used to it.'

'And now I'm worried this button is going to pop off.' With her hand, Clemmie indicated the button at her chest.

'It won't.' Moments later, the waistband of Clemmie's skirt turned over, her blouse tucked in behind it, and the belt fastened so tightly she worried she might not be able to sit down, Gwen stood back. 'What do you think?'

If it wasn't for her hair still being recognisable, Clemmie wouldn't have known her own reflection. 'It's—'

'*So* much better. I know. This mate of Jimmy's is going to take one look at you and think his ship's come in.'

He hadn't better, Clemmie thought, part of her wanting to burst into tears, the other part fascinated by the transformation. Was this how it felt to be Pearl? Was this what it took to appear confident and determined? Because if it was, she wasn't sure she wanted anything to do with it. On the other hand, look where being shy and retiring had got her. Besides, over these last few months she'd begun to think it was true what people said: nothing ventured, nothing gained.

–

'So, what did you think of the film?'

Put on the spot by Gwen's question, Clemmie debated how best to answer; with no idea what the others thought of it, she didn't want to risk saying anything that would make her look silly. On the other hand, if she didn't say something quickly, she risked looking daft for a different reason.

'I enjoyed it.' For the most part, it was true: while she would never admit it to anyone, this evening was the first time she'd been to the cinema and sat somewhere other than the stalls – and the cheapest section of the stalls, at that. Moreover, the film really had struck her as good; a brand-new mystery called *Alibi*, it was the story of police hunting for the killer of a woman who worked in a Paris nightclub.

'I did, too.' Shooting a sly glance at Jimmy, Gwen went on, 'James Mason is dead dishy.'

Jimmy affected indignation. 'Hey, if you're going to fancy the actors, I won't be taking you again.'

'So, it's all right for you to talk about that girl in the film last week—'

'Yeah, but I reckon even you'd admit she was something else.' With his hands, Jimmy mimed a curvaceous figure. 'Specially in that neggly… neggily…'

'Negligee.'

'Yeah, 'specially in that.'

'So, let me get this straight,' Gwen picked up again. 'You can ogle a woman in nothing more than a slip of lace, but I can't admire a fully clothed James Mason?'

'Sounds about right.' Squeezing his arm about Gwen's shoulders, Jimmy looked directly at her. 'You coming up home for a bit? Mum's on night shift.'

'So long as you make it worth my while.'

The sight of Jimmy and Gwen shambling away turned Clemmie's thoughts to getting home. It had to be very late, and she was dead on her feet.

'So… you want to go somewhere?'

Having completely overlooked that her date, a chap called Clive, was still there, she spun to face him; despite having sat alongside him through a programme lasting almost three and a quarter hours, she didn't know any more about him now than she had when they'd said hello. Standing there on the steps of the blacked-out Savoy, she was even struggling to remember what he looked like: heavily built; square shoulders; angular features framed by slicked-back hair. Tall, but no James Mason, that was for sure.

'I have to start work at seven.'

'I have to clock on at six.'

Bother. She'd thought that a good excuse. 'And it's quite a walk home—'

'I know a chippy that'll still be open.'

Clemmie's resolve wavered. She'd been unable to face supper on account of the knot in her stomach, and the thought of chips covered in salt and vinegar was enough to make her salivate. But if she did go somewhere with him, she would have to be on her guard; barely half an hour into the main film, his hand had landed on her leg. Horrified but not wanting to cause a fuss, she'd left it there. Moments later, she'd felt the fabric of her skirt being inched up her thigh. Still she'd done nothing. But when his fingers slid decisively over her bare flesh to arrive at the elastic of her knicker leg, she'd shoved them away. It hadn't stopped him trying again scarcely ten minutes later; in fact, she'd had to rebuff him another three times before he'd finally given up and sat stiffly for the remainder of the film.

'Is it on the way to Topsham Road?'

'Yeah. Sure. So, you want some?'

'Yes please.'

The chip shop turned out to be just a few minutes' walk from the Savoy, which did at least mean, she thought, as she watched him go in through the blacked-out door, that it was in the general direction of home.

'There's a park down here,' he said when he returned, his jacket smelling heavily of cooking oil, the cone of paper in his hand exuding the tantalising aroma of vinegar and hot newsprint. 'There might be a bench.'

Reliving the feel of his fingers on her leg, she shook her head. 'I'd rather walk. I can't afford to be too late.'

From the corner of her eye, she noticed him shrug. 'Fair enough. Chip, then?'

She'd thought he was never going to ask. 'Thanks.'

She supposed he might be all right; since they were walking side by side, she could really only see his profile. For a first date, the cinema struck her as a ridiculous place to go: you could neither properly study your date's appearance nor talk to him. So, how could you know whether you wanted to go out with them again? At least if you went dancing you had the chance to chat.

When he offered the bag in her direction again, she took another couple of chips.

'So, where do you work?'

'At a shop in…' She paused. 'Near where I live.' If she decided not to see him again, she'd rather he didn't turn up at Narramore's. He could find her through Gwen as it was. But at least if he showed up at Buckingham Crescent, she could always ask Miss Evercott to see him off.

In the darkness, she reached for another chip. Already they were losing some of their crispness.

When they were all gone, he screwed the newspaper into a ball, and when they arrived at the next street corner, he tossed it into a litter bin.

'Do you work with Jimmy?' she asked as they crossed the road. She might have decided not to see him again, but she could still be polite.

'Same depot, yeah. Used to be in the same shed but a few weeks back he moved to the other side of the yard. We still see each other after work at the Platelayers, though.'

Since she didn't know whether the Platelayers was a public house or a working men's club, she didn't reply. As they continued to walk, guided by the white paint ringing the lampposts and daubed on the kerbstones, she felt a light breeze and supposed they were passing the park he'd mentioned. But as she went to remark to that effect, he grasped her arm and she found herself being yanked sideways from the pavement. With no idea where he was taking her, she scuffled along in his wake, trying desperately to shake herself free. Unmoved, he tightened his grip.

'Let me go,' she yelled at his back. 'You're hurting me.'

When he showed no sign of releasing her, she dragged her shoes in the dirt and pulled against him, but he kept walking, powerful fingers pressing even more firmly into her flesh. Unable to see where she was going, she tripped over a tussock of grass, turning an ankle and yelping in pain; still, he kept going.

Without warning, he stopped dead and swung her about. Her back met with something hard; ridges like the bark of a tree pressed into her spine. She clenched her fists and tried to pummel his chest; he flattened himself against her. She opened her mouth to cry out; a vinegary tongue thrust its way between her teeth. She gagged. A clammy hand forced its way up her skirt. She writhed furiously. Grabbing one of her flailing wrists, he twisted hard, burning her skin. Heart racing with fear, she struggled to think. *Get away from him. How? You're trapped. Kick him. For God's sake, kick him.* Pinned beneath his weight, it was as much as she could do to wriggle her feet. Determined fingers clawed at the leg of her knickers. But for the tightness of Gwen's belt, the flimsy cotton drawers would have slid down her thighs. Instead came the sound of ripping. How was she going to stop him? He was so strong.

In desperation, she let her body go limp. With luck, he would think she was done resisting and was giving in. To her surprise, the weight of him pressing against her lessened. Carefully, so as not to alert him, she edged her hand from between their bodies. Then she grabbed a fistful of his hair and wrenched as hard as she could.

Undeterred, he jerked his head and it slid from her grasp. Pinned once again beneath his weight, her strength seemed to desert her. Feebly, pointlessly, she plucked at his shirt. He was too strong… she was too tired… there was nothing she could do…

The feel of hot angry tears triggered a memory of Charlie Warren. Shoving her repeatedly, he'd pinned her against the dresser and was looming over her, snarling. *Know what you need, you good-for-nothing bint? A dose of obedience thrashed into you, that's what. Be a bit swifter to do as I said after that, I can tell you.* But this animal towering over her now wasn't her stepfather; offering to dash up the hill to the off-licence for two bottles of brown ale wasn't going to do any good here, nor was promising to move a bit quicker next time. Her only option with this brute was to fight back; to somehow take her fear, turn it to anger, and catch him off guard.

With that, she saw a way. Silently she counted to three. Then she bit with all her might on his tongue.

He reeled away so fast, she fell to the ground.

'Jesus Christ! You little bitch.'

Gulping for air, she staggered to her feet and took off. 'Leave… me… alone!'

'What the ruddy hell was I supposed to think…' His cursing sounded so close she feared he was coming after her. '…you all done up like that. Bloody little tease.'

With no clue as to direction, she ran, full pelt, stumbling and lurching over the uneven ground. Where the hell was she? Beneath her feet, grass gave way to pavement. But in the moment it took her to realise it, she flew off a kerb, landing with a clang in the grating of a drain and buckling her knee. Without turning to look behind her, she gasped and limped on. At least she'd reached a road.

Lungs burning, she kept up a lopsided jog for as long as she could until eventually, clutching her midriff, she staggered to a halt. In her mouth, the lingering taste of vinegar made her retch. Doubling over, she spat in the gutter. Then, rubbing at her side to relieve the stabbing of a stitch, she eased herself upright and cast about. She seemed to have reached a junction. But where? Which one? She strained to see. Houses – flat-fronted like those in Worcester Terrace. Near the barracks? Close to the main road? Reach that, and she could find her way back to Buckingham Crescent.

Behind her, the clatter of a dustbin made her turn sharply. Cat? Fox? Heart pounding, she listened. That animal Clive? Hard to believe he'd follow her all this way, but she couldn't risk it. He'd been so enraged that if he caught up to her, she daren't think what he might do.

With the muscles in her thighs quivering in protest, she set off again. What was wrong with the man? Did he really think sharing a penny-ha'penny's worth of chips gave him the right to… to… force himself on her like that? Was that what men did? Were they all beasts and bullies like Charlie Warren? May had repeatedly assured her they weren't. Even Pearl said her father was *the worst of the worst*. But what if they were wrong? What if all men *were* just the same?

Fed up with being sliced in two by Gwen's belt, she paused long enough to wrestle the buckle undone and pull it off. Then she turned up the waistband of her skirt, tugged down the hem and buttoned her blouse. Perhaps it wasn't men that were the problem; perhaps, through letting Gwen get her all dolled up, she'd brought this on herself. *What the ruddy hell was I supposed to think… you all done up like that.* Perhaps he had a point; what *was*

234

he supposed to think? *Bloody little tease.* She'd heard boys at school talk about girls who looked *easy*. Well, never again would she wear mascara and rouge. She would even think twice about lipstick. And she definitely wouldn't have anything to do with stuffing her bra or getting her skirt to *swish about her legs* – no matter that it would get her a man. If this was what happened when you got one, she would go without. Her poor mother would be turning in her grave.

Exhaustion slowing her pace, she pulled out her handkerchief, spat on the corner of it and rubbed it over her lips. Then she folded it inside out and wiped it more widely around her mouth. If men were no better than farm animals, then thank goodness she'd found out now, before she'd bowled headlong into real trouble. In her last year at school, rumours had gone round about a girl ending up in the mother and baby home. *Filthy creature*, the mistress had denounced her in assembly. The narrowness with which she had just escaped a similar fate sent a shudder the length of her spine. *There but for the grace of God…*

Desperate now simply to be home, she trudged on in what she hoped was the direction of the main road. From now on, she would look to Miss Evercott as an example of how to conduct herself, not the likes of Gwen Brewer. Maybe not all men *were* like that Clive – she was certain Squadron Leader Dunning wouldn't be – but after this evening's close shave, she would rather end her days a spinster than risk finding out.

Chapter 16

Clemmie smiled. The second-hand jumper she'd found in the WVS shop was huge, and once unpicked would provide enough wool to knit not only a new long-sleeved sweater, but also a sleeveless one to wear over blouses. Given the difficulties of clothes rationing, there was finally an advantage to being slim. The yarn looked like two-ply Shetland and, if she made a start tonight, she should have two warm garments knitted before the weather took a turn for the worse; September could be such an unpredictable month. Granted, the garment reeked of camphor but, once the wool was washed, she was convinced it would knit up like new. Such a pretty colour, too; a very clever find.

Still smiling as she opened the door and stepped inside, she paused to listen. If that was a man's voice, Miss Evercott must be home early from work for once. And by the sound of it she had a visitor, too.

Deciding to stay out of her landlady's way, she tiptoed along the hall. But just as she went to go upstairs, the door to the drawing room opened and Dorothy came out.

'Ah, you're home.'

'Yes. Sorry. I'll go on up and stay out of your way.'

With a signal that Clemmie should stay where she was, Dorothy crossed the hall. 'Actually,' she whispered, 'it's a visitor for you – Squadron Leader Dunning.'

As everything seemed to blur, Clemmie tightened her grip on the banister. 'For me?'

Dorothy nodded. 'He arrived about ten minutes ago and asked if he might see you.'

What was Squadron Leader Dunning doing here? What could he possibly want with *her*?

'I didn't see his car outside.'

'His man Pearce has gone to take care of something, but he'll be back in a while.'

So many thoughts. So many questions. 'But—'

'So,' Dorothy said, her tone encouraging, 'why not take your things upstairs, splash your face—'

'Do I look dirty? I've been sorting stock in the shop.' Christ, what the devil was he doing here?

'Not at all. I just thought you might like to take a moment to freshen up.'

'Did he say what he wants? Is it the Americans?' The possibility now in her mind, she rushed on, 'Have they invited us there for a party? Only, they said they would, once they got settled in.'

'I don't believe so, no. But the sooner you go on up, the sooner you'll find out, won't you?'

Clemmie sighed. 'Yes, of course. You're right. I'll go and freshen up.'

'I'll tell him you've just this minute got in and will be down in a moment.'

'Yes. Thank you.'

At the top of the stairs, Clemmie hurtled along the landing to her room, threw the sweater on the bed, fought to undo the buttons on her blouse – only to give up and pull it off over her head – and then yanked open the middle drawer of her chest. In here somewhere was her lace-stitch jumper – the one in the colour that always made her think of bluebells. Yes, here it was. And luckily it was clean.

Having tugged it over her head and straightened it about her body, she darted along the landing to the bathroom, pressed the rubber plug into the basin and turned on the tap. Without waiting for the basin to fill, she lathered her hands with soap and washed her face. Turning off the water, she rinsed away the suds and reached for her towel. Her face dabbed dry, she pulled out the plug and leaned over the basin to check in the little mirror. Somehow, her hair was still reasonably tidy; all it really needed was a damp finger run over the odd loose strand.

That done, she stood back. Squadron Leader Dunning had come to see her, and she had no idea why. Well, as Miss Evercott had said, there was only one way to find out.

Descending the stairs, she reminded herself to stay calm but it was, of course, a waste of time; her hand trembled on the newel post as she reached the final tread. *Breathe, you stupid girl. Just breathe. And for God's sake, don't open your mouth without thinking first.*

Unable to put it off any longer, she opened the door to the drawing room.

'Here she is,' Dorothy said warmly and rose from the sofa. 'Come in, dear, and sit down. I'll go and make some tea.'

The first thing that struck Clemmie was the absence of the squadron leader's wheelchair; instead, propped up nearby were two crutches.

'You're walking?' she said, her tone betraying her surprise.

Squadron Leader Dunning smiled. 'Good afternoon, Miss Huxford.' Clemmie blushed. It had taken just seconds for her to make her first gaffe. 'Forgive me if I don't get up. And yes, I suppose my painfully slow shuffle does just about qualify as walking.'

'Sorry,' she said, feeling her cheeks colouring even darker. 'What I meant to say was good afternoon, Squadron Leader Dunning. It's just that…'

'Don't read too much into it.' He gestured to his legs. 'As I think I said to you a while back, from time to time I do have some use of them. Anyway, as I can't get up without a great deal of fuss, please, won't you sit down?'

When he indicated the sofa, she did as he said, careful to arrange her legs in a ladylike manner. 'So… you're keeping well then.' He certainly looked it, the light colour to his face suggesting he had seen something of the late summer sunshine.

'I am. And how are you?'

God, she hated small talk. 'I'm very well, thank you.'

'Miss Evercott tells me you've continued with your volunteering.'

She nodded. 'I have. We've just got— the WVS has just got a shop in Heavitree where we sell donated items to raise money. You'd never believe how busy it is. When we were getting ready to open, Miss Evercott said it wasn't to become like a rummage sale… that we would only sell the best-quality items.'

'And it's paying off.'

'It is.'

'Here we are then.' When Dorothy came through the door with the tea tray, Clemmie leapt to her feet. 'I'll be in the kitchen if you need anything else.'

When Dorothy had left the room and shut the door behind her, Clemmie sat back down. Now, she supposed, she would learn why he was here.

Deciding that if she didn't deal with the tea now her nerves might get the better of her, she indicated the tray. 'You take milk, don't you?'

'Just a dash. No sugar.'

It was no good: the silence was excruciating. 'Have you seen Major Hogue at all?' At least her question would give him something to say while she fussed with the teapot.

'I haven't, I'm afraid, no.'

Lifting his cup and saucer from the tray, she cast a glance at the way he was seated. 'If I put this there,' she said, getting to her feet and reaching to place it at the edge of what Dorothy called her *coffee table*, 'will that be all right for you?'

'It will be perfect.'

'Good.'

When she had settled herself back on the sofa, he looked across at her and smiled.

'Miss Huxford, please forgive my arriving out of the blue like this. I should imagine you must be astonished to find me sitting here.'

She attempted a smile. 'You could say that.'

'Trust me when I say that many's the time I've wanted to come and see you, but have repeatedly failed to summon the courage.'

Unable to help it, Clemmie frowned. 'You'll have to forgive me if I find that hard to believe.' If ever there was a person who had courage in abundance...

'But this morning, I made up my mind. And to ensure I was unable to back out of my decision, I told Pearce that no matter what I said when the time came, he was to pay no heed and bring me here anyway.'

'Gosh.' Then what the devil was this about?

'You see, there are a couple of things I want to say to you… well, and to ask you, I suppose.'

Clemmie's heart was now hammering so hard she felt certain he must be able to hear it. 'All right…'

'So, here goes. Firstly, the way I spoke to you at the end of the welcome dance was uncalled for. I should have thought more carefully about how I communicated my decision to stand down from the committee. We had become friends. And that is not how friends treat one another. And so, for my manner that evening, I apologise and ask that you forgive me.'

Listening to him explaining, Clemmie felt a twinge of disappointment. That the incident had been playing on his mind was heartening, his apology sincere. But then she'd always known he was a gentleman. That it seemed to be his reason for coming was something of a let-down.

'I've no need to forgive you. You simply told me what you'd decided to do. Your reasons were your own.'

'Nevertheless—'

'Truly.'

'Anyway, of greater importance than what I *did* say to you that night is the matter of what I *didn't*. So, might I say it to you now?'

With no idea what he was talking about, she gave a single nod. ''Course.'

'Miss Huxford – look, I don't suppose after all this time I might call you Clemmie?'

Deep inside, she felt something lurch. 'I'd like that.'

'And perhaps, after this – if I ever manage to get to the point I wish to make – you might see your way to calling me Andrew?'

Andrew. So that was his name. She'd often wondered. But what did he mean by *after this*?

'Um, well, I'll try.'

'Then, Clemmie, after much soul-searching, I feel I cannot go on without being honest with you. While, at the time, the matter of my health was of genuine concern to me, the main reason I decided to withdraw from the committee was because I had found myself unable to stop thinking about you. And the more time we spent together, the worse – if that is indeed the right word – the situation became. Indeed, it had reached the point where you were – *are* – all I can think about—' He thought about her? All the time? This wise and intelligent man had been thinking about her in the same way she had become preoccupied with him? Dare she believe it? 'And I was starting to find the situation difficult to hide. It was the first time I'd felt that way about anyone since my accident. As you might imagine, it put me in a difficult position. I'm paralysed – at least, some of me is. And you're young and bright. And pretty. And though I very much wanted to get to know you better, how could I? I couldn't ask you to go for a walk, let alone to go dancing. Even a trip to the theatre or the cinema is mired with obstacles – and that's without the difficulties of where, at the best of times, one can find to take a young lady in a bombed-out city. So, determining it was for the best, I chose to bury my feelings and remove myself from your company.'

Sensing he had more yet to say, Clemmie sat with her hands clasped tightly in her lap. 'I see...'

'But if I thought I was going to forget you, I was wrong; the manner of our parting only added to what has turned into abject misery.'

Thinking she might cry, Clemmie bit hard on the side of her tongue. It was a trick her mother had taught her to avoid crying in company. It rarely failed.

'So…'

'So why am I here?'

Unable to trust herself to speak, she confined herself to a nod and a single word in reply. 'Yes.'

'Because notwithstanding all that I've just said about my situation, I have come to realise that I can't just let you slip out of my life without at least knowing whether there is any chance whatsoever that you might – or *think* that you might – come to feel the same way. Had we met in different circumstances, I would simply have asked you out to dinner and risked having you rebuff me on the grounds that I am older than you, and no doubt too stuffy. But the moment I found myself without the prospect of seeing you, I rued not even giving you the opportunity to turn me down. Since that night, my concentration has been poor, my days dreary in the utmost. If it's not one hapless boy murdering Debussy, it's another reduced to tears over simultaneous equations.'

Still she had no idea how to respond. Part of her felt as if she was floating on a warm and fluffy cloud of delight while the other, more pragmatic part of her, felt nothing but terror. 'Oh.'

'In fact, it was the desperation of one of my piano pupils that made me decide to act. The boy in question is a talented player but, of late, has been struggling with one particular composer. His torment has even been making him talk of giving up. On more than one occasion, I have pointed out to him that you don't give up just because something is tough. His dream is to win a scholarship – and I believe him to be good enough to do so – and so I said to him, "Do you want to be a pianist? Do you want this scholarship, this dream?" And when he agreed that he did, I pointed out that the only way to achieve any goal is to stick at it. That was when I realised that I, too, was guilty of giving up – that I should at least see how you feel before letting you slip out of my life. And so, rightly or wrongly, here I am.'

While that was all well and good, Clemmie still didn't understand what he was hoping for.

'All right. But what is it that you—'

'What am I hoping will happen?' When she nodded, he went on, 'Well, I suppose I've come to find out whether there is any chance you might feel the same, and whether—'

'Yes.'

'There is? A chance, I mean? There is a chance that you feel the same?'

The depth of his surprise made her smile. By now, her heart was thudding so powerfully she thought she might faint. 'There is.'

'Then before I suggest we spend some time getting to know one another, there is much I must tell you. And you must give me your word that you will make no commitment until you have seen and heard all there is to… well, to see and to hear.'

This time, she laughed. 'All right.'

'You see, I feel it essential that we proceed slowly and with honesty. While my approach might seem clinical, the more you learn of my situation the more you will understand why it must be so. We must both – but you, especially – see everything for what it is. You do under-stand that, don't you?'

Struggling once again to quell tears, Clemmie nodded. 'I do.'

When his demeanour appeared to soften, she imagined it to be from relief. She was beginning to feel a little less tense herself.

'Why I couldn't have come clean with you before, I'll never know.'

'Fear,' she said. To her, it seemed obvious. 'Fear that things might not turn out as you hoped.'

'Indeed. You know, behind the controls of an aeroplane, I was never troubled by fear. Once in that cockpit, all I ever felt was a determination to keep my men safe and do what was asked of me. But coming here today, I have felt terror such as I never thought possible.'

'I think it's called being normal,' she said with a giggle.

'Part of what makes us human.'

'I suppose.'

'Well, look, I've taken a lot of your time, when all you probably thought was that you were coming home for a quiet evening and a bite to eat.'

No need to tell him what she had actually been expecting was to unpick a second-hand sweater and save the wool to knit herself two new ones. 'Something like that, yes.'

'Then I shall leave you to it… but not before I ask you one final thing. How would it be if you came to visit me at my home? We could call it coming for tea. You could see how and where I live. And I could explain to you about my regime of exercise, and how I cope with the more mundane aspects of daily life. Would that… well, do you think that might help you? I promise you we wouldn't be alone – Pearce would be there, too.'

The risk now was that she would grin so much he would think her simple. 'I'd like that very much.'

'Then how about tomorrow? Or does that smack of indecent haste on my part?'

'No,' she said, her mouth still curled into a warm smile. 'No, tomorrow would be lovely.'

'Then I shall send Pearce to collect you. Shall we say… three thirty?'

'Thank you, yes.'

'And in which case, might I trouble you to look through the window and see whether he has returned?'

Getting to her feet, Clemmie went to look out. 'Your car is there.'

'Excellent.'

Suddenly flustered by the question of whether or not to offer assistance, Clemmie dithered. But, while she was still hesitating, Andrew positioned his crutches under his arms and, in one practised movement, levered himself to his feet. 'Growing quite proficient,' he said when he saw her smile. 'I was determined that if I came here at all, it had to be without my chair and without Pearce to assist me.' When he gestured her ahead of him into the hall, she opened the front door, stepped back, and watched as he negotiated the step. 'Thank you for agreeing to see me and, more importantly, for hearing me out. You would have been well within your rights to refuse.'

With a smile, she shook her head. 'I wouldn't never have done that.' Having opened the gate for him, she stood aside and watched as he crossed the pavement to where Pearce was waiting to help him into the Wolseley.

'I'll see you tomorrow, then.'

'You will.'

When she stepped back indoors, it was to meet Gwen thundering down the stairs on her way out.

'Who was that?'

Watching her push her feet into her shoes, Clemmie determined to give nothing away. 'Just a friend of mine.'

'Yeah? Oh, and by the way,' Gwen looked back at her to say as she went to leave, 'you still haven't told me what happened with you and Clive. Only, according to him, you blew it.'

'Well, one of us did,' Clemmie said drily as she closed the door smartly behind Gwen's disappearing back. *But turns out the other one of us did exactly the right thing.*

Chapter 17

She did wish she had something nicer to wear. Just lately, it was something she found herself wishing more and more often. This afternoon, she particularly regretted not having had the time to pop into the WVS shop and see whether there was a dress that fitted because, yet again, she was wearing her plain navy-blue skirt and white blouse, and over her arm her one and only jacket. If there was a chance she was going to be invited out like this more often, she was going to need to find ways to expand her wardrobe. Visiting Squadron Leader Dunning – *Andrew* – in the same clothes she wore to work in the shop was lamentable. And that was another thing: how, after all these weeks of addressing him by his rank, was she supposed to start calling him Andrew? Using his first name felt so disrespectful that, when she tried practising aloud, the word refused to leave her tongue. However, since he had requested she use it, she would grasp the nettle and start the moment she saw him. *Hello, Andrew.* Oh, dear Lord, no. It just sounded all wrong.

Looking out through the window of the Wolseley, she realised that by having become so fixated on the matter of his name she had lost all track of where they were and of the route they had taken to get there. The dwellings past which they were now driving were detached and large and terribly smart, each a slightly different design from its neighbours while still featuring the same dark-brown tiled roofs, oversized casement windows, and partly white elevations. Behind low garden walls, each had flower borders and a lawn with a driveway running down the side.

Having turned slowly in through one of the gateways, Pearce was now bringing the motor to a halt alongside a recessed porch, beneath it a pale-green door with a semicircle of coloured glass near the top. While she had no idea what she'd been expecting – indeed, had been so preoccupied with the general turn of events that she hadn't stopped to consider the squadron leader's home at all – she was surprised that it should be so modern.

When Pearce came round to open her door, she got out and cast an incredulous glance along the road. That first time she'd walked along Buckingham Crescent, she'd felt as uncomfortable as she did now, the area having struck her as the sort where girls like her aspired to being taken on as char to the household of a junior manager in a bank. But here the houses were even grander, the roads even more quiet and leafy and, by virtue of being on a rise, even more removed from the grime and the bustle of the city. The centre of Exeter might be barely three miles distant, but she appeared to have arrived in a different world. Standing there in her simple skirt and blouse, she felt as though she'd taken a wrong turning and ended up in the realm of twinsets and pearls. 'Nobby' was the word Pearl would use for it.

Hearing the front door opening, she turned to see Squadron Leader Dunning – *Andrew* – on his crutches. Dressed in grey trousers and a sage-green woollen sweater, he looked somehow softer, certainly more at ease than he had yesterday. She regretted not feeling the same way.

'Clemmie,' he said, resting his weight to one side and smiling warmly. 'You came.'

Had he genuinely thought she might not? Of all the panic-inducing fears that had prevented her from falling asleep last night, declining to come at the last minute hadn't been one of them. She liked him. And if being made to feel like a fish out of water was the price of finding out how he lived, then so be it. If it transpired that their friendship was destined to remain just that, at least after today she could rest in the knowledge that she had conquered her discomfort and based her decision upon the facts.

''Course I came,' she replied to his observation. To her relief, now that she was here her nerves did seem a little less frayed.

'Come in, come in.'

'Thank you.'

When she stepped inside, it was to find herself in a square hallway, off which led several cream-painted doors and a staircase. On the floor were strips of wood laid in a repeating pattern; she had an idea it might be called *parquet*. In contrast to the floral-patterned wallpaper in the hall of Buckingham Crescent, the walls here were painted a pale cream colour, the lightness giving a feeling of space.

'Why don't I show you around?'

She smiled. 'I'd like that.'

'Through here, then,' he said, pushing open a door, 'is the drawing room.'

Entering ahead of him, she swallowed a gasp. On the far wall was a fireplace with a surround of chocolate-brown brick, above it a mirror in a gilt frame; but most eye-catching were the floor-to-ceiling shelves, crammed with books, to either side. In most homes, she imagined the sheer volume of them would overwhelm, but here the bay window, shaped like one half of a hexagon and giving on to the front garden, was flooding the room with light.

She turned to take in the furniture. Arranged in front of the fireplace, looking modern and comfortable, were a small sofa and two matching armchairs. And in the bay was a more upright chair with a footstool. There, she imagined, was where he sat to read something plucked from his vast collection.

'Have you read them all?' she asked, turning to look at him.

'The biographies and the fiction, certainly. But many are reference books that I peruse as the mood takes me, or when I'm in search of a specific fact or idea.'

Against the wall opposite the bay window – in contrast to the others, painted a similar shade to the sweater he was wearing – stood a gramophone cabinet; next to it was a narrow table bearing a photograph in a frame. Instinctively, she went towards it and bent to look. The couple in the picture were young, and from the flower in the man's lapel and the small bouquet in the woman's lap she suspected it to have been taken on their wedding day.

'Are these your parents?'

'On the day they married in 1904, yes. When I was sorting out their house – my father died four years ago – I came across that picture. I couldn't remember seeing it before and was struck by the way they were looking at one another.'

'They seem very much in love,' she said. 'Happy.'

'They do, don't they? Since I could find no other photographs of my mother – well, I'm not sure there were any – I decided to hold on to that one. She died when I was away at school and my memories of her are somewhat vague.'

'Did you enjoy school?' she changed the subject to ask. For all she knew, the loss of his mother was something he preferred not to talk about. The pain from her own mother's passing still had the capacity to floor her at times.

'I did enjoy it, yes. My father's decision to send me to such an academic hothouse was inspired. I thrived there. I absorbed knowledge like a sponge takes in water. But I also excelled at sports. Cricket, especially. I made a great many friends, too.'

While she couldn't picture the sort of school he described, she envied him the fondness of his memories. Given the chance of a proper education, might she have turned out differently? It was impossible to know.

She turned back to the room. 'Do you have any brothers or sisters?'

'I was my parents' only child, and a source of great joy. They'd been married eight or so years before I came along. My father was already forty, my mother well into her thirties. I think they'd almost given up.'

Detecting the wistfulness to his tone, she changed the subject yet again. 'This is a lovely room.'

'Thank you. Why don't I show you the rest of the downstairs?'

The room along the hall to which he directed her next was of similar size. As she went through the door she didn't know where to look first, but the feature that eventually held her attention was the full-length glazed doors and the view they gave over the back garden. Drawn to look out, she went towards them. Directly outside, a small brick-paved area was bordered by a low wall; sloping gently away beyond that, a lawn surrounded by curving flower beds packed with clumps of orange, spires of yellow, and towering blooms of fiery red. At the far end of the lawn stood a couple of trees. Despite the distance, she could make out ripening apples on one of them and what looked to be pears on the other. 'Goodness,' she breathed.

'I'm afraid I can't take credit for anything out there. The garden is Pearce's domain, and one over which I am more than happy to grant him free rein.'

'I've never seen a garden so beautiful.'

'Late summer and early autumn do show it at its best. Although, in the spring, down under the trees, all manner of bulbs poke up through the grass.'

Remembering she was supposed to be looking at the room, she turned back. Immediately behind her, at an angle to the doors, was his piano. 'You play,' she said, remembering him mentioning giving lessons.

'I play and I teach. Obviously, in a house of this size a concert grand is out of the question. But this one does have a lovely tone. If I play for you now, though, you'll never get to see the rest of the house, which I'm sure is of far greater interest.'

In fact, while the house was indeed captivating, at that moment she had a longing to hear him play something. Apart from teachers at school hammering out hymns for assembly or reels for country dancing, she had never met anyone musical.

Crossing the wooden floor back towards the door, she took in the small dining table with four chairs. In the centre of the table stood a low vase crammed with blooms she recognised from the garden.

'Your home is so light and bright,' she said as he beckoned her ahead of him into the hall.

'Precisely the reason I bought it. The house where I grew up had been built towards the end of the last century and was so terribly dark I vowed that when I one day had my own, it would have picture windows and be painted in light colours.'

'It's certainly both.'

'Come through with me and see the kitchen.'

The kitchen left Clemmie speechless: along two walls were cabinets with pale-green doors; there was a modern electric stove; further along, what she recognised as a refrigerator; under the window, a sink with shiny taps. And on the floor were black and white ceramic tiles laid in a chequerboard pattern. To the far side of the window was a partly glazed door, through which she could see a vestibule. The word that leapt to mind was 'stylish'.

'I've never seen anything like it,' she confessed. No sense pretending otherwise; make out she was used to such luxury, and she would quickly be caught out as a liar.

'The kitchen is another of Pearce's domains. If you go through that door, you'll find a bathroom. I had it built there so that during the day I don't have to trouble with the stairs.'

'That's very clever.'

'Tell you what,' Andrew said, not bothering to disguise his eagerness, 'why don't we go back through to the drawing room? I'll ask Pearce to bring us some tea. That way, we can sit and talk. And you can ask me anything you like. Then, before you go, you can have a look around upstairs. How does that sound?'

'Very nice,' she said. And it did. In the short time she'd been there, she'd already forgotten the state of high anxiety into which she'd worked herself beforehand; being with him in his own home made him seem less like a squadron leader and more like an ordinary man – not that he was ordinary in the everyday sense. Anything but.

'You go on through. I'll tell Pearce.'

'All right.'

Back in the drawing room, Clemmie stood looking along the rows of books. On one shelf was a row of spines all displaying the name Dickens. She angled her head to read the titles: *David Copperfield*; *A Tale of Two Cities*; *Oliver Twist*. The last one, she'd heard of.

Hearing voices in the hallway, she went to the sofa and sat down, taking care to arrange her skirt. As she did so, a recollection of that beastly Clive's hand tugging at her knicker leg knotted her stomach in disgust. How sorely she wished now that she'd never given into Gwen's pressing to go on that double date. It had been a hideous ordeal from first to last, and the memory of it still had the capacity to make her nauseous.

'Right, tea and apple cake on its way.'

She buried the memory and smiled. 'Thank you.'

'So, now that you've seen where I live, what are you desperate to ask me?'

'Well…' It felt awful to pry, but it was, after all, why she was there. 'I suppose I'd like to know about Pearce.'

'Of course. Entirely natural that you should wonder. Well, what can I tell you? At the outbreak of the Great War, he lied about his age so as to serve in the medical corps. By his own account, he was fearfully naïve but terribly eager, and saw a great deal of action in France. He had the misfortune to be gassed for his trouble. Back home in England, he tried a variety of jobs connected with medicine but, by his own admission, found it hard to settle. In the meantime, having for my part undergone initial examination and treatment following my accident,

I was sent to Torquay – to an RAF officers' hospital for convalescence and rehabilitation, aimed as much at the mind as the limbs.'

Wondering what this had to do with Pearce, Clemmie nevertheless nodded. 'I see.'

'When the time came for me to be discharged, the doctor overseeing my treatment asked what arrangements I had made for the help I was going to need. I supposed he envisaged it coming from within my family. When I confessed to not having thought about it – and to no longer having relatives to assist me – he told me about someone whose last position had recently come to an end when his elderly employer had suffered a stroke and died.'

Now she saw the connection. 'And that was Pearce.'

'Correct. And talk of the devil…'

When she turned in the direction of the door, she saw Pearce arriving with a tray. 'On the table, sir?'

Andrew nodded. 'Yes please. I'll let you know if we need anything else.'

'Very well, sir.'

Once they were alone, Andrew resumed his explanation. 'Pearce resides with me. He is my cook, my chauffeur, and in charge of my physical exercise. Not being terribly mobile makes me susceptible to all manner of ailments that come from not using my body to the same extent as everyone else. So, I start every morning with an hour of manipulation and stretching. Most evenings, I do a further thirty minutes. The regimen is gruelling, but I submit because I must.'

'I see. So…'

Noticing her hesitation, Andrew bade her go on. 'Whatever it is, please, do ask.'

'Well, does it work – the exercise?'

'In the sense that it probably prevents me seizing up entirely, then yes, it would appear to. Is it likely to cure me?' Pressing his lips together, he shrugged his shoulders. 'Medical opinion is divided. I have days when I truly believe I might one day conquer it, others when I despair, and doubt that my situation will ever be any different. I continue to put myself through the rigours of it because there is always hope.'

'What does Pearce think?' Knowing how he saw the situation might provide her with a broader view from which to draw her own conclusion.

'Pearce is not a man known for making predictions. His view is that it's generally best to just deal with the here and now.'

'Not a bad way to be.'

'It's one of the things I like about him.'

'How long have you lived here?' she asked as the question went through her mind.

'I bought this place after I was discharged from hospital and when, against my wishes, I was pensioned off from the RAF. That would be about eighteen months ago. I had a small sum left to me by my father and, on a monthly basis, my RAF pension pays the bills. My terms with Pearce are that he has bed, board and a small monthly salary. My earnings from piano lessons and tutoring mathematics go into the bank for what I call rainy days.'

'I see.' As she sat there listening, Clemmie realised she hadn't been expecting him to be quite so candid. Clearly, there was nothing he considered out of bounds.

'While by no stretch of the imagination am I wealthy, I *am* comfortable – certainly solvent.'

Comfortable, Clemmie thought, was not having to go out into the yard to use a toilet shared with half a dozen other households. *Comfortable* was not having to empty rat traps every morning or beat the mould from your clothes before you could put them on. But she knew what he meant. What she didn't quite understand from all of this was what he wanted from her. From what he'd said yesterday, she'd got the impression he was after more than just companionship. With Pearce living in, he didn't seem in need of a nursemaid or a daily. But how to find out without making herself look foolish?

'The thing is… what I mean is…' Golly, what garbled nonsense. In a bid to compose herself, she drew a breath and then started afresh. 'What I suppose I don't understand—'

'Is what my expectations are of you? If that doesn't sound too old-fashioned?'

She blushed fiercely. 'Your expectations. Yes, I suppose so.'

'Well, Miss Clemmie Huxford, I have no qualms in admitting that from my very first conversation with you, I was smitten. You are a lovely young lady. You are bright and cheerful, thoughtful and considerate. And did I say pretty?' She blushed more deeply. 'Were it not for my condition, I would long since have asked you to go out with me. At home later that first day, though, I told myself not to be foolish. As I think I said to you yesterday, it was absurd to imagine that a young lady as lovely as you would want anything to do with a husk of a cripple like me. But the more I tried *not* to think about you, the more I found myself doing just that. So, to answer your question, I should very much like you to be a part of my life. That said, clearly, I can't court you – at least, not in the accepted fashion. But, if the idea appeals to you, then I see no reason why we cannot get to know each other by means that suit the two of us. For instance, you can visit me – come to tea or to luncheon. We can read. I can… teach you to play the piano.'

His suggestion was so outlandish that she burst out laughing. 'You'd have your work cut out with that! The patience of all the saints in heaven wouldn't be enough.'

'I beg to differ. But anyway, it occurs to me that perhaps doing such things would give us a far better understanding of each other than could ever be gained from going to the cinema to see a film.' He wasn't wrong there. 'Or by going dancing and for dinners, fun though such things are. And if, in the fullness of time, you came to feel about me as I do about you, then I would ask you to marry me. Part of me longs to ask you this very moment. However, while that would satisfy *my* interests, it would show no respect whatsoever for yours. And I am not that sort of man.'

When he looked back at her, Clemmie struggled to know how to reply. 'I see.'

'Besides, I wouldn't dream of asking you without knowing for certain that you understood what marriage to me would mean. And by that, I don't just mean that I can't take you dancing.'

She smiled. '*There is always hope.*'

'Well, that's true. Safer, though, to assume there will be no miracle, and that not only will I never accompany you in a tango, but I will never be able to give you children, either.'

Sensing that he was waiting for her to react, she tried not to let her expression betray her shock. No children. *No children.* His condition was as bad as that.

'You're certain of it.'

His expression neutral, Andrew nodded. 'To be fair, you never know. But I've been told to view the possibility as extremely unlikely. And although I've left it all the way until now to tell you that part, I have at least done so.'

Exhaling a lengthy sigh, Clemmie lowered her gaze to her lap. A husband and children: for as long as she could remember, those were the two things she'd wanted more than anything else. So, having fallen in love – for she was sure now that's what this inexplicable feeling had to be – with a man who could never give her children, what did she do?

Slowly, she looked back up. 'Thank you. What I mean is, thank you for being honest with me.'

'Despite everything I've said, I feel bound to point out that in all other respects we would have a proper marriage. I'm not looking for a nursemaid. I have Pearce. And it would be my intention that he – or someone like him – remain with us. No, to finish answering your question from earlier, what I wish for, my dearest Clemmie, is love and happiness, and for you to have the same. I wish to cherish you and help you to fulfil your hopes in life. I wish you to have independence of thought and deed because, with that, I believe that together we could do a great deal of good.'

She still didn't know what to say. But for the children – or lack of them – what he was offering sounded idyllic; a life of love and comforts beyond anything she could ever have imagined.

'It all sounds lovely,' she whispered.

'But also, I am sure, a lot to take in.'

'A great deal, yes.'

'Look, how about I ask Pearce to show you around upstairs?'

'I shouldn't want to put him to any trouble.'

'He would be offended if you didn't. As it is, we have neither eaten his cake, nor drunk the tea he made for us.'

With a start, Clemmie stared at the table; how deep in thought must she have been to forget about a slice of cake? 'Then, yes, I should like to finish looking around.'

Standing in the hallway moments later, she tried to follow Pearce's explanation of the workings of a contraption that carried Andrew to the first floor without the need for him to climb the stairs.

'The first one of these machines was made about twenty years ago, in America,' he told her. The device in front of them comprised a folding seat and a footrest mounted upon a rail running up the staircase. 'This button switches on the motor and this lever carries the squadron leader to the top of the stairs and back down again.'

'That's real clever,' she said. 'I never knew such a thing.'

'Few people do.' When she smiled, and he smiled back, the crinkling of his eyes gave him a kindly warmth. As she followed him past the contraption up to the first floor, she wondered what he thought of her. She could wholly forgive him for thinking, heaven forbid, that she was a gold digger – a term she'd gleaned from listening to Pearl talking about a film. 'This is the bathroom on this floor,' he said.

When he opened the door, she peered in to see a bath, lavatory, washbasin, and the same pattern of black and white tiles on the floor as in the kitchen. The walls were tiled in plain white. As a room it was modern and clinical. Easy to keep clean. Feeling the expectation upon her to comment, she said, 'Very nice.'

'And this is the squadron leader's bedroom.'

When Pearce opened the door this time, she hung back. 'Are you sure he would want me to look?'

'He specifically asked that I show you everywhere. And if he is comfortable with that, you need not feel awkward.'

With a nod, she approached the doorway. Longer than it was wide, the room looked out over the front garden and had the same-shaped bay window as downstairs. In it stood an upright armchair identical to the one she had seen in the drawing room. There was also a single bed, to one side of it a small circular table bearing a lamp, and in the corner a tallboy. To the left of the bed was a metal-framed trestle with a padded top, where she supposed he underwent his treatment. All told, the room was plain and masculine.

'Thank you,' she said, and took a step backwards.

'It might seem spartan,' Pearce said, his comment causing her to wonder whether it might be wise to practise better concealing her thoughts. 'But there can be nothing in this room that might cause the squadron leader to trip and fall. No rugs, no trailing bedspread. No ornamentation.'

Was that a warning against interfering, she wondered? Was he telling her that any attempt to introduce what she'd heard referred to somewhere as *a feminine touch* would be unwelcome?

'I understand.'

'Miss Huxford, forgive me for asking, but what do you know of paraplegia?'

Since she would prefer not to show her ignorance and admit that, before today, she had never heard the word, she hesitated. But then a realisation dawned: here was her chance to get answers to the questions she couldn't ask Andrew himself; here was an opportunity she mustn't let pass simply for fear of looking stupid.

'Only the little bit Squadron Leader Dunning has told me,' she said with that in mind. When she went on to add an apologetic smile, she realised something else; this had to be why Andrew had encouraged her to come up here with Pearce in the first place – to learn more about his condition without having to ask him directly.

'Then perhaps it would help you to know that suffering an injury to one's spine results in rather more than just a lack of feeling in one's legs. In Squadron Leader Dunning's case, by not having total loss the damage to his spine is termed "partial". But don't let that mislead you. The impact of his crash resulted in impairment not only to his legs, but to other functions below the point of damage.'

Reminding herself that now was not the time for squeamishness, Clemmie forced herself to draw gentle breaths. 'I see.'

'For a person's limbs and organs to function, the brain must be able to send messages to them via the spine.'

It was something she hadn't realised. 'Right.'

'In the squadron leader's case, faint messages do get through. Some days more than others. Unfortunately, there can be no telling in advance how he will fare at any particular moment.'

'No, I've seen that.'

'Which is why it is critical that the squadron leader is active. For a start, to avoid withering his muscles must be exercised. In addition, his joints must be manipulated and put to as much use as much as possible in order to prevent osteoporosis.'

When he looked at her as though to check that she understood, she forced herself to be honest. 'I don't know what that is.'

'It's a term for weakening of the bones.'

'Bones. I see.'

'The squadron leader must also take medication to ward off infection, particularly genito-urinary complications. Although seemingly unrelated, and rarely catastrophic in an otherwise fit human body, in the squadron leader's case an infection of that sort could prove fatal. Thankfully, after the last war, valuable research resulted in new medication that reduces the possibility.'

'But his spine itself,' Clemmie ventured. 'It won't get better?'

'Impossible to say with any certainty. As you have seen for yourself, some days he has reasonable mobility, other days much less.'

It had been daft to ask, really; Pearce's assessment had been unlikely to differ from Andrew's own. 'I see.'

'Perhaps, given the research being undertaken in this area of medicine, new treatments will come along. Squadron Leader Dunning is still a young man, and otherwise healthy. But were you to ask me the odds of him making a full recovery with the treatments we have now, I would be forced to say I think it improbable.'

Improbable. While the prognosis was stark, she was grateful for Pearce's directness. 'Thank you,' she said. 'Always best to know how things stand.'

'Indeed. Would you like to finish looking around?'

Her mind still struggling with all she'd just learned, Clemmie glanced out through the door to the landing. Would she? Had anything she'd just learned changed how she felt about Andrew?

'Yes please. If that's all right.'

'Then this next room,' Pearce said, moving past her to open a door further along the landing, 'is spare at the moment.'

Spare at the moment. Spare until it became hers, she supposed, were things to progress that far.

The room in question, Clemmie noted as she went in to look around, was situated above the porch. It contained a single bed with small sets of drawers to either side and a modest wardrobe against the wall opposite the window. Since the room was unused, and she didn't feel she was intruding, she went to look out. The houses and their gardens on the other side of the road were neat and well cared for. Even when measured against Buckingham Crescent, it really did feel like another world. But, ignoring for a moment the implications of what she'd just learned about Andrew's health, was it a world into which she would ever fit? Surely the women behind those sparkling picture windows across the road were far more suited to this manner of living than she would ever be. Would she be accepted by them, or would her arrival here raise eyebrows? Would Andrew expect her to make friends with them or keep her distance?

Feeling how the weight of so many considerations was making her head pound, she lowered her shoulders and tried not to stand quite so stiffly. Then she directed her attention back to the little room. In size, it was more than three times the one she had in Buckingham Crescent, which, in itself, was the nicest place she had ever slept. But if she and Andrew married, how would she feel about never sharing his bed? How would she feel when, every night, she retired to this little room on her own? Did such an arrangement even constitute a proper marriage? Clearly, there was more to being wed than simply sharing a bed – and how much easier to be a wife in comfortable surroundings like these? In many ways, she would be mad to turn down the chance to make this her home, alongside a husband who wanted her to live life according to her own ambitions, and who would support her in the achieving of them. *I wish you to have independence of thought and deed because, with that, I believe that together we could do a great deal of good.* Considered in isolation, it sounded perfect. Except that it wasn't, was it? She might not know much about love and marriage – or even about men – but she did know that loving someone came with a physical longing; indeed, when she was with him, she'd already felt it stirring. And what woman, with a husband she loved, didn't want to have his children?

She glanced about the room. Was the price to pay for all this comfort and love just too great?

'Thank you,' she said to Pearce, purposely avoiding his eyes as she returned to the landing.

'You're welcome to see my room as well.'

'No,' she said. 'You're very kind to offer but that wouldn't be right.'

When she arrived back downstairs, and Pearce had gone out to start the car, Andrew turned to her and smiled. 'Did you see all that you needed to?'

'I think so.'

'Any questions you would like to ask me?'

She smiled. 'Plenty. But I have a lot to think about before I'm ready to ask them.'

'Naturally. Then I promise not to pester you while you reflect.'

'Thank you.'

'Thank *you* for coming. Would you like me to accompany you home? It would be no trouble.'

Her feelings all over the place, she shook her head. 'No. But thank you.'

'I shall invite you again soon. In the meantime, promise me you'll think about what I've said.'

'I will.' In truth, she would think about little else.

'And next time you come, we mustn't forget to eat.'

To her surprise, the smile on her lips became a light laugh. 'No. That wouldn't do at all.'

As she rode in the rear of the Wolseley back to Buckingham Crescent, it took all of her determination not to cry. How on earth was she supposed to choose between two things that came with such opposite and far-reaching implications? How on earth was she supposed to decide between what would undoubtedly be a wonderful life with a caring man, or having the children of whom she had always dreamed?

Quite simply, she couldn't. The choice before her was impossible. And completely beyond her to make.

Chapter 18

Clemmie sighed. She did so hate lying. But in this instance she had to put herself first. With all that had been happening lately, she'd forgotten she'd written to her sister about Cedric, and the envelope waiting for her when she'd returned from visiting Andrew had taken her by surprise – even more so her sister's reference to 'your quandary'.

Reaching into the pocket of her shop apron, she pulled out May's letter and reread the paragraph in question.

> *I, too, often wish we could talk. But if you like, and if you could find a way to do so, would you care to come for a visit? If you were here for a couple of days, the distance might help you see your quandary in a different light. If nothing else, we could certainly have a good old chat!*

In some ways, the timing of May's reply couldn't have been better: when she'd written to her, the quandary she'd been stewing over had concerned Cedric and his apparent claims for war damage to those properties in Magdalen Street. But now she had a far greater dilemma in the form of Andrew and his proposal. In that regard, a healthy dollop of May's common sense could only help. She'd *sort of* broached the subject with Miss Evercott but, ultimately, had shied away from discussing the more intimate aspects.

'You should *absolutely* go and see your sister,' Dorothy had said when Clemmie had mentioned May's invitation. 'If nothing else, there is surely no one who knows you better. I also happen to think she's right about the perspective to be had from the gaining of distance.'

The problem was, having decided to accept May's offer, she now had to tell Mr Narramore she needed two days off. And he wasn't going to be happy. He'd been savage cross about something these last few days as it was.

Hearing his weighty tread on the stairs, she stuffed May's letter back into its envelope and thrust it into her pocket.

'Morning,' she said lightly as her employer came through the door and stood looking about.

'Huh.'

His mood didn't bode well.

'Um, Mr Narramore…' Unable to face him directly, she lowered the line of her eyes to his chest; one of his buttons had popped undone and she could see pale flesh. 'I'm afraid I need to take a bit of time off. My sister is unwell. She lives out near Crediton and there's no one there to look after her. I only need two days. And only just this once.'

When she raised her head to gauge his response, she was horrified to see his face screwed up in disbelief.

'Come again?'

Had he genuinely not heard her? Given they were the only two people in the shop, and standing barely three feet apart, it seemed unlikely. Perhaps he just wanted to put her through the agony of having to ask twice.

'I'm afraid I need two days off.'

Cedric's expression hardened. 'Ain't convenient. Mrs Narramore's… gone up her mother's.'

Up her mother's? That couldn't be right: by Mrs Narramore's own telling, her mother was dead and had been for some years. More importantly, though, now he'd denied her request, what would she do? In her eagerness to see May, she'd never considered that he would refuse.

'Well, I really do need to go.'

'Do you, indeed? Ungrateful little cow, aren't you?'

His language made her flinch and she took a step away from him. The edge of the counter pressed into her back. If she was going to withdraw her request, now would be a good moment to do so.

'Ordinarily, I wouldn't ask. But I really do need to go. Like I said just now, my sister—'

'Then you better ask yourself just *how* bad your need really is.' When he closed the gap between them to tower over her, she could see the perspiration beading his top lip. 'Because I don't take kindly to being mucked about by anyone, but 'specially not by some strip of a schoolgirl. So, tell me, what's more important – this job, or your sister and her sniffles?'

Turning sharply from the rankness of his breath, she swallowed hard. 'Both of those are important.'

'And yet,' he said, lowering his eyes to within an inch of her own, 'only one of them pays you a wage. So, let me ask you again. What's it to be? Your supposedly poorly sister, or the wage that keeps a roof over your head and the food in your mouth?'

He was going to make her choose? When he knew that was unfair? All she wanted was two miserable days. She wasn't asking for a fortnight to go on a jaunt to the seaside. Given that he was up to no good, the man had a real nerve.

'Then I'm afraid it's my sister.'

Her response clearly not what he'd been expecting, Cedric glowered down at her, his arm twitching by his side as though he was minded to strike her. Rooted to the spot, she held her breath; only when he backed away did she breathe out.

'You certain about that?'

She gave the merest of nods. 'I am.'

'Then give me back my apron, walk out that door, and don't come back. I will not tolerate disloyalty. I gave you the chance to change your mind, so on your head be it. Go on. I will not be messed about.'

Golly, he was a bull-headed man. Nevertheless, unable to see an alternative, she untied the strings, lifted the apron over her head, folded it neatly and placed it next to the till. Stepping around him, she reached to the shelf for her handbag. Then, careful to avoid looking in his direction – she would not give him the satisfaction of seeing he'd made her cry – she raised the flap of the counter to leave.

A couple of paces across the shop, though, the temptation was too great, and with a sniff she turned back. 'All I needed was two days.'

Was that a flicker of regret that crossed his face?

'Since you're not working your notice,' he said hotly, 'you can forget your week in hand. Consider it the cost of letting me down.'

Having closed the shop door behind her, Clemmie stood on the pavement. While she might have come off worse, at least she still had her pride. She might eventually have the last laugh too because, first thing this morning, she'd seen a letter on the desk from the War Damage Commission. It was, it stated, *acknowledgement of your application for compensation in respect of losses incurred in the destruction of numbers 1 to 6 Hastings Terrace, properties in your ownership at the time of loss.*

So, yes, if anyone was going to pay a price, she was going to do everything within her power to make sure it was him.

–

'You going somewhere?'

Clemmie looked up to see Gwen leaning in the doorway and smiled. 'Going to see May for a couple of days.'

'May. That the older one?'

From where she was folding her sweater, Clemmie nodded. 'That's right. She's a housekeeper up near Crediton. They've had a fire on the farm and she's a bit down in the dumps, so I thought—'

'A fire? What, like from an incendiary, you mean?'

Clemmie shook her head. 'No, apparently one of the barns went up. She didn't say how.' When she turned to fetch a spare pair of knickers from the drawer, she could feel Gwen watching her. 'You all right?' she asked, turning back.

'Not really.'

Unable to miss the despair in Gwen's tone, Clemmie patted the bedspread and sat down. 'Want to tell me what's up?' In her heart, she hoped Jimmy hadn't thrown Gwen over for someone else. He might not have been the type of man she would have gone for herself, but she could see clear enough why Gwen had.

'End of next week, I'll be moving out.'

'Moving out? Where?'

When Gwen landed heavily beside her, Clemmie studied her expression. The pink blotches on her cheeks and the red rims of her eyes suggested she'd been crying – and recently, too. But why would Gwen be moving out? Where did *she* suddenly have to go?

'I'm expecting.'

'*A baby?*' As the words left her lips, Clemmie rued her stupidity. What else could Gwen possibly have meant?

'Yup. I'm expecting a baby.'

Desperate to avoid putting her foot in it, Clemmie tried to work out how long Gwen and Jimmy had been dating. If she remembered correctly, she'd started talking about him not long after she, Clemmie, had come to live there, which would make it around the end of May – three and a half months ago. 'And… is it Jimmy's?'

'Better bloody be. When I missed the third time, I went to see a doctor. That's how I'm sure.'

Golly. Gwen was deep in it now. 'So—'

'An' to save you the trouble of asking, it's his nan I'm going to live with.'

'Oh. So—'

'Jimmy went nuts. And when he told his mum, she said he needn't think I was going there to live. Thank God for his nan.'

'So, are you going to get married?'

'It's either that or the home for unmarried mothers. But *they'll* make me give the baby up. It's what they do. And if anyone thinks I'm going through the next six months of misery just to have some disapproving old cow take it off me at the end and hand it over to some stranger, they've another thing coming. Far as I'm concerned, Jimmy's been the one since the moment I set eyes on him.'

'I know.'

'I always joked I'd do anything to marry him. But not this…'

'No.'

'Worst of it is, when I told him, first thing he did was say he'd been thinking he might join up.'

'Join up? But I thought being on the railway put him in a reserved occupation?'

'It does.'

'So, he'd do the decent thing and marry you… but then up and leave?' Not only was Clemmie aghast, she was indignant on Gwen's behalf.

'I asked him, straight up. I said to him, "Why would you do that? With a baby on the way?"'

'What did he say?'

'Nothing. He just shrugged. And now I'm left thinking though he might do the right thing, he'll clear off straight after and that's the last I'll ever see of him.'

'Probably just the shock,' Clemmie observed. It was the only thing she could come up with that might go some way to explaining the man's behaviour.

'That's what Miss Evercott said.'

'You *told* her?'

Gwen nodded. 'Had to. She's been good to me. She pointed out how I need to bear in mind that while I'd already had some time for the news to sink in, the first Jimmy knew of it was the moment I told him… which was bound to have thrown him into a panic. She also said she's sure we'll work things out. But I don't know so much.'

'Are you seeing him tonight?'

With a shake of her head, Gwen pulled a balled-up handkerchief from the sleeve of her shirt and blew her nose. 'No. Anyway, thanks for not getting all preachy—'

'I wouldn't ever do that.'

'You'd be surprised how many folk will. And though it might be too late for me, promise you'll learn from my mistake. Don't go taking chances.'

While Clemmie wasn't entirely sure what constituted *taking chances*, the kindest thing seemed to tell Gwen what she wanted to hear.

'Promise,' she said, and patted Gwen's hand. 'And though I've only met Jimmy the once, I remember thinking how he seemed real taken with you.'

'I thought so too.'

'And for certain Miss Evercott is right to say the two of you will get along just fine – once everything settles down. If it's what you want, then it's down to the two of you to make a go of it.'

'Easily said…'

Gwen had a point; trite sayings helped no one. 'Mm.'

'…but now he's got no choice in the matter, I'm none too sure.'

'No.'

'Anyhow, I hope you have a nice time at your sister's.'

'Thanks. And I'll see you when I get back.'

Yes, Clemmie thought as she watched Gwen wander disconsolately back along the landing, for a relationship between two people to work it had to be what both of them wanted: not what one of them wanted and the other only wanted in part. It had to be the wish of both, completely and wholly. And therein lay her own dilemma: while Gwen wanted Jimmy but didn't want a baby – at least, not in the manner it had come about – she was going to have one anyway. And while she, Clemmie, longed in due course for several, she had fallen in love with a man unable to give her any. And no matter how creatively she tried to find an answer to the problem, she knew in her heart that it had to be one or the other: Andrew or children. And already, the prospect of having to choose was breaking her heart.

Chapter 19

Golly, May looked bright and healthy. Gone was the deep furrow between her brows, and in place of the usual dull greyness to her complexion was a golden summer glow. Clearly, when she'd written in her letters that life in the countryside suited her, she hadn't been exaggerating.

Blinking back tears of relief, Clemmie moved to wrap her sister in a warm hug. 'Oh, my goodness, May!' Hearing a sniff, she guessed May was similarly overcome. 'Lovely to see you.'

'Lovely to see *you*, too. Look at you, all… different.'

'Different?' Clemmie frowned and released May from their hug. 'I can't think how.'

'I suppose you just look real grown up.'

Detecting from May's expression that she was struggling to pin down what it was about her that had changed, Clemmie smiled. Her skirt, her blouse and her coat had all come from the WVS shop; one of the perks of volunteering on a regular basis was having first pick of the donations – in exchange, of course, for paying the proper price. By contrast, she'd had to use five coupons to get her neat little pair of low-heeled shoes: five coupons from the newly reduced annual allowance of just sixty. May's face, though, made it worthwhile: the scrimping and saving to make herself look a bit less schoolgirlish was paying off. Moreover, her smartened-up appearance should reassure

May that she was taking care of herself. That there was someone else for whom she also had the urge to dress smartly was a fact that, for the moment, she would keep to herself.

'About time I looked grown up,' she said. 'I'm not *so* far off nineteen.'

'I suppose that's what I forget. I hope you remembered to bring some old clothes to work in.'

Clemmie shrugged; finding clothes that she didn't mind getting dirty had been more problematic than getting new ones.

'Haven't really got any. But I did bring my old lace-ups. Though were it not for Miss Evercott, I doubt I would have thought to.'

'Never mind. I'll lend you a housecoat or something.'

'Thanks.' May always had been practical. And golly, it was good to see her.

'Come on, then, it's this way to Fair Maids.'

'Lead on.'

'While I was waiting for you to arrive,' May began as they started across the village green towards the railway bridge, 'I found myself struggling to believe it's not even four months since I arrived here. It feels so very much longer.'

Despite the two of them having never, until four months ago, spent a single night apart, it felt the same to Clemmie; where there had once been familiarity, there now seemed to be reserve. She supposed it was only to be expected; in those four months, her own way of looking at life had changed beyond all recognition. Why shouldn't the same be true for May?

'Waking up this morning,' she said, anxious for the stiffness between them to be gone, 'I thought the same thing. And though I don't know why, I worried how we'd pick up again, you know, after so long apart.'

May's reply was accompanied by a sheepish grin. 'Same here.'

At least it wasn't just her, then. 'I was sorry to hear about Mr Beer.' While the subject might be a difficult one, she felt it only proper to offer condolences. She could only imagine how distressing it must have been for May to lose her employer in a fire. 'Must have been dreadful hard for you.'

'It was,' her sister said softly. 'Still is, truth to tell.'

What was it May had written in her last letter about the situation – that she was still waiting to hear whether Fair Maids Farm was to be sold and, thus, to learn of her own fate? Clemmie knew from experience that to live from one day to the next amid such uncertainty was deeply unsettling.

'Still no word what's to happen to the farm?' she asked as they continued along the lane.

Beside her, May shook her head. 'Not yet. Though I can't imagine it'll be too much longer now. The solicitor has finally sorted out Mr Beer's money… and his accounts, so at least me an' Bonnie are being paid proper again.'

To Clemmie, the news sounded encouraging. 'That's something.'

But when May went on to explain about having been visited by War Ags – whatever they were – Clemmie found her mind wandering back to her own problems. It wasn't that she had no interest in May's situation, it was just that when she'd first written to her about being in a quandary, her concern had centred upon Cedric Narramore and his claims to the War Damages Commission for compensation. Since then, more pressing matters had been exercising her, in the shape of Andrew. Now she was here, though, she felt disinclined to talk about him. Perhaps, once she and May had caught up with all their other news, she would feel differently. There was plenty of time; she was here until Sunday.

Once May had shown her around the peculiar little farmhouse and the few outbuildings to have escaped the fire, Clemmie found herself furnished with a set of borrowed overalls and a pair of wellington boots. She was introduced to Bonnie, the land girl, and had accompanied the pair of them out to a field where seemingly thousands of knee-high plants were growing in long rows. Apparently they were beetroot, and now was the time to get them out of the ground.

'*All* of them?' she had asked May, her heart sinking at the scale of the task ahead of them. 'Just the three of us?'

'All of them.'

'In which case,' she had said with a sigh, 'hadn't we best get stuck in?'

To her surprise, as the day wore on, Clemmie found working outdoors soothing: in a nearby copse, the trees kept up a gentle shushing in the breeze; on her arms and face she could feel the warmth from the autumn sunshine; following the three of them across the field, a dozen or so starlings whistled and chattered as they pecked about in the bare earth. Moreover, the rhythmical nature of repeatedly pulling beets and tossing them into crates appeared to be stilling the clamour in her brain. To her surprise, she was beginning to relax.

She glanced across to May. To see her carrying on with such knowledge and authority was nothing short of astonishing. Having given little thought to her sister's life here, she could scarcely believe this was the same young woman who, after nine hours cleaning at the Sovereign Hotel each day, had come grumbling through the door every teatime on the verge of collapse.

'What do you think, Bonnie?' she heard her sister enquire when they all reached the end of yet another row. 'Will we be done for the chap coming to collect them at six?'

'Just about, I reckon.'

'Then how about we award ourselves a moment's break?'

'You won't catch *me* arguing.'

'Tell me,' May said once the three of them were perched on upturned crates, sipping tea poured into cups from a flask. 'What's it like in town now?'

Trying to picture the centre of Exeter, Clemmie shrugged. 'Not so very different really. The main streets have been cleared of rubble, and so some of the buses are back and running on their old routes again. But to be honest, I don't go in all that often and so I don't really know. The WVS centres have all been moved further out, and we're not supposed to travel unless we have to. *Is your journey really necessary?* and all that.'

'Mm.'

'But when I do go in,' Clemmie picked up again when, before long, they were wandering back towards the beet-root, 'it still seems strange, even now, not to be living there any more – not to be in the thick of all that bustle and commotion… not to be among all those people we knew like family.' *Family.* Was this her chance to introduce Andrew? No, not here. Not with Bonnie working alongside them, nor with May anxious to get the harvest finished. But maybe later.

'Strange for all of us,' May remarked. 'Maybe more so for you, though, what with you still being close by.'

'I heard the other day that Mrs Tuckett ended up going to her son's down near Topsham. She didn't want to – kicked up a right fuss, apparently – and her son and his wife didn't want to have her. But there was nowhere else for her to go.'

'Suppose not.'

Mentioning Mrs Tuckett – the old dear who had lived upstairs – turned Clemmie's thoughts to Albert Terrace, the contrast between the quiet normality here and the devastation in the city brought starkly into focus. 'You know, sometimes in my mind I still see pictures of what happened that night. They come without the least warning. I dream about it now and again, too.'

May looked across at her. 'So do I.'

'Wake up in a real panic sometimes. But then I suppose it would be odd if we didn't – dream about it, I mean. All that noise. All that trembling with fear.' The details of that night back in her mind, she recalled afresh the eerie whistling of the bombs as they dropped from the sky; the terrifying rumbling through the earth as they hit their targets; the horror of not knowing whether the next one – and those that would surely come after it – would fall wide of their shelter or be a direct hit.

'I shouldn't think we're ever likely to forget it.'

Eventually, when six chimes of a church clock drifted through the early evening stillness and the beet field was just an expanse of bare soil, Clemmie was sent back to the farmhouse to get cleaned up. But it wasn't until dusk, when the three of them had prepared and eaten a light supper and cleared away afterwards, that she and May were finally able to sit down together in the farmhouse's tiny parlour. Now was the moment, Clemmie realised, when May would expect her to disclose the reason behind her rather vague letter.

'Heavens above,' she groaned, still wondering how to broach the matter even as they were settling themselves into the two threadbare chairs in front of the fireplace. 'I ache even just sitting here.'

May's grin was an apologetic one. 'It's my fault. It was mean of me to put you to work like you were from the land club.'

Regretting that her insides felt so tightly knotted with apprehension, Clemmie waved away her sister's apology. 'Don't be daft. It was fun.'

'So,' May said. Clemmie held her breath. *Here it comes.* 'What's this quandary you wrote of in your letter?'

For a moment, the question hung awkwardly. Having discovered just how much May had on her own plate with matters here on the farm, to burden her further by telling her about Andrew felt selfish; with May not even knowing Andrew existed, to suddenly hear that he'd as good as proposed marriage would surely cause her all sorts of alarm. In her sister's shoes, she would probably react in the same way. For a start, May was bound to be bothered by his age. Then there was his paraplegia, not to mention the fact that, on the surface at least, they appeared to know very little about one another. And all of that was before they got to the other matter; the one that meant they wouldn't be able to have children. To May, that would surely seem the most troubling part of all.

Aware that she still hadn't answered her sister's question, Clemmie sighed. No, no matter how badly she wanted May's advice about Andrew, this wasn't the time to seek it. Her sister's world had been turned upside down in what was surely the cruellest way imaginable: a careless fire had destroyed part of the farm; her employer had died; her home and her livelihood were in peril. So, no, she couldn't have it on her conscience to add to her sister's burden.

Instead, she drew a breath and launched into an explanation of what she had uncovered about Mr Narramore, and what she supposed him to be up to.

'You can't just turn a blind eye,' May remarked when Clemmie had finished relaying the details. Hauling herself more upright in the other of the two rather lumpy armchairs, she went on, 'Wartime or no, if you don't tell the authorities then you're as bad as he is.'

It was nothing the passage of time and Clemmie's own conscience hadn't already told her. 'I know.'

'It's not as though you have to fear losing your job, not now he doesn't want you to go back.'

'No.'

'So, I don't see as you've a choice.'

But to Clemmie, the situation wasn't that straightforward. 'It's just that if I'm right, the upshot will be serious. He could go to prison, lose his shop. And Mrs Narramore depends on that, too.'

May's reply when it came was typically matter of fact. 'Then he should have thought of that before getting involved. From what you've told me, it seems clear he's stealing. Not only money from the government, but also from whomever really owned them houses. And if that's true, then prison is where he should be. There's not a shred of doubt in my mind.'

May was right; put like that, the facts appeared cut and dried. But her sister wasn't the one who had to report him; it would hardly be difficult for Cedric to guess who had snitched on him. Indeed, now that he'd sacked her he would probably assume she'd done it to get back at him. And then there was Jean Bodley; there was more to her than met the eye, as well. In fact, it wouldn't surprise her if the two of them were somehow in cahoots. That said, May was still right: Mr Narramore couldn't be allowed to get away with it. Even if all he got was a slap on the wrist, she would at least be able to rest easy knowing his scheme had been thwarted.

'You're right,' she said wearily. 'When I go home, I'll tell Miss Evercott. She'll know what to do.'

'Good. And what are you going to do for work? Will your Miss Evercott let you keep your room until you find a new job?'

Clemmie nodded. 'When I told her what had happened, she said not to worry about rent until I get settled again. She's incredibly thoughtful and generous like that.'

'She must be.'

'Though I'll admit I've not the least idea where to even start looking. It was hard enough last time. And I surely don't relish going to the Labour Exchange.'

'Can't say as I blame you. Look, why not give yourself a week? That way, if you find a job under your own steam the Labour Exchange need never know. And if it's in a grocer's or suchlike, they won't hassle you about war work anyway. Being employed in food is as good as being exempt.'

'I suppose.'

'It's what I'd do in your shoes.'

'Mm.'

Unfortunately, the shift in conversation to the matter of employment did nothing to ease Clemmie's guilt about keeping May in the dark over Andrew; after all, if in the fullness of time she did agree to marry him, then, as she understood it, she wouldn't be expected to register for war work anyway. Nor would she require a wage. But even if she did decide to come clean with May, where would she start? She could hardly just blurt out that a nice man she had met through a WVS committee had suggested they get married. Faced with that bombshell, how could May do anything other than panic and warn her against it? Besides, all she and Andrew had agreed for now was that they would get to know one another – which they were doing. She supposed there was even an argument to be made that, given the ramifications of the decision ahead of her, she should make up her own mind and not be swayed by anyone else, even May.

Raising her head, she looked across at the dim outline of her sister seated in the other chair. Not doing anything rash seemed good advice for both of them; haste, as their mother always used to warn, was the enemy of good judgement. And despite her sister not knowing what was going to happen to the farm now that the owner had died – apparently without an obvious heir – she still thought May shouldn't jump to the conclusion that once the place was sold, her position would come to an end. Returning to Exeter, when she otherwise seemed so happy here, wasn't a step she thought May should take lightly – certainly not before she knew what was to happen. In addition, unless she was mistaken, there was something going on between May and that chap Dan from the next farm over. *He looks nice*, she'd remarked to May when he'd come up to the fence to talk about something. *He is nice*, her sister had said. It was something she sensed May was choosing to keep close to her chest. So, yes, her sister could do without the added burden of learning about Andrew and his proposal. Tonight at least, she would say nothing. She would sleep on it and see how she felt in the morning.

Unsurprisingly, daylight found her just as uncertain, the morning after that, the same. And when, far too soon, it was time for her to head back to Exeter, despite having gone over and over the matter in her head and convinced herself that keeping quiet about Andrew was for the best, she still felt riddled with guilt: her sister would be so cross if she knew what she was keeping from her. She was glad she'd come to see her, of course she was, and especially to see her looking so well. But that didn't quell her regret at being unable to confide in her. Did that tell her something about the decision ahead of her? If only.

'You know, Clemmie,' May said, her voice breaking into her sister's ruminations as the two of them stood in the village, waiting for the bus to take Clemmie back to Exeter, 'Mum would be real proud of the way you've turned out.'

Feeling a lump hardening in her throat, and forced to wonder at the truth of her sister's assertion, Clemmie reached to give her sister a hug. 'Do you mean that?'

'I do.'

'*I* think she'd be proud of *you*. Unable to believe her eyes, happen, but jolly proud all the same.' May living on a farm? Mum would never have believed it.

'Mm. Well, anyway, look, here comes your bus.'

Bending to pick up her bags, Clemmie raised a smile. 'Thanks for the apples. And the beetroot.'

'When you eat it, you'll be able to picture pulling it out of the dirt.'

'I will. Though if there was a way to keep one as a trophy, I'd do that too.' With the bus pulling up alongside them, she hurried on, 'Promise me you'll write soon. The moment there's news about what's to happen with the farm, I want to know.'

'You make sure an' write too,' May said as she leaned to kiss her sister's cheek. Her smile, Clemmie couldn't help thinking, was rather a watery one. 'And just be careful.'

'I will. You, too.'

For reasons Clemmie could only attribute to guilt, the bus ride back to Exeter seemed to take far longer than the one that had brought her there. *Had* she missed an opportunity to help resolve her dilemma over Andrew? Or had she been right to keep quiet and work things out for herself? At least by deciding what to do about Cedric she'd soon have *that* load off her mind. As for the other thing, well, all she knew as she sat watching the green of the countryside trundle past was that she was no further forward in her thinking now than she had been seventy-two hours earlier. And for that, she had only herself to blame.

Chapter 20

'You're certain.'

'I am.'

'I'm not asking because I doubt your word – far from it. It's just that if we're going to do something about it, the day might come when you have to swear upon oath as to what you saw.'

Deeply unsettled by the prospect, but reassured by Dorothy's thoroughness in the matter, Clemmie nodded. With time to reflect after her visit to May, she was determined not to let Cedric Narramore profit from his scheme, which was why, this morning, she had chosen to confide in her landlady. 'Though I hope it won't come to that, yes, I was able to read what the forms were for, and also what Mr Narramore had written on them.'

'And you're certain the address was for the terrace where your friend lived – where she led you to believe the rightful owner also resided? You couldn't be mistaken about that?'

Clemmie shook her head. 'She wasn't a proper friend, but we did see each other at school every day. And yes, it's the same place. I'm sure of it.'

'Very well. Then I applaud your desire to act. Far too many people have come to see this war as an opportunity to make money. But while profiteering from the odd item of black-market goods is one thing, committing fraud is a far more serious crime.'

'Yes.'

'I'll have a word with Inspector Lethbridge,' Dorothy said, removing her glasses and folding them up. Looking about for her spectacle case, she spotted it on the windowsill and went to put them away. 'Without mentioning names, I will ask his advice on how to proceed. This evening, I will tell you what he says.'

'Thank you.'

'So, what are your plans for today?'

It was a good question. With no work to go to, her day – indeed, the whole of the week now stretching ahead of her – felt to have lost much of its purpose. 'I thought this morning I'd strip the beds and catch up with the laundry.'

'Oh, would you?' Dorothy scanned the room, spotted her handbag and went to pick it up. 'That would be terrifically helpful.'

'´Course.'

'And how about, with Gwen gone – silly girl, I knew it would end in tears – you move your things into her old room? It's a good deal larger than your little one.'

Uncertain she wanted Gwen's room, Clemmie nevertheless responded with a grateful smile. 'I'll think about it. I'll strip Gwen's bed and give the room a good airing anyway.'

'All right. Well then, since you're not on the rota for the shop today, I shall see you this evening.'

'You will, yes.'

The moment she heard the latch on the front door click, Clemmie pulled out a chair from under the kitchen table and sank onto it. Telling Miss Evercott about Mr Narramore was a huge weight off her mind; whatever happened now was out of her hands. If she did have to go the police and talk to them, she would worry about it when the time came. No sense meeting trouble halfway. She had plenty of other concerns waiting to fill the gap left by *that* worry. For a start, she'd lost her job. And then there was this: reaching into the pocket of her skirt, she pulled out a small ivory-coloured envelope she guessed had been delivered by Pearce. From within it, she withdrew a stiff little card. Embossed at the top was Andrew's address. Beneath it was his handwriting, a flurry of swooping curves. The style of it made her think of a bird in flight.

Laughing at her fancifulness, she reread his message.

> My dearest Clemmie,
>   I trust this note finds you well and that you had an enjoyable visit with your sister. Since I should very much like to see you and hear all about it, would you like to come for lunch with me on Monday? Just a bite to eat, here, at home. There is no need to go to the bother of confirming. Just arrive when it suits you.
>   With warmest wishes, and hoping you'll come,
>   Andrew

In many respects, especially since she was now jobless, Andrew was the answer to her prayers; certainly, any woman harbouring even the slightest mercenary streak would think so. But getting married simply to avoid having to find another job struck her as pitiful. Girls frequently married for less – and for worse, Gwen Brewer being a case in point. And she couldn't deny that having been raised in Albert Terrace, she would be pushed to do better: Andrew Dunning was nice to look at; he owned his own home – as well as a motorcar, even if he couldn't drive it himself. He was mature and settled, hardly likely to be flighty and chase after other women; he was knowledgeable and funny and interesting, as well as encouraging and endlessly patient with her. Viewed like that, what more could she want? In truth, it wasn't his injury itself throwing her into a quandary, but rather what it meant in terms of his ability to give her children; no matter how hard she tried, she struggled to picture herself without them.

She shook her head in confusion. Even were a lesser man to come along and give her the family she so badly craved, would he be someone with whom she would want to spend the rest of her life? Would he encourage her, cherish her, nurture her – because she was certain Andrew would do all of those and more? Or would another man, perhaps one like that Clive, merely expect her to fall dutifully into line with his beliefs, demand a hot meal be waiting for him the moment he came through the door every evening and her nightly compliance in bed? Worse than that, would he turn out to be a womaniser – something she suspected to be true of Gwen's Jimmy – or a gambler or a drunk, like Charlie Warren? Which was the lesser of so many evils? With so little knowledge of life, how was she supposed to decide?

Staring down at Andrew's card, she wished afresh that she'd plucked up the courage to discuss some of this with May; her sister might not have much experience of men but, through working all those years at the Sovereign Hotel, she did know something of the wider world. Well, too late now. Of greater importance right this moment was the matter of whether to accept Andrew's invitation to join him for lunch.

With another shake of her head, she let out a sigh. What did she have to lose? She liked him – a lot. And so, surely, the more she found out about him, the easier it should be to make her decision.

Noticing from his card that printed beneath his address was a telephone number, she hesitated. No: Miss Evercott said the telephone service was still unreliable and only for use in an emergency. Besides which, she didn't really know how to use it. She would take him at his word and just arrive.

A glance through the window told her that the morning was dry and bright, meaning she could take the bus part of the way and walk the rest to arrive around midday. But first, if she was going to keep her promise to Dorothy and get the laundry done, then she really *must* get her skates on.

–

Andrew's face lit up. 'Clemmie,' he said brightly as he opened the door. 'Come in. I wasn't sure what you would think, receiving an invitation from me at such short notice.'

At the sight of him back in his wheelchair, Clemmie fought down a look of disappointment. 'When I got home from visiting May,' she said as she stepped inside, 'I was a bit tired and cranky. Your card was a nice surprise.'

'Here,' he said, motioning to her jacket as she stood unbuttoning it, 'allow me to take that for you.'

Watching him put the garment on a chair beside the coat stand, she said, 'Is Pearce not here today?' On her way up the drive, she'd been struck by the absence of the Wolseley.

'He's gone out. I hope you won't mind but I'd previously asked him to attend to a matter of personal business for me. But in case he's not back in time, he's left us a light lunch.'

Unable to decide whether Pearce's absence caused her relief or concern, Clemmie nodded. 'All right.'

'I usually eat around one o'clock. But if you're used to dining earlier, we can always—'

'No.' In emphasis of her point she shook her head. 'One o'clock is just right.'

'Then why don't we go through to the drawing room, and you can tell me about your visit to your sister?'

'It wasn't terribly exciting,' she said, anxious that he shouldn't expect her to regale him with some great adventure. 'But I did learn how to harvest beetroot—'

'Goodness. Look, why don't you sit there?' He indicated the end of the sofa. 'And I'll position myself here.'

'It was lovely to see May,' she continued as she sat down. 'She has a land girl. Well, until recent she had two, but one turned out to be… well, trouble.'

'Ah.'

'So now she just has Bonnie, who's tinier than I am but twice as strong. More likely three or four times.'

'And your sister is well?'

'The picture of health.'

'Good.'

'And you?' she asked. 'Are you well, too?' She was hoping her question might lead him to explain why he was back in his wheelchair.

His response came with a heavy sigh. 'Since I have no wish to sound "woe is me", let's just say that the last few days have been difficult.'

'Oh.' *Please explain*, she willed him. *Please don't leave it to me to ask.*

'On Friday afternoon, I saw my doctor – the one responsible for my care since my discharge from the officers' hospital in Torquay.' Listening carefully, Clemmie nodded. 'Having had a jolly good week getting about on crutches, I had been hoping it was a sign of better things to come. To that end, I mentioned that I had met a young lady.' In the knowledge that he was talking about her, Clemmie blushed. 'And asked him whether anything about my recent progress might lead him to change his prognosis – for the better, I mean.'

'And what did he say?' In anticipation of his reply, she held her breath.

'To my dismay, his response was quite brutal. His words were something along the lines of "For God's sake man, you've got to let go of this idea that you're going to make some sort of miraculous recovery. Ignoring recent ups and downs, your condition is unchanged. You can never be a proper husband. That being the case, my advice remains. Stop clinging to false hope and let the poor girl go." And I regret to admit that his words have left me feeling rather… squashed.'

Clemmie could see why. What a horrible man.

'But isn't it his job to encourage you to keep trying?' she said, her indignation making her hot. 'To encourage you to have hope, to urge you to picture your condition improving and strive to bring it about?' What sort of doctor told someone to give up? Even a quack doctor knew better than that.

'You would think so. On the other hand, if there genuinely is no hope…'

'No hope?' Aware that her voice had turned screechy, she paused for a moment to draw breath. 'Does he know,' she continued more evenly, 'for certain, I mean, that nothing about your condition will ever change? Does he have proof? Because to my mind, if he doesn't, then to imply that all hope is lost is unresponsible of him.'

Studying Andrew's expression, she wondered whether she had overstepped the mark.

'My condition is such that there can be no proof either way.'

'Then don't listen to him.'

'Please, don't get me wrong, I haven't given up hope. But I will admit that his conviction on the point did somewhat puncture my resolve. And did leave me to wonder whether he's right. Have I been fooling myself to think you'd want to be tied to a cripple for the rest of your life?'

'With all due respect,' Clemmie began, rueing that her exasperation with the doctor was making her short, 'isn't that decision mine alone to make? It's certainly none of *his* business.'

'That is true. But picture, if you will, discovering that your friends and their husbands are going to a dance. In that moment, will you not long to go with them?'

Resisting the urge to disclose that, apart from Pearl – and possibly, she supposed, Gwen – she didn't know anyone likely to go dancing, she instead treated him to a forceful shake of her head. 'It's not something I can say I've ever craved.'

'Will it not bother you that our social life will be almost non-existent?'

'I don't think you can miss what you've never had.'

'Even so...'

'Look,' she said carefully. 'Some girls believe you got to kiss a lot of frogs before finding the one that turns out to be your prince. But believe me when I tell you how the prospect of putting myself through such a trial has only ever filled me with dread.'

'I wouldn't even be able to walk you back down the aisle once we'd exchanged our vows.'

'Since both of my parents are dead, I assumed I would marry in a register office.'

'Or carry you over the threshold when we got back here—'

'I daresay I can cross it by myself.'

When Andrew smiled, she sensed it was in amusement at her matter-of-fact tone.

'You're practical, I'll give you that.'

'It's not as though you're leading me on. It's not as though you've let me think recovery is just round the corner and that everything will be all sunshine and roses. You're not trying to lure me with false promises.' To her consternation, her anger over the doctor's words was refusing to subside. 'Moreover, it was *you* who told me about the perils of giving up.' When he frowned, she waved a hand and went on, 'You told me about your piano pupil, the one struggling with some or other difficult composer.'

His expression changed to one of surprise. 'I'm flattered you remember.'

'As I recall the tale, a certain wise man asked the boy how badly he wanted to win a scholarship.' Struggling to remember the precise details, she hesitated. 'But that if he still wanted it enough, then he couldn't let one tricky piece of music come between him and his dream. Leastways, I think that was the gist of it.'

'Your recollection is spot on.'

'So I suppose my point is that your dreams don't belong to your doctor. He can't achieve them for you. Nor, seemingly, does he have it within his power to improve your chances of them coming about. Only you can put in the effort – stick with it through thick and thin.' Instantly regretting the forcefulness of her tone, she flushed. 'Sorry.'

'Good lord, no, my dearest Clemmie, don't apologise. You're right. One hundred per cent. We are each master of our own destiny. But… do I deduce from the strength of your feelings on the subject that while you have been away your thoughts have… come down in favour of accepting me?'

In the time it took Clemmie to exhale, she realised that she had indeed made up her mind. If nothing else, there was a war on, and who knew whether a chance that was here today would still exist tomorrow, let alone next month or next year?

'I believe they have. Should you still feel inclined to ask.'

Beaming with delight, Andrew reached for her hands and grasped them tightly. 'Oh, my dearest girl. You beautiful creature—'

'It won't be easy, I know that.'

'You will be so loved. I shall make it my priority to ensure that whatever will make your life here comfortable, as long as it is within my means, you shall have it. You shall be neither nursemaid nor drudge. You shall be my wife, my equal, and I your dutiful husband.'

So why, Clemmie wondered as she sat with her hands in his, given the sincerity of all he'd just said, was the singing of her heart rather more muted than she might have expected? Why was the feeling in her chest more a cosy glow than a raging inferno? Squadron Leader Andrew Dunning was a wonderful man, was going to be a devoted and caring husband. She would never want for a thing. Apart, obviously, from one…

—

The afternoon flew. When Andrew showed her through to the dining room, Clemmie's eyes fell upon the table laid ready. At his request, she carefully removed the cloths covering the plates of food set out on the buffet. Seemingly, Pearce had been saving up rations: there was sliced tongue – more accurately, *two* slices of tongue; boiled potatoes chopped up with chives; a salad of cabbage and carrots in a creamy sauce; and a bowl containing lettuce, tomatoes and cucumber.

'The salad is the last from the garden,' Andrew said as he handed her the serving spoon. 'Pearce has a Dig for Victory patch down near the apple trees. He is surprisingly green-fingered.'

Helping herself to a modest portion from the bowl, Clemmie smiled. 'Can I put some on your plate for you?' Since it seemed she was going to marry him, she might as well start adopting a few wifely habits.

'Yes please. You know, one of the things I miss from a salad is watercress.'

'Ooh, yes.' In truth, it was something she'd only tasted once or twice when May had brought home a bunch left over from the hotel kitchen. Their mother had been surprised that someone so young should like it. 'Hot and peppery.'

'The hotter, the better. Sadly, it's also the wrong time of year now for radishes. I like those too.'

'So do I.' See, she thought, replacing the serving spoon on the rest at the side of the bowl, we do have things in common – even if it is only humble vegetables. And thank goodness for the chance she'd been given to lodge with Miss Evercott because now she knew how to properly lay a table, and the etiquette of presenting and serving food. Without that recently acquired knowledge, she would never have had the courage to even *think* about sitting down to eat in a home as posh as this one.

'Please,' Andrew said, gesturing her to the table, 'do have a seat.'

Noting the napkin laid alongside the place settings, Clemmie unfolded hers and spread it across her lap. The perfection with which the heavy linen had been starched and ironed raised in her mind the question of Pearce and of housework: when they were married, would Andrew expect her to do it, or would he expect her explicitly not to?

'So, ignoring that there's a war on,' Andrew said as he manoeuvred himself from wheelchair to dining chair, 'what are your favourite foods?'

From there, the two of them chatted with ease. When it came to ice cream, she liked strawberry, he preferred chocolate. When it came to eggs – oh, for a fresh egg, they both agreed – she liked hers boiled with soldiers, he liked his scrambled on hot buttered toast. And when it came to meat, her favourite was lamb, his, beef. For Clemmie, the discovery of such facts helped her feel more relaxed, and the two of them were soon laughing as though taking lunch together was a regular event.

'Do you have a taste for music?' he asked her at one point.

'I'm afraid I know nothing about it.' To her surprise, admitting to the fact didn't make her feel inferior.

'Well then, when we finish our meal I shall play something for you, and you can tell me what you think. If doesn't move you, I shall keep playing until we find something that does. There's a style of music to suit every taste. It's just a question of matching the one to the other.'

His suggestion sounded fun. 'All right.'

'Favourite season?' he enquired a while later.

'Summer. Always. Though spring would be a close second.'

'Other way round for me. But autumn shouldn't be entirely dismissed. Crisp frosty mornings. Clear skies. Bonfire smoke.'

About to say 'Guy Fawkes', she stopped herself for fear of sounding childish. Instead, she asked, 'Favourite hymn?'

'Heavens. There's a question. To sing? To play? To listen to as sung by a choir?'

'Your real favourite if you could only choose one.'

'Do you know, you're turning out to be as hard a taskmaster as Pearce.'

His remark made her laugh. 'I hope not.'

The afternoon drifted easily on. When she insisted on clearing the table and at least putting the left-over food in the refrigerator, and he guided her around the kitchen to make tea, she struggled to believe how at ease she felt. And content. Yes, she knew it wouldn't always be this easy; this afternoon wasn't a true test. Life didn't consist solely of lunches eaten while asking one another about their likes and dislikes. There were bound to be days when one of them was grumpy or irritated by a tiresome habit the other failed to curb, or when they were simply in plain disagreement over a matter. But she also had a feeling that, with a bigger problem never far from the surface, everyday niggles would seem trifling and insignificant. At least, she hoped they would.

'Now, on a more practical note,' he said as they sat in the drawing room drinking tea from dainty porcelain cups, 'to fulfil the proper formalities before I get down on bended knee' – The irony of his remark wasn't wasted on either of them; when he winked at her she grinned – 'from whom must I seek permission to marry you?'

His question stopped her dead. Golly. There was a thing: even at eighteen years of age, she didn't have the final say over whether or not she got wed. 'Well…'

'Only, I am aware that your parents are deceased.'

Deceased. Presumably, that meant dead. 'They are, yes.' But was Charlie Warren? Dear God, what a terrifying thought. Was he, as her stepfather, her next of kin? And if he was, would they have to try to find out whether he was still alive? The morning after that air raid destroyed Albert Terrace, Pearl was convinced he'd been killed. As was May. For her own part, she'd doubted they could have been so lucky. Well, alive or not, she wasn't going to let him ruin her new life. 'I suppose it would be my sister you'd have to ask.'

'Is she an adult – over the age of twenty-one?'

Clemmie nodded. 'She is.'

'Then since it would be jolly unfair of me to just put her on the spot, to expect her to simply consent without even knowing me, how about you invite both of your sisters here one afternoon for tea? Perhaps one weekend. You can introduce us, you can show them my home – the place that will become *our* home – let them see I have the means to support you, and then I can ask her permission.'

Clemmie forced a swallow. So far, apart from Miss Evercott knowing Andrew through the work of the welcome committee, her two worlds had never crossed. But May would have to meet Andrew at some point – and learn the news that they were to be married. So would Pearl, who, with her rather more worldly outlook and habit of calling a spade a spade, might prove the more difficult to win over.

'Yes, all right. That sounds a good idea.'

'Then, once we've cleared that hurdle, you and I can make plans – decide how long you want to wait before we tie the knot. Which, by the way, will be entirely down to you. And we can discuss arrangements here. You're bound to want to make changes.'

'Plans. Yes,' she said, hoping she didn't sound as dazed as she suddenly felt. 'You're right.'

With that, the sound of a motorcar coming to a halt, followed moments later by the sound of the front door opening and closing, brought their discussion to an end.

'Pearce,' Andrew said of the noises in the hallway. 'Will you excuse me while I go and find out whether he was able to carry out my request?'

''Course.' She must stop saying that: educated people, she had come to notice, people like Andrew and Miss Evercott, said *of course*. And so should she.

When Andrew had wheeled himself from the room, Clemmie rose to her feet. What an afternoon this had turned out to be. This lovely house was going to be her home and Squadron Leader Andrew Dunning – albeit *Ret'd.*, as she'd seen on his card – was going to be her husband. Clemmie Dunning. Should she perhaps start calling herself Clementine? Maybe she should ask Andrew whether, to the outside world, Clemmie didn't now sound a mite childish.

'Right, then,' Andrew said when he returned.

'Did Pearce succeed?' she asked, sensing from his broad smile that he had.

'Indeed he did. Now, you and I must agree when we are to host your sisters for tea.' Yes. She supposed they must. If nothing else, there was the matter of May's consent to be got. 'I suppose this weekend would be too soon.'

'May lives out near Crediton. She'll have to arrange to be away. And check how the buses run.'

'Yes. Of course. Then how about the weekend after? Sunday the twenty-seventh. Leave it any later and we risk the weather deteriorating and your sisters having to travel in inclement conditions.'

Just under two weeks. She *should* be able to persuade them, especially if she asked Miss Evercott whether May might stay one night in Buckingham Crescent.

'Yes. I'll write to May. And I'll try to see Pearl. She's so busy I never know where she is.'

'Excellent. I'll wait for you to let me know. And thank you, dearest Clemmie, for giving me such hope for the future. I just know that, together, we're going to have a wonderful life.'

On her way home, somewhat overwhelmed by the speed at which things were happening, Clemmie reminded herself to take one step at a time. Most pressing was the need to decide how much to disclose to May before she invited her to meet Andrew; unless she somehow set the scene for her sister, his proposal might appear to be one of unseemly haste. Before she could do that, she would have to work out how long to say that she and Andrew had been… well, what even had they been? Friends?

Secondly, there was the matter of the preparations for the wedding itself. And then, there were what Andrew had referred to as 'arrangements within the house'. He had said she was to become neither nursemaid nor drudge, and that Pearce would be staying on. But did that mean doing everything for Andrew that he did now? Clearly, there was more to understand about all of this than she'd realised. And all of it so very grown up.

Well, as she had decided earlier, she would tackle one thing at a time; allow herself to become overwhelmed, and who knew what daft decisions her steadily increasing panic might lead her to take?

Chapter 21

'Well, here we are, then.'

When Clemmie reached to unfasten the gate, the loudest thing she could hear was the sound of her pulse thudding in her ears. When she then stood back to beckon May and Pearl up the path to Andrew's front door, the astonishment on her sisters' faces served only to make it thud even harder.

'Here?' Pearl asked, her expression suggesting she feared falling prey to a prank.

'Yes. Here. This is where he lives.'

Barely half an hour prior to that, Clemmie had stood with Pearl at the bus station on Paul Street, waiting for the service from Crediton to bring May from Fair Maids Farm. This afternoon was the first time all three of them had been together since May had left to go and work there. On that particular morning, watching their sister get on the bus, both she and Pearl had thought her mad. Today, she worried that the two of them would think her just as crazy – if not more so. It was why, in the end, she had told them only that she had met someone, that he had proposed they get married, and that she would like them to get to know him. In response to the outpouring of questions with which they had both responded, she had elaborated to the extent of telling them his name, that he had formerly been a pilot in the RAF – but that an accident had brought his service to a premature end – and that he was now a tutor in music and mathematics.

Despite wondering as to the wisdom of it, she had also gone on to add that he was *a little bit older*. Having deliberately withheld mentioning his paralysis, she could only pray they didn't react with a display of shock. As it was, as she fished about in her handbag for the door key Andrew had pressed upon her, she felt so light-headed with nerves she feared she might pass out.

With a quick stab of the doorbell to announce their arrival, and silently cursing the trembling of her fingers, she slipped the key into the lock and opened the door.

'You have a key?' Pearl hissed.

'Yes, of course.' When Andrew had first handed her the key, he'd explained he was doing so because he wanted her to be able to come go as she pleased. After all, he'd gone on to add, his house was soon to be her home. This afternoon, she was glad she'd accepted it; being able to let herself in ought to show her sisters that Andrew was serious in his intentions.

'But you're not already living here, are you?'

'Of course not.'

May, she noticed, looked mildly sheepish. Was it possible something had come to pass between her and that nice chap Dan? If it had, then this afternoon's ordeal might go more smoothly than she had spent the whole morning fearing.

'Only, an older man with his own home, and you, a young girl…'

'Stop it,' May whispered. 'Whatever you're suggesting, being vulgar doesn't become you.'

'Quite so,' Clemmie remarked, smiling gratefully at May. 'Now then, come on in. You can hang your jackets on the stand and May, you can leave your overnight bag there, out of the way.'

From the direction of the dining room came the staccato tapping of Andrew's crutches on the parquet floor. And when he arrived in the hallway, she was delighted to see that he was wearing his sage-green sweater. With the collar of a crisp white shirt showing at the neckline, she thought it lent him a healthy glow.

'Good afternoon, ladies. I'm so pleased you could come.'

Instinctively, she went towards him. And when he kissed her cheek, she kissed him back. 'You're on your feet,' she said quietly.

With a smile, he nodded. 'I thought it would look better.'

That he should put himself through such torture on her account made her heart swell with love. Her sisters could form whatever opinions they liked; as long as May gave Andrew her consent, nothing else mattered.

'Andrew,' she said brightly and turned back to her sisters. 'This is the eldest of us, May Huxford. And this is my younger sister, Pearl Warren. May, Pearl, this is Squadron Leader Andrew Dunning.'

'How do you do, Miss Huxford.'

'How do you do.'

'How do you do, Miss Warren.'

'Pleased to meet you, I'm sure.'

'Won't you come through to the drawing room and I'll arrange for some tea?'

'Actually,' Clemmie said, 'why don't I do that?' Directing a sheepish grin at May and Pearl, she added, 'If they're going to tell you terrible things about me, happen I'd prefer not to hear.'

With a warm smile, Andrew nodded. 'Sounds like an opportunity not to be passed up. Ladies, please, won't you come through and sit down?'

In the hallway, Clemmie exhaled heavily. How on earth was she going to quell her rattling nerves?

'Miss Huxford,' Pearce greeted her when she arrived in the kitchen.

'Good afternoon, Pearce.'

'All set to make tea for you and your guests, assuming you would like some?'

Ever so slightly, Clemmie felt the tension in her neck begin to soften. 'Yes, please. Tea would be lovely.'

'And I've baked what passes for a chocolate cake, if you think that would go down well.'

Having tasted Pearce's cake on a previous occasion, Clemmie nodded. 'For certain it would. Thank you. Just the thing.'

'Very well. Then if you care to go and rejoin your guests, I'll bring it through. And by the way, perhaps try not to look so petrified.'

Such tender concern from him almost brought tears. Raising a watery smile, she somehow held them back. 'But I *am* petrified.'

'Try hard not to be,' Pearce said, carrying the kettle to the tap in order to fill it. 'Rarely do these occasions turn out to be as dreadful as we anticipate.'

'Thank you.' If only she believed him. 'I'll try an' remember that.'

In the drawing room, Andrew paused his explanation of something to look at her and smile. 'Everything all right?'

'Pearce will bring it through in a moment.'

'I was just telling your sisters how I came to end up like this.'

With May and Pearl occupying the sofa, Clemmie chose one of the armchairs on the other side of the occasional table, Andrew being seated on the more upright chair that ordinarily occupied the bay. Clearly, he had given the arrangements prior thought. Did that mean he was as nervous as she was? Embarrassed to even be entertaining the possibility, she contained a scoff; no, of course he wasn't. How ridiculous.

'I understand you're a tutor now.'

Clemmie relaxed a little further; May's remark was perfect in its politeness.

'That's correct. I tutor mathematics and music, both passions of mine—'

'Where did you meet?' Pearl's interjection, on the other hand, was altogether more pointed. 'Only, I doubt it was at a dance.'

As she tried not to let anyone see her wince, Clemmie saw May give Pearl a nudge.

'We were serving on the same committee,' Andrew took it upon himself to reply. 'The city corporation wanted to plan for the arrival of a United States Army Air Force group of fighter aircraft and personnel to be stationed at RAF Exeter. Your sister and I were appointed liaison in connection with a welcome event in the guildhall. In fact, the venue was your sister's idea.'

It would have been better, Clemmie thought, had the two of them not turned quite so sharply to stare at her – nor with such a degree of disbelief.

'I was only part of it on account of my landlady,' she explained, her tone verging on apologetic. 'Miss Evercott is the centre organiser for the WVS where I volunteer. She took me along for something to do.'

'I think she took you along,' Andrew said gently, 'because she believed you had something to contribute. And she was right.'

'You still doing mornings up that corner shop?' Pearl went on to ask next.

What had got into her, Clemmie wondered? It wouldn't harm her to show some grace. 'No, a couple of weeks back the owner decided he no longer needed me. Since then, I've been working in the new WVS shop in Heavitree. When I'm on shift there, I act as manager.'

'That where you got that skirt?'

Clemmie forced a swallow. Why was Pearl being so catty? 'It is. Since it was such a reasonable price and the right size, I couldn't let it go to anyone else.'

'It's very nice,' May said. 'I always think that shade of grey very smart.'

'Me too.'

'Ah, Pearce, thank you.'

Following the line of Andrew's eyes to the door, Clemmie fought back another urge to cry. She could only hope that tea and cake would give Pearl something to do other than be so *scerbic*. Or should that be *a*cerbic? It had been a favourite word of her headmaster's, and she thought it suited Pearl's attitude this afternoon to a tee. What had happened to make her so caustic, she couldn't imagine. While she'd always been plain-spoken, she wasn't usually *this* cutting. Perhaps she had her monthly and it was giving her cramps.

As Pearce placed the tray of tea things on the table, Clemmie wished she could tell what May thought of

Andrew. As nightmares went, this was turning into one from which she was desperate to wake up.

'Thank you,' she said to Pearce as he backed away.

'Please let me know, Miss Huxford, if you need anything else.'

'We will.'

As Clemmie poured the tea and passed around plates of cake, the silence was horrible. Now that she could have done with someone prattling on, no one had a thing to say. It didn't bode well.

'This is very good cake,' May eventually remarked.

It was Andrew who replied. 'The secret is a table-spoonful of golden syrup. It supplements the sugar and, in the absence of eggs, helps to keep it moist.'

'Did *you* make it?' Pearl asked.

Was she doing it on purpose, Clemmie wondered? Was she deliberately setting out to provoke Andrew into showing a crack in what she had no doubt marked down as a veneer, an act? And if so, why? Why would she do that? Moreover, why wasn't she using her napkin?

'I can't take the credit, no. It's one of Pearce's creations.'

Her slice of cake barely touched, Pearl put her plate on the table and looked from Clemmie to Andrew and back again. 'Can I use the lav?'

Cringing at her half-sister's continued lack of grace, Clemmie placed her own plate back on the tray and rose to her feet. 'Of course. I'll show you.' But the instant the two of them were out of earshot, perilously close to losing her battle with tears, Clemmie grabbed Pearl by the arm and dragged her along the hall. 'What's the matter with you? Why are you being so... so... so confrontational? You're not normally like this.'

Shaking herself free of Clemmie's grasp, Pearl glowered. 'I don't know what you're talking about. Like what?'

'So… offish.'

'I'm not offish.'

'Yes you are.'

'I tell you,' Pearl said, her eyes narrowing, 'I'm not.'

'Then what's the matter with you? Because something clearly is.'

'The matter,' Pearl hissed, 'is you an' him.' With her head, she gestured back towards the door. 'For a start, he's old enough to be your father.'

'Don't be silly. He's not even thirty.'

'And this house.' Stiffly, Pearl waved her hand about the hall.

'What of it?'

'For crying out loud, Clem. You've no business in a place like this. Can't you see what's going on here? Can't you see his game?'

Clemmie frowned. 'What are you talking about? What game?'

'For Christ's sake, look around you. You're his little experiment—'

'*What?*'

'You're the little orphan he's going to clean up and dress nice and… and learn to talk proper to see if he can pass you off for a lady—'

'*How dare you.*'

But Pearl wasn't finished. 'Either that, or it's you, trying to make up for never having a father—'

'Pearl Warren, you take that back!'

'Shan't do nothing of the sort. It's as plain as the nose on your face. You're just something to occupy him,

313

something to make up for the fact that no woman with an ounce of sense is going to sacrifice a normal life for *him*.'

'Stop it. That's not true.'

Pearl's glower hardened. 'For Christ's sake, Clem, open your eyes. I'm right and you know it. I mean, when the two of you go on a date, where does he take you, eh?'

Clemmie hung her head. 'He—'

'I mean, is he even able to, you know, *do it*?'

When Clemmie flushed, her entire body prickled with the heat of her embarrassment. 'Don't be so crude. That's none of your business.'

'Huh. So no, then, he can't. Thought as much. No, so I'll tell you what will happen here. He'll dress you up, parade you about for a while. But then, once he sees how all the silk and the jewels in the world won't ever conceal that you were born just up the hill from the canal, among the stench of the tannery and the foundry, and Thomas's boiling up offal all day and night—'

'Pearl, stop it.'

'—once he realises how dull you are, he'll lose all interest. Trust me. *You* might not know much about men, but *I do*.'

Unable to hold back any longer, Clemmie gave in to tears. 'You're wrong.'

'I'm not and you know it. Though clearly, trying to convince you is a waste of my breath. So, if it's all the same to you, I think I'll leave.'

When Pearl swivelled about and marched towards the coat stand for her jacket, Clemmie went after her. 'I wish you wouldn't. But if you're not prepared to give him the chance to show you the sort of person he really is, then I'm not going to beg you to stay. Nor do I think that, after the way you've behaved this afternoon, I'll be able to find it in my heart to invite you back. I never doubted you'd have concerns – either of you. I knew you'd have questions. One sister wanting to be satisfied that nothing is amiss for another is only natural. What I wasn't expecting is that you'd be so *mean*.'

Pointedly folding her jacket over her arm, Pearl scoffed. 'Satisfy myself nothing is amiss? Huh. Makes my flesh creep just thinking what's in store for you if you go through with this… with this madness. And if I never set foot through this door again, that'll be fine by me.'

'By me, too.'

'Fine.'

'Fine.' Golly, she was so cross even her tears had stopped.

When Pearl snatched open the door and strode straight down the path towards the gate, Clemmie stood watching her go. What on earth had got into the girl? She'd always had a fiery temper but this, today, was something new.

Closing the door, she turned to see May coming along the hall.

'Has she gone?'

'Yes.'

'You all right?'

'Not really.'

'I should like to say I don't know what came over her,' May said. 'But we both know how she can be if she thinks she's being upstaged. Never could stand being out of the limelight.'

Clemmie gave a dejected shake of her head. 'I know how she can act up. But today she was just plain nasty.'

'Wholly.'

Nasty, Clemmie reflected, was putting it mildly. Today, Pearl had gone too far. 'I don't suppose she's right, though, is she?'

May met her look. 'Right about what?'

'That I shouldn't be here. That if I think I can ever fit in somewhere like this, I'm just kidding myself.' If she *was* fooling herself, she could do with knowing now, before matters got away from her.

When May caught hold of her hands, Clemmie met her look.

'She's as wrong as it's possible to be. Truly.'

'You mean that?'

'I do. I might not know Andrew yet, but I can see what sort of man he is. As for whether you fit in here, well, that's down to you and him, isn't it?'

'I suppose.'

'If you ask me, Pearl's just jealous. Maybe some chap she likes has just given her the heave-ho, and she begrudges you your happiness.'

'Hm.'

May might be right. Perhaps it *was* jealousy. Perhaps Pearl couldn't stand that an educated gentleman like Squadron Leader Dunning could see *poor little Clemmie* for who she was – shortcomings and all – but still fall in love with her and want to marry her anyway. That she was out of her depth in his world and understood next to nothing of the fine and tasteful things with which he filled his days, she would readily admit. But that didn't make her dull, nor did it mean she couldn't, with his help, come to understand and appreciate and even enjoy them. For certain, if she never tried, she would never know.

When May put an arm across her shoulders, Clemmie let out a long sigh.

'Look. Don't pay her no heed. Ten to one, by the time she's traipsed back into town she'll regret having behaved so bad and be frantically trying to work out how to beg your forgiveness.'

'If you say so.'

'Besides, you can't help who you fall in love with.'

Intrigued by the tone of May's remark, Clemmie studied her sister's eyes. 'You got together with that nice neighbour of yours? That Dan?'

'Happen I have.'

'I knew it! So what's—'

'But him and me, that's for another day. Come on, your Andrew and I have just been having a little chat.'

Clemmie tensed. 'You have?'

'And it seems there's something he wants to ask you. But trust me when I say that first' – Putting her hand in the pocket of her skirt, May pulled out a handkerchief – 'you might want to dry your eyes.'

When Clemmie returned to the living room, it was to find that Andrew had moved to sit on the sofa.

With a smile, he patted the cushion. 'Your sister and I have just been having a chat.' As she sat down beside him, he reached for her hands.

'So she just said.'

'And since she's clearly a woman possessed of terrific judgement...'

Clemmie shot May a glance. 'She is?' What on earth was he on about?

'She has given me her permission to ask you something.'

Realising what was happening, Clemmie turned to see May beaming with delight. 'She has?'

'Daft apeth. 'Course I have.'

Feeling Andrew let go of her hands, she swung back to see him opening a small velvet box. Inside it was nestled a slender gold band set with an oval red stone in a halo of smaller white ones.

'Clemmie Huxford, the day I saw you, my world turned upside down. And if I'm truthful, it hasn't turned back the right way since. As you are aware from my clumsy attempt a while back to distance myself from you, the repercussions of what I'm about to ask you are something I have considered long and hard. But if there's one thing I've learned in this world, it's that life doesn't always go to plan, such that when a chance of happiness presents itself, one mustn't let it slip through one's fingers. And so, my dearest Clemmie, will you please do me the honour of becoming my wife?'

The speed with which the tension drained from her limbs told Clemmie all she needed to know. When Andrew had first declared his feelings, she had been beset by doubts. Since then, she had swung wildly in favour, then against, then back again. It wasn't going to be plain sailing, she knew that. But if they loved one another, then whatever the difficulties, she and Andrew would face them together. The time had come to trust her instincts.

'Yes,' she whispered, unconcerned by the tears of happiness pouring down her cheeks. 'Yes. I should like that very much.'

V. Safe Landings

Chapter 22

Clemmie sighed with relief. Golly, it was good to be home. While she was glad she'd gone to the effort of visiting May again so soon after her last trip to Fair Maids, the bus journey back to Exeter had left her with a stiff back and a pounding in her temples. Mind you, the problem with her back probably owed more to three days spent stretching to pick apples and lifting giant pails of them into the trailer. When her sister had written to invite her back for the harvest, the prospect of being away so close to the wedding had put her on the verge of declining. But, with the weather over the last few days so glorious, and with everyone there in such good spirits, she was glad now that she'd let Andrew talk her into going.

'It will do you good to get away,' he'd said when she'd expressed concern about accepting May's invitation. 'Change of scenery and all that. Besides, is it not possible your sister asked you because she would welcome your help? By your own admission, last time you were there you took to pulling beetroot as though born to the job. And one imagines harvesting apples is very much a case of many hands making light work.'

As usual, he'd been right; May had been delighted to see her again so soon, and grateful for the extra help. And for her own part, Clemmie felt that the different company, and a couple of days spent working out of doors, had done her good. As Andrew had said that day when they'd discussed their favourite times of year, the countryside in autumn was enchanting: the foliage on the trees had been a riot of russet, scarlet and amber; the air had been rich with the aromas of damp turf and mushrooms and overripe apples; the trees in the orchard had echoed with robins whistling melancholy refrains. Pausing at one point to stand and take it all in, she'd understood afresh why May had fallen in love with the place.

Dearest May. No wonder her mood last time had been so hard to fathom; turns out, the countryside wasn't the only thing she'd fallen in love with. Late yesterday afternoon, with the apple harvest safely in the barn, Dan had announced to everyone that, after lengthy prevarication, May had finally agreed to marry him. Until recently Fair Maids' neighbour, Dan was now its new owner, and to Clemmie's eyes he and May were clearly both besotted. Had she been shocked to arrive and find the two of them already living together as man and wife, 'practising', as May had put it? Shocked was something of an understatement. Her sister had always been so proper. But, as Dan had said over supper last night, how the two of them chose to carry on behind closed doors was nobody's business but their own. Besides, from reading between the lines, that they weren't already married wasn't for want of asking on Dan's part. No, as May had later gone on to confide, she'd taken her time accepting him because she'd wanted to be sure it was the right thing to do. And there was no harm in that. Of course, if her sister's radiant bloom foretold what Clemmie suspected it did, then next spring not only would her sister be a wife but a mother as well. And she couldn't be more thrilled for her. It was just a shame Mum hadn't lived to see her two eldest daughters married, one so soon after the other, or to have been able to get to know her two vastly different but equally doting sons-in-law. With a light sigh, Clemmie smiled. Yes, she was glad now that she'd made the effort to see her sister again.

Dragging her attention back to the here and now, she lifted her sponge bag from her little overnight case – the brand new one Andrew had bought to save her having to borrow Dorothy's again. When he'd given it to her, he'd said it was because she was going to need one for their honeymoon. He took mischievous delight in calling it that, despite it being just two nights in a seafront hotel near Exmouth. She was glad they were going, though. The prospect of spending their wedding night at home, with Pearce in his room along the landing, brought her out in a cold sweat. Their first night together was going to be, well, it was going to be awkward enough as it was. Andrew had hinted that they could still be *romantic and amorous* but, given the way things were, she had shied away from trying to work out what that might entail. Whatever he envisaged, unless miracles really did happen, next summer certainly wasn't going to see the two of *them* welcoming a honeymoon baby. Still, at least the Huxford family line wouldn't come to an abrupt end; it would live on through May's offspring, when she had them.

Offspring. Was marrying Andrew the right thing to be doing? Could she be happy as a childless wife? Until recently, she had convinced herself that she could be. But now, with May clearly on the road to motherhood, her conviction felt somewhat less robust. Andrew was a wonderful man, who was going to give her a life beyond her wildest dreams. But was he? Hadn't her dream only ever been to have a husband, a home – and children?

You can't help who you fall in love with, May had observed on the day she'd come to meet Andrew and see his home. But while that might be true, shouldn't the couple in question be certain that, by itself, love would be enough?

'Clemmie, dear?' Startled from her thoughts, Clemmie turned to see Dorothy in the doorway. 'Sorry to make you jump, but I saw from your jacket on the coat stand that you were home. How was your visit to your sister?'

Clemmie smiled. 'Lovely. Real hard work gathering up all them apples – I ache all over – but fun just the same. Oh, and May announced that she and Dan are to wed.'

'Goodness. Two weddings in the family.'

'Yes.'

'Well, when you've finished unpacking, why don't you pop downstairs? We can have a little sherry while you tell me all your news.'

With a frown, Clemmie glanced to her alarm clock. 'Isn't it a bit—'

'You know, I shall miss having you ask me whether it isn't a bit early.' With a smile, Dorothy went on, 'You must fear that once you've moved out, and there's no one to stand guard over the drinks cabinet, I shall start taking my little sherry with my morning toast.'

Clemmie laughed. 'Lunch, perhaps, but no, not with breakfast.'

'You know, back at the start of the war, my cousin Ralph – he's a wine merchant, and the one entirely responsible for my little sherry habit – had the foresight to put a dozen crates into storage for me. Thank heavens he did because without those, I would be down to the dregs, and in something of a panic.'

'Then thank goodness for Cousin Ralph.'

'Quite. Anyway, I've news about your Mr Narramore. So, as soon as you're ready, pop down.'

Clemmie cast a glance over her partly unpacked bag. If there was news about Mr Narramore, she would rather not wait to hear it. 'I'll come now. I can finish this later.'

In the drawing room with their sherries, the blackout already lowered against the gloom of a dismal afternoon and two lamps lit, Dorothy shared what she'd learned.

'This morning, Inspector Lethbridge telephoned to tell me that one of his detectives had arrested and questioned Mr Narramore.'

Clemmie felt something in her chest go thud. 'Oh.'

'Apparently, once presented with the facts, the man was quick to confess.'

Hit by a wave of relief, Clemmie exhaled a long stream of breath. If Cedric Narramore had confessed, then the possibility of him learning who had given him away was something she need no longer dread.

'So, he admitted to what he was doing.'

'According to Inspector Lethbridge, Cedric Narramore is the lawful owner of both the premises containing the shop and the adjacent property in Worcester Terrace, albeit the latter by way of a small mortgage. Until recently, Mrs Narramore appears to have been in the dark about both the mortgage *and* his relationship with his tenant – Mrs Bodley, is it? – with whom he has a son.'

Crikey. When she had wondered whether Mrs Bodley knew what was going on, she hadn't suspected *that*. 'Golly,' she breathed as the facts sank in.

'It was, it would seem, his wife's discovery of the boy that led her to threaten Cedric with divorce, and to tell him that any solicitor worth his salt would see him saddled with paying to support her for the rest of her life.'

'Heavens.'

'That's when Narramore claimed he panicked. For years, he had promised this Mrs Bodley that as soon as he had enough money he would leave his wife and get a little pub in the country, where the three of them could start a new life.'

To Clemmie, it seemed such a simple and endearing thing to want. It also explained why she hadn't seen *Mrs* Narramore for a few days, and why *Mr* Narramore had exploded with such force the day she'd asked him for time off. Goodness, what a tangled web.

'So, his plan was to claim compensation for the houses and then just disappear?'

'To a man in a corner, it must have seemed the perfect opportunity.'

'Well,' Clemmie said, staring into her *little sherry*, 'I'm pleased he's not going to get away with it.' Even if he had only acted from love.

'But perhaps a little saddened, too?'

Clemmie sighed. 'That as well.' If nothing else, Mrs Bodley's boy would likely now continue to grow up knowing little or nothing of his father. And she knew what that was like – how it felt to sense that other children had something you didn't; that something was missing from your life.

'Well, on a positive note, you can rest with a clear conscience. In fact, you can take pride in having stopped a crime.'

'Yes,' she said dully.

'And look forward to your wedding, and to a new life as Mrs Andrew Dunning.'

'Yes,' she repeated, wishing she could summon greater conviction. 'You're right. I have everything to look forward to.'

'Whereas *I* shall be faced with finding a new lodger.'

'I suppose so.'

'But not just any lodger.'

Looking across to see Dorothy smiling, Clemmie frowned. 'No?'

'No, I shall have to find one prepared to join me in taking a little sherry.'

'Oh. Yes,' Clemmie replied with a smile of her own. *Whereas I shall rather miss being the one with whom you take it.*

—

It made sense. With no work to go to, and so many domestic matters in connection with Andrew's home – with *their* home – to be decided, she might as well spend as much time there each day as she could. As Andrew had said, it would help to allay any concerns she might have. At the time, she'd withheld the urge to smile: *any* concerns? Clearly, he had no idea of the length of her list.

As usual, though, his suggestion had been a good one and, gradually, one by one, things that had been making her anxious became gradually more familiar.

'What do I say again?' she asked the first time the telephone rang and he suggested she answer it.

'You just say the number.'

Fixing her gaze on the digits printed on the dial, she lifted the black Bakelite handset. 'Three-one-two-nine.' Turning to Andrew, she smiled. 'Yes, he's here. Who's calling please?' Covering the mouthpiece with her hand, she said, 'It's a Gerald Cook.'

'You see,' he whispered as he took the handset from her and smiled. 'It's easy.' Raising the receiver to his ear, Andrew addressed the caller. 'Gerald, good morning. How are you?' After a moment's pause, he continued, 'Yes, miserable, isn't it?'

That was another thing she had come to realise: if she wasn't going to let him down, she had to pay more attention to the way she spoke. She would never be posh – saw no point even trying to be – but she'd noticed how educated people said 'isn't' as opposed to 'ain't', 'lavatory' in place of 'lav', and 'because' rather than the shorter 'cos'. The problem was remembering to stop and think before she opened her mouth; no sense correcting herself halfway through a sentence and drawing even greater attention to her gaffe.

Anxious also to start addressing some of the chasms in her worldliness, and aware that Andrew devoured war reports from the *Daily Telegraph* and plotted events on a wall map of Europe, she asked him about the Allies' progress and listened to him explaining about the various campaigns. Some of it wasn't easy to follow; the foreign place names proved impossible to recall almost the instant she'd heard them.

'On this occasion,' he said to her one morning as she stood watching him stick several more pins into the top of Italy, 'Bomber Command had one hundred and twelve Avro Lancasters take off from England, one hundred and nine of which returned unharmed.'

'I see.' To Clemmie, the loss of even just three aircraft and their crews was of greater significance than the number who'd made it back. She chose not to say so, though.

'If reports are to be believed, they dropped close to two hundred tons of bombs.' The mention of bombs made Clemmie shudder. 'Their target in this instance was here.' She followed the line of his finger to the northern coastline of Italy. 'Genoa – a vital port. Primary targets would have been her harbour, her shipyards and her railways.'

'Were the bombers successful?' she asked. Despite not really wanting to think about it, she knew it was important to understand more of what was going on; the war was, after all, the reason their marriage would be childless.

'Incredibly successful. Almost every target was either destroyed or else critically damaged. Thankfully, reports are that, over two nights of attacks, very few civilian lives were lost.'

'Thank goodness for that.'

'Quite.'

Something else he'd taken to showing her – this time capturing rather more of her interest – was how to read music.

'Think of it as a secret code,' he'd said as she'd sat on the piano stool with him beside her in his chair. That was something else she'd recently picked up: to Andrew, his wheelchair was his 'chair' – or sometimes, when she guessed he didn't know she was within earshot, his *bloody infernal chair*.

'A secret code,' she'd repeated as she'd stared at the sheet of music positioned against the rest. It wasn't hard to see what he meant; to her eyes, it was just rows of lines containing randomly arranged dots on stalks – some pointing upwards, others down; some solid, some hollow.

When he taught her that each line on the stave represented a different note on the instrument, she learned to remember their arrangement through the mnemonic

Every Good Boy Deserves Football for notes written on the lines, and the word FACE for those occupying the spaces. Not long into their first lesson, and with a chart resting immediately above the keys to show her which note on the piano was which, she had even played a one-fingered and rather halting first line of 'Twinkle, Twinkle, Little Star'.

'Well done,' he'd said. 'Now that you understand the basic principles, you're on your way to becoming a musician.'

Clemmie doubted it was that simple. Nevertheless, captivated by the way squiggles on a sheet of paper could be turned into a song, she asked him to teach her more. To her surprise and delight, by the end of the week he could put in front of her a piece of music and, without telling her what it was, she could play the one-fingered melody: 'London's Burning'; 'Old MacDonald Had A Farm'; 'Happy Birthday To You'. He seemed as delighted with her progress as she was.

Buoyed by her ability to pick up new things, this morning he had asked Pearce to drive them in the Wolseley to a quiet stretch of level road at the bottom of the hill. And once Pearce was despatched with his newspaper to sit on a bench in the adjacent park, Clemmie tried to get comfortable behind the steering wheel, Andrew beside her in the passenger seat ready to explain the controls.

'Accelerator, brake, clutch,' she repeated after him. 'Gear lever, handbrake.'

But driving didn't come as easily to her as reading music had.

'It's all right,' he assured her as she repeatedly stalled the engine. 'Clutches are tricky devils. The key thing to remember is "smooth". Once you get the hang of it you can do it quite quickly as long as you keep your action—'

'Smooth. Yes, *I know*,' she replied, her frustration bringing her perilously close to tears. 'I understand. But I just can't seem to do it.'

'Then we'll just keep trying. As with the piano, it's worth mastering.'

Eventually she did manage to pull away from the kerb, even accelerating to a speed that necessitated changing up into second gear. She even brought the Wolseley to a gentle stop, perfectly parallel to the kerb. But by that point, her shoulders and neck had become so tense that her head was pounding like a blacksmith's hammer.

'I can't do any more today.'

He covered her hand with his. 'Don't underestimate what you've achieved. For someone who's barely ridden in a motorcar, let alone considered the mechanics of its operation, you've done incredibly well. We'll make a driver of you yet.'

'Only,' she said with a hefty sigh, 'if I don't wear out your patience first.'

'Once you've mastered the basics, I'll ask Pearce to bring you out without me. I have it on good authority that when it comes to driving, husbands do not make the best teachers.'

Before long, Clemmie came to realise that the more time they spent together, the more confident she grew and the happier she became, such that, when Andrew began suggesting she stay for lunch each day before going to her shift at the WVS shop, she didn't hesitate to accept.

Another morning, on hearing the telephone start to ring, she didn't stop to think about that, either.

'I'll answer it,' she called from the kitchen, where she had been helping Pearce with the clearing up. 'Three-one-two-nine. Yes, he's here.' Thinking she recognised the voice, she asked, 'Who is it, please?'

'Say, would that be Miss Huxford?'

Her face lit up. 'Major Hogue! I thought it was you.'

'Yes, ma'am. And hey, I understand congratulations are in order.'

'You've heard?'

'Squadron Leader Dunning called me. Left a message one afternoon when I wasn't here. I must say that sure is some swell news.'

When Andrew arrived, she put her hand over the receiver. 'It's Major Hogue.' Uncovering it, she went on, 'Andrew's here now. I'll pass you over.'

Listening from the kitchen, and initially hearing a good deal of laughter, Clemmie smiled. But then she heard Andrew say, 'Well, that's a shame. From an operational standpoint, I see the wisdom of it. Clearly. But I wish now that we'd had the chance to catch up beforehand.'

And when she heard Andrew replace the receiver, she put down the drying-up cloth and went back through to the hall.

'What's the matter?'

'Major Hogue's unit is being redeployed along the coast to Sussex – not that he divulged the details, of course. And not that *I'm* telling *you*.'

'No, of course not.'

'Which means, unfortunately, that we won't be seeing him again.'

Struck by the profoundness of her regret, Clemmie sighed. 'I liked Major Hogue.'

'So did I.'

'I did wonder why we hadn't heard anything from him.'

'Likewise. Which was why I telephoned. Apparently, the thinking is that basing his squadrons closer to France will give his pilots greater experience of combat. All they've been able to fly from here is escort duties.'

'I see. And will moving them along the coast put them in danger?'

'Undoubtedly. Every mission brings danger.'

'Yes,' she said, her foolishness making her blush.

'I wished him Godspeed and sent him our love.' *Our love*. In Andrew's eyes, they were already properly a couple, with a combined love to bestow. 'I also made sure he knew that if he ever finds himself back in Exeter, we'd make him most welcome.'

'We would.' The sense she got from Andrew's tone, though, was that, while his invitation was extended with the utmost sincerity, circumstances made such a meeting unlikely. The war would move on; their lives would move on. And the sad reality was that they would probably never see Major Hogue again.

She was glad she'd met him, though – felt proud to be able to say that she'd had the pleasure of meeting several Americans and that, to a man, they had struck her as warm and friendly. Indeed, had it not been for the major's squadrons being posted here to start with, she wouldn't have met Andrew. And without having met him, who knew where she would be now? For certain she wouldn't be wearing his grandmother's ruby on the third finger of her left hand. But then neither would she keep finding herself beset by unshakeable doubts as to whether or not she was doing the right thing…

–

'Bit of a blustery old day.'

'Yes.'

'Still,' May went on to observe as she stood looking out through the window, 'least it's dry.'

Seated at the dressing table in Gwen's old bedroom, Clemmie forced herself to agree. 'Yes.'

While it was heartening that her sister had gone to all the effort to be there with her, at that precise moment she would have preferred to wrestle with her anxiety alone. Not that she would admit to the fact.

'Which is about the best you can hope for this time of year,' May continued. 'Suppose that's why so many women get wed in the spring – for the better weather.'

'Suppose so.' Dear God, grow any *more* nervous and she was in danger of being physically sick. How was that possible when all she'd been able to force down so far this morning was half a cup of tea?

'So, then,' May said, eventually turning back to the room. 'You're the first of us to wed.'

Clemmie raised a smile. 'Though not by long.' In a couple of weeks, the boot would be on the other foot; she would be the one chattering away and May would be the one with the knot in her stomach and the iron-like taste in her mouth.

'Don't mind telling you I was as good as speechless when Dan said he wanted us to be wed from up the church. Didn't have him down as one for that sort of palaver. On the other hand, I *wasn't* surprised he wanted to wait until we were done pressing the apples. But then that's what I like about him. He might not have a romantic bone in his body but find me a man who's more practical. And this *is* our first pressing. And there *is* a lot riding on it.

Like he said, though, once the job's done, he won't be so distracted, and we'll be able to have a right ol' knees-up.'

Clemmie raised another smile. Though her sister couldn't know it, they had both been doing the same thing – persuading themselves of the merits of marrying the man they'd fallen in love with. In a way, the discovery was reassuring; as her own recent sleeplessness had shown, being in love with someone was a far cry from being certain about marrying them. Not that she had any doubts about May and Dan; those two were meant for each other. Nor, if she was perfectly honest, did she have concerns about Andrew. It was just that—

Tap-tap.

In the doorway stood Dorothy. 'May I come in?'

Clemmie nodded. 'Is he here?'

'He is. He's come straight from dropping Squadron Leader Dunning at the register office. Handy that it should be close by. Anyway, you look lovely. That suit is perfect on you. I knew it would be the moment I saw it.'

Catching a glimpse of herself in the mirror as she got to her feet, Clemmie sighed. 'Thank you so much for buying it for me. I can't believe you used your own coupons. It's so generous.' Overcome yet again by the incredible kindness of her landlady's gesture, Clemmie gave her a hug. 'And thank you for everything you've done. Your offer to take me in changed my life. I mean it. It really did. Well, you've seen that for yourself.'

'It might only have been six months, but it has been a pleasure watching you blossom.'

'And the nice thing is,' Clemmie went on, determined not to cry and spoil the little bit of mascara she'd painstakingly applied, 'this isn't the end. I shall see you at the WVS.'

'I'd better. The shop would be nowhere near as organised without you. Anyway, I'll leave you two girls alone for a moment. But just bear in mind that Pearce is already pacing up and down outside.'

'Yes, of course.'

'You do look lovely,' May assured her once Dorothy had left. 'The colour of your suit really lights up your eyes.'

'And so clever that it's almost Air Force blue. I couldn't believe it when Miss Evercott said she had a gift for me and then handed me such a posh box. I can't think how I'll ever repay her.'

'It's a kindness, for sure. And practical enough that you'll get a lot of wear out of it afterwards.'

'I will, won't I? And thanks for lending me Mum's brooch. I didn't know you had it.'

'Truth be told, I'd forgotten, too. Couple of days before the air raids, I put it in my handbag to see about getting the pin fixed and then, with all that happened, I thought no more of it. Once I remembered, I only just had time to get it done.'

Running her fingers over the little marcasite shape of two swallows on the wing, Clemmie sighed. 'Do you think she'd approve?'

'Of you wearing her brooch?'

'Well, yes. But I really meant of Andrew.'

''Course she would. Once she'd got over the shock and found her tongue again, she'd have clucked and fussed over him like the son she never had.'

'I thought the same.'

'Well, there you are then.'

'Yes.'

'Yes.'

Why, Clemmie wondered, did it feel as though something was hanging unsaid? Why did she get the impression that May was hovering on the verge of taking her by the arm and saying, *Look, are you sure about this?*

'Well,' she said, when May made no move to do so, 'I suppose we hadn't better keep everyone waiting. Wouldn't want the registrar to think I'd changed my mind.'

'Here, just a minute.' Reaching across, May adjusted the tilt of Clemmie's matching pillbox hat. 'A little more… this way. There. That's better. You're ready.'

Ready.

In the years that followed, Clemmie never could recall the drive to the register office. She knew that Dorothy had ridden in the front, next to Pearce, and she vaguely remembered being alongside May in the back. She also had a faint recollection of them pulling up alongside the steps to the register office. The thing she did remember with crystal clarity, though, was the smile that spread across Andrew's face as he stood waiting in the doorway, supported that morning by just two ordinary walking sticks. His eagerness brought a smile to her own lips; it was then she'd felt the few final wisps of doubt evaporate into the chilly morning air. In that moment, she had known it was going to be all right. They loved one another. Anything more than that was just icing on top of the cake. And who, these days, after more than three years of hardship and war, had the luxury of icing on anything…?

Chapter 23

December 1943

'Ooh, how lovely. Warmth at last.' Crossing the dining room to the fireplace, Clemmie held her hands in front of the crackling flames. 'What I'd give for a new pair of gloves. My old ones are so holey my fingers freeze to the bone. Would it be cheeky to ask Father Christmas for a new pair? Or does he face the same old problem as we do with clothing coupons?'

Looking up from where he was sitting at the table, an array of pupils' homework spread out in front of him, Andrew sent her a wry smile. 'I suspect he does. In any event, if you recall, I did urge you to take the Wolseley.'

Clemmie stretched out her fingers. Slowly, they were beginning to thaw. 'I know you did. But my trip this afternoon wasn't only for the WVS. And though Dorothy gets me a tiny petrol ration, I can't have it on conscience to abuse it.'

'Few would have such scruples. Especially when it's this cold.'

'That's down to them,' Clemmie replied. 'Anyway, what is it that smells so delicious?' To come through the door each evening to the aroma of supper cooking was a luxury she never took for granted; now that Dorothy had put her in charge of not one, but three WVS shops, having Pearce prepare supper was a real boon. In fact, without him she couldn't have continued with the existing shop, let alone get the two new ones set up. And golly, how beneficial they were for WVS funds and the causes they helped.

Enjoying the feel of warmth seeping through her body, she sighed. Sometimes she couldn't believe how far she'd come: in the little over a year they'd been married, her life had changed beyond all recognition. In all ways but one, it was perfect.

'It's sausage casserole,' Andrew replied to her question about supper. 'But Pearce decided to treat us to an onion from his precious string in the garage, which probably accounts for why it smells particularly appetising.'

'Goodness. One of Pearce's onions *is* a treat.'

'Indeed.'

Noticing then that he was poring over an exercise book, she went on, 'Sorry. I'm disturbing you.'

'You most definitely are not. As usual when you go out, I've been looking forward to you coming home.'

'Was it your afternoon for the Hayden-Jones twins?' While it was rare for her to see any of her husband's pupils, a couple had become known to her by reputation.

'Unfortunately, yes.'

'Still flogging a dead horse?'

Andrew's sigh was accompanied by a despairing shake of his head. 'Is it wrong that I'd give anything to suggest Mrs Hayden-Jones save her money and spare her sons the agony?'

'Not wrong. But it might not do much for your reputation – as a tutor, I mean. I gather Mrs Hayden-Jones is a force and a half on the parish council.'

'She is, rather. Don't get me wrong, neither boy is without ability. It's just that where Anthony is getting there – albeit painfully slowly – Alexander just isn't academic. And although I couldn't say this to anyone but you, rather than struggle for Cambridge he really would be best served going straight into his father's business. The family would seem to make a decent enough living from it.'

'Hm.'

'Anyway. I shall give up on these for tonight.'

'Fresh pair of eyes in the morning?'

'Indeed. Besides, you're hovering here for a reason, aren't you?'

With a sheepish smile, Clemmie turned away from the fire. 'I shouldn't mind ten minutes' practice. As you're forever reminding me, it only takes a day without playing to get rusty.'

'Go on, then. I can listen while I pack up.'

'If you must. Just don't be too hard on me.' Settling herself on the piano stool, Clemmie flexed her fingers and then reached to open the cover of *Piano Pieces for Beginners*. 'I've only sight-read this piece before. And my hands are cold.'

'What have I told you about frame of mind?'

Drawing a breath, she straightened her spine and softened her shoulders. He might be teasing, but he was right. 'Don't think up reasons why you won't be any good, just start playing.'

'Precisely.'

She stared at the score in front of her. 'Ode to Joy'. To her surprise, it was turning out to be her favourite piece so far. And the moment her fingers struck the keys, she remembered why; although relatively solemn – where was the joy, she'd wondered the first time she'd attempted it? *It builds*, he'd assured her – its harmonies made her spine tingle.

'Very good,' he said as she came to the end of the first section. So intense was her focus, she hadn't heard him come up to sit behind her. 'I know I've said it before, but you really do have an innate feel for music.'

'Hm.'

When she rested her hands in her lap, he reached for the nearest and gave it a squeeze. 'My darling girl, have you ever known me to exaggerate?'

She shook her head. 'Not as a rule.'

'Tell you what, how about tomorrow we tackle the next section?'

She leaned across and kissed him. 'I'd like that.'

'But now, I think we had better go and present ourselves for supper.'

Tilting her head, Clemmie listened. 'All that clanging and banging generally *is* Pearce's way of letting us know he's dishing up.'

As they arrived in the kitchen – its cosiness on dark winter evenings drew them to take their supper there, rather than clearing the table in the dining room – coming from the wireless was the Greenwich time signal for six o'clock. As she usually did when she heard it, she glanced at her wristwatch; it had been a gift from Andrew on their first wedding anniversary, and she loved it as much as her engagement ring. Worn together, the two made her feel like a properly grown-up woman.

'When I explained to the lady in the jewellers it was a gift to celebrate that we'd been married a year,' he'd said to her on the day he'd fastened it round her wrist, 'she looked at me askance. "First anniversary is traditionally paper," she seemed moved to point out. But ever since I noticed you didn't wear a watch, I've wanted to get you one.'

At the final pip of the time signal, Clemmie smiled: the jewelled minute hand was pointing precisely to the numeral *XII*.

Given the usual lack of ingredients, Pearce's sausage casserole proved as tasty as it had smelled; their meal was spoiled only by the tone of the report being delivered on the BBC Home Service news bulletin.

> *'Elsewhere in Greece, in the central-eastern city of Kalavryta, reports have been received that in addition to setting buildings on fire, an advancing battalion of German soldiers executed around sixty men and boys. The murders are believed to have been carried out in retaliation for the recent killing of eighty German prisoners of war by members of the Greek Resistance. Later reports suggest that as part of the same reprisal, a nearby monastery was destroyed, and a number of monks and visitors killed.'*

'Monks and visitors,' Clemmie whispered, struggling to keep the tremor from her voice. Across the table from her, she noticed Andrew nod to Pearce, who reached to turn off the wireless. 'Just ordinary people. Not even soldiers.'

'Goodness will prevail,' Andrew assured her. 'By this time next year, I genuinely believe things will look very different. Several of the countries who allied with Germany did so because they bore grudges from the last war, specifically over land lost to Russia. But since Italy had her change of heart, other nations who sided with Germany are also beginning to look around them and wonder where *their* longer-term interests might best be served – countries such as Romania. And Bulgaria, who have shown an unwillingness to fight in Greece. And then there's Finland. All these nations must secretly be wondering how they would fare – how quick Germany would be to come to their aid – were Britain and her allies to suddenly target them with their combined might.'

Some time back, Andrew had assured her that the more she understood about the course of the war, the less afraid she would be. But although she regularly asked him to explain events she didn't understand, it was rare for her newly gained knowledge to bring comfort. It might be her patriotic duty to understand what was going on – what people like Andrew were still making sacrifices for – but there were times when she would rather bury her head in the sand and risk becoming one of those women who, through only ever showing an interest in babies and knitting patterns, earned their sex the unfair reputation of being fluffy-headed. *Babies*. And there was another thing.

'There was a poor girl in the shop today – terrible sad to see.'

'Poor in what way?' Andrew enquired.

She still liked the way that, whenever she started talking to him about something, he stopped what he was doing to listen. It made her feel important, showed that he respected her opinions.

'She was carrying a little boy. Turns out, just a day or two after he was born, the house where she was staying with her mother took a direct hit.'

'Like your own.'

'The same, yes. Except in this case, her mother had gone back into the house to fetch nappies and was killed by the only HE to fall in their area. Then, this year, back in the summer, her husband, who was with the army in North Africa, was taken sick and died. Diss… diss…'

'Dysentery?' Andrew prompted.

'Yes. That. She'd come into the shop hoping to get some clothes for the little one. Said he'd outgrown the last lot.'

'I suppose he would have.'

'But she didn't have enough money for more than a set of cotton rompers. So I took her out the back and gave her a few bits straight out of the donations box. I mean, surely that's what the donations are for – to go to those in most need.'

'I imagine the family who donated them would think her a worthy cause and be glad to have helped her out.'

'Yes. But when she left, I found myself wondering what will become of her. How will she go on? How can she go to work to earn money to keep body and soul together while her boy is so small? It seems a rotten start in life for him, too. After all, it wasn't as though she was unwed. She wasn't one of those girls who goes out in search of a good time and brings it on herself.'

'The civilian tragedies of war are always the hardest to bear. But today, you helped alleviate her most pressing concern. You might not be able to right every wrong but, thanks to you, and to the generosity of those who donate, one young woman now has one less worry. And if everyone was able to go home at the end of the day and say the same, then good would soon defeat evil.'

'I suppose.'

'Now, do you have room for a piece of yesterday's suet pudding? Because I think I might just be able to manage the smallest sliver.'

Trying to push aside her gloominess, Clemmie raised a smile. 'Just as well, because *the smallest sliver* is all Pearce is going to let you have.'

Unsurprisingly, the bowl of pudding with its ladleful of watery custard did nothing to stop Clemmie thinking about the young woman with her little boy – and not just because of her perilous circumstances, but because she *had* a little boy to start with. She and Andrew were fortunate to have a lovely home and few concerns about money; they were also more content than she would ever have thought possible. It was just a shame how that very same providence served to draw attention to the one little gap in their otherwise perfect lives.

–

Staring at the slip of paper she'd just pulled from the envelope delivered by the postman, Clemmie frowned. 'Well, this is a surprise.'

Across the breakfast table from her, Andrew glanced up from the *Daily Telegraph*. 'What's that, darling?'

'This letter,' she said, gesturing with the piece of paper. 'It's from Pearl.'

'Your sister.'

'Yes.'

'What a coincidence. Only the other day you were saying it's a long time since you've seen her.'

Perplexed, Clemmie continued to frown. 'She wants to meet me.'

'Well, that's good, isn't it?'

While it ought to be, Clemmie wasn't so sure. Since getting married, she'd only seen Pearl a couple of times – and only then because she'd bumped into her in the street. 'I suppose that depends on what she wants.'

'Does she have to want something? Is it not possible that with Christmas just round the corner, she would simply like to see you?'

While that might be true for many sisters who hadn't seen each other in a while, where Pearl was concerned Clemmie thought it improbable; more likely, her sister was after something. Either that, or she was in trouble. 'I don't know.'

'But you'll go and see her.'

'Yes. Of course.' In distracted fashion, Clemmie reread Pearl's note. It was certainly to the point.

> *Dear Clemmie,*
> *Meet me at Farthing's on Tuesday at four*
> *o'clock. It's important.*
> *Your sister, Pearl*

It also filled her with apprehension.

'Does she propose when?'

'Tomorrow afternoon. She suggests a tearoom May took us to a couple of times – you know, for a birthday treat, that sort of thing. I'm in the Heavitree shop tomorrow, so I'll finish early, go and see her, and come straight home afterwards. Since I've no idea how long I'll be, perhaps I could ask Pearce to make dinner half an hour later – if that's all right with you?'

'Fine by me, darling. I'm pleased you're going to see her.'

But Clemmie wasn't sure she felt the same way. The wording of Pearl's note suggested considerable urgency. But with no time to write back and ask what she wanted – not that Pearl had given an address – and with no telephone number for her either, she didn't have much choice but to go and find out.

Setting aside the odd little missive and reaching for the butter dish containing the block of margarine, she sighed. At least she didn't have long to agonise over it. By suppertime tomorrow, she would know exactly what Pearl was after.

–

'Table for one, miss?'

'No, thank you,' Clemmie replied to the young waitress who came to greet her as she stepped into the blacked-out tearoom the following afternoon. Gesturing to a table against the far wall, she went on, 'I'll be joining my sister.' With her dark uniform, and her auburn hair pinned high on her head, Pearl was impossible to miss.

'Very well, miss. But as I said to the young lady just now, we close at four thirty.'

'I understand. Has my sister ordered anything yet?'

'No, miss. But I did tell her all we've got left is potato scones.'

'Then just bring us a pot of tea for two, please.'

'Yes, miss.'

That there was nothing to eat really didn't matter; if Pearl was after money, they wouldn't be there very long anyway.

'Thanks for coming,' Pearl said as Clemmie approached the table.

'From your note it sounded urgent.' Pulling out the other chair, Clemmie sat down. Then she pulled off her gloves. Golly, the place was freezing. 'I ordered a pot of tea. I think we'll need it to keep warm.'

'Thanks. I didn't order because I weren't sure you'd turn up.'

'To be honest, left to my own devices I might not have. But Andrew thought I should at least find out what was so pressing.'

Pearl started to smile. 'Yeah. Sorry about my note. But I wanted to be sure you'd come.'

'Yes, well,' Clemmie replied, making a quick study of Pearl's appearance as she did so. 'Here I am.' Whatever her sister's reason for getting her there, she clearly wasn't unwell. Her ivory skin was as radiant as ever, her make-up a match for any illustration on the cover of a magazine.

'Marriage obviously suits you, then. You look very… neat. Very… wifely.'

Clemmie withheld a sigh; why couldn't Pearl be as direct as she usually was? '*You* look very glamorous. But then you always did.'

'Seen May lately?'

'Not since the christening back in the summer. But we write.'

'She okay? And the nipper?'

'Seems to be. She wrote just last week to say that any day now George will be crawling.'

'Suppose so. Six months old now, ain't he – her little George?'

George Frederick: it had been nice of May and Dan to name their son after two of his grandfathers – especially since he would never know either of them. But she was sure Pearl hadn't got her there to talk about May.

When the waitress arrived and proceeded to set down their tea things, the sisters watched. And when she left them to it, Clemmie resumed, 'So, what is it you wanted to see me about?'

'You happy with Andrew? The two of you together, I mean?'

It was such a peculiar question that it took Clemmie a moment to reply. 'Of course I am. Why would you ask such a thing?'

'Because I wouldn't tell you what I'm about to if… well, let's just say if you had regrets.'

Regrets. What on earth was Pearl going to say? Moreover, what business was it of her sister's how happy she and Andrew were?

'Regrets?'

'You know, you're not about to leave him because it isn't what you thought it would be.'

Leave him?

'Christ, Pearl.' Leaning across the table, she lowered her voice to a hiss. 'For what it's got to do with you, no, I assure you I am perfectly happy. Probably the happiest I've ever been in my life. No, not even probably. Definitely. We both are. My life – *our* life – is more than I ever had any right to expect. Andrew has encouraged me to do things I never thought possible. I play the piano. I drive the Wolseley. And Dorothy has made me part-time supervisor of all three shops. All that? At twenty? It's beyond anything I could ever have hoped for.'

'But what about a family?'

Now Pearl was just making her cross. 'What of it?'

'If you could still have one, would you want it?'

'You know the answer to that. Of course I would. Look, Pearl, I don't know what you—'

'And what about Andrew? Would *he* want one?'

Don't raise your voice, Clemmie reminded herself. *Not in public.* 'Since it is highly unlikely to happen,' she hissed angrily, 'it's not something we discuss. But yes, what man wouldn't?'

'Huh. You'd be surprised. I can't think Charlie Warren ever wanted *me*.'

'No, well, thankfully Andrew is nothing like Mr Warren. Few men are.'

'Look,' Pearl picked up again, her voice softer. 'The reason I ask is because—'

From there, Clemmie sat, astonished and aghast in equal measure, her thoughts swirling like water over a weir in the wake of a winter storm: tumbling; churning; roaring in her ears. Unsettling in their power.

Even a good while later, when she'd got off the bus at the bottom of the hill and was walking the last few hundred yards up the rise, the bitter wind whipping about her neck and flapping her coat about her legs, she still couldn't believe what Pearl was proposing. It was a dream of an opportunity; one that would make her life – *their* life – complete. But it was also outlandish. And risky. And for all she knew, Andrew would want nothing to do with it, which just made it all the more important that she use this last hundred yards or so to the front door to work out how on earth she was going to convince him the way Pearl had just convinced her…

Chapter 24

Ordinarily, she enjoyed liver and onions for supper. But tonight, even though it was crisply fried and served with mash and gravy just the way she liked it, Clemmie was struggling to do more than move it around her plate. The only thought in her head was how to put Pearl's idea to Andrew so that he would at least consider it and not think she'd taken leave of her senses. *Had* she taken leave of her sense? She didn't think she had – but *he* might.

The worst of it was that the more she tried to work out how to introduce the subject into the conversation, the more she became riddled with doubt. Already, Andrew had remarked that she seemed preoccupied. But when she had simply smiled and shaken her head, he had, as was his way, pressed her no further. Ironically, by respecting her privacy he had simply worsened her agony; had he encouraged her to divulge what was bothering her – or even attempted to pry it out of her – she wouldn't still be so rigid with fear.

For the umpteenth time since sitting down, she sighed. Her anxiety was only to be expected: the stakes were high; the chance Pearl had presented to her seemed perfect, if not the answer to a prayer. Unfortunately, it was also fraught with so very many difficulties she didn't dare raise her hopes. Even if, once she'd plucked up the courage to tell him, Andrew welcomed the idea with open arms, there had to be any number of obstacles lying in wait to thwart the endeavour. Hence her hesitation; if the opportunity was to stand any chance whatsoever, she had to present it to him in the best possible light. But how to do that? How to think clearly when her mind was in such tremendous turmoil?

Eventually, it was Andrew who broke the silence. 'I trust your sister was well.'

Forcing down a mouthful of mashed potato, Clemmie nodded. 'She was, thank you, yes.'

Reaching across the table, Andrew took hold of her hand. 'If you're not hungry, darling, don't make yourself eat it.'

'But to leave it is a waste of good food.'

'Perhaps so. But if you can't eat it, you can't eat it. If you find you're hungry later, you can always make yourself a sandwich.'

With a resigned sigh, Clemmie set down her knife and fork. Perhaps, once she had spoken to him properly and the subject was out in the open, her appetite would return, and she might fancy a little something later; in the refrigerator was the end of that tin of tongue. Or maybe she'd just make herself an Ovaltine.

'Yes,' she said. 'All right. I'm sorry.'

'Look, why don't we go through to the drawing room? In a moment, the BBC Northern Orchestra is performing Schubert's Symphony No. 5. We can sit and listen – it's quite a jolly piece – and then, afterwards, you can tell me what you think of it. It's due to start any moment and only half an hour long.'

No closer to finding the words to explain her preoccupation, Clemmie found herself agreeing. 'Yes, all right.' If nothing else, it would give her more time to think.

But the moment the symphony's first movement began – allegro, B flat major, according to her husband – Clemmie's thoughts once again returned to Pearl's proposal. To Andrew, the suggestion was going to come out of the blue, it being something neither of them had ever considered, let alone discussed; and it would take their lives in a direction neither of them had contemplated. And that had to be why she had no idea how to even introduce the subject, let alone fight its corner. And she did so very badly at least want them to consider it.

Vaguely aware that, on the wireless, prominence had shifted away from strings to woodwind, she looked across at Andrew; as he leaned back in his upright chair, eyes closed, his right hand was making tiny movements as though conducting a miniature orchestra set out in front of him on the occasional table. She would wait now until the programme ended; interrupt his enjoyment of the piece and she might not get the reaction she wanted.

When the symphony finally concluded, Andrew opened his eyes and looked across at her. 'What did you think? Were you able to detect a likeness to the work of another composer?'

Wishing now that she had been able to pay greater attention, she frowned, her reply when she gave it uncertain. 'Mozart… perhaps?'

'Spot on. Well done, you.'

Lucky guess. 'I have a good teacher.'

'*I* have a good student.'

Her smile fading, she drew a breath. If she was to do this before they went to bed, it was now or never.

'Andrew, the reason Pearl wanted to see me today was because something has happened. Something that made her think of us.'

Adjusting himself in his chair, Andrew inclined his head. 'That something being?'

'Well, the thing is, it's quite… odd. And I confess to not knowing what you'll think of it.'

'This *odd thing* that's causing you such uncertainty,' he said, pressing on the arms of the chair to raise himself up, 'would it be more easily explained were we to sit side by side on the couch?'

Getting up to assist him to move across to it, she nodded. 'It might, yes.'

Installed beside her, he took her hand. 'I'm all ears.'

Simply desperate now to be rid of her jitters, she dived in. 'There's a baby. A little girl. Six months old. Orphaned. Her mother was a friend of Pearl's who went to work in London.'

'And the father?'

'The girl wouldn't ever say.' Having now reached what was, to her mind, the hardest part of her tale, she hesitated for a moment before going on, 'So, the baby is to go to an orphanage. Unless…' Oh, dear God. How could she put this without instantly making him take against the idea? 'Unless a family can be found for her.' There. Surely that was enough of an explanation without her having to—

'And your sister thought of you. Of us.'

She nodded. 'Yes.'

'But of the baby's father, nothing is known.'

'Nothing. The girl always refused to say who he was.'

'No doubt married,' Andrew observed, somewhat stiffly for Clemmie's liking. 'And the girl's own family?'

'Her father was badly gassed in the last war and didn't live long afterwards. By all accounts, she never knew him. Her mother died some years later, Pearl doesn't know how.

After that, the girl was put into a children's home until she was old enough to leave school and go out to work.'

'An orphan herself.'

'Yes.'

'So, the baby has no family.'

'None that could easily be found, even were there a will to do so. Certainly, no family as would be inclined to take in a baby they didn't even know existed.'

'I see.'

'And it just seems so truly awful,' Clemmie continued, 'the same thing befalling the little girl as happened to her mother. Worse, even, since she'll never know either of her parents at all.'

'Awful indeed.'

'And I realise that when *my* parents were taken, I wasn't anywhere near so young as this baby, and that I did have my sisters. Even so, I know what it's like to feel, well, to feel abandoned.'

When he squeezed her hand, she heard him sigh.

'So, your sister thought that since we are destined to be childless we might like to give this little girl a home.'

Slowly, to convey that she understood the gravity of the suggestion, Clemmie nodded. 'We do have the where-withal. And the love.'

'But what if, by some miracle, we *were* one day to have children of our own?'

Wait – had he been given a new prognosis? Might that now be possible? Not wanting to get up her hopes, she refrained from looking at him. 'You told me to discount the possibility – to make my decision about marrying you on the basis that could never happen.'

'I did tell you that, yes. And one year on, I would say the same again.'

Her sigh was one of disappointment. 'So why raise the matter then?'

'I raise it just in case. I raise it to draw your attention to the implications for this little orphan should we, one day, and by some miracle, manage to have a child of our own.'

It was something she hadn't stopped to consider – why would she? Andrew had told her children would never happen.

'But surely, if children are out of the question, then they are out of the question. Is that not the basis upon which we are building our lives together?'

Continuing to hold her hand, he nodded. 'It is. And I'm sorry if I have upset you. But, in the circumstances, it nonetheless remains a consideration. As does the matter of whether, at some point in the future, we would wish to adopt for this orphan a sibling.'

Oh dear. Having thought she'd considered everything, she realised now she had done nothing more than simply try to guess at Andrew's reaction.

'I suppose,' she said carefully, 'these are all the things we would have to discuss – should you even like the idea to start with, that is.'

Yes, it seemed now that she had been naïve. But that didn't make adopting this little girl out of the question; it just meant they had to think of, and find out, everything there was to know.

Later that evening, removed to the dining table, they attempted to do just that.

'Health,' Andrew said, with which Clemmie wrote the word in her notebook below where she had written the heading, 'Questions About the Baby'.

'Health. Yes. Of course.'

'Is the child physically fit – I should want her to be fully examined by a doctor. There would be nothing worse than us losing the child to an illness that might have been avoided had we known to take care. And what of the mother? How did she die? If she had an inherited condition, might the child be suffering from it, too?'

Clemmie frowned. 'That might be hard to find out – if Pearl doesn't know, I can't imagine anyone does.'

'It is something I should want to know. I can't imagine how grief-stricken you would be should we go ahead and adopt this little girl only to lose her to the very disease that took her mother.'

Clemmie exhaled heavily. He made a good point. But then Andrew was nothing if not thorough. 'Of course.'

'And does the child have a name? Was her birth even registered?'

As she wrote the words 'name' and 'birth registered?' Clemmie nodded. 'Pearl never mentioned a name. So perhaps she's not been christened yet. She just said that she was a pretty little thing who Sylvia – Pearl's landlady, that is – thought was ready for weaning and showed all the signs of trying to start to crawl.'

'I seem to remember,' Andrew remarked as the thought appeared to strike him, 'that earlier this year, the government passed into law a new act on adoption. We would need to familiarise ourselves with it – and establish what bearing it might have.'

Her confidence fading, Clemmie wrote 'adoption law'. 'I should want it to be all official.'

'Absolutely,' Andrew agreed. 'But I have no idea whether, with the child having no living relatives, the process would be more straightforward, or less. And we would need to consider very carefully how the child would be looked after in the event of our joint demise – the matter of a guardian, and provision through our wills.'

More obstacles, Clemmie thought as she wrote the words 'guardian' and 'will'.

By the time their list had filled an entire page in her notebook, Clemmie's head was spinning. To make matters worse, she was no closer to understanding whether her husband wanted to go ahead and take the baby in or whether he was merely going through the motions until he found a reason to say no.

In the knowledge that she was unlikely to sleep unless she found out, she laid down her pen. The time had come to be bold.

'So, setting aside for a moment all these questions, is this something you would like to try and bring about, or not?' Goodness, how she was trembling. 'Only, if not, then…'

'To be honest, I am undecided. I want you to be happy – am willing to move heaven and earth to make it so. You know that.'

'I do.'

'But not at the risk of us entering into something half-cocked, or at the risk of making a mistake.'

'No.'

'That said, there *is* something we can do in the short term.'

With no idea what that might be, she met his look. 'And that is…?'

'Well, do you think your sister might be persuaded to bring the baby here, so that we might meet her? After all, while every question on that list requires an answer, surely there is none more important than whether we – whether you in particular – take to the poor thing? And she to us?'

In her chest, Clemmie felt her heart swell. There was a chance. He was prepared to see whether it might work. Golly, she loved him. 'I'll ask her. She gave me a note of the telephone number for her landlady. I'll go and call her. I'll do it now.'

When she got up from the table to go in search of her handbag, her feelings all over the place, she let out a little sob. Andrew's idea was just the thing to help them decide. They could spend some time with the little girl, see how they all got on. Of even greater comfort, though, was the notion that he was unlikely to have suggested the idea unless, deep down, he thought there was a chance they could do this.

And no, she wasn't putting the cart before the horse. But if these last eighteen months had taught her anything, it was that two things were true: if you put yourself out, you could achieve the most incredible things. And that sometimes, life sprung the most astonishing surprises. She had a husband she loved, a beautiful home, a life crammed with purpose and reward. And now, just possibly, the icing on the cake, she might soon have a daughter to raise, too.

Epilogue

June 1944

'I still say it would have been nice to know the actual day she was born – for us to be able to celebrate her birthday on the proper day.'

Crouching down to where their daughter was rocking on her toes as she clung to the front of the sofa, Clemmie smiled. 'Perhaps,' she said. 'But at least we know the month. And by picking the fifteenth, the most we can be wrong by is two weeks.'

While Andrew was right to say it would have been nice to know the date – and place – of their daughter's birth, of greater importance surely was the fact that, after six months of bewildering bureaucracy, the little girl was now officially theirs. She had never doubted they would be allowed to adopt her; the authorities were simply relieved that someone was prepared to take her in; had it not been for the dearth of details surrounding her birth, and the circumstances of the death of her mother, she would have been legally theirs a long time ago. But, as Andrew so often said, what did it matter? She was theirs now. Moreover, while they might know very little about the first six months of her life, they knew every single detail of the last six – and would know everything about every moment from here on. What was more, she had settled in without so much as a murmur. In fact, Penelope Jane Dunning had so quickly become a part of their lives that neither of them could remember a time without her. And today, they were celebrating that she was one year old.

'Shall I bring you the parcel, sir?'

Looking up to see Pearce in the doorway, Clemmie frowned. 'What parcel is that?'

'Ah, well.' To Clemmie's eyes, her husband looked distinctly sheepish. 'When you were out one day last week, a box arrived.'

'And you didn't tell me?'

'I wanted it to be a surprise.' Turning his attention to Pearce, Andrew said, 'Yes please, Pearce. Bring it down.'

'But you know what it is.'

'Haven't the faintest idea. But I can see from the post-marks on the box who sent it.'

Clemmie's immediate thought was that it had to be from May. Had Dorothy or Pearl been responsible, there would have been no need to send it by post. But when Pearce set down a package wrapped in brown paper, bound with string and sealed with a blob of wax, Clemmie knew straight away that she was wrong. At least one of the smudged franking marks said *United States Postal Service*.

'America?' she breathed, even more puzzled.

'Scissors?' Pearce said, offering her the pair from the kitchen.

'Thank you.'

The string cut, Clemmie pulled away the brown paper to find a sturdy cardboard box. And when she opened back the top, she discovered a stiff white envelope addressed to *Mrs A. Dunning*. Still not entirely certain that Andrew wasn't in some way involved, she cast a glance in his direction. His expression did contain a hint of mischief.

'I assure you,' he said, reaching to lift their daughter from where she was clamouring at his legs, 'I have no more idea than you do.' With the little girl settled on his lap, he went on, 'What do you think, Penny? What's inside the box Mummy's opening? A present for your birthday?'

Getting up from where she had been kneeling at the table, Clemmie settled herself beside them, opened the envelope and pulled out a single sheet of notepaper. Intrigued, she read the unfamiliar handwriting.

> *Dear Mrs Dunning,*
> *We have never met but my name is Lillian Hogue and, upon hearing you now have a little girl, my husband, Major James David Hogue with the USAAF, wrote to suggest I send a parcel for her birthday.*

'Major Hogue,' she said with a light laugh. 'You didn't tell me you two had been in touch.'

'We haven't,' Andrew replied. 'Not recently. I dropped him a couple of lines back in the spring. I wasn't even sure where he was. The army post office must have forwarded it. One would imagine that this last week or so, he and his squadrons have been caught up in the Normandy landings.'

Her rush of warmth for the major checked by her knowledge of what had been happening in northern France, Clemmie read on.

> *I understand it is hard to get baby things over there in Britain right now, and so I have filled this little box with items I hope you will find useful. Not all of them are brand new – the blanket was one my*

mother made when I was expecting Beth, our first.
But my three are all too grown up for it now. And
the buster suit was given to me for my youngest,
Donald, but he was already too big for it. As I
recall, I only put him in it the one time.

My dear Mrs Dunning, as a mother myself, if
I could be so bold as to offer one piece of advice it
would be this: children are a gift, but they grow
up so darn quick. Whatever else you do, be sure
to make the most of every moment with your little
girl. Please also know that you and your family
are in my thoughts, and that I pray every night for
God to watch over you all.

Yours sincerely,
Lillian Hogue (Mrs)

Her vision blurred by tears, Clemmie sniffed. What a lovely letter, and what heartwarming sentiments. Eager now to see what the major's wife had sent, she passed the letter to Andrew and, returning to kneel on the floor, lifted out the layer of tissue paper tucked over the parcel's contents. Astonished by what she saw, she gasped. Beneath it was a white openwork blanket.

Carefully, she lifted it out. 'It's beautiful,' she whispered, in awe of the skill required to create something so delicate. 'Look at it. You can feel the love in every stitch.'

'It is quite incredible,' Andrew agreed, reaching past Penny to put the letter on the table.

'How on earth could she bear to part with something so treasured?'

'Perhaps she felt it time someone new appreciated it.'

'Mum, Mum,' Penny gurgled and thrust out a hand to grab it.

'Oh – and look at these.' From within the box, Clemmie lifted out a set of three woollen vests, all trimmed at the neckline with pink satin ribbon. She held one up. 'By the time next winter comes, these will be just right. How clever of her to know the size.'

'I suspect,' Andrew said with a smile, 'having had three of her own, she's well placed to judge.'

Next from the box Clemmie pulled three white knitted bonnets and three pairs of socks; from beneath those, a bundle of towelling bibs. 'Seven of them,' she said, admiring the gaily coloured farm animals printed on the fronts, and the contrasting piping around the edges. 'I've never seen bibs so cheerful.' She held one up. 'Look at this bright cockerel. And this goat wearing a hat.' In her disbelief, she sighed. 'What a godsend. What thoughtfulness.'

'What else is there?' Andrew, it seemed, was equally overwhelmed.

She reached back into the box. 'Baby soap, some sort of skin cream… what's this? Oh, baby powder. And good-ness, look, safety pins.'

'I doubt anyone has seen any of those since before the war.'

'No. And oh! Heavens, look at this.' Starting to laugh, Clemmie pulled out a honey-coloured bear with a long snout, jointed limbs, and a red felt waistcoat with matching hat, through which were poking his ears. Holding it up, she moved an arm and waved one of his paws.

'I think,' Andrew said, taking the bear from her and jiggling it in front of the entranced little girl on his knee, 'we'd better call him Hoguey, after your benefactor.'

'Good idea.' As she continued to unpack the box, Clemmie grew more and more disbelieving: scarlet needlecord dungarees with a buttoned gusset; a pink and yellow flowered cotton dress with matching sunhat and two little cardigans – one pink, one yellow – a whole coordinating outfit, the likes of which she'd never seen. 'Oh, my word.'

When she held up a blue waxed cotton cape with matching rain hat, Andrew laughed. 'Penny Dunning, you're going to be the best-dressed girl in town. I shall be fighting off suitors left, right and centre.'

'Some of these are a little large,' Clemmie observed, laying the cape alongside the dresses on the table. 'Perhaps American infants are bigger.'

'The cape will be good in the autumn.'

Aware that Pearce had been watching from the doorway, Clemmie turned to send him a smile; for all the planning they had done ahead of Penny's arrival into their home, the thing they could never have anticipated was the softening effect she'd have on Pearce, tenderness being a trait he'd always kept well-hidden before. 'You're right,' she said. 'And the dresses will be perfect for next summer.'

'I expect that was what Mrs Hogue had in mind.'

'I expect so. Oh, and this must be the… what did she call it?' Reaching for the letter, Clemmie scanned the rows of handwriting until she picked out what she was looking for. 'The *buster suit*. I did wonder what that was. Seemingly it's rompers.'

'Is that everything?' Andrew asked, leaning across to peer at the little white cotton suit with its red piping.

'No, there's a box. But it's upside down, so I can't see what…' Carefully, she lifted it out. 'Oh, look, Penny, it's wooden alphabet blocks.' Having examined the lid, she held it up for the little girl to see. 'Lots of blocks for Daddy to build into towers and you to knock down!'

'Knock down my towers? Daddy's little angel? Never!'

Moving to sit alongside Andrew on the couch, Clemmie relieved her husband of their daughter and felt him slide an arm round her waist. 'Major Hogue struck me as a kindly man the moment I met him.'

'Me too.'

'He would have made such a good godfather.'

'He would have been perfect.'

'I still can't believe he would have thought to do *this*, though. It's so unexpected. Such a shame we shan't have him and Mrs Hogue as our friends.'

'Who knows,' Andrew said thoughtfully. 'Perhaps one day we will. Who knows what will happen once this war is over?'

'I shall write and thank Mrs Hogue. I'll do it this afternoon.'

'And I'll get Pearce to take a photograph of the three of us—'

'With Penny in one of her new outfits—'

'And we'll send it on afterwards.'

'Yes.' Exhaling a long sigh, Clemmie rested her head on Andrew's shoulder. The feeling of warm fuzziness that washed over her in moments like these was one she never took for granted. 'You know,' she said. 'We have a lot to be thankful to the Americans for.'

'The Normandy landings, do you mean?'

'No, you ninny.' Lifting her head, she met his look. 'I mean, obviously, yes, I'm grateful for what they're doing this very moment in France. But I meant closer to home – you and I.'

'You and I?'

'Well,' she said, and started to grin, 'without the arrival of Major Hogue and his men, there would have been no need for the welcome committee.'

'Ah. And without the welcome committee—'

'You and I would never have met. Not in a month of Sundays.'

'I would still be a sorry old retired pilot, living the dreary life of a bachelor whose legs don't work—'

'And I would probably be a factory girl, secretly yearning for better but unable to say boo to a goose.'

'But here we are. And I have you to thank for the sort of happiness for which I had no right to hope.'

She nestled back against his shoulder. 'And here *I* am, with the love of a fine man and the confidence to do things I would never have imagined.'

'And now we have a family, too.'

Yes, she thought, and gave a sigh of utter contentment. Despite the hardship and the deprivation, the worry, the fatigue, and the terrible losses, this war had turned out to be the making of her. And who would have thought *that* on that terrifying night, just over two years ago, when she and her sisters had clung together in that foul little underground shelter, praying for all they were worth that they would be spared to see another day? Not her, that was for sure. Those nightmarish air raids had turned her life upside down. And while the eventual upshot had caused her a dilemma like no other, through learning to take chances she had found happiness and fulfilment beyond her wildest imaginings. And for that, she would never fail to be grateful.

Acknowledgements

With grateful thanks to Kiran Kataria for her ongoing support, and to Emily Bedford at Canelo for her continued guidance and enthusiasm. Above all, thank you to my husband for his forbearance and unfailing belief.